A Woman of Secrets

By *Amelia Carr* and *available from Headline Review*

DANCE WITH WINGS
A SONG AT SUNSET
A WOMAN OF SECRETS

A Woman of Secrets

AMELIA CARR

headline
review

First published in 2011
by HEADLINE REVIEW
An imprint of HEADLINE PUBLISHING GROUP

1

Cataloguing in Publication Data is
available from the British Library

ISBN 978 0 7553 7002 3

Typeset in Joanna MT by Palimpsest Book Production Limited,
Falkirk, Stirlingshire

Printed and bound in Great Britain by
Clays Ltd, St Ives plc

Headline's policy is to use papers that are natural, renewable and
recyclable products and made from wood grown in sustainable forests.
The logging and manufacturing processes are expected to conform
to the environmental regulations of the country of origin.

HEADLINE PUBLISHING GROUP
An Hachette UK Company
338 Euston Road
London NW1 3BH

www.headline.co.uk
www.hachette.co.uk

To the brave men and women of the SOE

ACKNOWLEDGEMENTS

Sometimes I think that writing acknowledgements is more difficult than writing a book! I worry that I will leave out someone whose help deserves to be acknowledged, or that I'll publicly thank one of my 'experts' but will have made such a glaring error in using the information they gave me, that having their name associated with it will be a huge embarrassment to them.

I'm taking a big chance, then, in thanking Richard (Rick) Cross, who was the sergeant in charge of a police diving team (and a former colleague of my husband, Terry), and Dr Douglas Wardrop, who explained to me the different forms of leukaemia, their treatment, and the likely progression of the illness. I couldn't have written *A Woman of Secrets* without their generous help. I must admit, though, that I've used a little artistic licence here and there in the interests of the story – I hope they will forgive me, and once again, I stress – any mistakes are entirely down to me!

Thanking the lovely folk at Headline is much easier – they are all wonderful, unfailingly encouraging and super-efficient. Marion Donaldson, my editor, is an inspiration, and her back-up team, Kate and Frankie, are always there for me. I was sad to say goodbye this year to Sarah, when she moved on to pastures new, though perhaps 'goodbye' is the wrong word since she is now with Curtis Brown, who happen to be my agents. Then there is Helena, who is full of brilliant ideas for publicity, and the sales team who get my books on to the shelves.

A special mention here for Russell Moore, my local representative. Russell is brilliant, working like a Trojan on my behalf. Though my feet are covered with blisters and my right hand aching by the time he's dragged me — and I use the word advisedly! — from book-shop to bookshop for hours on end to sign stock, we still manage to have great fun. Thanks, Russell, you're a star!

My wonderful agent, Sheila Crowley, is always tremendously supportive. I couldn't get by without you, Sheila.

Last but not least, a huge thank-you to my family — Terry, my husband, for putting up with my obsession with whatever I'm writing, and for coming up with suggestions when I'm stuck, and my daughters, sons-in-law and grandchildren, just for being them.

I'm really lucky to be doing a job I love so much, and for having the support of so many wonderful people. Thank you all!

PROLOGUE

1947

She stands at the edge of the lake, a diminutive figure in a belted trench coat and black beret, worn flat on the side of her head. From beneath it, wavy dark hair tumbles over her collar, which she has turned up against the chill wind and fitful scuds of drizzling rain. Between her hands, stiff from the cold, she holds a small but surprisingly heavy box of dark blue leather, flipped open to reveal a gold signet ring, a silver locket containing a curly snippet of a baby's hair and an ornate medal in the shape of a cross, all nestling on a bed of dark blue velvet.

For a moment she stares at them, dark eyes narrowed, biting down hard on her scarlet-painted lower lip. She is thinking she should be feeling a rush of emotion for the lost loves the personal items represent, and perhaps pride in the honour conveyed by the medal, but she can feel nothing but the hollow pain of despair that sits like a cancer at the heart of her, which sharpens to unbearable agony at the sight of them. The memories they revive are all overshadowed by grief and guilt, a guilt she knows will never leave her, though the voice of reason that struggles to make itself heard might argue that she was not to blame; that desperate situations determine desperate responses. But it is of no comfort to her. What happened came about because of the choices she made. They are a burden on her heart – on her soul – that she knows will never lighten.

These mementos are a tangible reminder of everything she must

1

now leave behind. It is time to move on. For the sake of others, and for her own sake, the sake of her sanity. Time to close the door on that part of her life, which, short as it was, has affected her more profoundly than all the others that make up her twenty-six years on this earth.

She snaps the box shut, raises her head, looks out across the expanse of the lake. In the gathering gloom of a late November afternoon, the surface of the water is dark, rippled by the wind, mottled with the falling rain. Trees surround it on three sides, sparse in places, dense woodland in others, a natural muff holding the lake securely at its heart, just as the little locket holds the curl of baby hair and the gold ring encircled her finger. This seems a fitting resting place for the things that tie her to a past she must leave behind.

Before she can change her mind, she transfers the box to her right hand, arcs her arm back to its furthest extent, and hurls the box as far as she is able towards the centre of the lake. For a brief moment it seems to hang in the murky air, then it strikes the water with a barely discernible splash, and is gone.

She stands motionless, her eyes fixed on the spot where it disappeared. She wants to feel relief, or regret, but she is numb. Her cheeks are wet, but from the rain, not from tears. She has cried too many of them; those particular rivers have run dry.

She thrusts her chilled hands into the pockets of her trench coat, bows her head in a silent last goodbye to the treasures that meant so much to her, and the decoration that meant nothing at all.

Then she turns and walks back along the path that winter has cleared through the undergrowth, dead leaves mushing beneath the sturdy soles of her shoes, dead brambles catching at her stockings. Her past has been laid to rest in a watery grave, and though the requiem will go on, it is the future she must look towards now. A long, long future without the ones she loved most. But to which she owes a debt for the sake of those who love her now, and whom she may yet come to love.

Part One

ONE

MARTHA

2008

It's 8.30 a.m. and I'm at my desk in the Police Underwater Search Unit office at Almondsbury when the phone rings. I curse silently; I came in early to catch up on some of the mountain of paperwork that's accumulated and as yet I've made next to no impression on it. We've been busy the past week or so, as we often can be in summer. We cover a large area, Gloucestershire, Wiltshire and Dorset as well as Avon & Somerset, and people have a habit of gravitating towards water on warm days and long light evenings. In the past few days we've recovered the bodies of a lad who'd drunk too much and fallen into the docks in the wee small hours when the clubs and pubs were emptying, and, even more tragically, a foolhardy kid who'd gone swimming with friends in a flooded quarry. As the sergeant in charge of the unit, most of the form filling and report writing that follows falls to me. A sad task as well as a time-consuming one. But very necessary.

Still writing, I reach for the phone.

'Sergeant Holley.'

'Morning, MJ.'

My nickname. Short for Martha Jane. Some wag started calling me by my initials way back when I was a rookie beat PC, and somehow it's stuck. Well – it could be worse, I suppose. Policemen can be very rude and politically incorrect.

I recognise the voice immediately – the soft Scottish burr that

5

can turn whiplash sharp if the situation merits it. Jock McLaren, training sergeant at my first station, now inspector in charge of a division out in the sticks that covers my old home.

'Morning, Jock.'

'Busy?'

'Snowed under.'

'But enjoying it.'

'I wouldn't be anywhere else.' It's the truth. I love every moment of life with the team. Well – almost every moment. There are times in winter when I'm wet and filthy, chilled to the bone, when I think it would be nice to be in a warm, dry office, or even a response car. But it's not a sentiment that lasts long.

'I can't believe you're ringing to enquire after my welfare, though,' I say drily.

'And you'd be right, I'm afraid.'

'Go on. Where do you want us?'

'Bolborough Lake.'

Bolborough Lake. A place I know well. I sigh.

'OK, what's happened? A fisherman toppled in? Or kids swimming?'

'Nothing like that. There was a burglary last night at Bolborough House. The big place up on the hill, you know it?'

'I know where it is.' I've only ever seen it from the other side of the perimeter fence, though, and even then obscured by trees. A big old country house owned by local gentry, the same family who owned most of the surrounding land. 'The Woodhouse family lived there when I was a kid, but they're not still there, are they?'

'No, they sold up some years back. It was bought by an actor – Will Ford. You've seen him on TV, I expect.'

'I don't watch much TV.' But I do remember Lucy, my sister, telling me about it. There'd been great excitement at the time, with rumours that the new owner was a Hollywood star – Brad Pitt's name was bandied about, I seem to remember, and Russell Crowe. There was even a suggestion that Madonna had been seen in the vicinity. By their standards, this Will Ford was something of a disappointment.

'Go on,' I say.

6

'Well, last night the house was broken into and a lot of antique silverware was stolen. The burglar alarm went off, triggered a call to the security company and one of our response cars that was more or less just up the road got to the scene in time to see a couple of our local villains legging it. Our lads gave chase, down across the fields. They lost them in the woods round the lake, but we got the helicopter out and caught them on the other side of the valley. But they didn't have any of the stuff on them. And my thinking is they dumped it in panic and—'

'It's in the lake.'

'Seems highly likely.'

'You want me to take a look.'

'If you can. Any chance you could fit it in today? It would make my life a whole lot easier if I had the evidence before I charge them.'

I close my eyes briefly. There goes my clear run at the paperwork.

'OK, Jock. You've got it.'

Bolborough Lake. A place I've known since I was a child. When I was eight or nine, Lucy and I would trek the mile or so across the open country behind our house taking a picnic lunch – meat paste sandwiches, Jammy Dodgers, a bottle of lemonade – and eat it sitting on the grassy slope that led down to the lake. You can't see the water from that slope, it's hidden behind a thick tangle of trees, and neither can you see the underground stream that runs into it. If you're local, you just know which part of the field to avoid if you don't want to end up ankle deep in boggy ground.

When I was with Lucy we never went down to the lake; it was forbidden territory and Lucy, two years older than me, was obedient to the point of being a goody-goody. When I was on my own, though, I would go the rest of the way down the field, scramble beneath the barbed-wire fence, and through knee-high fern and undergrowth, right up to the strip of rough earth lapped by the algae-covered water. Sometimes I would even take off my socks and sandals and wade out on to a promontory of stones and boulders over which the lake flows into a cascading waterfall to form a river through the wooded area beneath. Even then I was always drawn by water, and unlike my sister, I wasn't a child who did what I was told if my inclinations were otherwise. I was something of a tomboy and definitely a rebel.

Nothing much has changed, really. I still like to be where the action is – I've tried everything from bungee jumping and a sky-dive for charity, to potholing and rock climbing, though water is the only love I've remained true to. And I'm still a rebel at heart. I've been hauled over the coals more than once for following my own nose rather than instructions from on high – I have a healthy disregard for career officers who graduate to flying a desk via the fast-track system and think all the answers come from a textbook. But miraculously, in spite of that, I've made sergeant and I'm in charge of the nine-strong specialist search unit. Because I'm good at my job, I like to think.

Unfortunately, I can't say the same about my personal life. My marriage broke up two years ago when I discovered that Nick, my husband – also a police officer – was having an affair with one of the civilian clerks in the CID office, though if I'm truthful, it was just the last act in a relationship gone sour, and I couldn't really blame him for looking towards greener pastures. Sad, though. Once upon a time we'd been so much in love, so determined to make our relationship work against the backdrop of a profession noted for the high proportion of failed marriages it spawned.

Mostly, of course, the problems arise because police wives get fed up with the long, uncertain and unsocial hours their husbands work; in our case the boot was on the other foot. We'd thought that, both being serving police officers, we'd understand and be able to work around the problems. Trouble was, when push came to shove, Nick wanted a wife waiting for him at home when he finished a long shift. A meal on the table if he made it at a halfway normal hour, someone to cuddle up to in bed if he came in at two in the morning, chilled to the marrow – Nick was a motorcycle cop, and eight hours on a motorbike when the thermometer is hovering around zero is guaranteed to induce a body temperature that needs some warming up. But of course the chances were I was at work myself, our shifts overlapping.

To make matters worse, Nick didn't just want a wife, he wanted a family. And I didn't. Well, not just then. I loved my work, and I knew I was in line for promotion and possibly the job of leading the underwater search team. Taking maternity leave would scupper that. Besides, when I was ready to be a mother, I wanted to do it properly, as my sister Lucy did, not shuttle a child about between childminders and often not even be there at bath and bedtime. But as yet I didn't feel ready to give everything up to change nappies and puree carrots and watch CBeebies.

I got my promotion. I was given the job I'd worked for, heading up the underwater search unit, with whom I'd worked for the past three years. And it really was the beginning of the end.

Nick said he was pleased for me, and perhaps he was, but it wasn't long before the cracks began to appear.

Disappointment that I'd committed myself, yet again, to the job instead of giving it up to be a good little wife and an even better mother, resentment that I was a sergeant whilst he was still a PC.

It was obvious enough to me, though neither of us actually put it into words. And it seemed so petty! Nick was doing what he wanted to do, just as I was. Why would he be jealous and resentful? But he was. I knew he was.

I've no idea how the affair with the CID clerk began, except that they were both based at the Divisional HQ – but I can guess. Nick's a good-looking chap; in his motorcycle leathers he's pretty damned near irresistible. And she is, to give her her due, a very pretty girl. Who probably threw herself at him. We used to joke that the civilian girls came to work at the police station in order to hook a handsome copper, and certainly there were so many romances and even marriages that the admin inspector said that in future he would only employ older women who looked like old boots. But with all the young, unattached talent around the place, she had to pick on my husband. A compliment to my taste, maybe, but one step too far.

When I divorced him, I really thought there was a good chance they might hook up. But they haven't. He did live with her for a bit, but no more. Perhaps she didn't like it when he had to work at weekends, Christmas, Easter, and all Bank Holidays in between;

perhaps she didn't turn out to be the little homemaker he wanted deep down even when he was taking advantage of her 36DD full frontal – not a breast enhancement in sight, or needed. I don't know and I don't care.

At least, that's how I kid myself. And if I still feel a pang of regret when our paths cross, I give myself a good shake and move on.

OK. So that's my failure as a wife dealt with. Now we come onto my shortcomings as a granddaughter, sister, paid-up member of the human race.

I've failed in that department, too. My sister makes that all too clear to me. Well, actually, she doesn't. She's too nice for that. But it's an inescapable fact that confronts me every time I visit, which is at least once a week.

My grandmother, Bea, who's in her late eighties, suffered a stroke just over a year ago, and became incapable of being left alone in the house that had been hers and Grampy's and where she brought up Lucy and me after our parents were killed when Lucy was nine and I was seven. Lucy, always determined to do the right thing whatever the cost, wouldn't hear of her going into a care home, or even sheltered accommodation, since the closest available is a good fifteen miles away. She converted the extension on her house, intended as a games room for her three teenage sons, and moved Granny in so that she could look after her herself. It must have meant a considerable sacrifice on the part of the family, and it is, without doubt, a constant burden on Lucy. Granny has never properly recovered the use of her limbs on the left side, or the power of speech, and needs a lot of understanding as well as help with basic day-to-day necessities like washing and dressing. Lucy had been hoping, I know, to go back to work now that the boys are more or less grown-up, looking forward to a life beyond baking, cleaning, being on hand to help with homework and providing a taxi service to rugby practice, judo, or whatever other activity the boys were currently involved with. With Granny to care for, her plans had to go on hold again.

Lucy never complains, but it makes me feel horribly guilty that she is shouldering the whole of the burden whilst my life continues in exactly the same way as it did before, and I can't help thinking she wouldn't be human if she didn't resent me for it.

So you see, my private life is something of a mess. Usually, when I'm at work, I'm able to forget about it. But today, as the eighteen-ton lorry that is the unit's mobile HQ rolls down a rutted track across open farmland, the only access for a wheeled vehicle to Bolborough Lake, I look at the fields sloping up on the far side of the valley and see the ghosts of two little girls, picnicking on meat paste sandwiches and Jammy Dodgers, and feel a pang of nostalgia for a long lost past of endless summer days when, it seems, the sun always shone, and a closeness between sisters that has all but disappeared. And make up my mind to try a bit harder to pull my weight.

How I'm going to manage it, though, I'm not quite sure. I adore Granny every bit as much as Lucy does, but there's no way I could care for her in the poky flat I took when Nick and I split up and sold the house, and no way I can give her the care and attention she needs. Maybe I could take her away for a holiday. But I'm not at all convinced she would want to go. Even before her stroke, she was very much a homebody. I don't think she's been far outside of Somerset in the whole of her life. Certainly I don't ever recall them going anywhere exotic when we were small, though I suppose they might have done, and when Lucy and I went to live with them, money was tight and the furthest we ever went was on day trips to Weston-super-Mare and Weymouth, though we did once have a week in a caravan in Barry, South Wales. But even then Granny didn't seem to enjoy it much. When we got back, she heaved a huge sigh of relief and put the kettle on for a 'nice cup of tea', even before taking off her coat.

'There's no place like home,' she said, standing there waiting for it to boil with the suitcases and our duffel bags piled up around her ankles.

So I can't see that now she is old and infirm, a week in a hotel, however luxurious, would be much of a treat for her. But it would be a change, and I expect the bracing sea air at Weston would do her good, besides which it would give Lucy a week off.

The lorry lurches to a stop, tilting a little to one side on the uneven, sloping ground.

11

'There we are then,' says Doug Hawthorn, a former professional deep-sea diver who is driving. 'Over to you, Cap'n.'

And I have to forget about my personal problems and give the job in hand my full attention.

I've decided that I'll dive, with Colin Bell, known as Ding-Dong, as stand-by diver and Tony Short, known as Shorty, and Carlo Morris as our handlers. Doug will oversee operations as supervisor. We get kitted up in our drysuits and check our equipment. When we're satisfied that everything is in order, it's time to go.

It's murky in the lake, the thick covering of green plant growth over the surface of the water close to the bank obscuring the sunlight, but at least we're unlikely to encounter the sort of hazards that are commonplace in canals and rivers in urban areas. Old refrigerators and microwaves, abandoned supermarket trolleys, broken chairs, you name it, someone will have seen fit to dump it. The poor access to Bolborough Lake means – hopefully! – that coming here to dispose of their rubbish would be, for most folk, more trouble than it's worth. Could be a stolen car submerged somewhere, of course – joyriders would get a kick out of racing down the bumpy track, and perhaps playing 'chicken' at the water's edge – 'Last one out's a wanker!' And once, on a training exercise at a flooded quarry, one of the team came up with an unexploded World War II bomb. Not a pleasant thought, since apart from the obvious danger, everything would have to go on hold while the bomb disposal unit was sent for.

I put such thoughts to the back of my mind and concentrate on searching, sweeping arcs with my right hand on the floor of the lake whilst holding the jackstay line with my left. Disturbed mud and silt rises, clouding the water and reducing visibility still further.

We've started by looking in the vicinity of where the burglars were last seen by the pursuing coppers, and estimated the distance they would have been likely to be able to throw the silverware haul, but Bolborough Lake is pretty big, and the perimeter a good three quarters of a mile, so I'm highly gratified when I encounter something that feels, through my thin gloves, like a metal plate.

I tug on my line to indicate I've found something. As I surface, I can see I was right – it's a silver salver. I pass it to Doug and dive again, swimming out to approximately the same distance from the bank as before, and following it to the east. I'm working on the assumption that the rest of the haul will be in more or less the same area, but possibly spaced out if, as seems likely, the lads were disposing of it as they ran. Sure enough, a bit further along I come across another salver, oval this time, and a silver candlestick.

And then what feels like a small case of some kind. Was there a trinket box on the list of missing items? I don't remember seeing it – platters, a condiment set, candlesticks and a candle snuffer, as far as I can recall. But perhaps the loser hadn't yet missed the trinket box. In any case, it's definitely not a native of the lake. I tug on my line again, gently rise to the surface.

The box isn't silver, it is covered in a dark fabric that has rotted in places. I pass it to Doug, flip up my mask.

'Good work, MJ,' he acknowledges me. 'Take a breather. Ding-Dong? Do you want to see what you can find?'

'Boss.' Ding-Dong is all wired up and ready to go.

I pull off my helmet, running my fingers through my hair, short-cut all over in a neat crop. When I was in my teens, I wore it long, and it was a thick curtain of dark waves that looked for all the world as if I'd paid a lot of money for expensive extensions. As a diver, hair like that just isn't practical and in any case, I like it this way, and I think it suits me. Long hair cries out for make-up to complement it, and I can't wear that either in my job. Just a flick of waterproof mascara and a touch of natural-toned lipstick is as girlie as I can get when I'm working.

Doug is handling the box, carefully.

'This doesn't look like part of the haul.'

'No.' I go closer to take a look. 'You're right.'

He prises the lid up carefully with his thumbs, whistles between his teeth.

There are two or three items in the box. One looks like a locket on a chain, another is a gold signet ring. But what really catches my eye is a medal in the shape of an elaborate cross, on a medal ribbon.

'What the hell is this?' I ask.

Doug's eyes narrow. He shakes his head. 'Never know what you're going to find, do you?'

'You're right there.'

'Ah – has Ding-Dong got something?'

'Great. This looks like being one of our more successful days.'

But as I go to the bank to see what Ding-Dong has come up with, it's the box I'm thinking of. How in the world did it come to be in the lake? Was it part of another haul of stolen goods from a burglary so long ago that the owner had long since given up hope of ever getting it back? I can think of no other reason for it being there. But it seems strange that the thief would throw away what were probably highly saleable items, unless, like last night's burglars, he was on the point of being apprehended. It's not really small enough to have been lost accidentally, either. Just the ring, or the locket, yes. But not the whole caboodle. Not a medal box into which the other items had been placed.

Well, however it got there, it would be nice if we could reunite it with its owner. It must be of huge sentimental value to someone.

The idea that we might be able to give someone back their lost treasures is a very satisfying one. A whole lot more worthwhile than returning collector's pieces to a man who can probably well afford to buy replacements at the next sale at Sotheby's or Christie's.

But not for one moment does it occur to me that this find may come to dominate my life. It is, at the end of the day, just another job. Far less harrowing than many that have gone before. And one which I can go back to my life and forget.

TWO

ANNE

'I have to talk to you about the college end-of-term fashion show,' Elaine, my PA, says. 'Do you think you'll be able to come in to the office, or shall I come to you?'

She sounds anxious and faintly harassed, which is not a good sign. Elaine is, by nature, calm, competent, almost completely unflappable, which is why she's so good at her job. She's had the head of fashion design at the school of art hassling her to firm up arrangements for their degree show, I imagine, and efficient though Elaine is, she doesn't feel qualified to make final decisions.

The degree show for third-year students is an annual event, for which my agency provides the models. It's a massive undertaking, staged in a marquee in the college grounds, with full lighting erected on scaffolding towers, a sophisticated sound system, and a champagne reception for dignitaries, talent scouts, boutique owners and other glitterati from the world of fashion, as well as the proud relatives of the twenty-odd graduates who are showing their final collections. It takes weeks of careful planning on everyone's part, and concentrated rehearsal in the week leading up to the shows to ensure everything runs smoothly. Paris or New York Fashion Week it might not be, but with my background as a sixties catwalk model, I aim to emulate the professional shows as closely as I can. You could say – and some do – that I'm too much of a perfectionist; for me, the smallest hiccup will mar the whole event, and normally I lay out my plans like a general preparing for battle.

Not this year. I've had too much on my mind to be able to concentrate on what is the biggest event in the agency's calendar. It's almost ceased to matter. There are things in life that make business pale into insignificance. Now, however, the stress in Elaine's voice triggers a frisson of guilt, that I'm expecting too much of her, and a brief concern for the agency that I built up from scratch and that I think of as my baby.

Would it be better, under the circumstances, to tell the college to find another agency to provide the models this year? The last thing I want is to give a less-than-perfect service, to have some foul-up happen because my eye is not on the ball. But equally, allowing another agency to take over what is a regular, and lucrative, job might mean losing it permanently.

The decision is, for the moment, beyond me.

'Could you come over, Elaine?' I say. 'Bring all the files and your laptop with you, and we'll run over the options.'

'Will do. This afternoon?'

I try to get my mind into gear. Sonia usually rests for a couple of hours after I've got her some lunch; the children have to be collected from school at 3.15.

'Could you make it about half one?'

'Yes. That should be OK.'

'I'll see you then.'

A brief pause.

'How is Sonia?' Elaine asks, a little belatedly.

'Much the same.' What else is there to say?

Down the line, I hear the other telephone begin to ring.

'I'll have to go. There's another call coming in,' Elaine says.

'Yes, sure.'

We don't want to lose business. Though in the last resort, what does it matter? What does anything matter?

Except Sonia.

I've always said I live a charmed life. A happy childhood, a good education at a fee-paying girls' school, a glamorous career, catwalk modelling in the days when the fashion houses wanted girls who looked like girls and not strings of spaghetti, a happy marriage, a lovely daughter, and a successful second career running my own modelling agency. The chips always seemed to fall my way. It scared me a bit sometimes – how could one person be so lucky? Might fate have something in store to knock me off my perch and redress the balance? But the moments of intro-spection never lasted long. Unlike my mother, who is, not to put too fine a point on it, rather highly strung, I have never wasted too much time worrying about things that might never happen. I thanked God I hadn't inherited her genes, accepted that mine was a world where the sun almost always shone and believed that, with a positive outlook, I could overcome any problems that might arise.

I know now that I was right to feel occasional unease at my seemingly indestructible good fortune. I was indeed racking up a debt to fate. Now it's payback time, and I'd willingly forfeit every-thing that has so far run in my favour if it would balance the account. But of course it's too late for that. Things don't work that way. I, who have always been able to sail with the wind, have run into the perfect storm, and the sense of utter helplessness, the fear and the dread, are driving me to the edge of black despair.

Nine months ago, Sonia, my beloved daughter, was diagnosed with acute myeloid leukaemia. She's thirty-nine years old, with two children, a boy and a girl aged ten and eight, and when she started feeling tired and ill and getting nosebleeds she thought she'd just been overdoing things, running a home and family in tandem with a demanding career as a solicitor specialising in family law. In her busy life she even begrudged the time to see her GP until she reached the stage where there was really no option.

The diagnosis was the most terrible shock, though with hind-sight, I suppose it shouldn't have been. In the beginning, though, we were all determined to be optimistic. Medical science can work wonders these days – she'd get through this, and we would back her every step of the way.

When Sonia was admitted to hospital for her month-long course of chemo, it was decided that I would go and stay at her home, so that I could be on hand to help Kevin, my son-in-law, with looking after the children.

We'd discussed it at length, Rod and I, and to begin with it was all I could do to talk him out of coming too.

'It's a logistical impossibility,' I said. 'You have to be within striking distance of your office.' (Rod is a partner in a firm of quantity surveyors). 'And you've just landed that contract for the new supermarket too.'

'The supermarket can go to hell. Sonia is far more important. I should have retired by now in any case.'

'But you didn't. You're like me – you enjoy working too much.'

'Not when I should be with my daughter.'

'I know that. I understand how you feel. But you can't just walk out and leave Angus in the lurch.'

'He'd understand. He'd have to.'

'It wouldn't be fair on him. We'll manage. It's different for me. There's nothing stopping me from working on my laptop at Sonia's, and Elaine can manage the day-to-day running of the office. It's much better if you stay here and hold the fort.'

I didn't add that I thought I could cope better at Sonia's without him. Rod, usually a tower of strength, had taken the news of Sonia's illness very badly indeed, and if he no longer had his work to give him a focus, I dreaded to think what he would be like. I absolutely cannot bear it when Rod crumbles. It's like seeing a ruined fortress. And it would make it all the more difficult for me to carry on and do what needed to be done.

And so eventually it was decided. I would go to Sonia's, Rod would stay at home. On condition that I would call on him if there was anything I needed, anything he could do.

It wasn't easy, but I hadn't expected it to be, and busy as I was, there was little time for the demons to come out to play. They did sometimes creep out at night, though, when I was alone in the small double bed with the unfamiliar poppy-strewn duvet and pillows much fatter than I am used to. Then I wept for the awful change in Sonia, who had lost so much weight she looked as if a strong breeze would blow her away, wept for the loss of her thick dark hair, wept for the exhaustion in her eyes and the forced brittle brightness of her once heart-warming smile. But by day I ploughed on with determined optimism.

'She's a fighter,' I said to anyone who asked. 'She's going to be fine.'

But now I'm not so sure. I'm still staying with her – when she came out of hospital, she really wasn't up to coping alone – and in the last couple of weeks I've seen her going downhill again. Frankly I'm worried half to death. She's due to have further tests next week. I'm very afraid they will show that she's relapsing, and it may well be that we're reaching the point where her only hope is a bone marrow transplant.

That, of course, is something of a lottery, especially given that we are such a small family. I suspect Rod and I will be told we're too old to be considered as possible donors, we're both only children, and Sonia doesn't have brothers or sisters either. When she was small, I was so busy with my career the time never seemed right, and to be honest, I didn't really want another baby. I'd been very sick the whole nine months of my pregnancy, so much so that I ended up in hospital. I had a horrendous labour – thirty hours of hell without an epidural – and then, when Sonia was born, she was a colicky baby who cried for hours night after night. I shrank from the prospect of going through it all again. I kept putting it off and putting it off and was actually quite relieved when I realised I'd left it too late. Why would I want another child anyway? I had Sonia, my lovely little girl, and she was more than enough for me. I adored her, wanted to wrap her in my love and attention, give her everything without having to share it out amongst siblings.

Now, though, I am tearing myself apart over what I think of, in the dark hours of the night, as my selfishness. If Sonia had brothers and sisters she would have a much better chance of finding a suitable donor for a bone marrow transplant. Siblings, apparently, are not only more likely to provide a match, but also the risk of complications is reduced. I know this because I checked it out on the internet. We haven't got around to it with the consultant as yet, or at least, Kevin hasn't told us that it's been mentioned. But I've been thinking about it, trying to check family trees for obscure relatives who might be a match in case it comes to that, and drawing blanks at every turn.

I've made discreet enquiries of my mother, too, though I've kept hidden from her just how ill Sonia really is. I'm very afraid the truth might trigger a bout of the depression she's suffered from periodically for most of her life. She'd want to help in any way she could, I'm sure; my mother has always had a keen sense of family. Then, when she realised there was nothing she could do, it would just make things worse. And if it did tip her over the edge, I don't know how I would cope with it, on top of everything else. I already feel I'm neglecting her – she still lives all alone in the huge old house that Dad had built as the family home, absolutely refuses to leave it and move into sheltered accommodation or nearer to me. But she has become very needy since he died two years ago, and with all this going on with Sonia, I can't get over to see her and make sure she's all right as often as I used to.

It's all piling up horribly. Sonia. My mother. Harry and Abigail, Sonia's children. Rod at home alone. Poor Elaine left to run the agency.

I feel I'm sinking under a weight that just gets heavier and heavier, as if I were drowning in a sea of confusion and anxiety. And utter helplessness.

All I can do is repeat the mantra, over and over.

Just as long as Sonia is all right, nothing else matters. Please, oh please, let us have good news next week.

But a horrible, nagging little voice whispers in my ear, and sick dread tugs at my heart.

I very much fear that there is worse to come.

THREE

MARTHA

My find made the papers: a full front-page spread in the locals – 'Mystery of Treasures in Bolborough Lake' – and a couple of columns in the national dailies. There were photographs, too, of the medal, a French Croix de Guerre, apparently, the ring and the locket, displayed against the faded and watermarked velvet, and of me – 'the police diver who recovered the treasures'. Not a very flattering likeness, but then, I defy anyone to look glamorous in a drysuit and hood, and I don't much like having my photograph taken at the best of times. But Amanda Coles, the ex-journalist who heads up our press relations department, was keen enough on the idea to put pressure on the chief superintendent, and orders from on high must be obeyed. I was wheeled out, albeit reluctantly, for the benefit of a chap with a digital camera who posed me in full gear against the backdrop of our van, and encouraged me with the patter he must have used a million times before. I suppose Amanda and the chief super thought it would be good publicity for the police for a change; I thought it was just damn stupid – and embarrassing. I only hoped it might help track down the owner of the medal, locket and ring.

How the box had come to be in the lake was as much of a mystery as who it belonged to, though speculation had it that most likely it was stolen property that had been dumped when the thief had been unable to find a fence to get rid of his haul. But why in Bolborough Lake? There was a good reason for the stuff we'd been diving for to be there; it had just been nicked from Bolborough House, and the burglars had a couple of burly local bobbies on their tails.

This was something different entirely. A Croix de Guerre would surely have been of interest to an unscrupulous collector somewhere, though it might have been tricky to dispose of, and the ring and locket must have been worth a few quid. Lists of stolen and lost property had been checked and no match found, at least as far back as records went. It was an inexact science, of course; the box had probably been in the water long before the days of computerisation, and trawling the dusty registers of days gone by would have taken too many precious man hours, even if the theft or loss had occurred in our area. The brains of some old retired officers were picked, but nobody who was still alive, and compos mentis, had any recollection of anything that fitted the bill, nor of anyone who might have been awarded a Croix de Guerre ever living in the locality. Really the best chance we had of finding out who the box and its contents belonged to was the publicity Amanda had generated.

It was quite likely, of course, that the recipient of the medal was no longer in the land of the living, but if they were, it would be nice to be able to return it to them. And if not, there might well be relatives who would be glad, and proud, to have it.

But it's almost a week now since *The Western News*, our regional paper, ran the front-page spread, and several days since the nationals picked it up, and nothing. Nothing, either, from the items on the local TV and radio stations. I wish to goodness someone would come forward – Amanda is talking now about me doing a live interview on Radio Bristol, and I can't imagine anything more horrifying. I was forced into a radio interview once before, when I was promoted to head up the diving team, and it was horrible. Not the fault of the radio station – they did their best to put me at my ease. A nice young chap in jeans and wire-rimmed spectacles collected me from reception, got me a paper cup of coffee and another of water, and yacked to me in between fiddling with switches and answering the telephone while I waited in the control room, or whatever they call it, outside the studio. The presenter was pleasant, too, shaking my hand, showing me how far to sit from the microphone and warning me not to drum my fingers on the desk or anything else that would go out loud and clear across the airwaves.

'Relax,' he said. 'We're having a little chat, that's all.'

A little chat! With thousands of listeners. Relax! When my throat was so dry I couldn't imagine that anything would come out but a croak, and the cup of coffee had made me desperate for the loo.

I was OK, they said afterwards; it was all absolutely fine. But it is not an experience I am anxious to repeat. I am beginning to wish I'd never found that blooming box. If I'd sent Ding-Dong down first, he might have been the one having to pose for ridiculous photographs and go on radio chat shows. He'd enjoy it, most likely. He's always the first to volunteer when they want someone to do a talk for a Rotary Club or a WI. Then again, they might still be pushing for me to do it. I am the sergeant in charge of the unit, and I am a woman. A bit of a novelty.

'People like to see a pretty face,' Amanda said.

The cheek of it! If that had come from the chief super, I'd have grounds for a complaint of sexual harassment. If I was one for that kind of crap – which I'm not. Mostly I take all the non-PC stuff that goes on in my stride. You have to if you want to fit in. And I can't honestly say I lose any sleep over it.

Lucy probably would. I remember once when we were young, a chap in the office where she worked began making suggestive remarks – or at least, Lucy thought they were suggestive – and she got herself worked up into quite a state about it.

'Just slap his face if he gets too fresh,' I told her. 'Even better – a knee in the balls. That would soon cool him off.'

She didn't take my advice, of course. She had a word with a senior manager. That put a stop to the innuendo, but it made for an awkward atmosphere and Lucy left soon afterwards for a job in a predominantly female office. She wouldn't have lasted five minutes in the police force. You really have to be able to give as good as you get – and I do, even if I never have had to resort to that knee in the groin or any other sort of physical retribution, though there have been times when I've been sorely tempted.

That newspaper photographer, for instance. 'Look at me, darling. Smile! Beautiful. And again . . . perfect! Ever thought of doing this for a living? You've got just the figure for it . . .'

Bloody cheek! Did he think I came down with the last shower? I hope to God they don't want me posing again in a hurry. But I think I could even put up with that as long as I don't have to go on the radio. Or TV. Shit, that would be even worse . . .

Lucy thinks it's all very exciting, however. Last week when I visited, she could hardly talk about anything else.

'I couldn't believe it when I opened the paper and saw a picture of you!' she bubbled. 'I bought three copies. And I very nearly jumped a traffic light, I was so desperate to get home and show it to Granny.'

'Not a good idea,' I said.

'Oh, it was only those temporary ones at the end of the road. They stick on red for hours, and there's never anything coming the other way.'

'You don't know that.'

Odd for me to be the one cautioning Lucy, instead of the other way around. But I absolutely believed her when she said: 'Well I didn't jump it, anyway. I just felt like it. I mean, all that stuff in Bolborough Lake – and you found it! It's incredible. And so romantic – and sad!'

She laid her knitting down in her lap, untangling the wool from around her finger and pushing the stitches well down the needles. Lucy always has some knitting on the go. This looked like a jumper for one of her boys, navy blue Aran. How on earth she memorises those complicated patterns is beyond me. I never got beyond garter stitch when Granny tried to teach me, and that looked like something the cat dragged in, a higgledy-piggledy hotchpotch of uneven rows and dropped stitches.

'Sad?' I echoed Lucy's choice of word as though I didn't know what she was talking about. Though I'd thought much the same myself, some imp of contrary mischief made me want to challenge her. Plus, truth to tell, I'm getting a bit fed up with the subject.

'Well of course it's sad! Those things must have meant a lot to somebody. The medal – that's a huge honour! Heaven knows what someone went through to win that. And a ring! And a locket with a child's hair! They're all really sentimental things. It's awful to think of them being lost, or stolen. I'd be heartbroken if it was me. Things like that are irreplaceable. Well, I think so, anyway.'

'That's stating the obvious.' That was Phil, Lucy's husband. He was watching a snooker match on TV with the sound turned down. 'You never throw anything away.'

'I do! Just not things that matter.'

'George's first baby shoes? God, woman, what do you want with them? He's a size nine now, and never wears anything but trainers and rugby boots. And all those boxes of cards and drawings . . .' He raised an eyebrow in my direction. 'She's kept every card they've ever sent her.'

'They *drew* them. And decorated them with stickers and glitter stuff . . .'

'The loft floor is going to collapse under the weight of it all one of these days.'

'Oh – go back to your billiards,' Lucy retorted amiably.

'Snooker. It's snooker.'

'Snooker, then. You'll never understand how important these things can be to a woman.' She looked at me for support, realised it was unlikely to be forthcoming, and turned to Granny instead. 'I'm right, aren't I, Granny? You've still got that necklace Mum made for you when she was a little girl, haven't you? The coloured beads strung on a length of plastic.'

Granny nodded and smiled faintly with the side of her mouth that still works properly. And there was a faraway look in her good eye; the other droops so that it is almost closed.

'I have. And the china . . . china *horse* she got me with her . . . oh, what is it? – her present . . . no, no, her *pocket money*.'

The words were a little slurred and hesitant, but at least she got there in the end. Her visits to the speech therapist seem to be working.

25

It breaks my heart, though, to see her like this. My Granny, always so strong, so capable and loving, reduced to a shell of her former self.

Where would we be without Granny? When Mum and Dad were killed, there really was no one else. Both were only children, and Dad's parents had gone to Spain to live when they retired, selling up the family home, buying a bijou apartment in a pleasant development in a mountain village and spending the difference like there was no tomorrow on the expat lifestyle of long boozy lunches and even boozier evenings. They wouldn't have had the space nor the inclination to take on two distraught small girls. If Granny hadn't stepped in, I expect we'd have ended up in a home, or with a succession of foster parents.

Granny, bless her, wasn't going to let that happen.

Lucy and I were away on a school trip when the accident happened. Mum and Dad had taken the opportunity to sneak a much-needed holiday while we were away, a week in Tenerife. Except that they never got there. Their plane ploughed into a mountainside as it came in to land, as I understand it. At the time we weren't told many details, or if we were, we were too shocked to take them in. All we knew was that Mum and Dad were not going to be coming home, and we couldn't take that in either. Sometimes I wonder if Mum had a premonition – I remember her hugging us very tight when she dropped us off at school that last day with our duffel bags and bed rolls, tin plates and plastic cutlery. I wriggled away, embarrassed at her overt show of emotion, and eager to join my classmates. It didn't cross my mind for even a moment that I might never see her again. But perhaps it crossed hers, though I would imagine that she was afraid something would happen to one of us, not the other way round.

I don't have much recall of those first days; it's mostly a nightmarish blur of taut white faces and people trying to be kind and Lucy and I feeling that our world had come to an end. But I do remember Granny and Grampy coming to fetch us. We sat one each side of Granny in the back seat of Grampy's old Saab 96; she had her arms round us both. We burrowed into her, crying, and I looked up and saw tears running down her cheeks too. That really shocked me – Granny crying! I think I knew then, if I hadn't known before, that this was real and it was serious, not some bad dream I would soon wake up from.

They took us home to collect clothes and belongings and I remember our next-door neighbour hightailing it indoors when she saw us drawing up at the gate. I couldn't understand it at the time; she'd been really friendly with Mum, and always made a fuss of Lucy and me. Now, of course, I know she was one of those people who run away from anyone touched by bereavement or tragedy because they don't know what to say. At the time, though, I was puzzled and hurt. Just another little hurt on top of the enormous one, but scratching at my raw grief like a thorn on an open wound.

When we'd gathered together clothes and other belongings, Granny and Grampy took us to Little Compton, the Somerset village where they lived. And so began the first chapter of the rest of my life.

The bedroom Lucy and I used to share when we went to stay became our home; the once immaculately tidy living room was soon littered with our toys and books, though Grampy did insist none of our clutter was allowed in the front room. 'We've got to have one place kept tidy,' he would say in what we called his policeman's voice – a lowering of his tone to a growl that you didn't argue with. He was a typical old-style village copper, was Grampy; good fun, one hell of a sense of humour, generous and kind, unless you got on the wrong side of him. Then – watch out! I loved him dearly – he was the reason I wanted to join the force in the first place. From the time when I was a little girl I loved playing with his whistle and truncheon – sadly, he'd never let me play with his handcuffs, though he did once put them on me when I begged hard enough – and I was fascinated by his endless repertoire of tales about villains and cute found dogs and gruesome sudden deaths, though Granny would try to shut him up when we got him started on those.

'The children don't want to hear such things!' she would say fiercely. 'You'll give them nightmares!'

But: 'We do! We do!' we would chorus. 'Tell us the one about the man who got burnt to a cinder! Tell us about the head that rolled down the road . . .' Nothing was too ghoulish – even Lucy, though she covered her face with her hands, would peep through her fingers, her eyes huge and round, as she relished every morbid detail. Those stories were a sort of real-life equivalent of watching Dr Who from behind the sofa.

Which brings me back to the front room. As I already mentioned, it was sacrosanct. When we went in there to watch TV, play Abba records on the stereo unit that was Grampy's pride and joy, we were allowed to take only one doll or soft toy each with us. Or the knitting Granny was trying to teach us. Not both. Needless to say, I never wanted to take the knitting.

Oddly enough, given our terrible loss, I remember those as happy days. Children adapt to their circumstances, I suppose. They are programmed to survive. And Granny and Grampy were not strangers to us; we'd visited them regularly, once a month for Sunday lunch and high tea, sometimes for a whole weekend when they babysat us while Mum and Dad went out to a dance or to see a film, and we'd stayed with them, just the two of us, for a whole week each school holiday. They'd take us on day trips to Weston-super-Mare or Bristol Zoo, and I'd help Grampy make marmalade when the Easter holidays were early enough to coincide with Seville oranges being still in the shops, and jam and chutney in the summer. Grampy was a great jam and chutney maker, and I loved helping him, using a wooden spoon to wrinkle the skin on the puddle of sweet plum or strawberry when he spread it on a saucer, and sticking labels on the filled pots, and fastening down the greaseproof paper lids with strong rubber bands. They looked so satisfyingly good when they were done, and lined up in a row on the top shelf of the larder. And the kitchen smelled delicious for days afterwards.

Really, I must make some jam myself one of these days – if I can get around to saving the jars, and buying the fruit . . .

I suppose, in those early days, living with Granny and Grampy seemed a bit unreal, a bit like being on holiday. We still half expected Mum and Dad to come and collect us and take us home. We hadn't really grasped that they'd gone for ever. And by the time we did, we'd sort of acclimastised. There were times, of course, when we got really upset and clung together, sobbing. There were times when I'd wake in the night, aching so badly for Mum that the pain would become physical, pounding in my head, griping in my stomach. Once, I packed my pyjamas and toothbrush and Betsy, my bedraggled blue bear, into my duffel bag and set out with the intention of walking the forty miles home. Wretched as I was, the whole thing had the aura of a great adventure, and planning it made me feel a whole lot better – resourceful and determined, the master of my own fate. I'd gone the best part of two miles, I suppose, when Grampy caught up with me, plodding along the grass verge in my wellington boots – I'd decided to wear them in case I got caught in the rain, or had to cross a muddy brook. Grampy was driving the police panda car, so a ride in that was my compensation for having my great adventure curtailed. He even put on the siren and flashing light – 'the twos and blues', he called them – as a special treat when he was sure there was no other traffic about, and listening to the chatter on the police radio made me forget my disappointment at having my plan scuppered.

Or perhaps I was just relieved that I didn't have to go through with it. After all, Mum and Dad wouldn't be at home when I got there – if I got there – would they? It would be just the house, locked up and empty. Or, even worse, there might be strangers living in it . . .

Perhaps starting at a new school was the most daunting thing about moving to Little Compton. But even that turned out not to be as bad as we expected. It was quite a small school, a village C of E, with a playing field as well as a good-sized yard, and a real old-fashioned brass bell on the wall beside the main entrance that one of the teachers rang every morning, at lunch break, and at the end of afternoon lessons. By the time we started there, both Lucy and I had a peg allocated to us in the cloakroom, marked by a card with our name on it, like all the others. Mine also had a picture of a starfish; Lucy, being two years older, had to make do with just her name.

Of course we missed our pals, but the other children were quite friendly – they'd been briefed, I expect, and in any case, we were quite a curiosity: the two girls whose parents had been killed. *In a plane crash! Abroad!* Years later, Esther Harrison, who became my best friend, told me that that had somehow added to the awful fascination. 'Abroad' seemed so much worse than if it had happened in England.

After a while – months, a year maybe – the extraordinary merged into the ordinary. Granny and Grampy occupied the space in our lives left by the loss of Mum and Dad. The unbearable moments of raw grief came less often, the fierce longing for what had gone forever paled to bittersweet nostalgia. There was 'then' and there was 'now', and the past was a foreign country with no frontier posts through which we could pass. We grew up, two surprisingly normal little girls. And I have no doubt that was mostly down to Granny. She was the one who was always there for us. The one who fed us and clothed us and listened to our problems and praised our successes.

For me, especially, she was the one who always seemed to understand – an empathy that, strangely enough, transcended even the bond I'd shared with Mum. Perhaps because I was older now than the small child I had been when Mum died, perhaps because Granny was older, with a lifetime's experience to draw on and more time to let things work themselves out. Or perhaps because we were alike. I don't know, I'm not one of those people who dissect every relationship and try to work out what makes it tick. I only know there was always a bridge of understanding between Granny and me.

I remember one occasion, early on, when I'd been having one of my down times. Something quite trivial had set it all off – one afternoon in school I'd broken my ruler by bending it to flick a paper ball, and, silly as it sounds, I shrank from telling my teacher. The thought of being told off, perhaps hauled up in front of the class as an example of how not to behave, was for me, in my fragile state, just horrible. I thought I might cry – already the tears were pricking behind my eyes at the prospect – and the shame would be more than I could bear. I hid the two pieces of snapped plastic in my desk, and as I didn't need a ruler for the rest of the afternoon, the problem was still unresolved and hanging over my head like a dark cloud when I came home. I was dreading going to school next day; I wanted Mum desperately.

'What's the matter with you, Martha?' Granny asked. I was moping about, didn't even want to go outside to play – very unlike me.

'Nothing,' I mumbled.

'I'm sure there is. You look as if you've lost a pound and found a penny.'

'That's stupid.' My lower lip was wobbling. I bit it fiercely, turned away to hide the tears that were gathering in my eyes. 'Just leave me alone!'

But the tears were spilling over anyway, my shoulders shaking.

'Oh, come here!' Granny went to put her arms round me; I shrank away.

I'm not a touchy-feely person; never was.

Granny didn't try to force me; neither was she hurt or affronted. She seemed to know instinctively how I felt. She just patted me on the shoulder, twisted a curl behind my ear, and fetched Betsy, my bear, who was sitting, askew, on the windowsill.

'Here's Betsy, my love. If you can't tell me what's wrong, you tell her.'

For a moment I resisted, not wanting to be thought a baby. Then I grabbed Betsy, holding her tight, burying my face in her scraggly blue fur. A lifeline to a safe, familiar place.

'Better?' Granny asked after a minute.

I nodded.

'So, are you going to tell me about it? Are you just sad, or is there something in particular?'

I told her. When I finished, she shook her head and smiled.

'Well, that's nothing to get so upset about. Miss Blackman isn't going to be cross with you about that.'

'It's not just that. It's . . .'

'You feel stupid, I know. That's the worst of it.'

I nodded.

'Look, all you've got to do is go straight up to her and own up and that'll be the end of it.' Her eyes twinkled. 'Just so long as you don't try flicking paper with a ruler again.'

'I won't,' I said solemnly.

Already I was feeling better. Just sharing my secret with Granny had done that. And she hadn't tried to smother me when I didn't want it, either. But I had the comfortable feeling she'd be there for me if I did. Granny understood me. I knew that on an unconscious level, and it was more comforting than all the hugs in the world could ever be.

Much later, I came to realise what a remarkable woman she was. How strong she'd been for us when she must have been torn apart by grief herself, by the loss of her only daughter. How strong, and kind, and wise.

Which is why now it's so awful to see her reduced to a shadow of her former self, unable to communicate properly, dependent for her basic needs on those who once depended on her. Old age is damn cruel.

I remembered the idea I'd had about taking her on holiday.

'How do you fancy a break, Granny?' I said. 'I've got some leave coming up. We could go away for a few days if you like.'

I saw the doubt in her one good eye, then saw her glance at Lucy.

'Oh, you'd like that, Granny, wouldn't you?' Lucy said, too quickly, too eagerly.

And Granny nodded, though the understanding between us is a two-way street, and I knew she wasn't really keen on the idea. But she knows she's a burden on Lucy, and she hates it. A holiday with me would give Lucy a breather.

'We could go to Weston-super-Mare,' I said. 'The sea air would do you the world of good.'

The corner of her mouth that still works properly twisted up.

'Sea? What sea?'

I laughed. Weston-super-Mare, on the Bristol Channel, is famous for the acres of mudflats beyond the beach; the tide hardly ever seems to be in.

'Shall I see if I can book a hotel, then? On the front? So you will see the sea sometimes, at least?'

Granny nodded again, and this time when our eyes met I could feel the old connection between us. She might not care for holidays, but she would like to spend some time with me.

So now I've got to see about fixing it up. Sooner, rather than later. And hey, that way I might just get out of this radio interview Amanda's rabbiting on about. Which has got to be a bonus, however you look at it.

FOUR

It's four thirty in the afternoon as our lorry pulls into the parking bay at Almondsbury. We've been on a bit of a wild goose chase today; we were called down to Dorset, where a small boy had gone missing. The local police wanted a lake near his home searched in case he'd wandered down there and tumbled in, but by the time we arrived he'd turned up, safe and sound. To my enormous relief. There's nothing worse than having to recover the body of a child.

We'd stopped off for a cup of tea in the Dorset nick, and even off our patch there was a fair bit of interest in my find in Bolborough Lake. It was the Croix de Guerre that did it, I expect. Hard-nosed policemen find it hard to get excited about sentimental items like a ring and a locket. But a prestigious French decoration is something else.

As I mentioned before, I'm getting heartily sick of talking about it, so I am not best pleased when, as I clamber down from the lorry, the local newspaper reporter who interviewed me before emerges from nowhere and collars me.

'Sergeant Holley.'

The reporter is a good-looking chap of about forty. Slim build, medium height – only a couple of inches taller than me, and I'm five foot seven, but with the sort of physique that suggests he works out at the gym regularly, or plays a sport. Some reporters I know look as if they get through too much whisky and too many cigarettes for their own good – not unlike some policemen, really. Not this one. He has cropped hair, receding a little at the temples, which actually opens up his face, a strong nose that looks as if it might have been broken at some time, and dark eyes that narrow when he speaks to you, giving him a sort of intensity. Against that, his style of dressing is throwaway smart casual – open-neck checked shirt with the sleeves rolled back to the elbows, loosely knotted tie, Italian-style loafers. All in all I might find him attractive if I wasn't so turned off by his profession. I absolutely cannot abide the gentlemen of the press. Vultures! Pushy, hypocritical, heartless, feeding off the gory details of the misfortunes of others.

Bit of a waste, really, one so dishy making his living prying into things that are none of his business. But I expect he finds his looks and manner quite an asset when it comes to winkling stories out of gullible young women – and maybe the not-so-young too.

Well, he needn't think for one minute he can fool me with his false charm.

'Yes?' I say shortly.

'Pete Holbrook.' He holds out his hand. I ignore it.

'Yes, I know. *Western News*, isn't it?'

His mouth quirks in a lopsided smile, those dark eyes narrow almost to slits and crinkles appear from the corners as he gazes at me intently. 'Come-to-bed eyes', we used to call them in the days when my girlfriends and I were young, free and single.

'I'm flattered you remember.'

'Oh, I've got the press pegged.' I gesticulate to the gear I'm carrying. 'Look, I'm really busy right now. And there's nothing I can tell you. You'll have to speak to our PR – Amanda—'

'You haven't heard, then?' he interrupts me.

That stops me in my tracks.

'Heard what . . . ?' I break off. Fool for giving him an opening!

'That the stuff you found in Bolborough Lake has been claimed.'

I feel the jolt of surprise run through me, but this time I'm better prepared.

'I've been out of the office all day, Mr Holbrook. I can't tell you anything. And I have no comment to make. Sorry.'

I turn away, away from those disconcerting eyes, heading across the yard. He follows me.

'No, but I can tell *you*, Sergeant Holley. I think you'll be interested . . .'

'You OK, MJ?' Doug calls.

'Fine.' I don't need protecting from a reporter who thinks he's God's gift.

I keep walking. So does he.

'It's a woman from Portishead. A Stella Leverton. She was involved with the SOE – the Special Operations outfit in the Second World War. Was an agent in France. That's how she came to be awarded the Croix de Guerre.'

'Thank you, Mr Holbrook. I'm sure I'll get the details if I want them.'

'That's not the best bit. And do you have to call me Mr Holbrook? My name's Pete.'

I stop, turn to face him.

'It doesn't matter what I call you. I've said all I'm going to say to you. OK?'

Another wry, upward twist of his mouth.

'Pity. I was hoping you could help me out on this one.'

'Not my job,' I say shortly. I've reached the door that leads into our office. I hold it open with one shoulder, manoeuvring my gear inside.

'She wants to talk to you,' he says.

That very nearly stops me in my tracks, but I know better than to be lured into letting the creep see it. I bundle my gear through the aperture, intending to push the door closed behind me. But his foot is in the way.

'Aren't you intrigued, Sergeant? I know I am.'

'Nope.' I give the door a push. 'I'd move your foot if I was you. Unless you want that poncy leather scratched beyond repair.'

He laughs. 'I've survived a lot worse than you can throw at me. Come on, Sergeant, do me a favour. Just five minutes of your time, and I promise you'll be as interested as I am.'

'Can you move please, pal?' Doug, also laden down with kit, is behind the persistent reporter. He has no choice but to give way, and gratefully I escape inside. Not even Call-me-Pete will follow me in here.

I hope!

'Well done, Doug,' I say as we go into our office and start stowing the gear. 'That fellow is a real pain in the ass.'

'Aren't they all?' Doug lifts our kettle, shaking it to ascertain if there's water in it, decides there is and switches it on. 'Do you want a cup of tea?'

'Why not?' I'm in no hurry to get home to my lonely flat, a microwaved meal and an evening of trying to find something worth watching on the telly. 'Did you hear what he was saying? The owner of the box I found in Bolborough Lake has come forward.'

'No kidding!'

'It seems it's an elderly lady who lives in Portishead. Who was an SOE agent in France in the war.'

'And she's the one who won the Croix de Guerre?'

'Apparently so.'

'Well, well.'

'And you haven't heard the rest. It seems she wants to meet me.'

Doug is searching among the used mugs in the sink for his — a cracked but highly valued monstrosity bearing the West Ham logo. For some unfathomable reason he supports their football team.

'Why the hell would she want to meet you?'

'Because I'm the one who found her treasures, I suppose.'

'You didn't agree to anything?' Doug has found the mug now and is rinsing it under the cold tap.

'What do you think? When have I ever played into the hands of the press gang?' I nod towards the sink. 'Is my cup there?'

'Looks like it.' Doug holds aloft a mug with bold blue and white stripes — the last survivor of a set Nick and I bought when we were first married. 'Want me to wash it up for you?'

'Thanks, I'll do it myself.' I'm pretty unimpressed with Doug's ideas of domestic hygiene, and he'll use the grubby tea towel to dry it, too. 'No, chances are he made up that part to try and get my attention, now that I come to think about it. You're quite right, actually. Why in the world would she want to meet me?'

As I admit it, I feel just the tiniest shard of disappointment. The thought of actually meeting a woman who had done something remarkable enough to win the Croix de Guerre is rather an enticing one. But it ain't going to happen. It's pie in the sky. Knowing I've reunited her with it, and with her other treasures, has to be satisfaction enough. If I've made her happy in her old age, I'm glad.

The kettle's boiling, the other members of the team are piling into the office. The chaps start talking football – there's some big local derby being played tonight, apparently. I switch off. But I'm still thinking about an old lady in Portishead who was once a special agent in occupied France when she was probably a lot younger than I am now. And though I'd never admit it to Pete Holbrook, or anyone else, come to that, I'm impressed. And intrigued.

When I get home, the light on my phone is blinking, indicating a message, or messages. I press the button, listening as I strip off my work clothes.

There are two. The first is from Lucy.

'Granny seems really excited about your offer to take her on holiday. Can we talk about it?'

I raise an eyebrow. 'Really excited' seems a bit of an exaggeration. It's Lucy who's 'really excited' at the prospect of a few days off duty, I suspect. But I owe it to both of them. I'll go online later, have a look at hotels, check out any special offers. Not that I'm mean, but I have a budget to consider. Police officers might be a lot better paid than they used to be, but I still don't have that much cash to splash.

Message two is Nick. A nerve tightens in my stomach at the sound of his voice, and I freeze, still as a statue, and clad only in bra and pants.

'Ricky Gervais is coming to the Colston Hall. Just thought you might be interested. See you.'

I click off the answering machine and stand, for a moment, with my finger on the button.

What is Nick playing at? Is he relaying information because he knows I like Ricky Gervais, or is he getting around to suggesting we should go together?

Recently, I've had the feeling he is trying to worm his way back in with me. I could be wrong – I have been plenty of times before – but he has been rather friendly. Whenever our paths have crossed he makes some quip, or allusion to our life together. Last week it was spaghetti bolognese.

'I'm making a big pot of your favourite Italian tonight,' he said.

For some reason, he'd come up to the traffic HQ that shares our base at Almondsbury; he was wearing his leathers, though not his helmet, and looking every inch the handsome police motorcyclist I'd fallen for.

'Good for you,' I said.

'Thought you might be having withdrawal symptoms.'

'I can live with it.'

'OK, OK, it was just a thought.'

I shook my head, walked away. But the truth is I *am* having withdrawal symptoms, of sorts, and not just for Nick's delicious concoction of minced beef, onion and whatever else he throws in – red wine, certainly. I do miss the fun and the company and the loving. What I absolutely do not miss is the pressure to be something I am not, and the suspicion, nay certainty, that he plays away. That I would not go back to for any amount of his sexual prowess, or spaghetti bolognese.

Now here he is ringing to tell me that Ricky Gervais is coming to the Colston Hall. Hmm.

I play the message again, but it leaves me none the wiser. Perhaps I am reading too much into it. Perhaps it really is just a friendly call. But if it's more . . .

No way, Nick, I mutter fiercely.

And wish, at the same time, that I could be more forgiving.

The call from Amanda Coles comes in at just after four.

It's been a quiet day today; I've actually managed to get most of my paperwork up to date, thank goodness, and I'm feeling pretty pleased with myself.

39

Hearing Amanda's voice on the other end of the line punctures my smug satisfaction, though, with a bolt of irritation. What does she want now? It takes me less than a minute to find out.

'Martha . . .' Amanda never calls me MJ like everyone else. 'There have been developments in regard to your find. In Bolborough Lake,' she adds, as if I could be in any doubt. 'The loser has come forward.'

'Yes, so I heard.'

'Oh.' She sounds a bit offended, as if news was her sole prerogative, then gets into her stride again. 'The thing is, she wants to meet you.'

'Yes. I heard that too. Except that I can't quite believe it.'

'Who told you?' This time she is seriously annoyed.

'The *Western News* reporter. Twenty-four hours ago. You're a bit slow off the mark this time, Amanda.'

She ignores this. 'OK. Well, whether you believe it or not, it happens to be true. She has specifically asked to see you so that she can thank you herself. And it seems to me it would be a perfect opportunity for some good publicity. It would make a very good picture, you and Miss Leverton – with the medal, of course.'

'Oh, I don't think so.'

'The ACC thinks so too,' she carries on, regardless. 'I happened to see him at lunchtime – we were at a civic reception at the Council House – and I ran it past him.'

'Shit,' I mutter. That's all I need, Amanda cooking up cock-eyed schemes with the top brass over a glass of sherry and a dish of salted peanuts. What is the matter with the woman? Why can't she just field criticism and supply journalists with the details of new initiatives, without behaving as if she were a stringer for the *Daily Express*? Bring back Bluey Morrison, the old PR officer she was hired to replace, that's what I say. Bluey did his job without bothering anybody and forgot about it when he went home at night. Amanda seems to eat, drink and sleep stupid ideas for getting the Avon and Somerset Constabulary in the news. Could be, of course, that that's why Bluey got edged out.

'What I'm thinking is just a photograph . . .'

40

'You're not getting me into my drysuit again for it. I'm not vain, but—'

'No, of course not your drysuit. Just normal uniform.'

'Well, cheers for that!'

'. . . and maybe a couple of paragraphs about Miss Leverton, how pleased she is to have her medal back, what she did to win it, that sort of thing. I've got a reporter who's interested . . .'

'I'll bet you have. His name doesn't happen to be Pete Holbrook, by any chance?'

'As a matter of fact, yes.'

'And – don't tell me – this was all his idea.'

Amanda bristles.

'Not at all. It was mine.'

Oh yes, pull the other one. When I turned him down flat, Pete Holbrook went to Amanda. He must have known she'd jump at the opportunity. And get the necessary permission from on high, too.

I can see where he's coming from, of course. An old wartime heroine reunited with her decoration is a good human interest story, and quite a meaty one, at that, if he can get her to talk about her former exploits. It could well turn out to be the sort of thing he could work up into a big feature for the nationals, a double-page spread in the *Mail on Sunday*, perhaps, if his contract with the *Western News* allows it. I've no idea how reporters work – I just know they can be pretty unscrupulous with the scent of fame and fortune in their nostrils.

What I can't understand, though, is why he's so keen to get me involved. I'd have thought he was perfectly capable of getting his story all by himself.

'So, can we talk times?' Amanda says. 'When would suit you?'

'I haven't a clue. I never know where I'm going to be, or what I'm going to be doing, from one day to the next.'

'What about tomorrow?'

'As I say, I don't know. Depends if a job comes in.'

'Suppose I ring you first thing in the morning? You'll know then . . .'

'Not necessarily.'

'If it looks like you've got a clear day, I'll go ahead and firm up the arrangements,' she persists. 'Otherwise we'll have to schedule it for your next rest day.'

'OK, ring me in the morning,' I agree with bad grace.

'We really should make it soon, while the story is still fresh in people's minds,' she says, more pleasantly now she's got me where she wants me. 'Besides which, Miss Leverton is really quite old. And you never know, when people are getting on a bit . . .'

Heartless bitch! Of course, she used to be a newspaper reporter herself, I remember.

'Point taken,' I say, hoping my cool tone will let her know how disgusted I am. Not that she'll care. Her sort have skins like rhinoceroses.

I'm still fuming when I put down the phone. But I'm also curious, and maybe just a little bit flattered. That an old-time heroine should actually want to meet me – a two-bit police diver who'll never, in a million years, get to do anything worthy of a Croix de Guerre. Who'll never, in all probability, amount to very much at all.

FIVE

The development of retirement apartments where Stella Leverton is living out the last years of her life occupies a prime location on the marina, looking out on to the sea, which is, today, calm and sparkling in the sun.

I park my Golf among the solid-looking but mostly new and well-cared-for saloons and estate cars, feeling a bit like a poor relation. It's my pride and joy, and it packs a good punch under the bonnet, but the number plate gives away the fact that it's six years old, and it's still mud-splattered from the heavy rain we had last week – so much for it being summer! Washing the car is not high on my list of priorities. Old and dirty though it is, at least it locks and unlocks with an electronic device, however. I press the button and flick the key away so it won't make holes in my pocket.

There's another car that looks slightly out of place among the genteel saloons – a Toyota RAV4. I squint at it suspiciously. I don't know what car Pete Holbrook drives – the first time I met him he had ridden with the photographer, saving expenses, and when he accosted me outside our HQ I was too hell bent on escaping him to notice an unfamiliar vehicle. But he could well be the type who'd go for a RAV4. Has he beaten me to it? Is he already pulling Stella Leverton apart at the seams? My hackles rise and I tell myself: 'Calm down. Count to ten. No point giving yourself a heart attack.'

I was right, though. I've only made it halfway to what looks like the main entrance to the apartments when I hear footsteps behind me. I half turn, see an all-too-recognisable figure gaining on me.

Today he's wearing a distressed leather bomber jacket over the ubiquitous open-necked shirt.

'Morning, Sergeant. You didn't get called out on any urgent business, then?'

'No.' *Worse luck*, I add under my breath.

'No bodies or weapons to search for today.'

'Not as yet.'

'What an exciting life you lead!'

I choose to ignore that.

'You got Amanda on your side, then,' I say instead.

'D'you blame me?'

'Yes, actually.'

'She's a pushover, that one.'

'From where you're standing, yes, I expect she is.'

'Go on. It's not such a hardship, surely?' He's looking at me with those narrowed bedroom eyes. I turn away and concentrate on the name tags on the entry phone.

Leverton. Miss S.

I push the bell. In the pause before it elicits an answer, I can feel his gaze on the back of my neck. It makes me uncomfortable. The speaker crackles into life.

'Hello? Who is it?'

'Shall I handle this?' Before I know quite how it happened, Pete Holbrook has taken my place in front of the entry phone panel.

'*Western News*, Miss Leverton. And Sergeant Martha Holley.'

In the briefest of pauses I feel myself bristling again.

'I'm opening the door for you now. Do come up.'

The voice, despite the crackles of static, is surprisingly firm, youthfuly almost.

There's the faintest of clicks from the door. I give it a push, determined not to relinquish all the action. It opens. Inside there's a staircase and also a lift. With the bit still between my teeth, I head for the stairs.

'Third floor, remember.' Pete, pushing the call button for the lift, sounds faintly amused. 'See you up there.'

Annoyed, I backtrack.

The lift, freshly painted and pristine, is a far cry from the ones in council blocks. It purrs upwards. I stand facing the door, avoiding looking at him. When it comes to a halt we set out along a carpeted corridor. One of the doors is ajar. An elderly woman stands in the doorway.

'Good morning!' she calls.

Stella Leverton, I presume.

For a woman who must be about ninety, she is very well preserved. A smooth oval face, iron-grey hair drawn back tightly into a knot at the nape of her neck. A slash of scarlet lipstick and the faintest hint of blusher on her still-full cheeks. She's wearing dark loose-cut trousers and a brightly patterned floral overshirt. As we approach, she fixes Pete with a stern gaze, unmade-up eyes sharp beneath slightly hooded lids.

'I thought I made it clear, young man. It's Sergeant Holley I want to talk to, not you.'

Pete raises both hands in a gesture of surrender.

'Fine – fine! I'm just the chauffeur.' Liar! 'I won't say a word, I promise.'

'But you'll be writing everything down in your notebook, I expect. Or recording it on a pocket tape machine.'

He flips open his leather jacket, all injured innocence.

'No notebooks – no tape recorders. OK?'

I wonder if he's lying again. It seems a warm day to be wearing a heavy jacket. Who knows what he's got hidden in the pockets?

'Hmm.' Miss Leverton looks him up and down, no more satisfied than I am. Presumably she didn't survive as a special agent in occupied France by being gullible. But after a moment she relents.

'Very well. Since you're here. But if you misbehave in any way, I shall ask you to leave at once. And I shall immediately telephone your editor to make a formal complaint. He is very well aware that I have expressly requested no publicity.'

'Understood.' Pete has the look of a small boy called up in front of a very strict headmistress.

'And absolutely no photographs.'

'Not my job. I stood the photographer down.'

I feel a flash of relief. Good for Miss Leverton. She certainly has put Pete Holbrook in his place. Obviously she's no more keen on having her picture taken than I am.

'Very well. On that understanding . . .' She stands aside, opening the door wider. 'Please come in.'

Beyond a minuscule lobby is an equally minuscule hall with four doors opening off it. One looks like a broom cupboard, one is presumably the bedroom and one the bathroom. The fourth door stands open.

'In here, if you would. My sitting room.'

I'm instantly surprised by how spacious it is, though given the upmarket rent this place no doubt commands, I suppose I shouldn't be. Up here on the third floor the view from the huge wraparound window is spectacular, right out over the sea.

The room is nicely furnished – neutral-coloured floor-length curtains and carpet, two brown leather armchairs, a chaise longue, a small, highly polished dining table and upright chair, a low coffee table. The only piece that looks old, apart from the chaise, is a small writing desk – yes, definitely an antique. The room is sparklingly clean and smells of fresh furniture polish and freesias – there's a bunch in a vase on the table. None of the unpleasant odours of an old person's home here. And none of the clutter I've come to associate with old people either. No family photographs, no trinkets or mementoes, just a carefully chosen ornament or two, and a couple of what look like library books and a neat stack of glossy magazines on the coffee table.

There's no sign, either, of the box I found, or its contents. I'd have thought, after having been deprived of it for so long, Miss Leverton would have it on display, especially since she was expecting us – or me, at any rate.

'Do sit down. Would you like coffee?'

'Thank you, that would be very nice.' I feel as if I'm on my best behaviour.

'Not for me, thanks,' Pete says.

Miss Leverton doesn't so much as raise an eyebrow, just smiles faintly. She's probably thinking, as I am, that he'd prefer a beer or a whisky.

She disappears to the kitchen, moving with surprising spryness for someone of her age. I perch self-consciously on the edge of one of the leather chairs, and Pete goes to the window, looking out at the stunning view.

'This place must be worth a small fortune!' he says in a low voice.

There's no time for me to answer, even if I wanted to. She's back, carrying the Pyrex jug from a coffee-making machine, which she sets down on the table. Another trip to the kitchen, and she's back with a tray already laid up with cups and saucers, milk, sugar and a plate of shortbread biscuits.

'How do you take it?' she asks me.

'Black, please.'

She pours, black for me, milky for herself, then puts them on the coffee table within easy reach. I spoon a couple of measures of demerara sugar into mine and stir. Miss Leverton does not. One of the reasons she's remained fit, no doubt.

'Yours must be a very interesting job,' she says.

'Not nearly as interesting as yours was,' I say daringly.

That faint smile again. 'Interesting? Hmm. I'm not sure that's quite how we thought of it. Necessary, very necessary to the war effort. Dangerous, certainly. Do you know that the life expectancy of an SOE wireless operator in occupied France was just six weeks, and a courier not much more? Many, many of the women who crossed the Channel never came back. They were tortured, then executed. But there you are, these were desperate times. We did what we had to do.'

Her tone is dispassionate, and I'm amazed she can talk about it so matter-of-factly, when you think of what she must have gone through, the friends she must have lost. But then again, I suppose she could never have done what she did if she didn't have a core of steel. I've seen old soldiers on TV, talking about how terrible their war was, tears running down furrowed cheeks for their lost pals, and here was this old lady dismissing what she'd done in much the same way she might talk about a visit to the supermarket. It goes to prove what I've always thought. That when it comes down to it, women are a whole lot tougher than men. Not as strong physically, perhaps, but boy, are they resilient!

'We did a lot to help girls like you get where they are today, of course,' Miss Leverton says, as if picking up on my train of thought. 'Before the war, a woman's place was very much in the home. The war proved she could do as good a job as a man. A female police sergeant would have been unthinkable in those days, and a diver . . . !'

'I'm very lucky to be doing a job I love,' I say. 'But to do what you did . . . I'm not sure I'd be up to that.'

'You'd be surprised what you're capable of when the devil drives.'

'And what were you capable of?' Pete asks.

I'd wondered how long he would be able to keep quiet.

Miss Leverton fixes him with another of her hard stares.

'I thought we'd established that my experiences are not for public consumption.'

'You won the Croix de Guerre. Our readers—'

'I have not the slightest interest in impressing your readers. I simply wanted to meet Sergeant Holley and thank her for recovering something very precious. I rather hoped she would come alone,' she adds pointedly.

'I'm very glad you've got it back,' I say. 'It must have been a dreadful loss – and the other things in the box, too . . .'

I break off. Miss Leverton's hard stare is on me now, but she says nothing. I'm beginning to feel very uncomfortable.

'How did you come to lose it?' I blunder on. 'Was it stolen?'

'Not stolen, no.' Her eyes move from me to Pete Holbrook. 'I'm sorry, but I don't feel able to speak freely in front of this gentleman. It really is very unsatisfactory. I had hoped . . . but under the circumstances . . .'

The shrill beep of my radio-cum-mobile phone interrupts her. She glares accusingly at the offending object.

'Sorry,' I say, feeling even more uncomfortable. 'I really need to . . .'

'Of course. You are on duty, I assume, Sergeant.'

I get up from the chair, move to the doorway so my back is turned towards Miss Leverton and – more importantly – Pete Holbrook.

'Sergeant Holley.'

'MJ? It's me.' Doug's voice. I move a little further out into the hall.

'Doug.'

'How is it going?'

'Awkward.'

'Do you need a get-out?'

Bless him! Doug is a real pal.

'Possibly. Do we have a call-out, then?'

'If you want one. What do you fancy – a gun or a knife thrown in the city docks? A floater in the river? The choice is yours.'

I can feel the corners of my mouth twitching. I work hard at keeping the amusement out of my voice.

'I see. Right. Well, I'm in Portishead at the moment, but I could be there in . . .' I make a show of checking my watch, though I don't think either Miss Leverton or Pete can see me. 'Say forty-five minutes?'

'Nice one, MJ.' Doug isn't bothering to hide his amusement, but then he doesn't have to.

'OK, will do. Thanks for letting me know.'

I snap my phone shut, turn back to the sitting room. As I do, I notice for the first time a framed photograph hanging on the wall of the hallway. The daylight streaming out from the living room is hitting it squarely and I see that it is of three young women, arms linked, smiling into the camera. One is wearing a suit with a tight straight skirt and a jacket nipped in at the waist, the other two summer dresses topped with fitting cardigans. Their hairstyles are quite glamorous, but unmistakably old-fashioned – sausage curls across their foreheads, full waves pinned back from their ears and tumbling to their shoulders. One of them, I guess, is Miss Leverton in her heyday. Perhaps the others are friends from her days in the SOE; the picture certainly looks as if it dates from the early forties. But judging by their carefree smiles, it would have been before they went to France. When they were in training together, perhaps. Yes, one of them is almost certainly Miss Leverton, though which one I haven't a clue. And the other two . . . perhaps they were among those who never came back.

A knot of sadness lodges in my throat. I'd really like to ask her about that photograph. But she wouldn't tell me. Not in front of Pete Holbrook. And besides, now that I'm supposed to be needed for some urgent job, there really isn't time.

'I'm sorry, I'm going to have to go,' I say.

'Ah, what a pity.'

Pete doesn't seem to think so. He's realised he's wasting his time, I guess. He heads for the front door, anxious, no doubt, to be on the trail of a story where he isn't frustrated at every turn.

Miss Leverton touches my arm, an unspoken indication that I should hold back.

'Will you come and see me again, Sergeant? Alone?' It's not so much a request as a command.

But for some reason I don't feel as cornered as I might have done. The brief snippets of what her life must once have been have fascinated me; seeing that photograph, the only one on display in a home bereft of any other memorabilia, has aroused my curiosity. A photograph of three smiling young women, two of whom may well have died soon afterwards.

To be honest, I don't know very much at all about the war. No great surprise there – it had been over for the best part of thirty years before I was born. I've seen films, of course, with square-jawed heroes talking in strange clipped accents which make them seem as unreal, unnatural, as Dr Who's Daleks. I've seen TV footage of Dunkirk and the D-Day landings, the sort of thing they wheel out every time an anniversary comes around, which seems to be pretty well non-stop. 'Forty years ago today . . .' 'Forty-five years ago today . . .' 'Fifty . . .' But until now it has all seemed so much ancient history to me.

Now, though, there is this woman who was part of it all, not just as someone who lived through the Blitz and food rationing and all the rest, but who did dangerous work right under the noses of the

Germans in occupied France. Who had somehow survived. Who had done something so extraordinary that she had been awarded the Croix de Guerre.

Against my will, I'm beyond intrigued. And I can't help but wonder about her personal life, too. In the case I rescued from the lake there was a ring and a locket with a baby's curl in it. Once, a lifetime ago, there had been people she'd loved, and who had loved her. What happened to them? From what I've seen, if doesn't look as if she has any family. She's 'Miss Leverton' and she doesn't wear any rings. There are no pictures on display of children or grandchildren. Perhaps whoever gave her the ring was killed in the war; perhaps the child's curl belonged to a much-loved niece or nephew, I don't know. But all of a sudden, I want to.

It's really odd, but it's almost as if there's an unseen bond linking me somehow to this intriguing lady, and it's drawing me in.

'When could you come?' she asks.

'I have a rest day next Wednesday . . .' I can't believe I'm saying it. Hadn't I absolutely bridled when Amanda suggested I should visit Miss Leverton on my rest day?

She nods.

'Next Wednesday. Yes. That would suit me. Why don't you come about four? We'll have tea and get to know one another.'

Afternoon tea! I didn't know anyone had afternoon tea any more.

'OK.'

'I'll look forward to it.' That faint smile again, red lips, the colour she used to paint them sixty years ago, I guess, a scarlet gash in her smooth pale face.

I nod, leave the flat, walk back along the carpeted corridor, wondering why on earth Miss Leverton is so keen to see me again. Perhaps she's lonely. Perhaps by agreeing to come back I'm letting myself in for more than I've bargained for. I certainly don't want to put myself in the position of feeling obliged to become some sort of companion. But it's too late to back out now. I've promised I'll visit her next Wednesday, and I have to admit I'm curious.

Pete Holbrook is waiting by the lift.

'Well, that was a bit of a waste of time.'

'I expect you're used to that.'

'You could say. Not unlike police work, really.'

'I wouldn't have thought journalism was much like police work.'

The lift arrives, we get into it, and Pete pushes the button for the ground floor.

'You're wrong there, Martha. I'd say it's a lot the same. Chasing loose ends that lead nowhere. Waiting for a break. Following leads . . . I think we've got quite a bit in common.'

I shrug. 'If you say so.'

The lift grinds to a halt. We walk out of the main entrance door into the sunshine. I turn in the direction I parked my car, expecting Pete to head over to his. He doesn't. He's still walking alongside me.

'Goodbye, then,' I say pointedly.

'Have dinner with me, Martha,' he says.

That really stops me in my tracks.

'What?'

'Let me buy you dinner one night. Or just a drink if you'd rather.'

'You must be joking!'

'Nope.' He grins, a grin that's halfway between mischievous and guilty, and he's looking at me with those narrowed come-to-bed eyes. 'Did you really think I was that desperate for a story?'

'You certainly seemed to be.'

'And it never occurred to you I might have an ulterior motive? More to do with a very attractive police sergeant than a poor old lady?'

'Frankly, no, it didn't.'

'So – now I've come clean, how about it?'

I really, truly, can't believe this.

'In your dreams,' I say rudely.

'Oh dear. So it really was a wasted morning.'

''Fraid so.'

'Pity.' But he doesn't look dejected, just a bit rueful.

'Hadn't you better get going?' he adds wickedly. 'I thought you had an urgent call to attend.'

'Oh . . . yes . . .'

'Anything that might make it worth my while to follow you?'

But I know from his tone and his amused expression that he knows full well my call to duty was a fake.

'Absolutely not,' I say.

'See you around, then.'

'Not,' I say coolly, 'if I see you first.'

But as I head for my car, I glance over my shoulder. He's walking in the direction of the SUV, easy strides, hands in the pockets of his leather jacket, and I can't help thinking it's a great shame he should have the sort of shitty job that turns me right off. He's too sure of himself by half; no doubt he thinks he's God's gift; like all journalists he's probably hard as nails. Well, yes, like policemen too – he wasn't so far off the mark when he said there were similarities between the professions. But then I've no intention of getting involved with a policeman again either. Though at least they only pry into other people's lives with the intention of righting wrongs, solving crimes and maintaining law and order. Not for the edification of their nosy readers. Not just to peddle gossip and shift as many copies of their scandal rags as possible.

But it's rather a pity that I have such a hearty dislike of the so-called gentlemen of the press. There's no doubt about it, Pete Holbrook is rather a hunk, and I have the feeling he'd be a bit of a challenge, too. Under other circumstances . . .

Ah well, such is life.

I fish my electronic car key out of my pocket, press the button and see the answering wink of my sidelights.

I climb into the Golf, put the key into the ignition and head back to Almondsbury. Already I've forgotten about Pete Holbrook. Instead, I'm thinking of Stella Leverton and the hell of a life that she led thirty-odd years before I was born.

SIX

ANNE

It's been a horrible day that started badly and just got worse.

Kevin had to leave early for work, and it was left to me to get the children off to school. I had the devil's own job getting Harry up – he was playing games on his Nintendo when he should have been going to sleep last night, I suspect – and Abigail was kicking off because we'd run out of her favourite breakfast cereal and there were no chocolate brioches left either. I offered her a choice of bagels, or toast and marmalade, or lemon pancakes, but she turned her nose up at all of them before demanding scrambled egg. A healthy option, I know, but more work for me when I was already fighting a losing battle with the clock.

When Harry eventually came down, the two of them started squabbling because he accused Abi of having taken some of the set of cards he's collecting – Dr Who's Enemies, I think – and then he informed me he had to play football after school and would need his kit. I eventually found it, still in the dirty clothes hamper in the bathroom, and had to do my best to get the creases out and hope no one would notice the grass stain on the shorts that gave away the fact that it hadn't been washed.

There was more squabbling about whose turn it was to sit in the front of the car, and by the time I deposited the pair of them at the school gates with only minutes to spare, I was totally exhausted as well as stressed, feeling I'd just battled through a whole day rather than only just beginning it.

Back at Sonia's house, I cleared the kitchen and living room, which looked like the Wreck of the *Hesperus*, and took Sonia a cup of tea and some milky porridge – she has a mouthful of ulcers, a side effect of the chemotherapy, that make it difficult and painful for her to eat anything solid. She was looking dreadful, huge dark circles under her eyes, and her skin like tissue paper stretched thinly over her cheekbones. She admitted she hadn't slept well – unsurprising, given all she's going through both physically and mentally – but she made a huge effort when I went into the room, dragging herself up into a sitting position against the pillows.

'Oh Mum – were they being a pain?'

'Harry and Abigail? Of course not. They were fine,' I lied.

'I hope so. I thought I could hear . . .'

'They were just being children. Nothing I can't handle. Harry thought Abi had pinched some of his Dr Who cards, that's all.'

'Oh, I think he left them here when he came in to say good night to me . . .' Sonia reached across to the bedside table. The skin on the back of her hand looks like tissue paper too, pale and almost translucent.

Sure enough the cards were there, lying between the magazines, box of tissues and various medications.

'That's good. That'll save more ructions when they come home . . .' I stopped short, wishing I could take back the words. The last thing I want is Sonia knowing that I'm actually reaching the end of my tether. But it was too late.

'Oh Mum, I'm sorry.'

'Don't be so silly,' I said shortly. 'We're managing perfectly. All you have to do is concentrate on getting well.'

Sonia gave a little snort, halfway between a laugh and a sob.

'What would I do without you, Mum?'

There really was no answer to that.

'Is there anything else you want, darling?' I asked instead.

'No. Just to feel better.' Her bottom lip wobbled; she bit down hard on it. 'Mum, I'm fine. You go and get on with your work – I'm sure you need to. I'll eat this, then I'll get up and have a bath.'

Ill as she is, Sonia refuses to remain in bed unless she is having a really bad day, and insists not only on getting bathed and dressed but putting on a bit of make-up too. I like it that she makes the effort and I do believe that you actually feel better if you look halfway decent, but it's just another worry all the same. Whether she's safe to be left alone in the bath, whether she'll exhaust her tiny reserves of energy.

But the problems at the agency were weighing heavily on me too. Besides the final collection for the school of art, which actually Elaine is coping with magnificently, there are a couple of other jobs, one supplying models for a wedding fair, the other some glamour girls for a drinks promotion, and I can't expect her to organise those as well. I needed to make some phone calls, get the right girls for the work briefed. Elaine also brought me a huge stack of mail when she came over for our meeting, which included several applications from young hopefuls who want us to put them on our books, along with their portfolios. That has to be way down my list of priorities, but I don't like keeping them dangling longer than I can help. I remember all too well what it's like to watch for the postman or wait for the telephone to ring when you're desperate for a break.

When I'd completed yet another stint of clearing up, fed Goldie, the family retriever, and loaded the washing machine, I got out my laptop and files and mobile, and settled down at the kitchen table to try and make a start on the jobs I had lined up.

Some days work goes well, some days it's nothing but a frustrating round of leaving messages on answering machines and getting nowhere fast. Today was one of those days. Goldie was angling for a walk, too; she was alternating between pawing me, and going to the door with her lead in her mouth and sitting there looking soulful, which was beginning to get on my nerves. Upstairs, I could hear Sonia moving about and the bathwater running, which made mincemeat of my concentration. I had to keep one ear open in case she called me for assistance.

The washing machine finished its cycle; I loaded the wet laundry into the basket and hung it out in the garden. Came back and tried to make a few more phone calls, still with limited success, checked the pile of mail Elaine had brought over for anything urgent. Goldie was still bothering me; when Sonia came downstairs, fragile but coping, I admitted defeat and took the dog out. I'd get no peace, I knew, until she'd had her run, and I hoped the fresh air might clear my head a bit.

It didn't.

Back home, I made a fish pie that I thought Sonia might be able to manage. Half the day gone, and though I'd been rushing around since before seven, I felt as if I'd achieved nothing. Perhaps after lunch, when Sonia was resting . . .

But no. Just as I was trying to concentrate again, my mother phoned.

When my mobile rang, I hoped it might be one of the girls I'd tried to contact returning my calls, and I almost wept with frustration when I heard my mother's voice.

'Anne? Where are you? I've been ringing and ringing, and you didn't answer. I was getting quite worried.'

'I'm at Sonia's, Mum, and my phone hasn't rung until now.'

'Oh – I was ringing your home number. That girl at your agency said you weren't there, so I thought . . .'

'You know I'm at Sonia's, Mum.'

'Well, yes, now you say . . . I just get confused, Anne. I never know where you are.' Her tone was plaintive.

'There's nothing confusing about it. I'm at Sonia's, and you can get me either on her phone or my mobile.'

I knew I sounded bad-tempered, but quite honestly, that was how I felt. 'I'm up to my eyes, Mum. Was there something you specially wanted to talk to me about, or can it wait until later?'

'Well, I was rather hoping you might be coming over to see me.' Her tone was huffy now, a little affronted. 'The bulb's gone in the downstairs lavatory again, and I want you to put in a new one. I'd do it myself, but I don't want to climb up on a chair and fall.'

'No, you mustn't climb on chairs, Mum. Do you *have* to have a light in there? It doesn't get dark now until well past your bedtime . . .'

'Well of course I want a light in there! I can't leave it like that. You never know when it might be needed.'

'Isn't there someone you can ask, then? A neighbour . . . the milkman . . . ?'

'Oh, I expect I'll find somebody if you're not going to help me out.' Her martyred tone now, the one that really gets to me. 'But surely . . . I haven't seen you now for nearly three weeks. It's only half an hour in the car. I'd have thought—'

'Mother, I'm at Sonia's. It's an hour plus from here.'

'Oh well, if you don't want to be bothered . . .'

My nerves were being wound tighter and tighter, a spring coiling inside my chest.

'You know it's not that.'

'Do I? It seems to me I'm a long way down your list of priorities. I'm not getting any younger, you know.'

This was going nowhere, an argument I could do without.

'I'll ring Rod and ask him to come over and see to your light,' I said wearily. Rod will be less than pleased at having to turn out and drive twenty miles; he likes to be able to relax with a glass of whisky when he gets home from work, and he's not a great fan of my mother. They've never seen eye to eye, and since Dad died and Mum has become more needy than ever, he's been growing steadily more impatient.

I know what he'll say. 'You mean you want me to go all the way to Compton Drew to change a light bulb?' And: 'I don't know why your mother insists on staying in that great big house all on her own. If only she'd move into a nice little place somewhere nearer to us it would make a lot more sense, and be a darned sight easier for you.'

He's right, of course, but there's no way my mother is going to move. She's lived in that house ever since she and Dad were married – in fact he bought a swathe of land and had it put up, a place big enough to accommodate a growing family in comfort, nay, luxury. Except that no other children besides me came along. It was heaven when I was growing up, of course – all those rooms and a huge garden to play in, wide lawns, hidden corners, a summer house, even a tennis court. To be honest, it holds so many happy memories for me that I'd be very sad myself to see it sold to strangers, though common sense tells me that that really is the only sensible course of action. The cost of the upkeep is horrendous, and it's eating away at the dwindling investments Dad left. But I know Mum wouldn't hear of it.

'This is my home,' she says. 'The only way you'll get me out of here is in a box, feet first.'

So we carry on, doing what we can from a distance and helping her budget for a cleaning lady, Thelma Jacobs, who comes in three mornings a week, and someone to keep the garden tidy, once a month in winter and fortnightly in the summer.

It occurred to me – surely tomorrow was one of Thelma's working days? Couldn't the light bulb wait for her to do it? But I didn't say so. I'd offered Rod's help now, and if that made Mum happy I wasn't about to upset the apple cart any more than I already had.

It didn't make her happy, though it did go some way to appeasing her.

'That's all right then. And while he's here, perhaps he'd have a look at the front door. It's sticking again. All the wet weather we've been having, I suppose.'

'I'm sure he will if you ask him,' I said. 'Now I really must go, Mum. I'm going to have to fetch the children from school soon.'

'Can't Sonia do that?' Mum asked.

'No, Mum, she can't. I have to go.'

'Oh well, if you must.' She sounded sniffy again. 'I really would like to see you, though. When you can find the time.'

'Yes, all right,' I said, smothering a sigh.

The problem is, of course, as I mentioned earlier, that we haven't told Mum just how ill Sonia is. I'm dreadfully afraid that if she knew the truth, she might sink into one of her depressions.

To the best of my knowledge she's suffered that way all her life, though of course when I was a child I didn't understand what was going on. All I knew was that sometimes Mum would be snappy instead of her usual happy, loving self, silent and withdrawn, losing interest in just about everything. It was only as I grew older that I came to recognise the warning signs, like the heaviness in the air before a thunderstorm: the excessive worrying over things that really didn't matter at all, the reluctance to leave the house, the tiredness and the ready tears.

I remember asking Dad about it once, when I was about thirteen or fourteen. Mum had been a bit odd for days, locked into that strange, private world, hardly seeming to hear me when I spoke to her, letting the telephone ring unanswered. Then, this particular evening when we were washing up, I knocked a glass off the draining board. It smashed on the tiled floor and Mum went ballistic.

'Oh no! That's one of my best glasses! They were a wedding present! How can you be so clumsy, Anne?'

'I'm sorry . . . I'll clear it up.'

'No you won't. I'll do it . . . Oh, I can't believe this . . .' She went on and on, working herself up.

'For goodness' sake, Margaret!' Dad had come into the kitchen to see what all the fuss was about. 'It's only a glass.'

'It's not only a glass. It's . . .' Suddenly her eyes were filling with tears. 'And you can stop looking at me like that, both of you!'

And with that she threw the dustpan and brush across the kitchen and ran out into the garden. Stunned and guilty, I was going to follow her, but Dad stopped me.

'Leave her alone, love. That's the best way.'

'But . . . she's crying. What's the matter with her, Dad? I don't understand . . .'

Dad sighed. 'It's just the way she is. Highly strung. Leave her alone and she'll get over it.'

And she did – until the next time. Mostly these depressions lasted only a few days, or a couple of weeks at worst, though there was one particularly bad bout when I was accepted for a year's course at the Elspeth Calleshaw School of Charm and Modelling in London.

To begin with, Mum had been very supportive. Dad, I think, was disappointed when I said I really didn't want to go into the sixth form at the private girls' school I'd attended since the age of ten. He had ambitions for me to do my A levels and go to college or even university. But I couldn't see the point. Ever since seeing a fashion show in the restaurant of a big department store in Bristol, I'd wanted nothing more than to become a model. Wearing all those lovely clothes, sashaying amongst the tables where admiring ladies drank cups of coffee as they decided on their new season's wardrobe, seemed to me the height of glamour. But it also seemed eminently achievable. I knew I was considered attractive with my thick wavy hair, blue eyes, a tiny twenty-three-inch waist and long legs, and in any case, I'd been spoiled enough to believe I could have anything I wanted.

Mum had helped me, finding out about so-called 'charm schools' and persuading Dad that if I was not interested in pursuing academic studies, his money would be better spent on a year's course at one of them. She even came to London with me for the interview, and seemed very impressed by Miss Calleshaw.

But then, who wouldn't be? I was terrified of her, absolutely in awe.

Miss Calleshaw was the very epitome of grandeur, with all the authority and unshakeable self-belief of a woman who was the principal of the legendary school she had founded. She moved with the upright grace that would support a whole stack of books piled on top of her head – something I would have to learn to do. She knew how to get in and out of a limousine, knees pressed tightly together so as not to show so much as an inch of inner thigh, how to drink tea in polite company, how to greet titled ladies – royalty even! Her most successful pupils went on to become catwalk models for some of the most famous fashion houses in the world.

If Mum had any concerns about me going to London at the tender age of sixteen, Miss Calleshaw laid them to rest. Her girls were expected to behave like ladies. They were chaperoned at all times, and they were taught how to discourage unwelcome advances without any unpleasantness. Miss Calleshaw raised an arched eyebrow disapprovingly as she explained this; I could well imagine it would deter any would-be suitor, however ardent, and Mum seemed satisfied too.

As the time for me to leave home approached, however, I saw the warning signs that she was going into one of her black holes. I was terrified she was going to change her mind and side with Dad, try to persuade me to stay on at school.

On several occasions she seemed to be attempting to open a difficult conversation, but it never came to anything. She just relapsed into the deep, unbreakable silence that surrounded her like a dark cloud. Dad told me later that it had lasted for quite some time after I left – I suppose it was what would be called 'empty nest syndrome' these days. But by the time I saw her again, at half-term, she was brittlely cheerful, and by Christmas she was absolutely fine – gay, chattering, anxious to hear every detail of my experiences so far.

Throughout my modelling career she was the same, delighting in my success, full of pride. The moods seemed to have lifted at last. Then, oddly, she suffered another one, just after Sonia was born.

'I'm the one who's supposed to get the baby blues,' I said, trying to tease her out of it.

And: 'Take no notice of me,' she said. 'Just concentrate on the little one. They're more precious than you know.'

Prophetic words indeed.

I have to say, she has been much better since she got older. In fact, since Rod and I moved to Bristol, when Sonia was five, I don't remember her having a really bad bout. Even when Dad died she coped remarkably well, and she began going out more than I ever remember her doing when he was alive – he was always too busy with the business to have much of a social circle. She joined a bridge club and a flower-arranging class, and even started going to church regularly instead of just Christmas and Easter.

That's gone by the board rather of late, though, as she's aged and become less mobile. And I really do fear that the worry of knowing Sonia is so desperately ill could very well throw her back to the dark days. It may well be, of course, that the time will come when we have no option but to tell her the truth, and it will be the most dreadful shock for her. But for the moment I don't want to think about that. For the moment it's all I can do to cope with all the rest of the things that are going on in my life.

It's half past nine now and Kevin is still not home – he rang at about six to ask if we were OK, as he really needed to stay late at the office. If it were anyone other than Kevin I might have been annoyed, but I know that whatever it was that had come up, it must be important. Kevin isn't the sort to use work as an excuse to get out of domestic duties; he worships Sonia and the children, and though he has a very demanding job in distribution management, he goes out of his way to arrange things so that he can be there for school concerts, parent/teacher evenings, and sports days. He's a good husband and father and I know he's devastated by what is happening to Sonia. Added to which, I have a very soft spot for him. So of course I told him not to worry about being late, we were fine, and I'd make sure there was a whisky waiting for him when he eventually made it home . . .

I got the children to bed, and when she went up to say good night to them, Sonia didn't come back down again. She'd decided to rest in her room, I guessed, rather than having to face the stairs again later.

Left alone, I've been managing to deal with some more of the agency mail, but quite honestly I'm exhausted. I'll just go and make sure the children are asleep – I don't want Harry playing on his Nintendo half the night again – and then I'll make myself a cup of hot chocolate and try to relax for an hour or so before going to bed.

I kick my shoes off at the foot of the stairs, and creep up in my stockinged feet so as not to disturb anyone. I look in on Abigail first – she's fast asleep, long dark hair fanned out across her pink frilled pillowcase, duvet kicked back, gingham pyjama-clad legs curled up to her chin, thumb in mouth. I rescue Timmy, her floppy ginger monkey, from the floor beside her bed and nestle him next to her on the pillow, pull the duvet up over her, drop a kiss on her soft smooth forehead and creep out again, pulling the door to behind me. Then I go to Harry's room.

As I suspected, he's still awake and playing with the Nintendo by the light of his bedside lamp.

'Harry, you are supposed to be going to sleep,' I chide him.

'Oh . . . ohh . . .' It's a long-drawn-out wail.

'You'll be good for nothing again in the morning. Put it away now, there's a good boy.'

'Just this one game . . . I've nearly finished . . .'

'No. Lights out. Now!'

'Mummy always lets me finish the game! Just another minute . . . please!'

I relent. 'All right. But make sure it is just another minute, not ten. I shall be back to check up on you very shortly.'

'Thanks, Grandma. You're ace.'

I shake my head and leave him to it. I must be getting soft in my old age. I'll go down and get my hot chocolate ready, set out the whisky bottle, a jug of water and a tumbler for Kevin, who must surely be home soon, and then come back and make sure Harry has done as he's been told.

As I reach the door to Sonia's room, I hesitate, wondering whether to go in and see if she's OK or leave her alone. Then I hear what sounds like a muffled sob. That makes up my mind for me. Perhaps I should pretend I hadn't heard, go back downstairs and give her some privacy. But I just can't. Sonia might be almost forty years old, but she is still my baby.

'Sonia?' I say softly from the doorway.

She doesn't answer, but her shoulders are shaking. Such thin shoulders now, the bones jutting through the thin fabric of her nightdress.

'Sonia . . . oh darling . . .'

I cross to the bed, sit on the edge, take her in my arms. She's sobbing uncontrollably now; I'm afraid Harry will hear her.

'Hush, darling, hush . . .'

Her face is buried in my chest; I think that it seems like only yesterday when she nestled, just so, as a baby. I feel as if my own heart is breaking.

'Sonia, darling, don't. You'll make yourself ill.'

'I . . . am . . . ill . . .' The words choke out between sobs.

'But you'll make yourself worse. Please, darling . . .'

She raises her head a little.

'I'm so scared, Mum.'

'I know. I know you are. But it's going to be all right.'

'What if it's not?' Her voice falters again. 'What if I'm going to die?'

64

'Don't talk like that, Sonia. Don't even think it.'

'I can't help it, Mum. I don't want to die! I want to be here to see the children grow up . . .'

'You will. You will!'

'But if I don't? What's going to happen to them?'

'The children will be fine. We'll take care of them, darling, you know that. But it's not going to happen. You're going to get well. You'll be here to see them go to senior school, have their first loves, get married . . .'

I wish I felt as sure of that as I'm trying to sound. But I have to stay strong, stay positive. It's all I can do to help.

'Oh Mum, I hope so . . . I hope so . . .'

I hold her close; she cries some more. But she's quietening now, swallowing the blackest of her despair, for now at least.

I pass her a tissue from the box on the bedside table.

'I must go and make sure Harry isn't still playing on that Nintendo.'

A moment of normality in a world gone mad.

'Yes. Yes, do that, Mum.' She blow her nose, wipes her eyes.

In the doorway, I stop and look back at her, my darling daughter, and wish with all my heart that I could change places with her.

But I can't. Life isn't like that.

And it is just so unfair.

SEVEN

MARTHA

Well, it's Wednesday – my rest day – and I'm heading over to Portishead to see Miss Leverton. I'm still torn between wondering what I'm getting myself into and overwhelming curiosity as to how the box I found came to be in the lake, what Miss Leverton did to win the Croix de Guerre and how the ring and locket tie in to the private life that has ended up with her living all alone in a luxurious retirement apartment bare of any personal mementos but for a photograph of three girls who had apparently been friends back in the 1940s. I'm also curious as to why she is so set against any publicity, but inviting me back to talk.

The only thing I can think in answer to the last question is that she is desperately lonely, and saw in me something of a kindred spirit, and that, in turn, makes me wary. I don't want to find myself obliged to befriend her. I can't bear feeling trapped in any way; it makes me run a mile. One of the reasons my marriage failed, I expect. One of the reasons I'm resisting what I think might be an attempt by Nick to get back together. I can't face finding myself back in the position of feeling guilty because I don't want to be tied down by domestic duty and children. And I certainly don't want Miss Leverton drawing me into visiting regularly. She strikes me as the sort of lady who's used to getting her own way. Hard to refuse. I shall have to be very careful, and very firm. It's quite enough that I feel bad about not doing enough for Granny, who is really as much my responsibility as Lucy's, without adding an old lady who is nothing whatever to me.

No, that sounds horrible, as if Granny is a burden I don't want, and nothing could be further from the truth. I love her dearly and want to spend time with her. It's the guilt that my lifestyle doesn't allow it that makes me feel bad. It's about me, not about her. But at least I'm trying to do something about that. I've been online, found a nice hotel right on the seafront at Weston-super-Mare, and booked us in for a week at the end of June. I just hope the weather cheers up! Since the lovely spell we had in April, it's been very unsettled.

It's like that today, cool, overcast, rain threatening, and as I drive along the marina the sea is grey and choppy, disappearing into a fuzzy mist where it meets the heavy grey sky. Not the kind of weather you want on holiday. Not the kind of weather you want in summer full stop!

I turn into the car park outside Miss Leverton's apartment block, find a space and pull into it. Then I look around warily, half wondering if I'll see a Toyota RAV4 amongst the staid and respectable saloons and estates. He wouldn't, surely – would he? But to be honest, I wouldn't put it past him.

I'm talking about Pete Holbrook, of course.

I saw him yesterday, and he was as infuriating as ever.

We were searching the river Avon in Bath, for a second day. An old man has gone missing from a care home, and was last seen wandering in the city. Quite apart from the fact that he's frail and suffering from dementia, he's without the medication he needs daily – he's diabetic, I think, and may well have a heart condition too. To be honest, I don't give much for his chances.

Anyway, a full-scale search is in operation, and as part of that we've been looking in the river. So far we've found nothing but the usual rusted Sainsbury's trolley – shouldn't think they'll want it back – a mountain bike, ditto, a dog's lead, an old gas boiler and a plastic carrier bag containing a car battery; it's unbelievable what people will heave into the river rather than taking it to the council tip. But the body of a poor demented old man, no.

Pete Holbrook was sniffing around, though, ever hopeful.

'Sorry, but you're going to be disappointed,' I said to him when he approached me.

Those bedroom eyes teased me shamelessly.

'On what count, Sergeant?'

'Weren't you hoping to be on hand if we fished a body out of the water?'

'Nice to know you have such a high opinion of me. I hope the poor sod turns up alive somewhere. No, actually I thought you might have been talking about something quite different when you said I was going to be disappointed.' His mouth quirked. 'Have I got that wrong?'

'Meaning?' I knew very well what he meant, but I wasn't going to let on.

'Meaning, have you changed your mind about having dinner with me?'

'No chance,' I said briskly.

'Not even a drink? I know a great place down on the Watershed. You'd be in your element.'

'Don't you ever give up?' I challenged him.

'Not usually. Persistence is in my nature. It's what makes me a good newsman.'

'It's what makes you a wanker,' I said disparagingly. 'And if I was you, I'd give up and go home before you get a good soaking. This rain has set in for the day, and you're not dressed for it.'

He glanced down ruefully at his jacket, which already had dark patches like stains where the rain, which had started in the last half-hour, had soaked into the leather.

'I'm touched by your concern for me, Sergeant.'

'You're welcome.' I was well protected against the weather myself, in a police-issue waterproof and baseball cap – I'd supervised today's operation rather than diving myself, and for some reason I couldn't pinpoint, but which was making me prickle with annoyance, I was rather glad I wasn't wearing my drysuit and hood. Vanity, I suppose, though I've never thought of myself as vain.

'I've got to go. I've got work to do,' I said.

'See you then, Sergeant.'

I snorted, walked away, and when I turned back for a crafty look, he was gone. Somehow, though, I didn't think I'd seen the last of him. By his own admission, he was nothing if not persistent, and that last, amused comment had sounded more like a threat – or a promise – than just a clichéd throwaway farewell.

Which is why I'm looking around the car park outside Miss Leverton's apartment, half expecting to see the RAV4 appearing like the demon king in a pantomime on a cloud of acrid smoke. It doesn't, and I tell myself I'm getting paranoid. Pete Holbrook is no stalker, just an overkeen reporter who also happens to think he's God's gift. He can't resist trying it on with every woman he meets, and if he thinks it will help him get a better story, or even an exclusive, so much the better.

I press the button beneath Miss Leverton's name; the entry-phone crackles.

'Hello?'

'It's me, Miss Leverton. Martha Holley.'

'Oh good. Do come in, Sergeant.'

The buzzer sounds; I push open the door.

I'm on my way.

And suddenly, uncharacteristically, I feel rather nervous.

It's a good thing I didn't cry off coming. Miss Leverton has clearly gone to a lot of trouble. The small dining table is covered with a lace cloth and set with bone china cups, saucers and plates. Tiny sandwiches are piled on a matching platter and an assortment of small fancy cakes and pastries are arranged on a two-tier cake stand.

I feel as if I've stepped back in time to an age before I was even born. I don't think I've had afternoon tea in my life unless you count the high teas we used to have as children – ham or tinned salmon, lettuce and tomatoes straight from the garden, followed by stewed fruit and custard, or a slice of one of Granny's fruit cakes or Victoria sponges. Bread was a hunk cut from a crusty loaf and spread thickly with butter – no worries about cholesterol or calories then, jam was home-made. These cakes were clearly bought from a very expensive shop, and the sandwiches, denuded of crust and cut into dainty triangles, are as different from Granny's doorsteps as a Buckingham Palace garden party is from a faggot-and-peas supper after a police divisional skittles match. The sandwiches are cucumber, I wouldn't mind betting.

'I'm so very pleased you could come,' Miss Leverton says. 'Can I take your jacket?'

I'd worn my Berghaus – my own, not police-issue waterproofs – in anticipation of yet more rain. I could hardly sit down for afternoon tea wearing it, and in any case it was very warm in the apartment, as it so often is in old people's homes. But it didn't seem right to let a woman of eighty-plus run around after me either.

'Just tell me where . . . ?' I say as I shrug off the jacket.

'There's a peg in the hall.'

As I go to hang up the jacket, my eye is drawn to the picture of the three smiling girls. With any luck I'll find out soon which one is Miss Leverton, who the others were, and what happened to them.

I go back into the living room. Miss Leverton is fussing over the table, tweaking the arrangement of the china to make room for an ornate trivet.

'You're ready for a cup of tea, I expect.'

'Oh . . . yes . . . thank you.' It comes out sounding awkward; something about her manner is making me feel like a kid again, allowed to socialise with the grown-ups for the first time. Which in turn makes me bolshie. Why the hell should I be intimidated by an old woman just because she won a decoration for bravery, and lays out afternoon tea as if she were expecting the Queen?

While she's in the kitchen, I make up my mind. I'm going to take the initiative here.

She comes back with a teapot covered with a quilted cosy and sets it on the trivet.

'I'm puzzled,' I say, 'as to why you wanted me to come back today.'

She glances at me, sharp eyes lasering around my face so that I feel like a courtroom exhibit being pored over by a conscientious jury. Then:

'I thought you were curious about the items you found in the lake,' she says.

Back to square one. She's wrong-footed me again.

'Well, yes, I am . . . You said they weren't stolen, so I'm assuming they must have been lost . . .'

'Lost. Yes. Perhaps that's nearer the truth.'

'But Portishead is quite a long way from Bolborough . . .'

She smiles. 'I haven't always lived in Portishead, you know. I retired here because I liked the location of these apartments.'

'So at one time you lived . . . ?'

'I knew Bolborough well. In fact, once upon a time I was engaged to be married to Hugh Woodhouse. The son of the family who lived in Bolborough House.'

'Oh – right.' I try to sound blasé, but actually I'm impressed. I remember the Woodhouses living in Bolborough House when I was a child, though I knew them only by sight. They were gentry, we were proles. I've got a feeling there was a title; certainly the Woodhouses were treated with great respect in the district.

There's a mischievous twinkle in her eyes suddenly; I think she's rumbled me.

'It's all a very long time ago and things have changed. The Woodhouses had to sell up, you know. Bad investments and the upkeep of the place ate up what money they had . . . and I'm not sure that Hugh didn't run up gambling debts too . . . But you're not here to talk about that.'

'No.'

She's looking at me speculatively. 'I think we have a great deal in common, you and I.'

I look at the delicate china, the fancy cakes on the two-tier stand, the neat triangular sandwiches. At Miss Leverton in her below-the-knee navy blue skirt and pink ruffled blouse, old enough to be my grandmother. A great deal in common? We come from different worlds, different time zones.

She smiles faintly. 'You don't agree?'

Again, I'm at a loss. There's no way I can put what I was thinking into words without sounding offensive.

'I'm talking about spirit, Sergeant. Or may I call you Martha?'

'Yes . . . yes, of course.'

'And I would like you to call me Stella.'

'Oh, right . . .' But I can't imagine doing it. In this day and age, when everyone calls everyone else by their Christian names, it should come naturally. But this old lady will certainly always be Miss Leverton to me.

'Even today, yours is quite an unusual job for a woman,' she says, picking up the thread of conversation where she had left off. 'You are a pioneer in a man's world, I imagine. And in my own way, so was I. Now . . .' She lifts the teapot in one hand and with the other places a small silver strainer in one of the cups. 'I would think the tea is nicely brewed by now.'

I watch in fascination as tea leaves collect in the silver strainer. Why the hell would anybody bother with all this palaver when you can dunk a tea bag?

'And do please help yourself to sandwiches . . .' She nudges the plate in my direction.

'Yes, silly as you may think me, I do rather recognise you as a kindred spirit,' she goes on as I bite into soft white bread and yes, as I guessed, cucumber. 'I would very much like to know how you came to become the sergeant in charge of a diving squad. That's my price for telling you the story of the Croix de Guerre, which I am sure you are interested in hearing. Is it a good bargain, do you think?'

'Umm . . .' I might not be used to formal tea parties, but at least I know not to talk with my mouth full. That's something Granny drummed into us when we were small.

She raises an eyebrow at me. 'Perhaps you would prefer me to go first?'

I swallow my mouthful of sandwich.

'Well, yes . . .' I'm not entirely sure I like this bargain. It sounds to me as if I might have been right in thinking she is lonely and looking for a companion. She wants someone to talk to about her past, and she also wants to pick my life apart for her own satisfaction.

'This is strictly on the understanding that what I tell you goes no further, of course. I hope I can trust you not to share any of it with your newspaper reporter friend.'

'He's not my friend.'

'Oh. Forgive me. I didn't mean to presume . . . But I really would be most upset if any of this gets into the pages of his newspaper, or any other publication for that matter. We signed the Official Secrets Act, you know, and although it all happened a very long time ago, I still like to think I can be true to my word. And quite apart from that, there are many aspects of the story that are very personal.'

'I promise I'll treat whatever you tell me in confidence, Miss Leverton,' I say.

This time she doesn't tell me to call her Stella; her mind is elsewhere, I think. There's quite a faraway look in her eyes, as if she is already on her way back to the past.

'Very well.' She sips her tea, replaces the cup carefully on the china saucer. 'You've heard of the SOE, haven't you – the Special Operations organisation who worked in France during the occupation? Yes, of course you have. You mentioned it when you were last here. And you may or may not know that all agents had a code name, which was to be used at all times to protect their true identity.'

'I think I've heard that, yes . . .'

'I am going to tell you the story of an agent whose operational code name was Pascale. Actually it was her real name, too – albeit a second Christian name. Her mother was French, you see. When she was a little girl, playing the make-believe games children do, she always thought of herself as Pascale – so much more romantic than her very ordinary, very English first name.'

'I think Stella is a pretty name . . .'

But I get the impression she's not really listening to me.

'Pascale . . . much more romantic for an alter ego. And the obvious choice when it came to deciding upon a code name. Though of course every agent had at least two other alter egos – the name she was known by during training, and the ones in which her papers were made out, the identities she assumed whilst she was in the field. Oh, by the way, do please help yourself to sandwiches and cake. I might well forget to offer them . . . it's very easy to lose yourself in the past, you know. One of the strange things about getting old. One forgets what happened last week or last month, but what happened sixty and more years ago is as clear as crystal. And the telling might, I fear, take some time. You're not in any hurry to leave, I hope?'

'No . . .'

'Good. In that case, I'll begin.'

For a surreal moment I think of the old children's story programme on the radio – what was it called? *Listen With Mother*? When the presenter started: 'Are you sitting comfortably? Then I'll begin.' I suppress an urge to giggle. But there's nothing funny about Miss Leverton; that faraway look is back in her eyes and I have the feeling I'm going to learn far more than just the basic exploit that won her the Croix de Guerre. For some reason, my skin prickles.

'Pascale,' I say. 'Your code name was Pascale.'

'*Her* code name,' Miss Leverton says. 'I'd prefer it that way.'

There are obviously things she wants to forget as well as things she wants to remember. Well, I'm prepared to go along with that.

I nod, bite into my cucumber sandwich, which really is rather delicious, and wait to learn the story of a ring, a locket and a Croix de Guerre lost for goodness how many years in Bolborough Lake.

Part Two

EIGHT

PASCALE'S STORY

Bath was still burning on the day Pascale was headhunted to work undercover as an agent for the SOE in occupied France.

For two consecutive nights the city had been bombarded by Dorniers, He111s and Ju88s, diving low to deliver their high explosives in the clear moonlight, made bright as day by chandelier flares and incendiaries. Some had even machine-gunned the streets to hamper the emergency services in their work.

Well over a thousand people had died and many more been injured, though that morning it was too early for final figures – bodies were still being dug out of buildings that had been reduced to piles of rubble, along with trapped survivors. Beautiful and historic buildings were in ruins, among them the Assembly Rooms. Some were still burning; several water mains had been damaged, and with so many blazes all over the city, the emergency tanks were unable to cope, so that half-contained infernos leapt back to life as the pumps ran dry.

No one had expected a West Country town to be the target for such a devastating attack. Evacuees had come here from London in the belief that they would be safe in the heart of the Somerset countryside. The authorities were also convinced that Bath was unlikely to be targeted, and had relocated the Admiralty operation there, lock, stock and barrel, taking over buildings in the city and constructing camps on the outskirts. But they had reckoned without reprisal raids.

At the end of March, British aircraft had bombed Lubeck, and a few days before the raid on Bath, Rostock. There was a good reason for this: supplies and equipment were being stockpiled in ports on the Baltic in preparation for the attack on Russia that the Germans were planning. But Lubeck and Rostock were both heritage cities, with many beautiful, centuries-old buildings, and the Germans, understandably upset by the wholesale destruction, were determined to have their revenge. They took it by bombing English heritage cities — Exeter and Canterbury, Norwich, York — and Bath. All cities recommended for their architecture in tourist guides written before the war by Karl Baedeker. For that reason, the raids became known as 'the Baedeker raids'. And Bath, which had hitherto suffered only from stray bombs meant for the aeroplane works and the docks in Bristol, or dumped on a homeward flight from some sortie to an industrial region further afield, suddenly found itself the target of an enormous attack.

It came, that weekend in April 1942, almost literally out of the blue. And the devastation it wreaked was all the more shocking for that.

On the morning of Monday, April 27th, Pascale was at her desk in one of the hutments on the Admiralty site at Foxhill. Before the war – before her life had changed for ever – she had worked for the Revenue and Customs; now she had exchanged dull columns of figures for even duller technical jargon. It amused her that she'd had to sign the Official Secrets Act – she didn't understand a word of the stuff that landed on her desk and certainly would never have been able to pass any of it on in conversation. But at least she was doing her bit for the war effort. And the mind-numbing boredom of copy-typing what was, to her, nothing more than incomprehensible hieroglyphics was a means of escape from the grief that might otherwise have overwhelmed her. Whilst she was struggling to decipher the hasty scrawl of some engineer or boffin, there was no time to think of what she had lost; ensuring that she hadn't made any mistakes in the code names and numbers held the memories at bay.

That Monday morning, as always, the long, low room in the

prefabricated building was silent but for the clatter of typewriters banging out a constant rhythm. The desks of the dozen girls who worked there were arranged in neat rows, schoolroom fashion, and far enough apart that the typists were unable to overlook their neighbours' work. In any case, talking was strictly forbidden. At the front of the room, facing them, Miss Grundy, the pool supervisor, was ensconced behind a larger, more substantial desk where one deep wire tray held the stack of documents and letters waiting to be typed up and another the work the girls had completed and returned. Official-looking internal transit envelopes sat on the back left-hand corner of the desk waiting for the post boy.

There was no continuity in the work the girls did. When you'd finished one piece you gave it to Miss Grundy for checking and took the next document or letter from the top of the pile in the in-tray. A few of the files were stamped with the dull red 'Top Secret' or 'Confidential'; these were singled out to be dealt with by the pool's 'head girl', a prim, sour-faced woman named Mrs Singer who had come down from London with the Admiralty when they relocated to Bath; otherwise it was pot luck whether you landed a job that was straightforward or horribly complicated.

Miss Grundy had come down from London too. She was a dragon of a woman with heavy features, grey-streaked hair drawn back into a severe bun, and thin, scarlet-painted lips. She wore mannish tweed suits and laced brogues, but her fingernails were painted the same scarlet as her lips and adorned with so many rings, Pascale found it hard to believe she had ever been a typist herself. The weight of them, added to the weight of the typewriter keys that had to be depressed deep into the body of the heavy old machines, would have been like moving boulders, and those immaculate fingernails would never have survived the metal rings on the keys. But then again, perhaps Miss Grundy's nails were as indestructible as the lady herself. She was redoubtable in every way; even her voice was deep and rolling, and it cut like a foghorn through the clatter of the typewriters when she called some hapless girl to her desk to point out a mistake in the work she had submitted, or admonish someone who was, in her word, 'slacking'.

Everyone was expected to work continuously, moving seamlessly from one job to the next. Permission even had to be asked, and obtained, for a visit to the lavatory. The girls barely glanced up when anyone came into the room; to do so would be to risk a reprimand. Even the ones who had been on fire-watching duty the night before and had had only a few hours' sleep still tapped away diligently, and when a tall, bespectacled man entered the office and approached Miss Grundy's desk, none of them took the slightest interest. If they noticed him at all, they would have assumed he was an engineer, or even a departmental head bringing in an urgent job that couldn't wait for the post boy.

Certainly Pascale, struggling to make sense of the spidery writing on the document propped up in front of her, was so engrossed she was totally unaware of him, and she did not even hear the supervisor call her name until it was repeated in tones that echoed round the prefabricated building.

'Are you deaf, young lady? Come here at once, please.'

Pascale rose from her chair, straightening her grey flannel skirt and tucking her powder-blue cotton blouse more neatly into the waistband. She made her way between the rows of desks to the front of the room, wondering what she'd done this time. She was a good typist and took pride in her accuracy, but these documents were so technical it was easy to make a mistake and not know it. It must have been something pretty bad if this rather important-looking man had come in person to complain about it. She didn't know him, but then she didn't know many of the Admiralty officers and personnel – the typing pool was a lowly oasis far beneath such exalted circles.

'This is the girl you are looking for.' Miss Grundy's tone was clipped and disapproving; beneath her thick layer of face powder she had turned faintly pink. To Pascale she added: 'Mr Waters has a job for you.'

'Oh!' Pascale said, startled but relieved.

'Yes, but it's at the Empire, I'm afraid,' the bespectacled man said apologetically, referring to the Empire Hotel in the heart of the city, which had been taken over as the Admiralty's main operational centre. 'Is that all right?'

'Well of course it's all right!' Miss Grundy was bristling. 'My girls do as they are told, Mr Waters. If one of them is needed at the Empire, then she'll go there, no question. Though if it's an assignment that's going to run on, I hope you'll ensure I get a replacement. We are very busy.'

'I'm sure a replacement can be found if necessary,' Mr Waters said placatingly. 'And I am very sorry to take one of your girls at such short notice. But in times like these, I'm afraid there are some jobs that must take precedence.'

'I understand that, of course.' Miss Grundy smiled tightly. She looked directly at Pascale. 'I imagine you were in the middle of something. If you bring it here, I'll reassign it.'

Pascale's eyes widened. 'You mean I'm to go *now? Today?*'

'I'm afraid so.' Mr Waters smiled at her tentatively. 'I hope there's no problem?'

'No . . . no, not at all. But . . .'

'There's a car waiting for you up at A Block.'

'So perhaps you'd bring me what you were working on and collect your things,' Miss Grundy, determined to regain control, instructed sharply. '*Now.* We don't want to keep official transport waiting.'

Totally bemused, Pascale returned to her desk, fished her handbag and the packet of sandwiches she had made for her lunch out of the drawer and retrieved her cardigan from where it was hanging on the back of her chair. She was aware of the other girls taking an interest now, casting covert glances in her direction. They were wondering where she was going in the middle of the morning, she supposed, and the ones in the front row, who had been close enough to overhear the conversation, would be asking themselves why she had been singled out for this special job, whatever it was. There would be a few ruffled feathers, for sure. In particular, Mrs Singer, the head girl, would be bound to be miffed that the top-secret job had not been put her way.

Pascale permitted herself a wry smile, which broadened as she clipped together the confusing documents she had been working on, tore the half-covered sheet of paper from the Remington and crumpled it into a ball. Whatever job they had for her at the Empire, it couldn't be as dull as this technical stuff – could it? She marched back down the aisle and deposited the incomprehensible document on Miss Grundy's desk. Then she smiled again, this time at Mr Waters.

'I'm ready,' she said.

'It was a very bad raid last night, wasn't it?' Mr Waters said conversationally as they walked down the narrow corridor, past post collection points and the various stations where staff were required to sign in and out each day. 'Were you at all affected by it?'

Pascale grimaced. Of course she'd been affected by it – how could anyone fail to be, with enemy bombers overhead, dropping their deadly loads, and the city ablaze? And for her in particular the raids had stirred up the morass of emotion she was trying very hard to lock away in a place where it could not run amok and undermine her efforts to live as near normal a life as was possible under the circumstances, threaten her sanity even. But she didn't think that Mr Waters meant that.

'We didn't have any bombs where I live,' she said.

'And that is?'

'Half a mile or so up the road from here, actually. Close enough for me to be able to walk to work.'

'Ah.' He opened the outer door of the hutment, officially known as C Block, stood back to allow her to go through, closed it after them.

'So what is this job?' Pascale asked.

'I'm afraid I've no idea. I'm just the messenger.'

'Oh.' Pascale was becoming ever more confused.

'They'll explain when you get to the Empire. You are to ask for Mr Brown. Room 405. Have you got that?'

'Mr Brown. Room 405,' Pascale repeated.

They walked along the main service road that bisected the site, a swathe of mown grass that had once been a meadow but was now criss-crossed with concrete paths leading to the hutments. The sun was high and bright, reflecting in prisms on the glass of the windows, warming whitewashed walls.

An impressively large black motor car was parked at the side of the road outside A Block. A girl in ATS uniform emerged from the driver's side as they approached, opened the rear door and stood aside, hands clasped behind her, back straight, head erect.

'Good luck.' Mr Waters smiled at Pascale, looking for a moment as if he might offer her his hand, then changing his mind.

So – he wasn't coming with her. But then why would he?

'Thank you.' Pascale climbed into the car; the ATS girl slammed the door shut and went around to get into the driver's seat.

'This could be a bumpy ride,' she said cheerfully in an accent Pascale could only describe as cut glass.

The car pulled away; through the rear window Pascale saw Mr Waters standing on the path that led to A Block, watching them go. She settled back against the smooth leather, cardigan lying across her knees, handbag clasped tightly in her lap, and wondered again what secret work she was to do at the Empire, and why she had been singled out for it.

It soon became evident why the ATS driver had warned of a bumpy ride. Two nights of intensive bombing had left the streets strewn with rubble, fallen trees and telephone wires, and some, which had been particularly badly hit, or where there were still unexploded bombs, were closed altogether, forcing them to make detours.

In the centre of Bath the devastation was horrendous – collapsed buildings, some still burning, heaps of fallen masonry, bomb craters. Pascale gazed in horrified fascination, unable to tear her eyes away from it all, though the sick hollow in her stomach warned her that the sights would stir her sleeping demons again.

As the car pulled up in front of the Empire Hotel, she could see it had suffered some damage – a lot of windows had been blown out, and some workmen were busy at the ones on the ground floor, fixing white cloth on wooden frames to cover the gaping holes. But in spite of it the building looked as majestic as ever, standing proud amid the destruction.

Pascale gathered her things, but before she had time to open the car door the ATS driver was there, standing smartly to attention – as if I were royalty! Pascale thought. She thanked the driver and climbed the steps leading up to the vast front door of the grand old hotel that was now the HQ of one of the nation's greatest institutions.

Two sweeping staircases led up from the vestibule of the Empire, but the porter assigned to show Pascale the way advised her to take the lift. He unshuttered the doors, clanked them back into position and the lift shuddered into action, lumbering upwards. When it came to a halt, Pascale found herself in a broad, carpeted corridor. As she walked along it, she thought how odd it was to hear the clatter of typewriters coming from rooms that had so recently been occupied by privileged guests, and wondered if she would be working in one of them before the day was out.

At a door bearing the number 405, the porter left her. She tapped on it and a man's voice boomed from within.

'Come!'

Pascale opened the door and went inside. The room, high-ceilinged, with elaborate stucco cornices, had been transformed into an office. Filing cabinets and shelving lined the walls, a huge Civil Service-style wooden desk was backed up to wide bay windows, which were miraculously still intact. Pipe smoke hung in cirrus clouds in the sunshine that streamed in through those windows and infused the air with a sweet scent that instantly reminded Pascale of her father.

The man who rose from a leather swivel chair behind the desk was, however, nothing like her father, who had been a bear of a man – a cuddly bear, Pascale had always thought – with grizzled grey hair receding from a kindly face, who had always favoured baggy cardigans, open-necked flannel shirts and well-worn cord trousers.

This man was tall but slimly built, thick dark hair Brylcreemed back from a high, patrician forehead, and with a pencil-thin moustache defining his upper lip. He wore a dark suit, white shirt with well-stiffened collar, and a boldly striped tie that might have been regimental. An artfully folded handkerchief peeked from his breast pocket.

Sharp eyes appraised Pascale, making her uncomfortable. She

tucked a strand of hair, thick, dark and impossibly wavy, behind her ear.

'Mr Brown?'

'Yes.' He crossed the room, closing the door, which was still ajar, and indicated a hard upright chair drawn up at an angle to the desk. 'Won't you sit down?'

Pascale perched on the chair, pulling her skirt down to cover the neat darn in her stocking where she had caught a ladder. Mr Brown returned to his own chair, pushing it back from the desk a little and leaning back against the padded leather, legs crossed.

'I expect you're wondering what all this is about,' he said, almost conversationally.

'You have a job for me, I understand. But I am curious about it, of course. And why I've been brought down from Foxhill when you have typists here at the Empire.'

Mr Brown reached for his pipe, lying in an ashtray in the middle of the paperwork on his desk.

'To take your second point first, we don't have any girls here at the Empire with your qualifications.'

'But surely . . . ?' Pascale was surprised by this. She had certificates to show that she had passed her typewriting exam at 50 wpm with honours, and achieved a respectable 90 wpm in Pitman's shorthand, but that was hardly exceptional. The shorthand speed hadn't even been good enough to secure her a secretarial job in the Civil Service – their minimum requirement was 100 – and though she was proud of her typewriting skill, there were plenty of girls as fast and accurate as she was.

'I'm not talking about your secretarial qualifications.' Mr Brown tapped his pipe on the edge of the ashtray.

Pascale frowned. 'Then what . . . ?'

'We'll get to that in a moment.' He returned the pipe to the ashtray, took a packet of Senior Service from a desk drawer and held it out to her. 'I think I might have a cigarette. Would you like one?'

'Thank you.' Pascale didn't smoke much, and certainly not at work, where smoking in the typing pool was frowned upon, if not actually forbidden. But in this unsettling situation she thought a cigarette would be welcome, and she had the distinct impression that this pipe-smoking man was having a cigarette instead to create some camaraderie between them.

The lighter – solid silver by the look of it – flared, the cigarettes lit.

'So, my dear, I'd like to talk a little bit about you. You are half French, I understand.'

Pascale nodded, breathed out a mouthful of smoke.

'Yes. My mother was French. She and my father met when he was over there in the last war. He was in the army. They fell in love and married. But I don't see—'

'And you spent holidays in France with your grandparents?'

'Yes, I went to Poitiers every year for most of the summer when they were still alive. But—'

'So I'd be right in thinking you are bilingual?'

'Well, yes. Maman spoke French to me from the time I learned to talk. She wanted me to be fluent so there would be no language barriers between me and my grandparents.'

Pascale was beginning to think she knew where this was leading. For some reason they were looking for an interpreter. That must be it.

'Good.' The cigarette was burning away between Mr Brown's fingers, confirming Pascale's suspicion that he really would have preferred his pipe. 'I understand you are rather athletic, too.'

'*Athletic?*' she repeated, startled and puzzled again.

'Didn't you represent the country in cross-country running?'

'When I was at school, yes. I haven't run for years.'

'And you played for the hockey team, didn't you?'

'I did all kinds of sport, but not at the same level.'

'Still good enough to be in the school teams.'

'Well, yes, but . . .' Pascale broke off. 'You seem to know an awful lot about me, Mr Brown.'

'It's my business to know these things.' He smiled faintly, stubbed out the cigarette, half smoked, held her gaze directly once more. 'You asked me what kind of job I had in mind for you. I'll come to that now. But perhaps first I should explain. I don't actually work for the Admiralty. I work for quite a different department. And I would also like to make it clear that what passes between us must not go outside these four walls. You have already signed the Official Secrets Act, I presume?'

Pascale nodded, frowning.

'Excellent. Now, as you are aware, the Germans are occupying France – or the part of it that is not under Vichy control, and that, too, is of course effectively enemy territory. But there are groups of French patriots who are doing everything they can to make things difficult for the Germans, and the purpose of the department I work for is to assist them. One of the things we do is sabotage – blowing up bridges, that sort of thing, or at a more mundane level simply upsetting their organisation. Our other main concern is helping the French resistance workers to set up reliable groups, keeping them supplied with whatever they need, that kind of thing. We need liaison people for that, people who speak French well enough to be able to pass themselves off as natives, blend into the background, as it were. And that, of course, is where you come in. You come to our attention as just the sort of girl who could be very useful to us.'

Pascale was staring at him incredulously, scarcely able to take in what he was saying.

'You mean . . . you want me to go to France . . . as some kind of messenger?'

'Broadly speaking, yes. Exactly what role you are best suited for would be something that would be decided during your training.'

'Training,' Pascale repeated flatly.

'Well, yes. Obviously we don't send our people into an occupied country without them being fully prepared. Even then . . . well, it's only fair to warn you at the outset that what you would be doing is classified as dangerous work. Highly dangerous. The Germans are not at all happy about our efforts to undermine them, and they can react very violently, brutally even. Now, I realise what I'm proposing will have come as something of a shock to you, and I don't want to put you under pressure. The decision must be yours and yours alone. But at the same time I would urge you to give it serious consideration.

As I say, people with your qualifications are few and far between. It's not just a question of being able to speak fluent French, it's about being able to pass oneself off as a native. The accent must be absolutely authentic. Your mother is from Poitiers, you say?'

'Yes.'

Mr Brown made a note on the pad on his desk.

'What I'd like to do is recommend you to the people who run our preliminary courses. That would give us a chance to assess you – see whether you're suitable in other ways – and you a chance to see what you make of it all. But I don't expect you to give me an answer right away. You'll need a day or two to think things over. We'll arrange a position here at the Empire while you do so in order to keep your cover story intact. I'm going back to London this evening, but I shall be in Bath again next week. We can talk then, and you can let me know your decision.'

'No,' Pascale said.

Mr Brown looked at her sharply.

'No – I don't mean "no, I won't do it". I mean I don't need time to think. If I can be of any use . . . well, I'd like to be.'

'Really? Are you sure about this?'

'Yes. Quite sure.' Pascale was feeling oddly excited suddenly, as if something had exploded deep within her, sending a sense of purpose creeping through her veins as fresh green shoots erupt through barren earth at the onset of spring. For so long now she had felt numb and dead; suddenly she was alive once more.

'I love France,' she went on. 'I looked on it – still do – as my second home. Well, I am half French, after all. My grandparents are both dead now – they died before war broke out, and though I hate the fact that I've lost them I'm so glad they've been spared all this. But I still have relatives in France, though I don't have contact with them any more, and I can't bear to think of them having to live under German occupation.'

Mr Brown's eyes narrowed. 'Poitiers is, of course, quite close to the Free Zone.' He said it conversationally, but Pascale had the feeling he was testing her understanding of the situation.

'Well, yes,' she agreed. 'But I can't help wondering just how free it really is. I can't imagine the Germans would be content to keep a low profile there unless they were pretty sure that things were being run the way they want them to be.'

She broke off, tucking her hair behind her ear. 'I don't really understand all that's going on – my grandparents weren't in the least political, just patriotic, and I've had too many things on my mind to think about it much. But I do know that we have to win the war if France is ever again to be the place I knew and loved. And if there's anything I can do to help, then I want to do it.'

Mr Brown nodded, looking rather pleased.

'You sound quite passionate about it. But I'd still like you to take the week to think things over. It's not something to be decided lightly. If you still feel the same way when we speak again, then I'll set things in motion. I'll arrange for you to be commissioned as an officer in the FANYs – the First Aid Nursing Yeomanry. That's the cover we use for almost all the girls who work for us. In the mean-time we'll keep you here at the Empire. How does that sound to you?'

'It sounds fine.' The excitement stirred again, tightening her chest, prickling on her skin like nettle rash.

'We'll set you up in an office with a typewriter, which I'd like you to bang away on from time to time, though I don't imagine you'll be able to concentrate on any real work. *The quick brown fox jumped over the lazy dog* will do.' He smiled thinly; Pascale realised this was his idea of a quip.

'You must behave absolutely normally – that's vital,' he went on. 'And you do realise you must tell no one about this?'

A nerve jumped in Pascale's stomach; suddenly she felt very alone again. But that was something she'd grown used to over the past year.

'Really, Mr Brown, I have no one to tell, even if I wanted to.'

For a moment, an expression that might almost have been compassion flickered across his face. 'Quite so,' he said.

NINE

It was the fact that she was quite alone now that was the single most important thing influencing her snap decision to go along with Mr Brown's suggestion, Pascale knew.

For over a year now she had been languishing in a void that seemed to have stripped her of purpose, of her identity even. The grief, when it came in great overwhelming waves, was almost welcome – at least she was feeling something, not merely existing like an automaton swathed in a thick blanket of unreality. At least when she wept, the tears were proof that she had not dried up inside to a husk that could be blown away on the wind; the physical pain in her stomach as she was racked by sobs linked her to reality. It was the emptiness that was destroying her now, the loss not only of her family – her child, for God's sake – but of her reason for being, both now and in the future. Chance, fate – call it what you will – had robbed her of all that. She was no longer a mother, a daughter, she was a lost soul trapped in a wasteland from which there seemed no escape. To the outside world she appeared resilient, stoic, brave; inside her own skin it was very different.

The effort required to carry on called for a resolve that drained her; she'd lost interest in everything and couldn't face any kind of social interaction. She'd cut herself off from friends, unable to bear their sympathy, but at the same time unable to join in meaningless chatter. Now, for the first time in more than a year, something had pierced that all-pervasive fog of grief, brought her alive, given her a sense of purpose.

The prospect of being able to do something more for the war effort than fire-watching and copy-typing incomprehensible documents was exhilarating, especially if it meant she could help her beloved France in some small way. And the danger Mr Brown had mentioned didn't frighten her. It was a link, somehow, to those she had lost, so that it was almost exhilarating. Danger? Maybe. But what did that matter? Her mother and Lynne shouldn't have been in danger, but that hadn't saved them.

The bomb had been a fluke. Just why it had fallen on the block of shops in the quiet suburban street in broad daylight had never been properly explained. Certainly the German plane was being chased at the time by the fighters scrambled to defend the aeroplane works at Filton, just up the road in Bristol, from a daytime raid. Perhaps the crew had simply decided to dump their load, simple as that; it was the most popular theory. And really the reason scarcely mattered – the result was the same.

A direct hit had utterly destroyed a tobacconist and sweet shop and the hardware store next door. Both Marianne, Pascale's mother, and Lynne, Pascale's little daughter, had been in the hardware store, or so it seemed. Pascale knew that Marianne had intended to go there to buy tacks to make the blackout curtains more secure, and of course would have taken Lynne with her. The wreckage of Lynne's pushchair was discovered under the fallen masonry on the pavement outside, and when rescue workers finally managed to excavate the crater that was all that remained of the shop, just enough evidence had been found to identify Marianne as one of the victims. The tiny body of the year-old Lynne was never recovered; a policeman had explained to Pascale, as gently as possible, that it would have been utterly destroyed by the force of the explosion and the fierce fire that had followed.

All Pascale had left of Lynne now was a snippet of hair in a locket that she wore constantly on a chain around her neck, long enough for the locket to nestle unseen between her breasts, as close as it could be to her heart. When the pain of loss overwhelmed her, she would slip it out, holding it between finger and thumb like a talisman, snap it open and look at the little curl, remembering – the kiss of silky hair against her cheek, scented with baby soap, soft peachy skin, tiny fingers clasped around her thumb. Lynne had been born with a full head of hair; by the time she was ten months old, Pascale had trimmed it to keep it from looking untidy, and wrapped one of the curls in tissue paper and put it in the smallest drawer of her dressing table along with other treasures, some dating back to her own childhood. 'Her first haircut,' she had said to Marianne, choked with love and pride in her beautiful little girl.

After the bomb, after her unbearable loss, she rescued the curl from its hiding place and put it in the locket Kurt had given her. It seemed fitting. Not only could she keep the precious curl close to her at all times, what remained of Lynne rested safe inside a locket that had been a gift from her father.

Sometimes when grief made her maudlin, Pascale found herself thinking about the twist of fate that had seen her baby killed by a German bomb. Suppose it had been Kurt flying the plane that dropped it? A million to one chance, of course, really so unlikely as to be beyond sensible consideration. Kurt might not be in the Luftwaffe at all; he might be in the desert with Rommel, he might be one of the crew on a destroyer or a U-boat. He might be dead.

But one thing was certain. Though he might not have been the airman who unleashed the bomb that killed her child, one of his countrymen had been. Kurt was German; Kurt was the enemy. They were on opposite sides of the great divide. But for all that, she could not hate him.

She hated the Nazis, of course. She hated Hitler, whose grandiose schemes for creating an empire that would rule the world had started all this. But she couldn't hate Kurt, couldn't imagine he would ever willingly kill anyone. To her, he was still the handsome blond boy she had fallen in love with, courteous, considerate, with hidden fire beneath the ice-cool exterior. Who loved and respected his parents, his family, his country. Who had left her because he had to, not because he was running away from his responsibilities. He hadn't known she was pregnant – even *she* hadn't known when he left. But even if he had, she couldn't see that it would have made any difference.

Kurt was German, she was English. The threat of war had come between them and the reality of it put paid to any hope of resuming their relationship. Regretful but resigned, Pascale had accepted that Kurt would never be part of Lynne's life.

Now Lynne was dead, the last link severed. A twist of hair in a silver locket was the only reminder she had of either of them. And the unwilling admission, in the dark hours of the night, that she had been the author of her own fate.

She'd been so young, so impossibly young – just seventeen. And though it hadn't seemed that way to her at the time, so was he. He had come to Bath to work in the hotel trade; to her, just out of her secretarial course and in her first job as a typist with the Civil Service, he seemed incredibly grown up, as well as a romantic figure.

She met him on a lunch break from her office. As was her habit on fine days, she had taken her sandwiches and a bottle of lemonade to a bench in the Abbey Churchyard, and as usual she was alone. She hadn't made any real friends in the typing pool; in fact the rather hostile environment had come as quite a shock to her. At school she'd been popular – perhaps because she was good at sport, she thought wryly – and she had enjoyed the secretarial course too, relishing her new-found freedom. But the girls in the typing pool were quite a different breed. They were all older than her – or so it seemed – far more sophisticated, and rather catty. They had their well-established cliques, and she was not part of any of them. They made her feel like an outsider, and it was not something she was used to.

It was a pleasant day in the summer of 1938. The rain that had fallen earlier in the morning had cleared away and the sun was shining, giving the old Bath stone from which the abbey had been built a golden glow. Pascale spread her gabardine raincoat on the seat, which was still slightly damp, and started on her sandwiches. Egg today. One of the girls in the typing pool had wrinkled her nose at the smell coming from the greaseproof-paper packet and likened it to the fumes at Green Park railway station, but Pascale liked egg sandwiches. They were her favourite.

She liked Agatha Christie novels too – something else the girls scoffed at – and was working her way through the entire list. The one she was reading now was *Cards on the Table*, a Hercule Poirot mystery, and she was so engrossed she didn't even notice when a young man sat down at the other end of the bench until he spoke.

'This is a very beautiful city.'

Pascale glanced up, surprised, not even sure if the remark, uttered in a guttural accent, was directed at her. But the young man was certainly looking in her direction. Pascale sized him up, and liked what she saw – fair hair cropped short, a classically handsome face, eyes of a clearer blue than she'd ever seen before in a man. He was wearing a sports jacket and open-necked shirt, and an expensive-looking camera – certainly not your average Brownie box – hung on a strap around his neck.

'Yes, it is,' she said, and then: 'Are you here on holiday?'

'Holiday? No, I am here to work. But today is my day of rest. So I explore as if I were a tourist.'

'You're *working* here?' Pascale said. 'What do you do?'

'I wait at tables. At the Royal Grove Hotel.'

The Royal Grove, a very grand hotel, on a leafy square in the centre of town.

'Oh, I see.' Pascale took another bite of sandwich.

'I am here to learn more of the hotel business,' the young man said after a brief pause. 'My father owns such establishments at home, in Germany, in the Black Forest. I am expected to manage one when I am older and he wants me to gain experience in every part of the trade. And to improve my English, too.'

'Your English is very good,' Pascale said. 'I don't know a word of German. Though I do speak French,' she added, anxious, for some reason, to impress him.

'I, too, speak French. And a little Italian.'

'Goodness.' There was no answer to that.

'And you – do you work here too?'

94

'Well . . . yes.'

'In a store, perhaps?'

'No, an office. I'm a typist.'

'And you live nearby?'

'Not far. I come in every day on the bus.'

'You are very fortunate to work surrounded by such beauty, and such history, too! The Romans were here, were they not? What did they call Bath? Aquae Sulis? For the hot springs, I am told. I have not yet visited the Roman Baths, but I intend to do so soon. You will know them well, of course.'

'I suppose so . . .' Pascale had been to the Roman Baths once, on a school trip, and could picture only vaguely the steaming green waters, the sculpted archways and pillars. Her lack of interest in the history on her doorstep left her feeling vaguely ashamed.

'You must know every special place,' the young man went on. 'You are indeed fortunate.'

'Yes, I suppose I am.' Pascale glanced at her watch; the forty-five minutes allowed for lunch went by so quickly, and she mustn't be late back at the office.

'Perhaps,' the boy said, 'you could show some of them to me.'

Pascale's heart gave a little leap so that for a moment it felt as if it were beating in her throat. But she wasn't the sort of girl to allow herself to be picked up on a city bench by a perfect stranger, especially not a foreigner. If he had been French, maybe . . . that would have been different . . .

'Oh, I don't think . . .' she said, in a tone that meant 'no'.

'I would behave in a very proper manner. And there would be other people all around. We wouldn't be alone.'

Pascale laughed. 'You're very persistent.'

He shrugged. 'Maybe. But if I am not, then it is not only the sights of Bath that I shall be denied. It will also be your company.'

A faint colour tinged Pascale's cheeks. She was flattered – more, she was tempted. But even so . . .

'I come here most days when it's fine,' she said boldly. 'But my lunch break wouldn't give me time to show you around the city. In fact . . .' she checked her watch again, 'I have to go.'

She bundled up the remains of her sandwiches into their greaseproof paper wrapping and thrust the package into her bag.

'Then perhaps you will show me just some of it, as time allows.'

'Perhaps.'

She got up, walking across the sunlit churchyard without so much as a backward glance. But something like excitement was sending little darts of warmth through her gut, and Pascale was smiling at nothing in particular.

The next day she was aware of bubbling anticipation as she made her way to the seat in the Abbey Churchyard, and as she unpacked her sandwiches – cheese today, not nearly as nice as egg – she watched the entranceways through the pillars and between other buildings, hoping in vain to see the fair-haired boy amongst the shoppers and sightseers. She was disappointed when he did not appear, but reminded herself that he had said yesterday was his day off. If he had to wait at table he would be kept busy – the Royal Grove was a popular venue for lunch. It could be a whole week before he came – if he came at all.

And why would he? He'd probably just been flirting. Though she was only seventeen, Pascale had already had experience of that sort of thing: boys who asked you to dance at socials at the church hall, held you so close, especially in the last waltz, that it was embarrassing as well as darkly exciting, said they'd see you next week, and then ignored you, larking about with their pals or moving on to romance some other pretty girl. But she couldn't stop thinking about him, all the same.

On the second day it was drizzling again on and off, not really the weather for picnicking, but she went to the Abbey Churchyard just the same, though she told herself she was being foolish. She ate her sandwiches under the awning of a shop, and eventually returned to her office damp and disappointed. By day three, she had all but given up. Her usual bench was occupied and she had to take a seat on another one until the elderly couple who'd been sitting on hers vacated it. She moved quickly, so intent on staking her claim to the seat before someone else beat her to it that she did not see him until he was right beside her.

'Good afternoon, Fräulein.'

She jumped at the sound of the guttural accent, swung round, heart leaping.

'Oh – hello!'

'So – were you avoiding me? Trying to hide away where I would not find you?'

'No! Of course not! The bench was taken . . .' She broke off, scolding herself for sounding so eager. 'Why would I hide, anyway? I wasn't expecting to see you.'

'I said I would come.'

'That was days ago. I'd forgotten all about it.'

'Oh, I am sorry. I thought I explained. Sometimes I have to work all through the day.'

'But not today.'

'Today I serve at breakfast and at dinner. So, are you going to show me Bath as you promised?'

'I don't remember promising anything of the sort,' Pascale said archly.

'This beautiful place, for instance . . .' He nodded in the direction of an impressive building across the churchyard from the abbey. 'What is this called?'

'That's the Pump Room. It's very grand. But . . . how long have you been in Bath?'

'I have been here for almost three months now.'

'Well, I can't believe you've been here so long and not know that is the Pump Room.'

'Ah, Fräulein!' He assumed a hurt expression, though his very blue eyes were twinkling. 'Are you saying I do not speak the truth? I am offended. Deeply offended.'

'I'm saying I don't know you at all.'

'Then perhaps,' he said, a smile twitching at the corners of his mouth, 'that should come first. The Pump Room, the Roman Baths, they can wait. But it is not true that you know nothing about me. You know a great deal. That I work at the Royal Grove

Hotel. That I come from the Black Forest. That I have been in Bath for three months.'

'I don't know your name.'

'My name is Kurt Liebermann. I am twenty years old. I have two sisters at home in Germany, Ingrid, who is a year older than me, and Angela, the little one, who is seventeen. Now you know all about me, it is your turn.'

'Well . . .' Pascale's mind was racing, and she was suddenly very flustered. How could she tell him she was seventeen when he had just referred to his sister, who was the same age, as 'the little one'? 'There's really nothing to tell,' she said defensively. 'I don't have any brothers and sisters.'

'But you must have a name.'

'Well of course I do.' She lifted her chin and took refuge in her alter ego. 'It's Pascale.'

'That is a pretty name.'

'Yes,' she said, 'I think so too. It's French. My mother is French.'

'Really?'

'Yes, really.' But she didn't want to add that her mother had met her father when he was a soldier in France, didn't want to draw attention to the fact that once, not so long ago, their two countries had been at war. Especially since she'd heard talk recently about the German chancellor, Herr Hitler, how he was trying to take over other countries in Europe and that it might lead to another war

Though she didn't really understand what was going on, and tried not to think about it, Pascale couldn't believe it would come to that. According to her mother, the war had been so terrible, no one could possibly want another. Her father she could never remember mentioning it. In fact he had always retreated into silence if anyone brought it into the conversation, sometimes even left the room and went off out to the garden, where he could be seen wandering aimlessly around staring into space. His ill health was as a result of what he'd suffered, her mother had explained; he'd been gassed in the trenches, and his nerves had suffered too. He couldn't bear the bang of fireworks on Guy Fawkes night and had once chased some boys who were letting off squibs in the road outside the house, shouting at them in a way that was quite unlike her father. But at least he was alive; thousands had died. A whole lost generation, the maiden ladies left with no young man to marry living proof of it. There were three spinster sisters in the house next door but one to Pascale – the Misses Clarke – and they were never very friendly towards Marianne. They resented the fact that a foreigner had stolen one of their surviving English boys, Pascale suspected.

Now, however, she thrust any thought of that terrible war, or the worrying prospect that there might be another one, to the back of her mind. Kurt was in England, wasn't he? Surely that meant that the threat of hostilities was no more than scaremongering.

'There really isn't time for me to show you around Bath now,' she said. 'And I'm sure you've already seen the sights that are close by.'

'So let us arrange to meet when there is time.'

Pascale pretended to hesitate.

'All right,' she said at last.

'When are you free?'

'When are you?'

'I have to work all day on Saturday. Perhaps on Sunday afternoon?'

Again Pascale pretended to consider.

'I should think that would be all right.'

'So where shall we meet, and at what time?'

'Here,' Pascale said. 'Say . . .' she did a quick calculation: Sunday dinner at 12.30, a little time to help Marianne wash the dishes and clean the oven, 'three o'clock?'

'Better make it three thirty. I think I should be able to be here by then.'

'I hope so,' Pascale said. 'I don't want to come into town on a fool's errand.'

He looked puzzled, then smiled.

'A fool? You? I do not think so', he said.

It was, of course, just the beginning. Those summer months would be etched forever in Pascale's memory as a time of discovery and enchantment. The feelings that Kurt aroused in her were like nothing she had ever experienced before, as if she were dancing in the air with the whole world spread out beneath her, new and exciting and filled with promise. Kurt was handsome, courteous, considerate, the perfect Prince Charming to her Cinderella; his foreignness added an extra dimension to the mix, making him seem impossibly romantic. Her heart sang when she thought of him – which was constantly; her body was so sensitised that his slightest touch set her nerve endings prickling. When they went to the cinema and he held her hand under cover of the darkness, her whole awareness was centred on the wonderful feel of his fingers curled around hers; she had only the vaguest idea of what was going on on the screen. When he kissed and held her, she revelled in the warm pressure of his lips on hers, marvelled at the way they seemed to be breathing in unison, as if they shared the same heart and lungs, as if they were one, not two at all.

It wasn't an easy relationship to conduct, of course, given the unsocial hours that Kurt had to work, and in the beginning Marianne had raised objections. She had a distrust of Germans, which was, Pascale supposed, a legacy of the war. She couldn't forget they had once overrun her country, and she couldn't forgive the damage they had done to Pascale's father's health, which was steadily deteriorating. He could barely walk to the end of the garden now, though he was not yet forty years old. Yet strangely he was far more accepting of Kurt than was Marianne.

Pascale overheard them talking about it one day.

'I don't like it, Will,' Marianne was saying. 'Why couldn't she find a nice English boy? Or a French one? Why does she have to go out with a German?'

'Well – he's the one she fancies, I suppose.'

'But a German! Pah! Look what they did to you!'

'That's not Kurt's fault,' Will said. 'And it wasn't their fault, either, the ones that were fighting in the trenches. They were just obeying orders. You can't blame them.'

'I can! I do!'

'That's nonsense. They were just boys, like we were, doing a job. They were the same as us, only in a different uniform and on the

100

other side. Look at the first Christmas of the war – us and them, playing football together in no-man's-land. And they were singing carols, just like us. Leave the girl alone, can't you? She's seventeen years old, for goodness' sake, and I don't suppose it will last anyway. Let her enjoy it while she can.'

Certainly Pascale was enjoying it, though she desperately hoped her father was wrong about it not lasting. She couldn't imagine a life without Kurt – he was the air she breathed, and the thought of losing him was too dreadful to contemplate.

Afterwards, looking back, it seemed impossible to believe that they were together for such a short time. The importance of those months in defining the pattern of her life made them loom so large they dominated everything that had happened before and would happen afterwards. Kurt was a whole era, the death of her childhood, her baptism into the adult world. Yet in reality, what had begun in June was over by September, and Pascale's world crumbled with the first of the falling leaves and the sharp tang of autumn.

'I have to go home, *liebling*,' Kurt told her.

It was a Monday evening – Monday was invariably his day off. They had planned to see a film, but when they met, on the Old Bridge, where Pascale's bus came in, Kurt said he needed to talk to her. The seriousness in his tone and the set of his finely chiselled features made alarm tick in her throat.

'What's wrong?' she asked, the catch spilling over into her voice.

'Let's go to the park. We can talk there.'

It was a fair walk from the Old Bridge to the Victoria Park. They walked in silence, holding hands, and all the while Pascale's stomach was churning. They went into the park through the gate where two stone lions with a ball between their paws stood guard on plinths. When she was little, Pascale's father had told her that when the lions heard the abbey clock strike the hour, they threw the balls to one another. Pascale was entranced; she wanted to wait so as to be there to see it. She felt dreadfully let down when her father explained that because the lions were carved out of stone, they would never hear the clock strike, and decided to ignore what he had said, just as she had for a long time ignored the dreadful suggestion from a school friend that there was no Father Christmas and the stocking at the end of her bed was really filled by Maman and Daddy.

Today, however, Pascale did not so much as glance at the lions. She could think of nothing but that Kurt had something very serious to talk to her about.

'Kurt, tell me what it is, please!' she begged as they walked between shrubs and trees with the last of the evening sun filtering through the branches and making the swathes of parkland gleam a dull pinkish gold.

He told her.

Tensions were rising between England and Germany, with disquiet over Herr Hitler's plans to annexe Czechoslovakia and abhorrence of his treatment of the Jews, and the talk that it might come to war was gathering credence. The management of the Royal Grove Hotel had decided they could no longer employ a German to wait at their tables – there had been complaints from customers, and in any case they could not be held responsible for Kurt's safety if things turned nasty. He had been dismissed, and was to go home to Germany at the end of the week.

'This week!' Pascale was trembling; although it was a warm evening, her blood felt as though it had turned to ice.

'I am afraid so. But perhaps it is for the best.'

'No! I don't want you to go! Oh Kurt, you can't! You can't go!'

'I have no choice.'

How could he be so calm about it? So controlled? When she felt as if the world were coming to an end? Tears were gathering in her eyes, burning in her throat.

'I will write to you, I promise.'

Write to her! What substitute could a letter ever be for being with him? And besides . . . how long would it be before he met someone else, a German girl who was flesh and blood, not just words on a page.

'You can't go! I can't bear it! I'll miss you so much.'

'And I will miss you. But it has to be, liebling. I cannot stay here when I have no work. I would have had to go home soon, in any case. My father expects me to put my training to good use in his

102

hotels. I've always known that, and so have you. It's just sooner than I thought, that's all.'

'Couldn't I come with you?'

'Oh liebling, you know that is impossible.'

'Why? I could work there like you've been working here.'

'You are being silly.'

'No I'm not! I'm perfectly serious!'

'And so am I. One day, perhaps, when all this talk of war is over. But not now, as things are.'

'You don't want me to go with you.' The tears were gathering again.

'Of course I do. Oh, don't cry. Come here.'

He pulled her into his arms; she buried her face in his sweater, soft and smelling of fresh soap.

'I love you, Kurt.'

'And I love you.'

'Do you? Really?'

'Really.'

They were kissing, clinging. Desperation, the terrible fear of losing him, surged through Pascale, along with a sense of urgency. When his hand moved to her breast, she didn't try to stop him as she usually did, only clung to him more tightly, pressing her body against his.

'Don't,' he said, his tone low and guttural as he eased a little distance between them.

She ignored him, pressing close again, her overwhelming need greater than her caution.

A soft dusk had fallen; the park was deserted now. They sank to the grass, not noticing that it had grown damp with dew. And as Kurt pushed up her skirt and rolled on top of her, Pascale thrust aside the qualms that picked, even now, at the seams of her consciousness. Nothing mattered but that she should prove to Kurt how much she loved him; nothing mattered beyond finding a way to keep him with her.

But of course, there was no way. With passion spent, everything was just the same as it was before. She and Kurt might have become

103

lovers, but he was still leaving England at the end of the week. She might have allowed him to make love to her, instigated it even, but she couldn't change the way things had to be.

Kurt went home to Germany and Pascale was left behind.

A few weeks later she realised she was going to have his baby.

TEN

Pascale was in total turmoil. She veered between terror and wild elation – if she was having Kurt's baby, then surely they would be together, wouldn't they? But she had heard scarcely a word from him since she'd kissed him goodbye at Bath Spa station when he left for Dover and the onward journey home, just a short note telling her he had arrived and was now working in one of his father's hotels. The note was signed 'with love' – such inadequate words! – but already it was crumpled because she'd read and reread it so many times, and slept with it under her pillow.

She'd written to him several times, though she hadn't mentioned her suspicion that she might be pregnant. She was too afraid that she might frighten him off. But when she missed her second period and began feeling horribly sick in the mornings – a nausea that sometimes lasted all day – she knew she could wait no longer. She wrote again; when she took the letter to the post office, the woman behind the counter stared at the envelope for long seconds, lips pursed, eyes narrowed suspiciously, then turned the same hard stare on Pascale, who flushed a deep red, right down to her neck. She knew what the woman was thinking: why was she writing to a German when the political situation was growing more tense by the day? But that was the least of her worries. The only thing she really cared about was letting Kurt know of her condition, and getting a reply to assure her he would stand by her.

But no reply came. And whilst she waited, rushing home from

work each day in the hope that at last there would be an airmail letter for her, something dreadful happened. Her father got pneumonia. For three days and nights the house was full of his painful gasps for breath; there was no escaping it. Even downstairs in the scullery at the back of the house you could still hear it.

On the third night, his heart could take no more.

Pascale had gone to bed and fallen asleep, utterly exhausted. When Marianne woke her, just before three, the first thing she noticed was the silence.

'He's gone,' Marianne said. She sounded dazed, standing there beside Pascale's bed in her red woollen dressing gown with her arms wrapped around her as if she were trying to hold herself together.

Instantly, Pascale was wide awake.

'Oh no!' It came out on a sob.

'Can you . . . will you go for Mrs Dobson?'

Mrs Dobson, who lived in the next street, was the person everyone sent for in the event of a death. She had been a nurse before she had her family; now she laid out the dead.

'Now?'

'The sooner the better. Before . . .' She broke off, collecting herself. 'I told Mrs Dobson yesterday we might be needing her, and she said to call any time of the day or night.'

Pascale was shocked that her mother already had arrangements in hand. Ill as her father had been, she'd refused to give up hope, had told herself that he would get over it, as he always had before. She'd just wanted that awful rasping noise to stop. Now it had, but for the wrong reason.

She got up; the room, dimly illuminated by the light on the landing, spun, and she realised she felt very sick. Pausing occasionally to press her hand over her mouth, she struggled into her clothes – skirt, stockings and a warm jumper. Then she rushed to the bathroom and retched over the sink.

'Are you all right?' Marianne asked from the doorway.

'It's just the shock . . .' Her mouth tasted bitter from the horrid orangey-yellow bile.

106

'There was no way back for him this time, *petite*,' Marianne said. 'Would you rather I went for Mrs Dobson?'

'No – no, I'll go,' Pascale said hastily. 'I'm dressed now.'

Strangely, although she felt dreadful, she *wanted* to. She didn't want to be left alone in the house with her dead father.

She bundled herself into her coat, buttoning it up to the neck and tying the belt tightly around her waist. Then she went out into the cold, clammy fog that shrouded everything so that the street lights were nothing but pinpricks surrounded by fuzzy haloes and the houses on the other side of the road loomed shapeless and ghostly.

Pascale felt as if she was living a nightmare. Her father was dead; she was pregnant. 'One in, one out,' the old saying went. It seemed to echo around her, muted by the fog but inescapable. Pascale retched again, and the retch became a sob.

Somehow she regained control of herself. One thing at a time. Fetch Mrs Dobson. Don't think of anything else. She wiped her mouth with the back of her hand, swallowed hard, and rapped on Mrs Dobson's door until a light came on in an upstairs window and she heard footsteps on the stairs.

'Oh Lord, has he gone?' Mrs Dobson's hair was in curlers; she was wearing a thick dressing gown over a voluminous flannel nightgown. 'You'd better come in while I get dressed.'

'It's all right, I'll wait out here,' Pascale said, afraid that she might be sick again.

She wasn't. Not physically. But she *was* still sick at heart. For the loss of her father. And for the terrible predicament she was in.

She couldn't bring herself to tell her mother. Marianne was so grief-stricken over Will's death that Pascale shrank from inflicting this upon her. Of course, she was grieving too, she had adored her father, and saying the words that would make this other nightmare real was quite beyond her. She no longer enjoyed the swings to wild elation; she'd still received no reply from Kurt and was almost past hoping for one. Perhaps something had happened to prevent him replying – if he'd ever received her letters; perhaps he didn't want to. Either way the result was the same. She was in this on her own, and she didn't know what she was going to do.

In the end it was Marianne who broached the unbroachable subject. They were washing up the dinner things – they ate their main meal of the day when Pascale got home from work. When Will was alive, Marianne had eaten with him in the middle of the day, saving a helping of whatever they were having for Pascale and warming it up on a plate over a saucepan of simmering water when she came home. Now, Marianne cooked fresh for both of them at half past six. Today it had been a lamb stew, made the French way, though, since it was midwinter, without the handfuls of herbs she liked to throw in. She was at the sink, elbow deep in soap suds, when she suddenly stopped what she was doing and turned to look directly at Pascale, who was drying a glass.

'Is there something you want to tell me?'

Pascale felt her stomach lurch. She put the glass down carefully on the oil cloth-covered kitchen table, her back turned towards Marianne.

'Is there?' Marianne persisted. 'Come on, I'm your mother. You can tell me, whatever it is.'

Pascale said nothing. She bowed her head, unable, still, to find the words.

'Oh, chérie, do you think I am blind as well as stupid? Do you think I don't know? You have been a silly girl, I think. And now . . .'

Pascale's shoulders stiffened around the sob that was threatening to escape and she glanced sideways at her mother with eyes that were full of shame.

Marianne sighed deeply, shaking her head. She put her hand on Pascale's arm, her fingers making a snail-trail of bubbles on the rough blue wool of her jumper. She took the tea towel from Pascale, dried her hands on it, and turned her daughter towards her, drawing her head on to her shoulder as if she were a little girl again, holding her so close that the swell of Pascale's stomach, which she had tried so hard to hide, was there between them.

'You should have told me long ago,' Marianne chided. 'You shouldn't be going through this alone. It was Kurt, I suppose, and now he's gone home to Germany and left you in a pickle. Well, it's no use crying over spilt milk. What's done is done.'

'I've written to him,' Pascale said, 'but he doesn't reply.'

'I thought as much. That's what all this rushing for the post has been about.'

'I can't understand it, Maman. How could he not reply? I thought he loved me. That's what he said.'

'Pchew! They all say that.'

'No . . . no, it wasn't like that. Nothing happened until the night be told me he was going away, and it was more my fault than his . . . He wasn't like that, Maman.'

'Then perhaps there is a reason he does not reply to your letters,' Marianne said, although she didn't sound entirely convinced. 'Perhaps he has not received them. With all that's going on . . . maybe the authorities are intercepting mail from England.'

'I did wonder that . . .'

'Whatever, we can't waste time worrying about it. There is too much else to think about. Let's get this washing-up out of the way, and we'll sit down and talk.'

Pascale could hardly believe her mother's matter-of-fact response, but then, wasn't that Marianne all over? And in any case, she'd already guessed what was going on, so she'd had time to get used to the idea.

They finished washing, drying and putting away the dishes, then Marianne made a pot of tea and they took it into the living room and resumed their places at the dining table.

'Have you thought about this at all?' Marianne asked.

Pascale laughed, a short, humourless snort.

'I've hardly thought about anything else. Except Daddy, of course.'

Tears filled her eyes, just speaking his name.

'Yes, well, perhaps it's a good thing he knows nothing about this. It would break his heart . . .' Realising that she was distressing Pascale, Marianne bit off the words, concentrating instead on trying to be practical.

'So – do you want to keep this baby, or do you want to have it adopted?' she asked, pouring tea.

'Well I can't keep it, can I?' Pascale pressed her hands together, rubbing at her ringless fingers.

'I suppose adoption would be the best way,' Marianne said. 'Better for your reputation – you could go away for a time, and nobody here need know the reason why. I'd say you could go to France, to your aunt Cecile, but with things as they are at present, I'm not sure that would be a good idea. But we'll arrange something – if that's what you want. But is it? Parting with your baby, never seeing it again, never knowing if it was well and happy . . . it would be very hard, chérie. I lost a baby, when you were two years old . . .'

Pascale's eyes widened. 'I never knew that!'

'There is no reason why you should. Oh, it's not the same thing, I know. I had no decision to make – it just happened when I was four months gone. We never talked about it, your father and I, but that doesn't mean I don't think about him. Often, and especially at the time of year when he should have been born – I always think of him as a boy, though of course I'll never know for certain. I gave him a birthday, and each year on that day I thought of him at the age he would have been, pictured him growing up . . . I know how I felt, and I never knew my baby. I can't imagine how much worse it would be if I'd given birth to him, held him in my arms, fed him. You'd go through all that and then they would take him away from you. Is that what you want, chérie?'

Pascale chewed on her lip.

'Oh Maman, I don't know. What choice do I have?'

'If you do want to keep the baby, we'd manage somehow. I'd help you. Look after it while you went to work – if they let you keep your job, that is. If not, you can find another. And we have plenty of room here. The little front bedroom we can make into a nursery.'

Again Pascale was astonished at the thought her mother had given this.

'But . . . what would people say?'

It wasn't a question she was proud of asking, but already she'd experienced great washes of shame and no one even knew yet that she was pregnant. There was such a terrible stigma about having a baby without being married – 'letting yourself down', people called it. They even turned their noses up at girls who went on to marry the father of their child – 'a rushed job' – because they had gone with a man who wasn't their husband. Plenty did, of course, but no one admitted it, and getting caught out was the ultimate crime.

Marianne shrugged, a very Gallic gesture she had never lost though she had lived in England for the best part of twenty years.

'I do not much care what people say. Well – I do, I suppose, but I care more about what is right for you and your baby. They will talk to begin with, yes, but soon they will find something else to gossip about. We just have to hold our heads high and let them see we are not ashamed. They are no saints either, if the truth be known.'

'Oh, Maman . . .'

'I know, it will not be easy. But there you are. Not many things in life are. It's up to you, chérie. You have to decide. Think about it. But you know I am here for you. I will always be here for you.'

Pascale reached across the table, took her mother's hands, spreathed and red from washing sheets in the big stone sink.

'I am so sorry, Maman.'

'It's a little late for that.'

'I know, but . . . how can I put this on you? And so soon after Daddy . . .'

Marianne's lip trembled; she bit down on it fiercely.

'Don't, chérie. As I say, you must think about it very seriously. Decide what you want to do.'

'What would you rather I did?'

Marianne smiled faintly.

'I wish it had never happened, of course, I'd be lying if I said otherwise. But it has. And if you want the truth about what I think . . . I have just lost your father, who was the love of my life. I don't think I could bear to lose my grandchild too.'

'Oh, Maman . . .' A wash of gratitude and love brought Pascale to the verge of tears again. She really did not yet know what to do for the best, but at least her mother had given her an option.

'Drink up your tea before it goes cold,' Marianne said. 'And don't cry, chérie. If you do, I shall cry with you.'

*   *   *

111

There were plenty of sleepless nights, plenty more discussions over pots of tea or coffee before Pascale came to her decision, but eventually it was made. With her mother's support, she would keep her baby. Whatever the problems, whatever the consequences, she didn't think she could bear to part with it. And when Lynne was born, on a hot June day in the summer of 1939, she knew she had done the right thing. Already she had been subjected to all kinds of abuse – sacked from her job, stared at disapprovingly in the street, spoken to with rude cruelty by the midwife, who, when Pascale had been in labour for more than fifteen hours and begged for help with the pain, had told her tartly that it was her own doing, she should have thought of the consequences before she 'messed about with some man'. But when she held Lynne in her arms, touched her lips to that unbelievably thick shock of silky-soft hair, felt the tug of warm, rosy lips on her swollen nipples, the love she felt was so utterly overwhelming it made her weak.

Maybe she had lost Kurt – he was no more now than a sad, sweet memory – but this new little life more than made up for it. Perhaps one day, when all this trouble between Germany and the rest of Europe was over, he'd come back – she still thought that some kind of censorship had intercepted their letters – and they would be together again, a family. If not . . . she had Lynne, and really that was all that mattered.

Lynne was just three months old when war was declared. Bath was flooded with evacuees from London, parties of children who arrived at Bath Spa station, their names on cardboard labels pinned to their coats as if they were so much luggage, to be trailed around the city by WVS workers anxious to find them billets before nightfall. Two – a pair of little sisters – were taken in by Marianne's next-door neighbour, and the WVS women gave Marianne a hard time for refusing to take any herself.

'We have a baby in the house,' Marianne said firmly. 'I don't want strange children and their germs here, giving her goodness knows what!'

The Admiralty moved to Bath, taking over the Empire Hotel and other buildings in the city and erecting hutments on several sites. Pascale managed to get a job in the one that was closest to her home. The people from London were less censorious about her status as an unmarried mother; they were anxious to find competent, trustworthy staff, and Pascale's Civil Service background made her an ideal candidate. Just what they would have thought had they known her baby's father was a German was, of course, another matter, but at the time she was registering Lynne's birth, Pascale had asked for the entry to read 'Father Unknown', and really no one had known about her affair with Kurt. He'd never been to her home, so the neighbours hadn't seen him, and since she'd had no friends amongst the girls at the tax office, none of them knew either. If Kurt had ever told any of his colleagues about them, she didn't know, but she thought it unlikely, given his natural reserve, and in any case she'd never met any of them.

Whatever enquiries the Admiralty may have made about her background, obviously nothing had come to light. Her typing skills and the fact that she'd already been a government employee – albeit a fallen woman – carried the day. Good as her word, Marianne cared for Lynne whilst Pascale was at work, and both seemed to thrive on it.

To her shame, Pascale was slightly jealous of the time Marianne got to spend with Lynne, and the bond that existed between the two of them. It was Marianne who claimed to have heard her first word – though gratifyingly it was apparently Ma-ma – when she was just eleven months old; Marianne to whom she took her first tottering step a few weeks after her first birthday. But they were pinpricks of regret only. Pascale made the most of the time she was able to spend with her little daughter – 'the prettiest baby in all of England', as she proudly described her. She got up early each morning to cuddle Lynne before leaving for work; she rushed home in the evenings to bathe her and put her to bed, and often sat beside her cot long after Lynne had fallen asleep, holding one small finger through the bars and marvelling at the beauty of her.

At weekends she pushed her out in her pram, and later, the pushchair she managed to buy from the second-hand columns of the evening paper. The neighbours, who had been shocked and disapproving in the beginning, now seemed to have grown used to the idea that Pascale's baby had no father. They cooed over Lynne, who obligingly smiled back at them, commented on her beautiful hair and her deep blue eyes, even gave her little treats – a fluffy ball made of ends of knitting wool wound together and tied on a length of ribbon, a good-as-new toy rabbit, a little board book with brightly coloured pictures of everyday objects. The two evacuee girls doted on her, coming into the garden to hang over her pram when she was parked outside for her daily dose of fresh air and sunshine – Marianne no longer worried about germs; and a girl who had come down with the Admiralty from London – Pascale knew her only as Peggy – and who was in lodgings nearby, told Pascale she really envied her.

'I'm very lucky, I know,' Pascale said. And truly meant it. Though war was raging in Europe, it had as yet scarcely touched her life. Kurt seemed like a distant dream now, insubstantial and unreal. Her world centred around Lynne, her adored baby. And when she worried for her, they were the normal everyday worries of a mother for her vulnerable little one, and, sometimes, for the world she would grow up to inhabit. But Pascale felt confident that England would win the war. It was only a matter of time.

By the time Lynne celebrated her first birthday, the war was also a year old. Norway and Denmark had been invaded; Holland and Belgium had surrendered; Italy had joined the war on the side of the Nazis. The fall of France had caused Marianne enormous distress – she was dreadfully worried about her relatives in the area around Poitiers, and knowing that her beloved homeland was under the control of a foreign power offended her fierce pride.

'Just imagine! A swastika flying from the Eiffel Tower and the Arc de Triomphe – whatever next?' she said, practically wringing her hands. 'I suppose we must put our trust in Monsieur Pétain. He saved us before, in the last war. But to be truthful, I'm not sure I trust him. He's gone soft in his old age, I think.'

The Battle of Britain, too, had begun, with the Luftwaffe bombing cities and airfields, and the fighter planes of the RAF scrambling to defend them. Bristol had been hit – the docks and aeroplane factories were a prime target – but Bath, nestling in the valley bowl and surrounded by swathes of open countryside, seemed relatively safe. It was assumed the planes that flew overhead were taking their bombs elsewhere. Only the most cautious folk went to the shelters when the siren sounded, and Marianne, Pascale and Lynne were not among them. Marianne in particular loathed the cold, damp shelters, which she said would be the death of them all, and unless they actually heard explosions close by, they stayed at home, sheltering in the cupboard under the stairs until the danger passed and they could go back to bed.

Their lives were affected in other ways, of course. There was food rationing, there were gas masks that smelled of rubber and were supposed to be kept within easy reach at all times – even Lynne had a little one in a cardboard box. And there were all kinds of rules about showing lights.

Like every other household, their windows were all blacked out so that no light showed, a marker for enemy bombers. Marianne had got hold of the correct material, thick, black and heavy, and made the curtains. But for some reason, the one at the living room window refused to stay in place. The night before the catastrophe, Archie Stevenson, the rather officious ARP warden in charge of their street, had knocked on the door and told an indignant Marianne that she was in breach of regulations. A chink of light could be seen – didn't she know she was putting her family and everyone else in the road in danger of attack by the enemy?

'I suppose I'd better go to Mr Packer's tomorrow and see if I can get some longer tacks,' Marianne said as she and Pascale stood on dining chairs trying to secure the offending blind. 'I think it will hold for now, but it's going to come down again before long, and we can't sit here in the dark, whatever Archie Stevenson says.'

'It would be pretty miserable,' Pascale agreed. 'And I certainly wouldn't be able to see to sew by the light of the fire.'

She was making a little dress for Lynne from a length of parachute silk, and intended to try her hand at smocking the bodice when it reached that stage.

'Knowing him, he'd be knocking on the door and complaining even about that,' Marianne said shortly, and it was true, the flickering flames from the coal fire did make dancing shapes in the dark. 'No, I'll go to Mr Packer's tomorrow. He'll have something to fix it. He's got everything in that shop of his.'

Pascale laughed. As a child she had been fascinated by the array of goods Mr Packer stocked. Outside, on the pavement, were bags of seed potatoes and daffodil bulbs; inside you had to pick your way between lawn mowers, watering cans and Aladdin paraffin heaters, whilst behind the counter wooden boxes lined the wall instead of shelves, filled with nails, screws and washers. There was a strong but indefinable smell about the shop, a pungent aroma of all the things Mr Packer sold; Pascale had often thought that if she had been blindfolded and dumped in the hardware shop, she would have known instantly where she was.

'I don't know how he ever manages to find anything,' she said.

'But he does.' Marianne picked up the dress Pascale was working on. 'This is going to be lovely. Lynne will look a picture in it.'

'Yes, she will, won't she?' Pascale smiled with pride.

She had no way of knowing that her little daughter would never wear it – that indeed, it would never even be finished. That by this time tomorrow, both her mother and Lynne would be dead and the dress would be packed away in brown paper, a poignant reminder of what she had lost.

All for the sake of a few tacks to secure a drooping blackout curtain.

ELEVEN

After her second interview with the mysterious Mr Brown, things moved swiftly.

Pascale still lived in what had been her parents' house. Though the memories of happier times sometimes made it almost unbearable, it had never occurred to her to sell it and move on. It was her home, the only one she'd ever known; her father had bought and paid for it, and as long as she could afford the rates and the bills for gas and electricity, she intended to remain there, close to her roots and her ghosts. But still, even after more than a year, the emptiness when she returned from work had the power to shock her sometimes. The complete darkness in winter when she let herself in at the front door – no welcoming glow of light from the living room; the silence, no clatter of pans or crockery from the kitchen, no wireless tuned to the Light Programme; the post, if there was any, lying on the mat where it had fallen after shooting through the letter box, all underlined the fact that nobody but her lived here any more. A sort of malaise would overcome her, at least until she had switched on the lights and taken off her coat, and sometimes even longer, a haunting sadness for what had been and could never be again.

That afternoon, however, when she returned from her pretend job at the Empire and found a square, official-looking envelope lying on the hall mat, her reaction was entirely different. The block of pica type bearing her name and address appeared to have been the work of the same sort of machine that she used, though considerably newer; her stomach clenched and a shiver that was part excitement and part nervousness prickled over her skin. She picked it up and tore it open, but with the only light coming through the mullioned glass panel in the door, it was too dim in the hall to be able to read what the letter inside said.

She took it through to the kitchen and snapped on the overhead light, since she hadn't opened the curtains before leaving for work that morning. The single sheet of white paper trembled a little between her fingers as she read.

She had been appointed an ensign in the FANYs. And she was being called to a preliminary training course at a country house in Essex on Friday of the following week.

Pascale read and reread the letter, the nervous excitement fluttering again. Until now, the whole arrangement had seemed a little unreal, with the aura of a particularly vivid dream. This letter was palpable, and a sense of shock was washing over her like a strong incoming tide washing over a sandy beach, driving and sucking at the insubstantial grains of sand. What had she done? What was she letting herself in for?

She stood with the letter in one hand, the other pressed over her mouth as she took deep steadying breaths and the momentary panic passed to be replaced by an exhilarating determination.

This was her chance to be of real use.

She could do it. She would.

The country house was a grey-stone Palladian mansion set in an expanse of parkland through which a broad drive cut an arrow-straight swathe. The taxi that Pascale had been forced to take from the railway station came to a halt on a gravel turnaround where broad steps led up to an impressive front door. The driver unloaded her small case, which he had – rather unnecessarily, Pascale thought – placed in the boot, and hovered while she found the fare. He was expecting a tip, she supposed, but she really didn't know how much she should give him. She'd never taken a taxi in her life before; never been in a situation where tipping was called for, come to that.

In the end she settled on a florin, still worried that it might be too little or too much.

As the taxi pulled away, she started towards the steps, which were flanked by two stone statues, not unlike the lions who guarded the Victoria Park in Bath, Pascale thought, except that these looked more like large dogs. But before she could reach them, footsteps crunching on gravel and a voice calling 'Hello-oh!' made her pause and look round.

A man had appeared from around the corner of the house. Though he wore a tweed sports coat and brown corduroy trousers, his bearing was military, and a neatly clipped greying moustache and severe short-back-and-sides haircut reinforced the impression.

'The first of our arrivals!' His voice was deep, with just a hint of a Yorkshire accent. 'I'm Leonard Curtis. And you are . . . ?'

Pascale told him.

'Ah yes. You're to be known as Lise, if I'm not mistaken.'

Pascale frowned, puzzled, and he went on: 'All our girls have alter egos. It's something you have to get used to, so we start as we mean to go on. Lise is just the name you'll use while you're in training, but it's a useful exercise for a number of reasons. Now, let me take your bag . . .'

He picked up Pascale's little case and led the way up the steps.

'Go on in. I'll just check which room you're having and then you can get unpacked and freshened up. We shall start serving tea at four thirty.'

The hall in which Pascale found herself was impressively large, but surprisingly bare. The flagged floor needed rugs, she thought; the solid oak table and dresser cried out for jugs of fresh flowers; the great curving staircase needed a runner of some kind. There was a clipboard on the table; Leonard Curtis consulted it and nodded.

'You'll be sharing a room with Marie and Simone – those are their training code names, which you should all respect. You don't mind sharing, I hope?'

'No . . . of course not.' Pascale had never had to share a room before, but she imagined she would have to get used to much worse.

The doorbell jangled suddenly, echoingly loud in the vast empty hall.

'Excuse me.' Leonard Curtis went to answer it, and Pascale heard him talking to someone, saying much the same things he had said to her, then a tall, elegant girl with reddish-brown hair falling in a provocative bang over one eye came into the hall. Though the afternoon was warm, she was wearing a grey chalk-striped suit and a small felt hat, and she carried a black suede handbag. The suitcase that Leonard Curtis was holding for her was pale grey, large and smart. Pascale was suddenly horribly conscious of her cotton frock and cardigan, and most especially of her battered brown leather case.

Curtis looked from one to the other of them.

'Can I introduce you two? Lise . . . Simone.'

'Hello.' The newcomer held out a gloved hand. Pascale took it, a little self-consciously.

'Hello.'

''Right. Let me show you to your room, then.'

A suitcase in each hand, Curtis led the way up the broad staircase and along a landing where the floor sloped alarmingly in places. With one foot he pushed open a door that already stood ajar.

'Here we are.'

The room was reasonably sized, the walls papered in a design of overblown peonies and roses, which had faded in places and darkened in others, and the curtains were heavy dark red chenille. With the three single beds, a washstand and a wardrobe crammed into it, the room felt cluttered, and the rugs on the bare board floor looked threadbare and worn. But the view from the window was spectacular – the parkland Pascale had driven through, and beyond it a thick copse of trees in full summer leaf.

'So – which bed would you like?' Simone asked generously.

'Well – I'd choose the one by the window. But I expect you'd like that one too.'

'Mm. Tell you what – shall we toss for it?'

Pascale laughed. 'OK. I don't think I've got any small change, though. I gave it all to the taxi driver.'

'You *paid*? For your taxi?'

'Well . . . yes. Didn't you?'

'I told them to charge it. I think they do quite a lot of work for the bods here. You must be sure to claim it back on expenses.' As she spoke, she was rifling through her purse and extracting a half-crown. 'Here we are. Heads or tails?'

The coin was already spinning in the air. Simone caught it expertly and flipped it on to the back of her hand, covering it with a tightly closed fist.

'Oh – heads,' Pascale said.

'Heads it is. The bed by the window is yours.' Simone dumped her handbag on the bed next to it, fetched her suitcase from where Curtis had left it by the door, and lifted it up on to the bed too. 'I'm going to get out of this dratted suit and into something cooler. I had this crazy idea that I should look respectable, being on government business as you might say, but somehow I don't think it's going to turn out to be that sort of do. Did you notice the assault course on your way in?'

Pascale shook her head.

'Over beyond the trees. By the lake. At least it looked like an assault course to me. And I'm absolute rubbish at that sort of thing. Are you?'

'I don't know. I've never done an assault course.'

'Who has? But you look as if you'd be good at it.'

Pascale wasn't sure whether this was a compliment or not.

Simone had slipped out of her skirt. Beneath it she was wearing French knickers in what looked like cream silk, with insets of real lace. Pascale, unpacking, thrust her cotton floral-print nightdress under the pillow out of sight.

'So, what's your qualification for being here?' Simone asked, shedding her blouse to reveal a camisole that matched the French knickers.

'Qualification?' Pascale echoed.

'Yes – apart from being sporty. You must be bilingual, I assume, or you wouldn't have got this far. It's certainly the only reason I have. Apart from having lived and been educated in France, I can't see that I have a single thing to offer.'

121

'You lived in France?' Pascale said, interested. 'Where?'

'Paris. My father was in the diplomatic service. And after he got another posting, I stayed on. Because of a man, of course. He turned out to be the most frightful bore, and with quite the wrong politics for my liking. A communist! I ask you!'

'Oh, how awful . . .' Pascale had no firm opinion on the matter, but it seemed to be the reaction Simone was expecting.

'Ghastly! Especially now. The trouble they're causing . . .' Simone shook out a tea dress, examining it for stubborn creases. 'And then I met someone else. Someone rather wonderful. In fact, we're unofficially engaged to be married. And it was through him that I came to get involved in all this . . .' She broke off abruptly. 'I mustn't say any more; everything's supposed to be top secret, isn't it? But . . . let me put it this way. He's one of us . . . if we ever get to be an "us", that is.'

'Oh!' Pascale was impressed.

'So what about you? How come you're here?'

'My mother was French.'

'*Was?* Is she dead, then?'

'Yes.' Pascale didn't want to be drawn into a conversation about the tragedy that had changed her life. 'That's a very pretty dress.'

'Mm, yes. But we have to take care of our clothes now, don't we? Heaven knows when we'll be able to replace them. I only hope they'll provide us with something suitable to wear if we have to do awful things like that assault course. I've no plans to ruin a perfectly good pair of trousers scrambling over fences and through tunnels. Right.' She had slipped into the dress and was running a comb through her hair. 'Perhaps we'd better go down and see what afternoon tea has to offer. I must say, I'm starving. Are you ready?'

Pascale slicked on some lipstick and rolled her lips together.

'I think so.'

'Let's go then, and begin to find out what's going to be expected of us as special agents. It's rather exciting, isn't it?'

'Well yes, I suppose it is,' Pascale said, and wished she had half the self-confidence and *joie de vivre* of her room-mate.

*   *   *

Pascale, Simone and nine other girls gathered in the dining room, exchanging awkward greetings and summing one another up. None of them, however, was Marie, with whom they were sharing a room.

'Perhaps she's decided it's not for her,' Pascale suggested.

'And who could blame her?' Simone pulled a face at the soggy tomato sandwiches and slices of alarmingly yellow sponge cake, thinly spread with blackcurrant jam.

Hardly had she spoken than a small plump girl with strong features, a sallow complexion and jet-black hair came bursting into the room.

'I am so sorry that I am late. My train was delayed.' Her heavily accented voice left them in no doubt: this girl was not English, but French.

'Never mind, you're here now.' The matronly woman who was overseeing the meal – a housekeeper? Chaperone? – bustled over to the tea urn and filled a cup. 'You're Marie, I expect. Come and meet your room-mates, Simone and Lise.'

'You're French, aren't you?' Simone asked her.

'You knew.' Marie looked slightly affronted.

'Well, yes. Where are you from?'

'My home is a little mountain village in the south-east. When France fell, I escaped over the Pyrenees and came to England. My family is still there – my brother Pierre is trying to organise resistance in the area, and an escape line for British pilots. We thought maybe I could become a contact of some kind.'

'Your English is very good,' Simone said.

'I spent some time in England before the war. I was going to teach English in French schools, that was my dream. But now . . . well, everything has changed, has it not?'

When afternoon tea was finished, Leonard Curtis suggested the girls familiarise themselves with the grounds. They set out in knots of twos and threes, Pascale, Simone and Marie already bonding into a unit. They found the assault course Simone had mentioned, and a lake with rowing boats pulled up on the bank, and various pieces of rough equipment, which consisted mostly of planks of wood, empty oil drums and coils of rope, gathered together in a clearing where the copse met the water's edge.

'Good God, I hope we're not going to be expected to get ourselves across the lake with that load of old rubbish!' Simone exclaimed, horrified, but Pascale couldn't help thinking it might be fun.

At seven o'clock there was an introductory talk and briefing, then dinner was served – a watery vegetable soup and a shepherd's pie, the contents of which Pascale preferred not to guess at, followed by a jam roly-poly pudding.

'No burning the midnight oil, ladies,' Leonard Curtis advised. 'You've an early start in the morning.'

Back in their room, Pascale noticed that Simone had propped a small framed photograph on the cabinet beside her bed. A man in RAF uniform. She didn't like to stare, but Marie had less inhibition.

'Who is *that*?'

'My fiancé, Paul.'

'He's in the RAF?'

'Yes. Except that at the moment . . . Oh, there I go again, saying more than I should. Can we change the subject before I get myself into dreadful trouble?'

There was a slightly awkward silence, during which Pascale wondered if there was really something Simone should not be saying about her fiancé, or if she was simply trying to be mysterious. Then Marie sighed wistfully.

'He is very handsome!' She picked up the photograph, showing it to Pascale. 'Isn't he handsome, Lise?'

Pascale took in dark hair slicked back in a side parting from a pleasant face, a long, straight nose and generous mouth. 'He looks very nice, yes.'

'You are very lucky, Simone,' Marie said.

Simone smiled, showing a softer, almost vulnerable side to her rather daunting character.

'Yes, I know I am.'

Remembering how she had once felt about Kurt, Pascale envied her.

The three girls chatted for a while, but Pascale's eyelids were drooping. The voices of the other two sounded a long way off and became a dull, meaningless blur.

For the first time in months she drifted off easily, and the ghosts of the past seemed not to have followed her. She slept soundly, a heavy, exhausted, dreamless sleep.

Next morning, after an early breakfast of porridge and toast, it was time for the assault course that Simone was so dreading. To her relief, however, they were issued with suitable attire, including plimsolls that reminded Pascale of the 'daps' she had worn for PT at school. Predictably, although she was relieved that her own quality clothes would be spared the rigours of the assault course, Simone sniffed the plimsolls, wrinkling her nose in disgust, and groaned as she donned the trousers provided, which were coarse and scratchy.

The girls were divided into two teams, and much to Pascale's amazement, Simone put her forward as their team leader. Though she wasn't entirely confident, Pascale rose to the challenge and rather enjoyed it, especially when her team romped home the victors,, muddy, breathless and battle-scarred, but triumphant.

Less enjoyable was the session, later in the day, with the psychiatrist, the aptly named Dr Brain. Pascale was not looking forward to the inevitable questions about her personal life; she didn't want to revisit her devastating loss in the company of a stranger.

In the event, however, she found it quite cathartic. Since Lynne and Marianne had been killed, she'd avoided talking about it to anyone, but Dr Brain's detached manner made it a great deal easier than she had imagined it would be.

'Do you think you'd have been willing to join the SOE if your daughter were still alive?' he asked, when they'd gone through what had happened.

Pascale considered.

'I honestly don't know. I think I would still have wanted to help, if I could be of use, but I'm not sure I'd have been prepared to leave Lynne and go into France. I'd have been too concerned that I might not come back and she'd be orphaned.'

'Did her father have no contact with her?'

Pascale's mouth tightened into a hard line.

'I don't want to talk about her father.'

'And if I insisted that you must?'

'I'm sorry, but my answer would be the same. In any case, I can't see that it's relevant. Lynne's dead. She's no longer in the equation.'

She was surprised at how hard she sounded, when the terrible grief was just a heartbeat away. But she had compartmentalised it somehow.

'What matters now is that I can concentrate on whatever it is I'm asked to do, without any family commitments,' she said in the same cool tone.

'You want to die, is that it?'

'No, of course I don't!' Again, Pascale was startled by the immediacy and vehemence of her reply. 'It's just that knowing it wouldn't matter to anyone if I should be in danger sort of . . . sets me free.'

'I see.' Dr Brain pulled open a desk drawer and drew out a sheaf of papers. 'Now, I want you to have a look at these pictures and tell me what you see.'

This was stupid, Pascale thought, as she worked her way through increasingly obscure patterns that she was supposed to interpret.

Even more stupid was the word association test that followed – it reminded her of a party game. And then, quite abruptly, it was all over.

'Excellent.' Dr Brain smiled thinly at her, the first time any expression had crossed his face since she had entered the room. It took her by surprise, and since the smile was not reflected in his eyes, cold narrow slits behind his rimless spectacles, the effect was a little grotesque.

'We're finished?' Pascale asked.

'I think so.'

'So how did I do?'

Those cold eyes scrutinised her face for a moment; the forced smile gone now.

'I think I shall be recommending you for further training. It seems to me you have all the emotional attributes necessary. Now, will you ask the next girl to come in, please?'

Pascale experienced a little blip of satisfaction. Until that moment she had not realised just how important it was to her that she should make the grade. Though she'd barely begun, she knew that to go back to her old life would have seemed like being returned to an arid desert or a solitary prison cell.

England and France might need her, but it was a two-way bargain. This development had given her the opportunity to begin to live again. And she was going to grasp it with both hands.

'Shall we share a taxi?' Simone suggested. 'We're all going to the railway station, aren't we?'

The course was over; now all they had to do was to go home and await the official verdict on whether or not they had been accepted for further training.

'Not me,' Marie said. She was stuffing the last of her things into a tapestry holdall. 'Jeanne – you know, the one who was a dancer in Paris – has offered me a lift.'

'Good heavens, you are honoured!' Simone raised an eyebrow.

Jeanne, who had arrived in her own Austin 7, was a glamour girl and perhaps the least likely of all the new recruits, but she had actually acquitted herself well in all the tests, which was a little galling to some of the others, who had, rather spitefully, been hoping to see her make an idiot of herself.

'We got talking; she practically passes my door,' Marie said, a little defensively, as if she had somehow betrayed Simone and Pascale by accepting Jeanne's offer.

'So it looks as though it's just you and me,' Simone said to Pascale.

'But with any luck we'll all meet up again,' Pascale said. 'If we've passed muster, that is.'

'I do hope so,' Marie said.

'Me too.' Though she had known them only two days, Pascale felt closer to Simone and Marie than she had felt to anyone in a very long time. Their shared experiences and their commitment to what they were hoping to do had created a bond, she supposed, though superficially they were all so different and their lives so far had little in common.

'Well, I think the three of us should have a photograph for a memento,' Simone declared. She rummaged in her suitcase and pulled out a Brownie box camera. 'Come on, Marie, at least come down with Pascale and me and we'll see if we can find someone to take it for us.'

Marie protested at first, but Simone was not one to take no for an answer. The three girls went downstairs and Simone approached Leonard Curtis, who was hovering in the entrance hall, and asked him if he would do the honours. Outside, in the sunshine, with the grounds of the mansion as a backdrop, the girls posed, arms around one another, as he levelled the camera and pressed the button that would for ever immortalise the moment.

The taxi Simone had booked had arrived; Pascale and Simone said their goodbyes to Marie.

Wearing the costume she had arrived in, Simone was once more the sophisticated girl-about-town and Pascale was in awe of her all over again as she directed the driver to place her expensive suitcase and Pascale's battered one in the boot of the car. If only she had a tenth of Simone's self-confidence and sangfroid, she thought. She took the strap that hung beside her, trying hard to appear as self-possessed as Simone, but it wasn't until they reached the station and boarded the train that she began to relax, back in an environment to which she was more accustomed.

The carriage with its plush seats worn shiny and threadbare in places, the grubby antimacassars and the pervasive smell of soot and cigarette smoke was a great leveller. Her old suitcase was stowed out of sight on the rack above the frames that had until recently displayed pictures of seaside destinations, but were now empty in the interests of national security. The carriage they had chosen was empty; Simone took a window seat whilst Pascale opened a window and leaned out, watching the activity on the platform. The engine was taking on water from a cast-iron tank at the side of the track up ahead, sending clouds of steam into the clear late afternoon air; a porter trundled a sack truck laden with what looked like a mail bag towards the guard's van; the guard himself stood on the platform, furled green flag at the ready as he waited for the impending departure.

Suddenly a woman came running on to the platform through the wicket gate that led to the road outside. In her arms was a small child, whose legs kicked against her side as she ran.

'Wait – please wait!' she called breathlessly to the guard. He remained motionless but for a pointed show of looking at his pocket watch, but the porter, who had now thrown the mail sack into the guard's van, abandoned his trolley and went to her assistance.

'It's all right, missus, it won't go without you.' He took her bag, which was slung over her shoulder, and opened the door of Pascale's carriage, so that she had to step back sharply and take her seat. He helped the woman up the step and into the carriage and followed with the bag, a large hessian carrier embroidered with bright wools in a design that looked as if it was intended to portray a Dutch doll, which he hoisted on to the rack.

The woman, clearly flustered, thanked him, sat down on the seat facing Pascale and settled the child beside her – a little girl of just about the age Lynne was when she was killed. Her hair was straight where Lynne's had been curly, pulled from a side parting across her smooth forehead and secured with a white satin ribbon bow, but like Lynne's, it was fair, and her face had the same chubby innocence.

Pascale's heart gave a great lurch and for a moment she gazed at the child, mesmerised. Then, as emotion rose in her throat, choking her, she turned away abruptly, staring through a hot mist out of the window. The intense effort required to hold back the threatening tears called for all her concentration, but still stabs of memories pierced the fog, sharp and painful as red-hot needles. She covered her mouth with her hand, swallowing hard, willing herself not to betray her terrible grief, and after a few minutes she regained control of herself. She couldn't look at the child, though. Instead she continued staring out of the window until – heaven be praised! – the train stopped at a little halt and the woman and child got out.

She did look then, watching them disappear down the platform. When they were out of sight, she heaved an audible sigh and turned to see Simone watching her. Embarrassed, she looked quickly away, and for a moment neither girl spoke. Then Simone said: 'Are you all right?'

Pascale couldn't trust herself to answer, simply nodding, her face still turned towards the window.

'You're not!' Simone said. 'What's wrong?'

'Nothing,' she managed.

'Oh come on! I can see there's something the matter. It was that little girl, wasn't it? You were perfectly fine until they got into the carriage and then . . . Well, I saw the way your face changed.'

The tears were threatening once more.

'Just leave me,' Pascale murmured thickly.

'I will not! For goodness' sake – you're in a dreadful state. Come on, tell Auntie what's the matter. Maybe I can help.'

'You can't help,' Pascale said wretchedly. 'No one can.'

'Nothing's so bad if it's shared. It can't be anything so terrible, surely.'

'It is.' She was silent for a moment, and then, quite suddenly, the silence was too much for her. For so long her grief had been bottled up inside her, she felt she would burst with it.

'OK,' she said harshly. 'If you want to know. She reminded me of my daughter.'

'Your *daughter*?'

'Lynne. My little girl.'

'You have a *daughter*?'

'Not any more.' Her voice cracked. 'She's dead. She was killed.'

'Oh my God. Oh my dear, I am so sorry! That is . . .' For once, Simone seemed lost for words. She moved along the seat, taking Pascale's hand in both her own. 'When . . . ? How . . . ?'

Head bowed, voice shaking, Pascale told her, and although by the time she had finished she was crying again, the relief of being able to talk about her loss was enormous.

'Oh, my dear . . .' Simone pulled Pascale towards her, putting her arm around her, and for long minutes Pascale sobbed into her shoulder. When at last the tears stopped, she sat up, blowing her nose, attempting a grim, humourless smile.

'I'm sorry. Your lovely costume . . . I hope I haven't . . .'

'Never mind my costume. That's the least of your worries. It's too dreadful. I had no idea . . .'

Pascale swallowed hard, mopping the last of the tears from her cheeks.

'That's the way I want it. Simone, you mustn't tell anybody about this. You won't, will you?'

'Don't the authorities know?'

'Oh yes, they know of course. But I don't want the other girls to. I don't want everybody talking about it. Especially I don't want them talking to *me* about it. As long as it's not mentioned, I can cope. Usually I do, but that little girl . . .' Tears pricked again. She took a moment to compose herself. 'Promise me, Simone, you won't say anything to anyone.'

'I promise. But you must promise me, if you do ever want to talk, if you just want a shoulder to lean on . . . I'll be there. At least, I hope I will be! As long as we can be in touch, you can be sure you're not alone.'

'Thank you.'

'No problem. Now look, we're almost into London. You'd better do something about your face. Here . . .' She reached for her bag, extracted a powder compact and lipstick and handed them to Pascale.

'Oh, I couldn't use your—'

'Of course you could. No arguments, right? I don't like being argued with.'

Pascale chuckled wryly. 'No, you don't, do you? The Germans won't know what's hit them!'

'Come one. Stop talking and attend to your appearance. You'll have half London running for cover if they see you like that.'

There was a closeness between them now even more profound than the comradeship Pascale had felt earlier. When they left the train, they walked down the platform arms linked, and as they parted at the entrance to the Underground to go their separate ways, they hugged.

'See you soon,' Simone said. 'And until then – chin up, right?'

'Right. See you soon. And thank you, Simone.'

'What for?'

'For being a friend.'

'Oh . . .' Simone shrugged, embarrassed. 'It's nothing.'

'Don't you believe it,' Pascale said.

And somehow she knew that the friendship that had been forged on the train journey was one that would last a lifetime. However long, or short, that might turn out to be.

TWELVE

Pascale, lying flat on her stomach, steadied the gun against the heel of her semi-curled hand as she had been taught and squinted through the sight until she was certain she was lined up to the target, then pulled the trigger. Damn! Missed again! Or missed the bull's eye anyway. At least this time her shot had clipped the white surround. But it wasn't good enough, as the instructor, a burly little man with the stentorian bark of a sergeant major, was quick to point out.

'For crying out loud, woman! You need your eyes testing!' he snarled. 'This ain't a bleeding shooting gallery at a bleeding funfair. Your life's on the line, not a bleeding goldfish in a bleeding bowl!'

'I'm trying!' Pascale retorted, her frustration with herself making her irritable.

'Then try bleeding harder.'

Pascale did; the shot went even wider than before. It was no good, she was never going to be Annie Oakley – though she had managed to put a bullet in the straw-stuffed swinging dummy in the small-arms class. Thank goodness there *were* things she'd excelled at – the gruelling cross-country run, for one, and martial arts for another – or she'd probably have been sent home in disgrace by now.

It was a week into the training course proper, and for the most part she was enjoying it. Besides Simone and Marie, who had both also been recommended for further training, there were several other girls from the introductory course, as well as some men.

133

Pascale had been delighted to find her two friends there – especially Simone – though initially she was a little anxious that Simone might want to talk some more about the confidences she had shared when they were last together. But Simone didn't mention it. Apparently she was going to leave it to Pascale to raise the subject if and when she wanted to, and Pascale was grateful to her for that. She didn't want to talk about it. She'd unburdened herself once and that was enough. Now it was time to get on with the job in hand. But the closeness between them, though unspoken, remained. A bond had been forged, and Pascale felt that in Simone she had found a real friend.

The three girls had managed to wind up sharing a room again, though it had meant a little arm-twisting, as Marie had initially been allocated a different billet. But Simone had talked their roommate into doing a swap and then persuaded the powers-that-be to allow it.

'We're the Three Musketeers,' she said airily. 'They can't split us up – I won't have it.'

Pascale hadn't been hopeful – they were, after all, officially FANYs now, and as such, subject to orders. But it seemed the authorities were prepared to bend a little in the interests of morale; whatever Simone said to them had certainly worked. She was a force to be reckoned with, and Pascale hoped that some of Simone's easy self-confidence would rub off on her.

Certainly she was taking note of the way Simone spoke and behaved, which seemed to Pascale to be the epitome of breeding. It wasn't that she was ashamed of her own background, on the contrary, she was proud of it, and proud too that she – a very ordinary girl – had come so far. But there was no doubt that Simone had the knack of making people sit up and listen, and that could be very useful if she could learn it.

The training course was once again in a country house, this time just outside a tiny village on the outskirts of Exmoor. Word was that the SOE had commandeered similar houses all over England and in Scotland too for the purposes of training recruits, and Pascale thought she had been very lucky to wind up here. It was less than a four-hour journey from home and the setting was almost unbearably beautiful, with the rolling hills sloping down to the smooth waters of the Bristol Channel, sparkling blue in the summer sun.

She loved the moors, too, where paths curled through waist-high gorse and bracken, though it had seemed a less than friendly place on their twenty-four-hour cross-country. Then the scratchy undergrowth had torn at her aching legs, convincing her several times that she had been bitten by a snake as Yvonne, one of the other girls, had been. Yvonne had been whisked off to hospital and had not yet returned to the course – 'Blood poisoning,' Simone had whispered ominously. By day the sun had beaten down relentlessly, reddening Pascale's cheeks and blistering the tip of her nose, and when it went down and they were still plodding on by the light of the moon and stars, there were unseen potholes to stumble into and places where the ground fell steeply away, either to the sea or, when they were inland, into wooded river gorges. By the time they were back at training camp, their feet were sore and swollen, their heels rubbed raw; they were exhausted, hungry, filthy and covered in bites from the armies of tiny gnats that flew in clouds under the trees. But Pascale couldn't remember when she'd last enjoyed herself so much. Twenty-four hours and barely a thought for all she had lost; twenty-four hours with nothing but survival and staying awake on her mind. She experienced a stab of guilt that she was betraying Lynne and her mother by her forgetfulness, and determinedly pushed it to the back of her mind.

This was for them. All for them. Their memorial. And, she admitted, for herself too. And last but not least, for England and for France.

The other activities that made up their training schedule were many and varied. They were taught to handle a rowing boat; they were taught how to floor an attacker with a judo throw, and how to kill a man with their bare hands. There were lessons in Morse code and in the use of a wireless transmitter. There was detailed instruction in all aspects of explosives and in particular the so-called 'jelly' that could blow up a bridge or a railway line. There was map-reading – something else she found difficult, though she wasn't sure why. She could plot a course from A to B with no trouble at all, and memorise symbols and place names. But the contour lines and the shadings made little sense; try as she might, she couldn't visualise how the flat paper – well, flat apart from the raised and dog-eared folds – translated into undulating countryside.

That was nothing, however, compared to the dreaded firearms training, and Sergeant Walters – Wally, as the girls called him in private – was fast despairing of her.

'You're bleeding hopeless, miss,' he told her. 'Cor blimey, I wonder you haven't killed the lot of us with all those stray bullets. Just get out of the way and let somebody else have a bleeding go. They can't be any worse than you, unless they're blind and got no use in their bleeding hands.'

Feeling utterly fed up, Pascale scrambled to her feet, dusting down the knees of her trousers. Her place was taken by Marie, who looked as if she meant business, her mouth pursed determinedly, a kirby grip straining her hair away from her olive-skinned face. Marie was good, very good – but then she'd learned to shoot in the countryside around her home; been handling a rifle since she was seven years old.

She took aim now and pulled the trigger; the bullet flew arrow-straight towards the bull's eye, clipping the bold black circle that outlined the very centre of the target.

'See? That's how it should be bleeding done!' Wally threw at Pascale over his shoulder. 'Now, get back here and try again.'

That afternoon Simone had a visitor. When the girls returned to the house after yet another session at the practice range he was waiting, leaning against the stone balustrade that edged the terrace, a good-looking man in cords and a country-style checked shirt.

The moment she saw him, Simone's incredulous delight told the others exactly who he was: the RAF officer from her treasured photograph – her fiancé.

'I don't believe it! What are you doing here?' Once again, endearingly, she was transformed from cool sophisticate to a girl in love.

'Come to make sure you're behaving yourself, of course.'

'The cheek of it!' But she was flushed and laughing. 'I didn't even know you were back in England! Oh Paul, this is just the best surprise ever!'

Pascale and Marie exchanged glances. *We're not wanted here . . .*

'We'll see you later,' Pascale said.

As she and Marie went into the house, she cast a glance over her shoulder to where the two lovers were standing, very close together. Lucky Simone, Pascale thought enviously, to have someone in her life who could make her come alive, a dream to cling to when things were tough. Her own loneliness and loss ached in her, a yawning emptiness that nothing, not even her determination to succeed in this new adventure, could fill. And mixed with it another emotion she could barely identify – a will-o-the-wisp craving to revisit the sensation of expectancy and awareness of the summer she'd spent with Kurt. She wasn't ready to be involved with another man yet, but briefly she found herself looking forward to the day when she would be. And rather hoped that he might be a little like Simone's Paul.

There was no sign of Paul when the girls assembled for dinner, but there was still a glow about Simone.

'Has your fiancé gone now?' Pascale asked her as they were served bowls of potato soup, tasteless, colourless lumps drowning in a pale stodgy sea.

'Yes. It was a flying visit only. He really shouldn't have been here at all – wouldn't have been if he didn't have friends in high places.' Simone was crumbling a piece of gritty bread between her fingers. 'Actually, he's SOE too. And . . .' she lowered her voice, 'he's been in France.'

'Ah!' Pascale looked at her expectantly, but Simone shook her head.

'I can't say any more than that. I shouldn't be talking about it at all, even to you. And to be honest, I don't know very much. Just that he had to come back to England for some reason, and I expect he'll be going to France again soon.' She dropped the piece of bread into her soup, stirring it round with her spoon. 'I can't help wishing . . .

well, that when I'm trained I might be sent to his circuit . . . wherever that might be. I miss him so much.'

'Would the powers-that-be allow that?' Pascale asked.

Simone shrugged. 'I honestly don't know. I think there's some kind of rule about husbands and wives not working together, but we're not married . . . yet. And I don't suppose we will be until the war is over. So you never know.'

'For your sake, I hope it works out,' Pascale said. And truly meant it.

The training course was almost over, and apart from her inability to shoot straight – though she had improved somewhat, she was still far from being a crack shot – Pascale thought she'd acquitted herself reasonably well. Certainly she'd excelled in the sporting activities and unarmed combat, and done nothing to disgrace herself in the classroom, where she'd learned the ranks and regiments in the German army and how to identify enemy aircraft. She thought she'd held up quite well, too, under the faux interrogation in a dank cellar by two men she'd never seen before who were pretending to be officers of the Gestapo. Now only the parachute course remained.

'I'm really looking forward to it!' Pascale said. It was the evening before the first day's instruction, and the girls had been allowed some time off. They had chosen to spend it in a little pub in a nearby village, and though they had to hike the three miles along country lanes after their rigorous training, that was no hardship. Now, over pints of cider, they were reviewing all that had happened so far, and anticipating what was to come.

'I'm not sure about it,' Simone said, sipping her cider. 'I'm really not very good with heights.'

'Rubbish! You'll be fine!' Pascale encouraged her.

'Oh . . . I'm not sure. Supposing I throw up over the training sergeant's boots?'

Pascale and Marie laughed. The thought of Simone doing something so improper was unimaginable.

'The worst he can do is make you clean them,' Marie said.

'What I'd give for the chance to throw up over Wally Walters!'

Pascale mused. 'At least he wouldn't be able to complain about my aim then!'

'Perhaps you'd shoot straighter if they had a cardboard cut-out of him as a target,' Marie suggested.

'I think I just might! Shall we drink to that?'

They were all laughing, but Pascale cast an anxious glance at Simone. She really was very nervous about the parachute training. Pascale wished she could say or do something to reassure her. But really there was no way to help. In this, as in everything else they were undertaking, each of them was, in the end, on her own.

'Honestly, Simone, you'll be fine,' she said.

Simone smiled grimly.

'We'll see.'

The parachute course took place at a small private airfield an hour's drive from the course HQ. On the first day, once they'd been taught how to fall on landing, the girls queued to make their first jumps from a tower. From ground level the tower didn't look too intimidating, but once you'd climbed the ladder and were standing on the platform, it was quite a different matter, Pascale discovered, and her heart went out to Simone, who was looking decidedly green. From the platform the ground looked a very long way down, yet it was close enough to be horribly real and solid. She felt dizzy, suddenly, and her stomach seemed to be held in place only by the harness of the parachute. But she had to do it – fail, and she would be reduced to being the chauffeur for a brigadier, probably.

She took a deep breath and launched herself into space. Knees together, arms folded, hit the ground and roll . . .

The moment she landed, she was back on her feet, longing to do it again. It was exhilarating! If it was this good from a fourteen-foot tower, how much better would it be jumping from a plane?

And it was. Next day, when they took to the air, Pascale found it far less frightening to look down on the patchwork of fields from the belly of the plane, and even Simone seemed to be taking it in her stride. Pascale gave her the thumbs-up and peered out expectantly at the countryside far beneath them. She felt detached, as if she were a bird, not a nine-stone girl about to belly flop into oblivion. When the order was given, she launched herself into space, made a textbook landing and scrambled to her feet to watch the others floating down through the warm, clear air.

Simone, however, was less fortunate. As if her fear had attracted the attention of a whimsical fate, a gust of wind caught her parachute as she landed, dragging her across the rough turf. When she had disentangled herself and tried to get up, her face contorted with pain. Pascale ran to her assistance, but Simone was dismissive.

She'd sprained her ankle, rather badly, but it was her pride that was hurt most.

'How could I be so stupid?' she castigated herself later when the three girls were back in their room. She was sitting on the bed, her injured foot resting on the small dressing table stool, while Pascale and Marie packed her things as well as their own.

'You were scared. I expect you tensed up,' Marie offered.

'Well if so it was the stupidest thing ever. The medics say it's going to be several weeks before I'm fit for active duty. I can't believe I've got this far only to end up kicking my heels at home.'

'You'll be fit in no time,' Pascale said, trying to cheer her up. 'You'll beat us all to France, I expect.'

'Hmm. Just as long as people don't think I'm chickening out . . .'

'Honestly! Who's going to think that? Of you, of all people! It was an accident, for goodness' sake.'

'It shouldn't have happened.' Simone was silent for a moment. 'It makes you think, though, doesn't it? One little mistake, and I'm crocked up.'

Pascale, packing her sponge bag, knew what Simone was driving at, and wasn't surprised when she went on: 'Aren't either of you just a little bit frightened?'

'Not me! I am going home. To help my family,' Marie said stoutly.

But Pascale nodded. 'A little bit, yes,' she admitted. 'To be honest, I think it's rather foolish not to be. Oh, maybe not you, Marie. As you say, you're going home. But I do wonder sometimes if I'll be up to the job. And I wonder how I'd hold up if I was captured and tortured. I'd die rather than give the Germans information that would put my friends in danger, but if they were doing terrible things to me . . . I just don't know.'

'Exactly,' Simone agreed.

'I just didn't expect you to feel that,' Pascale said. 'You're so strong, Simone. Apart from not wanting to do the parachute jump, you never seem to have any doubts at all.'

'All a front, my dear,' Simone said bluntly. 'Of course I'm frightened. I'm just better at hiding my feelings than you are. It doesn't mean I don't have them.'

Pascale thought for a moment of the kindness Simone had shown her, and the way she had been around Paul, how her face softened when she looked at his photograph or spoke his name. She couldn't hide her emotions then; the strength of them stripped away the mask of self-possession. And now, being forced into inactivity through her own failure to make a good parachute landing, no longer the leader of the gang, had had the same effect. Simone might appear supremely confident as well as sophisticated, but beneath that carefully preserved veneer she was not so different.

Pascale stuffed the wash bag into her battered suitcase and put her arms round Simone.

'We'll be OK,' she said, with more confidence than she was feeling.

Then, realising she was excluding Marie, she reached out and pulled her into the tight little circle.

'Watch out, Jerry. The Three Musketeers are coming!'

It was a moment of determination, exhilaration even, that marked the occasion. Whatever the dangers that lay ahead, the three girls were determined that when their chance came, they would do all they could for King and Country. The bond between them was one that would endure through all the dark times that lay ahead.

THIRTEEN

The air was still warm from the heat of the summer's day, the shadows cast by the hotels and houses that flanked Portman Square long and sharp on the dusty paving stones.

As Paul Randall walked along the street, he counted off the numbers on the doors or etched in the stone beside them. He'd been here before, but not often enough to be sure which of the buildings was the one he was looking for. To him they were all so similar in appearance, grand old residences that had, for the most part, been turned into flats. It was this anonymity that had recommended it to the SOE, he imagined – a place where agents could be seen by the home staff. Their HQ, of course, was in Baker Street, but the exact location was a carefully guarded secret, and ordinary agents such as himself were rarely allowed to go there. When he had first been recruited, he had been interviewed in a basement in Whitehall where the labyrinthine corridors were policed by uniformed soldiers, but that had been returned to the military now, abandoned in favour of rented apartments.

When he found the number he was looking for, he checked surreptitiously over his shoulder to ensure he was not being followed. Unlikely here in London, but after the months he had spent undercover in France, caution had become second nature. The street was deserted but for an elderly woman with a shopping bag; satisfied, he opened the door and went inside.

The communal hallway was cool and dim, the only light filtering in through a stained-glass panel above the door. He went up the stairs and knocked on the door of the first-floor flat. High heels clattered on bare boards, and the door was opened by a young woman in a crisp white blouse and tailored skirt. Paul hadn't met her before – the last time he'd been here, the gatekeeper had been a dragon of a woman who'd looked quite capable of taking on Herr Hitler single-handed, he'd thought.

'Paul Randall,' he said. 'I think Major Dickens is expecting me.'

'Oh yes, of course. Come in. I'll tell the major you're here.'

She disappeared into the inner office, which had once been a bedroom, and Paul smiled to himself. This girl might be a good twenty years younger than the dragon, but her brisk efficiency suggested she could be every bit as fearsome as her predecessor, and might even look like her once the bloom of youth had faded. They were a breed apart, these women who had been hand-picked to keep the wheels running smoothly for the top brass. But then, he supposed, they needed to be.

A moment later she was back.

'If you'd like to go in . . .' She held the door open, standing to one side, then following him into the office. 'Shall I make a pot of tea, Major? Or would you prefer coffee?'

'No, it's all right, Ruby, I expect Paul would like something stronger. I know I would.'

The man, tall but slightly built, with a thin dark moustache, was half hidden by a cloud of fragrant smoke. He put the pipe down in an ashtray and came around the desk, extending his hand to Paul.

'Good to see you, Randall. Sorry I missed you when you first got back from France, but Major Tennant has given me all the details of your debriefing. Take a seat, won't you?'

Ruby left, closing the door behind her, and the major fetched two glasses from an official-looking cabinet and extracted a half-bottle of brandy from one of his desk drawers.

'Not the best stuff, I'm afraid, but it's all I could get hold of. You'll join me, won't you?'

'Thank you – yes, I will.'

With the drinks poured, the major returned to his chair on the opposite side of the desk to where Paul was seated, sipped his brandy and reached for his pipe. It had gone out now, but he made no attempt to relight it, simply sucking on the stem.

'So, what have you been doing since you got home?' he asked conversationally.

'Not a great deal,' Paul admitted. 'I've been to Sussex to see my mother – I only got back to London this morning.'

The major nodded. 'Recharging the batteries is very important, though. Especially given the circumstances . . . You've done a good job, though.'

Paul grimaced. 'I'd hardly call losing three key members of my circuit doing a good job.'

'Bad business, I agree.' The major sipped his drink thoughtfully. 'But these things are always going to happen, unfortunately. You can't blame yourself.'

'I'm afraid I do, though. I'd had my suspicions about a certain individual for some time. A man called Thierry Gaultier, a railway worker – but then you already know that from my report to Major Tennant.'

'Yes, but I'd still like to hear it in your own words. If you didn't trust him, why didn't you cut him out of the loop?'

'It was just a gut feeling. I had no proof. On the contrary, he was falling over himself to be useful – providing us with traffic movements, consignments of German ammunition, that kind of thing. In fact, I think it was his eagerness to assist that made me uneasy. But the rest of the group vouched for him, said they'd known him all their lives, and they were certain he'd never betray us. They even included his two brothers-in-law, for God's sake. And if I'd risked a mutiny and excluded him, I doubt it would have worked. He was too closely connected for a blank-out to be effective. Besides which, he already knew too much. What I should have done is dealt with him myself – arranged a convenient accident. That I didn't is my greatest regret. But even that might not have saved three good men.'

He broke off, his eyes shadowing as he thought of it. His group had been recovering an arms cache that had been dropped the previous night. He'd been there when the crates had come floating

144

down from the belly of an English plane; he'd helped lug them across the open field to a copse where they could be concealed to await recovery. But he hadn't been there when the rescue party had embarked on their mission, or when the Germans had swooped. A puncture in his bicycle tyre had delayed him; he'd arrived just in time to hear the shots and see his men being arrested.

Gaultier hadn't been there either; he'd pleaded a change to his shift pattern that would keep him at work at the time the others were moving the arms. That in itself was enough to make Paul sure he was right to suspect the man. But it was the force in which the Germans had turned out that confirmed it for him. That they should have simply chanced upon the operation was almost beyond belief. An odd patrol, yes. There were plenty of those. But a whole fleet of armoured vehicles? No, Paul was in no doubt but that they had been betrayed, and little doubt as to who was responsible, though how Gaultier would be able to live with himself – and his two sisters, who were very likely widows by now – he could not begin to imagine.

But then, what was happening in France was all rather surreal. The divisions were so blurred, and far beyond the simple fact that the country was split into two by the demarcation line – occupied France in the north and west, Vichy France, nominally still under French control, in the south and east. On both sides of that line there were so many factions at work, both politically and culturally. There were the Pétainists and those who looked to de Gaulle for salvation, there were the fascist sympathisers and the communists, who hoped the war would mean the end of the old order. There were those who wanted to resist, those who preferred to keep their heads down, and those who simply couldn't comprehend that it could be dangerous to trust their politicians, their policemen, and the people they had known all their lives. It was a hotchpotch of seething defiance and sullen acceptance, a tinderbox waiting to burst into flames.

'No, it's no use blaming yourself,' Major Dickens reiterated. 'It's a dangerous game we're playing, but a very necessary one.' The half-bottle of brandy hovered over Paul's glass. 'A refill, old chap?'

Paul raised a hand to indicate no and pulled the glass slightly towards him. He could certainly have drunk as much brandy as the major could spare, but the newly acquired habit of keeping a clear head was something else it wasn't easy to shake off.

'You are willing to go back, though?' One of the major's eyebrows raised slightly, a dark question mark that made his angular face look a little lopsided.

'Of course,' Paul said without hesitation. 'What's happened has only made me all the more determined. We've got to beat those bastards.'

'Good.' The major nodded, satisfied. Paul was one of his best men; he couldn't afford to lose him. 'You do realise, though, that I can't send you back to the same area. The whole of that sector is out of the question as far as you're concerned. You're known there, and your cover has been blown to smithereens. We'll try to re-form the circuit, of course, but I'm afraid it will be down to someone other than you to do it.'

'Yes, I do realise that,' Paul said regretfully, unable to quash the feeling that he had somehow let down not only his team but the whole population of what had been his area.

'Do you know the west at all?' the Major asked. 'Charente and Charente-sur-Mer?'

Paul grinned, nodding towards the brandy bottle.

'Yes, as a matter of fact, I do. I picked grapes there one year when I was a student to earn a bit of cash.'

The major nodded, also allowing himself a brief smile.

'Exactly. As I'm sure you know, the demarcation line runs directly through that area – Poitiers in the Occupied Zone, Limoges on the Vichy side. At the moment, nothing is properly organised there. A few locals have been carrying out some sabotage, I understand, just minor stuff – tearing down telephone lines and interfering with trainloads of supplies. But from what I can make out, there's no real direction. We'd like to set up an efficient circuit with a strong leader. That's where you come in. Provided, of course, that you don't think you'd be recognised from the time you were working there.'

'I very much doubt it,' Paul said. 'It's a long time ago now, and the only people I had much contact with were lads like myself – college students – and none of us local to the area.'

'You'd be prepared to take the risk?'

Paul was silent for a moment, thinking. The renegade groups the major had spoken of could well pose a problem; they were very likely hotheads who wouldn't take kindly to being told what to do or not to do by an outsider. If they persisted in their rash attempts at resistance, they could endanger the whole operation. Besides which, with the demarcation line dividing the area, opinions and loyalties were almost certain to be even more diverse than in the parts of France that sat firmly on one side or the other. It would be more difficult to be sure who were your friends and who your enemies.

But he liked the idea of setting up a circuit from scratch. Some of those hotheads, if they could be disciplined, could well be good men. They'd know the area like the back of their hands, and there was no doubt but that they were motivated by a love of their country and a hatred of the Boche, as they called the Germans. He would be able to hand-pick his lieutenants and answer only to his own instincts as to who he could trust. The responsibility was enormous, but after what had happened on his last assignment, it really was the only way he was prepared to work.

'So let's get this straight,' he said. 'You want me to organise a new circuit in the Charente area.'

'That would be your primary objective, yes. But there's something else, too.'

'Which is?'

'We'd like to establish a new escape route. As you know, our Allied airmen are given lists of safe houses they can memorise for use in the event that they are shot down. At present we have no such addresses in the area immediately east of Charente, and no *passeurs* to help them on their way down the line. I'd like you to take that on board too – every man we can get out safely is a man who can fly again.'

The coldness of the sentiment struck Paul – the major was talking about the missing pilots as he might about inanimate pieces of equipment, not men in distress in a foreign land. But that was the nature of war; for a battle commander it had always been thus.

'So, what do you say?' the major asked, reaching for his pipe again and tapping the bowl against the ashtray.

'OK so far. Am I going in blind, or do we have any contacts in the area?'

'Aside from the rag, tag and bobtail of local resistants, you mean? Actually, we do. Does the name de Savigny mean anything to you? They are a very old French family living just the Vichy side of the line. They own a lot of the land around there – in fact the village of Savigny takes its name from them – and they produce damned fine cognac from their own vineyards, have done for generations. Ring any bells?'

'Actually yes. Savigny.' Paul's eyes narrowed as he recalled that long-ago summer in Charente. 'The château on the hill. I do remember it, though it wasn't the vineyard I was working for. There's a Baron de Savigny, isn't there?'

'There is indeed.' Again the major's eyebrow lifted and his eyes levelled meaningfully with Paul's.

'He's not my contact, surely?' Paul said, though he thought he already knew the answer. 'A French baron? How on earth . . . ?'

'He's married to an Englishwoman, who just happens to be the sister of a friend of mine. It's possible, of course, that they are collaborating – or pretending to. When the welfare of all the people who live on your estates is at stake, it would be prudent. But my friend is certain where their true loyalties lie, and he says his sister was never the type to roll over and give in to authority. He's pretty sure she'd be only too willing to help. If she is, and her husband too, you'd have an ideal base for your operation and a good deal of up-to-date local intelligence too. I'm thinking that one of the identities we provide you with should be connected in some way to their business. How much do you know about the production of brandy?'

Paul chortled. 'Beyond the fact that your fingers get stained and your arms ache when you're picking grapes? And that it's a very nice drink? Next to nothing. The best bet would be for me to pose as a peasant looking for work.'

148

'A peasant will certainly be one of your identities. But we need something more . . . something that would be acceptable in polite society. I'll talk to my friend again, see if he can come up with something, and in the meantime I suggest you read up on the production of brandy.

'Now, to get on to other matters. The plan is to send a couple of other agents in to work with you – strictly under your command, of course. There will be a pianist – a wireless operator – and I have just the chap for that. Claude Bussy. He was a French seaman, spent some time after the armistice holed up in Casablanca on the *Massilia* with a lot of VIP passengers who thought they were going to be establishing a base offshore from mainland France. It was never going to happen, of course – Pétain had deceived them. But I digress. Bussy was a Gaullist from the outset. He managed to escape, and made his way to England via Spain and Gib, eager to do his bit to help the Free French. So you'll have at least one native Frenchman to assist you.'

'You're certain he can be trusted?' Paul asked warily.

'His credentials are as strong as they possibly could be. You'll have the chance to talk to him before you go in, and when you have, I think any doubts you might have will be laid to rest.'

Paul nodded. If the major was so certain of this man's allegiance, then he thought he was prepared to go along with it.

'The second member of your team will be a courier,' the major went on, 'and in our opinion it should be a woman. Women arouse less suspicion than men, and whereas two men creeping off together can make a German – or anyone else for that matter – think that something is going on, a man and a woman doing the same smacks of nothing more sinister than l'*amour*. And we have some dashed good girls in training. The reports I've received suggest they will be every bit as effective in the field as a man. Better perhaps. Less ready to act in a foolhardy manner. But then you've seen that for yourself, haven't you? You paid a visit to our Exmoor training camp a few days ago, I understand.'

'Yes, I did,' Paul said, a little shocked, though he knew he shouldn't be, at the extent of the information the major had at his fingertips. 'And yes, you're right. They're a promising bunch.'

'One in particular, I dare say,' the major said wryly. 'I'm not sure that would be such a good idea, Randall. Personal involvement can lead to problems. And in any case, I've just been informed that the young lady in question is out of the equation for the moment, but I expect you know that too.'

Paul frowned. He'd heard nothing from Simone since he'd last seen her.

'What do you mean – out of the equation?'

'Ah. You don't know. Apparently she sprained her ankle rather badly on her parachute course. An awkward landing.'

'Is she all right otherwise?' Paul asked anxiously.

'As far as I know. Her pride was what was hurt most as far as I can make out. And she'll be disappointed, of course, that she'll have to wait for her ankle to mend before she can be of any use to us.'

'I'll bet she's disappointed,' Paul said, imagining Simone's frustration – she had been so eager to see active service – and feeling very sorry for her.

'These things happen, especially with a novice,' the major said. 'But even if I thought it was a good idea, which I don't, it's obvious there's no way she could join you as your courier, given that I want you to leave for France as soon as possible once we've tied up the last few remaining ends, and while this good weather holds.' He shuffled papers on his desk. 'Now, I've got the details here of a couple of girls who may well fit the bill. Perhaps you'd care to glance through them and tell me what you think. I want you to be entirely happy with your team and I've already foisted Bussy on you. I think you should have an input when it comes to your courier.'

He opened a folder and pushed some paperwork and photographs across the desk.

'This is actually the one I favour.'

Paul suppressed a smile. The major would have his way, no doubt, whatever he said. He looked at the photograph and recognised the girl as one of Simone's friends. Simone had said she had done very well at cross-country and the assault course. Her athleticism could well come in very useful; a courier might have to cover long distances on foot or by bicycle.

He scanned the report. Bilingual (French mother). Test results: all good. Psychologist's report: very favourable. Ability to shoot: not so good, but rated against all her other attributes, he thought he could live with that. Hopefully she'd never be called upon to use a gun; it was a last resort, in any case. If it came to a shoot-out, there was every chance you were a dead man (or woman), whether you could take one or two of the enemy with you or not.

Paul made up his mind.

'She seems very suitable.'

The major nodded approvingly. 'A good choice, I'd say. Actually, I interviewed her myself – at the Admiralty HQ in Bath – and I was very impressed from the outset. She's had a difficult time in her private life, and coped with it very well. In fact I'd say it's made her entirely single-minded. Right, that's settled then. And now, my dear chap, are you sure you won't have another brandy?'

Paul took one last look at the photograph, at the heart-shaped face framed by thick nut-brown hair, and pushed the file back towards the major.

'Go on then, you've twisted my arm,' he said, and wasn't sure whether he was talking about the brandy, or the girl who was to be his courier.

FOURTEEN

In the belly of the Whitley, Pascale was half sitting, half lying against the fuselage. She was uncomfortably aware of the bulk of her parachute and her heart was thudding in time with the throb of the heavy engines. Although she was well wrapped up, the cold had eaten into her bones, and she sipped gratefully from a cup of tea one of the RAF sergeants on board had poured for her from a Thermos flask once they were safely airborne.

This was surreal. Though it was what she'd been training for, she found it hard to believe it was actually happening; she expected to hear Wally Walters yelling at her at any moment: 'Sit up straight!' or: 'Mind what yer doing with that tea, you stupid girl!'

She glanced around the bomb bay. In the gloom, she could make out several wooden crates with parachutes attached stowed against the opposite side of the fuselage. Her luggage would be in one of them, Claude Bussy's – and his wireless equipment – in another, whilst the rest, apparently, contained supplies that had been asked for by the resistance in the area where she was to be dropped.

Beside her, Claude Bussy himself sat close enough for their shoulders and thighs to touch. He was a thin, dark-complexioned young man, so typically French he might almost have been a caricature.

'Don't be afraid, _chérie_,' he had said to her when they had first met. 'I will look after you.'

Pascale had bristled. 'I don't need looking after, thank you very much!'

He had only laughed.

'But I shall do it all the same. Me, I am a chivalrous Frenchman. And you are a very pretty young lady.'

Pascale wondered how closely they would be working together. As a wireless operator he would probably have messages to pass to her, but it was also likely that he would be moving around quite a bit. Certainly it wasn't safe to keep transmitting from the same place; it was too easy for the Germans to pick up the signals and swoop.

The person she would be working closely with was the circuit leader. Who was, according to the cover story that had been concocted for her, supposed to be her husband. In the throbbing belly of the plane, she ran over the details once more.

Her papers named her as Madame Sylvie Jestin. She was a biologist, married to the acting manager of a vineyard. The new identity added to Pascale's feeling of unreality.

She leaned her head back against the fuselage of the Whitney and let her thoughts drift back over the equally surreal week she had just lived through.

The assignment, coming so soon after the completion of her training, had taken Pascale by surprise. She'd thought there might be an interminable wait – if she was ever sent into France at all. There was another surprise in store when she was called to the flat in Portman Square and discovered that the Major Dickens she had come to see and Mr Brown who had interviewed her at the Empire Hotel were one and the same.

He had smiled at her astonishment, shaking her hand and offering her a chair.

'You're a little shocked, I see,' he said amiably. 'We do have to take certain precautions with security in our line of work until we're certain of the people we're dealing with. It seems, though, that I made the right decision as far as you're concerned. You've done well. Come through all your training with flying colours.'

'I'm not sure about that,' Pascale said, thinking of her far from perfect marksmanship.

'Well, according to the reports, you've done frightfully well. And

I can tell you, too, that you were hand-picked for the job we have in mind for you. Group Captain Randall chose you himself.'

Pascale frowned. She didn't know a Group Captain Randall; certainly there had been no one of that name amongst her instructors. But then she hadn't known that Mr Brown was Major Dickens, either.

'Now. Let's have a cup of tea and I'll tell you what we'd like you to do.'

The tea was brought in by the smartly dressed – and rather intimidating – young woman who'd been manning the desk in the outer office. Major Dickens offered Pascale a cigarette – 'You do smoke, I seem to remember?' – but this time lit his pipe rather than joining her. Then he settled himself more comfortably in his chair, legs crossed, leaning back against the studded leather, and began to explain the details of the new circuit, which was, it seemed, to be called Avocet, and what Pascale's role would be.

'Basically, your job will be to help Captain Randall,' he said easily. 'Mostly, I would imagine, you'll simply be a courier, but I'm confident that whatever he asks you to do, you'll be up to it.'

'I certainly hope so,' Pascale said, a mixture of eagerness and apprehension making her stomach churn.

The major had gone on to talk about the area she would be operating in, and the 'pianist' who would be flown in with her. Group Captain Randall was already there, apparently, and would have been for a week or more before their arrival. Cover and accommodation had been provided by a Baron Louis de Savigny, a sympathiser, and also the owner of a great swathe of the countryside, including the vineyards whence came the grapes for the fine cognac he produced. The group captain was posing as some kind of manager brought in by the count to assist him in the production of the cognac; Pascale was to be his wife.

'You'll be given more details, of course, before you go, and time to memorise them,' the major said. 'Now, there's just the matter of what we are to call you. Besides your cover name – Sylvie Jestin – we like our agents to have a code name. It makes for greater security in the unfortunate event of possible capture by the enemy.

When you were training you were known as Lise, weren't you? It's usual to choose a different name for the field, but I can see no reason why you shouldn't stick with that if you'd like to. We don't have another Lise as yet. What do you think?'

Pascale took a last pull on her cigarette and ground it out in the ashtray.

'Could I be called Pascale?' she asked tentatively. 'It's my real second Christian name, but nobody knows that, and I'd like to have something of my own, if it isn't against rules.'

The major considered for a moment.

'All right, if that's what you want. Pascale it is.' He made a note on the pad in front of him. 'Now, what I'd like to do, Pascale, is to hand you over to Verity Lascelles. She's my right-hand woman, so to speak. She'll take care of everything from here on in.'

Pascale's heart gave a flip that seemed to echo in her throat.

'Now all that remains is for me to wish you the very best of luck.' The major rose, holding out his hand.

The interview was over.

Verity Lascelles was a stocky woman with greying hair, cropped almost as short as a man's, heavy jowls and a thin, unsmiling mouth. She spoke in a clipped way with an accent that suggested an upper-class background, and she was a hard taskmaster.

She talked Pascale through every detail of her cover story, gave her a day to learn it, then questioned her on it as thoroughly as if she was a German interrogator. She arranged for Pascale to be seen by a dentist, who replaced all the fillings in her teeth with gold ones that could pass for French. She kitted her out with clothes of the sort that Sylvie would be likely to wear, all French made, or with French labels sewn in, and which Pascale thought were disappointingly drab. In her experience, Frenchwomen took a great pride in their appearance, but she supposed that smart things were difficult to get hold of the way things now were and probably didn't fit her new persona anyway. Finally, on the day she was due to leave, Verity took Pascale to a flat in yet another anonymous building, where she once again checked every detail of her appearance – her make-up, the contents of her handbag – before delivering her to the major for a final briefing.

'If everything goes according to plan, you'll be met by a reception party from the sector we're dropping you into,' he told her. 'But just in case something should go wrong, here are some contact details.' He pushed a piece of paper across the desk towards her. 'Will you memorise them, please?'

Pascale's brain had gone into overdrive, but learning random facts had become second nature to her now. She studied the notes for a minute, then pushed the paper back towards the major.

'Got it.'

'Good girl. Well, that's about it. You're on your way, Pascale.'

'Yes,' she said, 'I suppose I am.'

'Nearly there now,' the RAF sergeant said. 'You know the drill, don't you? We'll drop the supplies off first, then go round again, and it's your turn.'

He and the other sergeant were beside the drop hole; together they heaved it open. A blast of icy-cold air made Pascale shiver, and the roar of the plane's engines was deafening.

'Anything?' She lip-read the single word one sergeant mouthed to the other, and saw him shake his head.

A sharp pang of fear knotted her stomach. She knew what they meant. There were no welcoming lights. No one to meet them. They would be alone in enemy territory, forced to find their own way. She tried to recall the names and addresses the major had given her to memorise, but her mind was a total blank, and her fear ratcheted up a notch. She tried to breathe deeply to calm herself; it would come back to her. She was good at learning things like that. It was just the stress of the moment that had made her forget.

And then the sergeant raised his thumb, a tiny gesture, but the most welcome Pascale had ever seen, and the two men pushed out the first of the crates, following it in quick succession with the others. With each delivery she felt the jerk in the plane's fuselage as the straps that could open the parachutes paid out, and it seemed to echo in her throat like a nervous tick.

The Whitley began to climb again, banked, and went around to come in once more over the landing area. She and Claude went forward, squatting beside the gaping hole and waiting for the signal. When it came – a small red light on the wall above the hatch turning green – the sergeant gave Claude a hearty push and he was gone, disappearing into the blackness beneath.

Her turn, and suddenly Pascale was absolutely calm. She sat, legs dangling as she had been taught, thinking of nothing but the moment, seeing nothing but the light, a red eye in the gloom.

It turned green. 'Good luck, love,' the sergeant said, and heaved her clear.

For the first dozen feet Pascale's senses were numbed by the buffeting of the cold night air, which took her breath and brought tears to her eyes. Then the parachute opened and she was floating in great arcs, not so much a leaf on the wind as a piece of flotsam caught in a whirlpool. The ground came rushing up to meet her; the moment her feet touched, she flexed her knees and rolled, but the wind still in the billowing silk dragged her like a rag doll over the rough ground. When at last she came to a stop, breathless, disorientated, her face grazed and her mouth full of dirt, she lay still for a moment. The torch bobbing towards her in the darkness might have been nothing more than an optical illusion – 'seeing stars', as people called it. But then dark forms took shape against the backdrop of moonlight and a husky voice murmured: '*Bon soir, ami.*'

Pascale felt a surge of relief; she might even have laughed if she'd had enough breath. And with the relief came exhilaration.

She was here. She was in France. It was as unbelievable as everything else that had happened. Except that it was true.

The reception party that had gathered in the long open space, flanked on two sides by thick copses, were a motley crew from widely differing walks of life and with an age range that spanned forty years. When the message had come through on the illicit wireless: 'The swallows are flying south tonight', they had each been contacted and made their way to the village near the drop site, gathering in cafés and bars in small groups of twos and threes so as not to attract attention. When the message was repeated a couple of hours later, word was passed from café to café that it was time to go. They had made their way in the darkness to the drop site, where they blackened their faces. Maurice Lejeune, son of the farmer on whose land the site was, supervised the laying out of the lights in the required 'L' shape – four men spaced out at a distance of a hundred metres.

When they first heard the engines of the Whitley, there was a small problem – René Pondard, a portly local butcher, thought he also heard the engine of a motor vehicle somewhere in the vicinity, but by the time the Whitley droned overhead, Maurice had decided it was only the roar of wine in the old man's ears – he was known to be a little too fond of the bottle. The torches were hastily lit, the big plane came in low, and six crates sailed to earth. The men whose job it was to recover them leaped into action, detaching them from the billowing silk and dragging them to the shelter of the copse, where, but for the one containing the personal luggage and wireless equipment of the two agents, they could be hidden until it was safe to recover them.

The Whitley climbed, banked downwind and completed a perfect circuit to come in again.

Two more parachutes billowed, one after the other, but with human figures dangling from them now instead of bulky crates. Maurice ran towards the one that landed nearest to him, grabbing at the parachute in an attempt to stop it dragging the jumper across the rough ground. It came to rest; the jumper punched the button to release the harness, and lay absolutely still for a moment. Then she rolled over, scrambling into a sitting position, and the moonlight illuminated a heart-shaped face that was, in spite of being grazed and dirty, very pretty.

'Are you all right?' Maurice asked, still holding on to yards of off-white silk.

'*Oui, je pense . . .*' I think so.

'*Bon.* And welcome to France,' he said with an ironic smile.

Though it was a long while now since she had been in France, Pascale felt instantly at home. She and Claude were taken to the farmhouse where she was to stay the night and Claude was taking up temporary residence. By the time the rest of the reception party had arrived and she and Claude were reunited with their suitcases, the farmer's wife, a stout, bewhiskered woman who looked forbidding but who greeted them with rough conviviality, had sausages and fresh farm eggs sizzling in the pan, and as the delicious aroma filled the kitchen, Pascale realised just how hungry she was. They ate around the scrubbed wood table, washing the food down with a rough but not unpleasant red wine, and Maurice Lejeune talked Pascale through the plans for her onward journey.

She was to travel to Angoulême, where 'Michel', her 'husband', would meet her, by train; he would have her suitcase waiting for her at the station, so as to avoid any suspicions that might be aroused should she be seen lugging it along the lanes. She'd have to find the station unaided, as none of the men would be free in the morning to escort her – it was vital that life went on as normal for the members of the cell so that they didn't attract unwelcome attention. He outlined the route Pascale should take, and checked her papers to make sure they appeared authentic.

Pascale's eyelids were drooping with tiredness by the time the men were ready to call it a night. She climbed the stairs to the attic bedroom that had been prepared for her and fell exhausted into the narrow bed. She had half expected the events of the day to be seething around in her head, preventing sleep, but when she pulled the sheets up to her chin the only image on her closed lids was of Lynne. A faint smile lifted the corners of her mouth, and thinking of her beloved lost daughter, Pascale fell asleep.

Next day, after a breakfast of bread fresh from the oven, Pascale set off. Though there was only a light German presence in the Free Zone, she was well aware that the local police could be overzealous and every bit as dangerous as the Boche, and as she walked down the rough track towards the country road, she felt horribly conspicuous. But the track and the road, enclosed on both sides by high hedges, were deserted, and she reached the railway station without seeing a single living soul.

When she had found the stationmaster's office and retrieved her suitcase, she purchased a ticket to Angoulême from a bored-looking clerk who didn't so much as give her a second glance. She hoped the border guards would be as uninterested – Angoulême was in the Occupied Zone – and that she would be able to hide her nervousness the first time her papers were inspected.

And she hoped too that the train wouldn't be delayed. She didn't know what she would do if she missed the pre-arranged meeting with Group Captain Randall – her husband, Michel, as she must think of him now, she supposed. Though she'd memorised the address of the Château de Savigny, she didn't relish the idea of having to find it unaided. But there was no point worrying about it. She'd just have to cope.

Pascale bought herself a cup of coffee, took it to a hard wooden bench, and settled back to await the arrival of the train.

Since his arrival in France, Paul had been busy with the setting-up of the basis for his new circuit, which he had code-named Avocet. The de Savignys, whilst pretending to collaborate, had proved more helpful than he had dared hope. Not only had they put a roof over his head, but they had helped him to concoct a cover story to account for his wife joining him at the château, one that he thought was ingenious enough to be totally plausible.

At the end of the nineteenth century, the vineyards of Charente had been devastated by plague. The disease had been carried by a louse, *Phylloxera vastatrix*, and the outbreak had caused the vines to wither and die. The de Savigny vineyard had only been resurrected when the then baron had replanted it with rootstock from the New World, a variety that was not only resistant to disease, but also ideally suited to the chalky soil of Charente.

Now suppose, Baron Louis de Savigny had suggested, fears were raised that a new plague was taking hold of the vineyard? It wouldn't be difficult to fake – a surreptitious excursion with a bottle of chemicals would have the vines dying off overnight. It would be a cause for huge concern for a producer of fine brandy such as he, and it was very feasible that he would call in an expert to try and find the cause of the outbreak before it took hold. Suppose Paul's wife should be a botanist whom he'd met at college and married? Surely it would be the most natural thing in the world for Paul, as the vineyard manager, to call on her for advice?

As he and Louis explored the plan together, Paul realised it had quite a few advantages. Though he didn't suppose Pascale knew the first thing about botany, it was unlikely that the enemy did either. He couldn't imagine that the commandant in charge of the district, Franz Buhler, was a scientist, and in any case, Buhler's French was far from fluent. He could converse on everyday topics, yes, but scientific jargon would be way beyond him. As for the local police, they were simple country men with only a rudimentary education. Though they knew the countryside, they would have no interest in rare insects or obscure plant diseases.

Another advantage was that Buhler was likely to be upset at the thought of the vines succumbing to a fatal disease. The general was extremely fond of his congac – making him a gift of as many bottles as he could drink was one of the ways of keeping him sweet – and Louis de Savigny had never palmed him off with inferior blends, falsely bottled and labelled, as some of the other producers were wont to do. Certainly Buhler would be as anxious as anybody that a cure be found before the disease spread.

And lastly, the deception would give Pascale an excuse to roam freely about the countryside, talking to farmers, retrieving messages from 'post offices' and scouting for fields that would make suitable landing sites. All in all, Paul thought it could work out very advantageously.

Whilst preparing the ground for Pascale's arrival, Paul had also set to work on his other objectives. With advice from the baron on who could be trusted, he had begun building a network of agents, and also made a start on setting up an escape line: a parish priest who was loyal to the cause and willing for the crypt of his church to be used as a hiding place for Allied airmen until they could be passed on; farmers with straggling barns and outbuildings and a burning hatred of the German invaders – the Boche. There was, of course, a limit to how far he could personally arrange the line – he couldn't check it out all the way to Switzerland or the Spanish border. For that he would have to rely on each member of the chain establishing the next link for themselves. But as far as he'd been able to go, things were looking promising.

He was feeling relatively satisfied as he drove into Angoulême to meet Pascale in the car the baron had put at his disposal, a Citroën that, although nominally for the use of the baroness, the baron himself drove more often than not, so that it was a familiar sight on the roads around Savigny. Paul chugged along following a country bus and making no attempt to overtake it – he was in plenty of time and there was no point in doing anything that might attract attention to himself.

His only fear was that Pascale's train might be late. Today was market day in Angoulême, and he wanted to meet her while the square was still busy with shoppers so that they would be less conspicuous.

Briefly he wondered how he would have felt if it had been Simone who had been coming in to work alongside him, and concluded that, sorry as he was for the disappointment and frustration she must be feeling at being forced into a lengthy wait to begin active service, he was, on the whole, rather glad that she was out of the picture. Though he was sure she would make a first-class agent, he knew he would have felt uncomfortably responsible for her. And there was something else . . . a gut feeling he couldn't quite put a name to but that was on a far more personal level. When he'd visited her at the training camp, he'd been aware of something missing – an absence of the feelings he used to have for her.

It was due, probably, to the experiences he'd lived through since he'd last seen her, he thought. He'd learned to shut out emotion in order to survive and do as good a job as he could. Plus, losing the three members of his circuit had affected him badly. Yet none of that quite explained the lack of pleasure he'd felt on seeing her, or the fact that he felt no urgent desire to be with her again.

Well, never mind that now. Paul was not a man given to introspection, even under normal circumstances, and at present he had more than enough on his mind without worrying about his feelings, or lack of them, towards Simone. His most immediate concern was meeting Pascale, and getting her back across the demarcation line to the château without incident so that he could brief her fully on the additional background that had been invented for her.

Could she pass herself off as a biologist? It was up to him to convince her that she could. Up to him, too, to ease her into her new job and give her the confidence to carry out the assignments he already had in mind for her, and others that would crop up in the future. Then he would just have to sit back and trust her.

He reached Angoulême, parked the car, and walked to the agreed meeting point in the town square.

Pascale picked her way between the market stalls, now virtually empty, though optimistic customers still lingered. To her left, in a small paved area, a group of sun-wizened old men squatted over a game of boules; another gaggle sat smoking and talking. She scanned the square anxiously, her suitcase making her feel horribly conspicuous, her feet hurting already from the clumpy shoes she'd been given to wear.

A hand touched her elbow; she stiffened, swinging round. Then, as she recognised the man who had visited Simone at the Exmoor training camp, her eyes widened and she only just managed to bite back an exclamation of surprise which might, disastrously, have given them both away.

'Sylvie,' he said. Not a question, but a convincingly warm greeting from a husband to his wife.

'Michel,' she replied faintly.

He took her suitcase from her, kissed her on both cheeks. 'Your train was on time, then?'

'More or less.'

'Come on, the car's this way.' His arm slid around her waist, guiding her through the thinning crowd.

She went with him, trying to act as she supposed Sylvie would, but at the same time struggling with her surprise that the agent she would be working with, whose wife she was supposed to be, was in fact Simone's fiancé.

In the car, she glanced around cautiously, as if half expecting someone to be hidden in the rear seat, before she said, almost accusingly: 'We've met, haven't we?'

'Briefly, yes. You trained with Simone, didn't you?'

'She was my best friend. She said that you . . . but I never expected . . .'

'Look, we haven't got time for small talk,' he said brusquely. 'There's a lot I need to fill you in on.'

Perhaps unreasonably, Pascale felt rebuffed.

'About me being your wife, you mean? I do know that. My papers—'

'About you being a biologist. An expert on the control of diseases affecting vines.'

'A *biologist!* An expert on *what?*'

'Just shut up and listen.' A sideways grin took the edge off his words, but still Pascale felt a little like a naughty child. 'It won't take us long to reach the border, and you never know who might be at the château when we get there. So concentrate, Madame Jestin.'

Pascale clamped her mouth shut, tried to swallow the edge of resentment at the way he had spoken to her, and listened.

FIFTEEN

Pascale's first sight of the château, perched high on the hillside above what Paul told her was fifty hectares of vineyard, made her draw breath. It was beautiful, like something from a fairy tale. A drive, lined on either side by tall, graceful cypress trees, led arrow-straight through half a mile or so of parkland and sweeping lawns to a paved courtyard where a fountain played. The château itself was turreted and perfectly proportioned. When she'd first agreed to become an agent of the SOE, she'd imagined she would be hiding out in dingy attic rooms or isolated farms, like the one where she had spent the previous night. That she was to be based in such opulence was almost beyond belief.

As Paul drew up at the foot of a flight of broad stone steps, the great door opened and a man came out.

'Baron Louis de Savigny,' Paul said softly.

The baron was, Pascale judged, of late middle age, tall and spare, with a full head of iron-grey hair and a thin, aristocratic face dominated by an aquiline nose and high forehead. To her surprise, however, the clothes he wore were less impressive – an open-necked shirt, frayed on the collar and cuffs, and baggy cords that had seen better days. He was carrying a walking stick, and as he came down the steps and approached the car, Pascale noticed that he had a pronounced limp.

'Madame.' He inclined his head towards Pascale in a courtly bow. 'I am honoured to meet you.'

Then he turned to Paul. 'I should warn you, we have company tonight.'

Paul swore.

'Tonight! I was hoping we'd have a little longer for Sylvie to settle in.' Already he was using her cover name with confidence; it was imperative that it came naturally, Pascale knew. But his grim tone gave her pause for thought and she wondered who the expected company might be. She didn't have long to wait to find out.

'You've already seen for yourself the sort of man Buhler is,' the baron was saying. 'He thinks there's a cachet in socialising with nobility. He likes his cognac, he likes his comforts. And we can't afford to upset him. When he drove out here this afternoon, more or less inviting himself to dinner, I really had no choice but to agree – and pretend to be pleased about it.'

Pascale was looking from one to the other of the two men, puzzled and alarmed.

'Buhler is the commandant in charge of the district,' Paul said, confirming her awful suspicion.

'And he has to be humoured.' A woman had come around the corner of the house and joined them. In her middle to late fifties, she was still slender, and beneath the wide brim of the straw hat she wore, her face was surprisingly smooth and unlined. She was carrying a garden trug filled with roses; she transferred it now to her left arm and held out her hand to Pascale.

'Welcome, my dear. I'm Alicia de Savigny. And you are . . .'

'My wife, Sylvie,' Paul said with just the hint of a wry smile.

'Of course.' Alicia's very blue eyes met Pascale's with something midway between conspiracy and amusement. 'Sylvie. It's a very pretty name. You've chosen well.'

'I didn't choose it, actually,' Pascale said, and was immediately afraid that she sounded unfriendly. These people were, after all, risking their lives to shelter British agents.

Alicia smiled, not apparently offended in any way.

'It's a good thing you weren't landed with something ghastly, then,' she said. 'Bad enough that you're forced to wear the sort of clothes I don't imagine you'd normally be seen dead in.'

Pascale glanced down at the shapeless skirt and clumpy shoes, comparing it with the elegant trousers and shirt Alicia wore – clearly expensive, clearly purchased when such things had been readily available.

'You could say that,' she said ruefully.

'Let's go inside.' Alicia placed a hand on Pascale's elbow. 'Paul will show you your room and then we'll have a cup of tea. Unless, of course, you want to spend some quiet time together so that Paul can brief you thoroughly.'

'I think that might be wise,' Paul said. 'We've covered the basics on the way back from Angoulême, but if Buhler is coming to dinner . . .'

They all moved off towards the house, Paul, carrying Pascale's suitcase, bringing up the rear.

Inside the château it was cool and dim. A spacious entrance hall was furnished with a heavy old armoire and a bureau. On it stood a crystal bowl of yet more roses; the scent of them hung heavy in the air. From the hall, a broad staircase led up to a balustraded gallery; Alicia guided Pascale towards it.

'I'll let Paul show you to your suite. I think you'll be comfortable there. The château can be very cold and draughty in winter, but at this time of year . . .'

'You're very kind.' Once again the feeling of unreality had descended; it was almost as if she were a guest at a country house weekend, not an agent here to undermine the German occupation.

At the very end of the corridor a door stood ajar; Paul pointed her towards it.

'Here we are. The guest suite. And just in case you were worried about having to share with me, let me set your mind at rest. I've been living here in luxury the last week, but now you're here, I'll let you have the bed and make do with the chaise in the sitting room.'

'Oh – you don't have to do that!' But in fact, Pascale was rather relieved. She had been wondering what the accommodation arrangements would be for a so-called married couple and hadn't relished the possibility of enforced intimacy.

'Let it never be said that I am not a gentleman,' Paul said drily. He carried her case into the bedroom and placed it beside the big canopied bed. 'Now, I'll leave you to freshen up and change, and then we'll go through the story again. It's vital that you're familiar with it. Buhler's French might be far from perfect, but we can't take any chances.'

'No, we can't.' A tic of nervousness had started in Pascale's stomach. 'I certainly didn't expect to spend my first evening in France with a German commander.'

'Staying here, it would have happened sooner or later,' Paul said laconically. 'Might as well get it over and done with.'

'Mm.' Pascale wasn't so sure about that.

'Look at it this way. Who would imagine for a moment that a British agent would be brazen enough to sit down to dinner with a German commandant? Be bold! It's a better smokescreen than creeping around in the shadows. And besides . . . as Louis said, Buhler likes his comforts, thinks he's on to a good thing having access to the best cognac in Charente, and gets a boost to his ego hobnobbing with French aristocracy. But he's got an eye for a pretty face too. Charm him, and you'll have him eating out of your hand. Given his position here, that's bound to work to your advantage.'

Pascale swallowed the knot of nervousness that stuck in her throat like a boiled sweet swallowed whole by mistake, and summoned a wintry smile.

'I'll do my best.'

'Good girl.' He squeezed her arm, and for a brief moment Pascale was startlingly aware of his physical presence, a frisson of something that might have been engendered by the dangerous situation she had found herself in so soon, and the need for comfort, or by something else entirely.

'Right. I'll leave you to it, then. But don't take too long titivating. We've got a lot of business to attend to.' He threw her an encouraging grin, left the bedroom, and closed the connecting door behind him.

Pascale stood for a moment, both hands pressed to her mouth, then sighed, gathered herself together and began to strip off her unflattering and travel-weary clothes.

*   *   *

Considering the circumstances, dinner was passing off without any moments of serious discomfort. After their intensive briefing session, Paul and Pascale had gone down to the salon for a pre-dinner drink to give Pascale the chance to meet the other members of the family before the German commandant arrived.

The baron, his wife and his son, Charles, were already enjoying a glass of wine in the salon when Paul and Pascale made their appearance, and Charles's wife, Giselle, joined them soon afterwards. Charles, heir to the baronetcy, was also slimly built, with the same aristocratic features as his father, and although not as tall, there was an athleticism about him that suggested hidden strength. Giselle was an elegant young woman who, in spite of the stringencies of wartime, still managed what looked like a Parisian chic. It was to Antoinette, Louis' daughter, though that Pascale was instantly drawn. Plump and curvy, she had sympathetic brown eyes and a generous mouth. She greeted Pascale in a friendly fashion, and Pascale felt instinctively that she had found an ally, though nothing more than formal acknowledgement passed between them.

Did the younger generation know that she and Paul were British agents? she wondered. Or were they being fed the cover story for their own safety? She couldn't imagine Charles would be taken in by it – apparently he worked with his father running the vineyard and the cognac production – and she would have thought Giselle must know the truth too. But perhaps Antoinette was unaware – perhaps that accounted for her open friendliness. For the moment, though, whether or not they knew scarcely mattered. None of them was going to deviate from the fiction this evening, even in private.

General Buhler was a little late in arriving. Pascale's heart came into her throat as he entered the salon, a slightly built man of medium height in the uniform of an officer of the Third Reich. Somehow she had expected a blond bear of a man; Buhler was almost disappointingly ordinary. Sandy hair was combed self-consciously over a thinning spot on the crown of his head; his hands were small, soft and white. But his eyes, behind the glass of his rimless spectacles, were Aryan blue, and cold and hard as chips of zircon, and his lips were a tight line in his thin face.

'I hope I have not kept you waiting,' he said in clipped tones and an almost comically bad accent. 'I was delayed by matters that could not wait. There was an attempt last night to destroy the telephone lines just outside Savigny. The culprits have now been apprehended and brought to my HQ. Two young local men we have been watching for some time. I wanted to interrogate them myself before passing them on to be dealt with. I don't like this sort of thing happening in my sector. I had hoped, Louis, that you had made the people on your lands see sense.'

Louis de Savigny sighed, not allowing his dismay to show for a moment.

'I had hoped so too. My apologies, Franz, for their stupidity. But I'm afraid there will always be hotheads who cannot accept the situation, or are just looking for adventure. Here, have a glass of wine. I'm sure it will help you feel better after what must have been a most trying afternoon.'

The commandant's lips compressed in a tight smile.

'I am sure it will, Louis. I only hope it will teach a lesson to others who think they can make fools of us. I don't want to be heavy-handed, but I don't want people like that thinking they can make trouble and get away with it either. I won't allow it.'

'Of course you won't, Franz. You have a position to maintain. As have I. I'll speak to the villagers again, tell them they must obey your orders.'

'Good.' Over the rim of his glass, those ice-cold eyes were on Pascale. 'You have another guest this evening, I see? One I have not yet met.'

'Indeed. Allow me to introduce you to Madame Jestin – Sylvie – Michel's wife. It's most fortunate that she has been able to join him. She is going to help me, I hope, with the problems I told you about the other day. The threat of disease to my precious vines. You've seen for yourself how some of them are dying where they stand, and I am very much afraid the canker will spread if it is not addressed quickly. Sylvie is an expert in the field – a highly respected botanist and biologist.'

Somehow Pascale managed a smile. She didn't like the spotlight being turned on her, and she didn't like the way Buhler was looking at her. Lascivious. It was the only word to describe it. But it was imperative that she do nothing to antagonise the man, or give him the slightest cause for suspicion.

'I'm very pleased to meet you, General,' she said.

'And I you, madame. I don't believe I have ever met a botanist before.'

Pascale heaved a silent sigh of relief.

'It's not a very social occupation, General. I'm afraid we talk more to plants than we do to people,' she said disingenuously.

'If that is the case, it is a very sad state of affairs.'

'Oh, I don't mind really,' Pascale said. 'Especially when it gives me an excuse to be with my husband.' She tucked her arm through Paul's, smiling up at him. As their eyes met, there was a moment of shared understanding, a wordless communication, and Pascale felt exhilarated suddenly.

'I'm afraid our different careers means we are separated too often,' she said with another wicked twinkle. 'The baron's misfortune is all to my advantage. Though I do hope I can help him find a solution,' she added solicitously.

'As do we all. If de Savigny cognac should fail . . .' Buhler shook his head gravely.

The baron refrained from pointing out that since the best vintages were aged for anything up to fifty years in the cellars beneath the château, the supply was unlikely to run out in Buhler's lifetime.

'Shall we go in to dinner?' he suggested.

Pascale was greatly relieved to find herself seated between Charles and Giselle on one side of the long refectory table, with Antoinette directly opposite her, flanked by Paul and the General. Louis and Alicia sat at the head and foot of the table, and the clever arrangement meant that neither Pascale nor Paul was close enough to the General for him to engage them in one-to-one conversation.

The meal was good, if not quite up to the pre-war standards the de Savignys had enjoyed, and despite the tension knotting her stomach, Pascale found she was ravenously hungry. The eggs and

171

sausages she had eaten last night were a distant memory, and apart from the hunk of bread at breakfast, she'd had nothing today.

Once or twice there were awkward moments when the General referred to the disease that was affecting the vines, and Pascale was desperately afraid he might begin to question how she was going to go about pinpointing the cause and preventing it from spreading. But on each occasion either Louis or Alicia intervened, steering the conversation to safer topics, and she was saved from having to pretend to a knowledge she did not possess.

She was also very aware of the general's eyes upon her, appraising her narrowly from behind his rimless spectacles, and his attention made her uncomfortable. But she didn't think it was because he was suspicious of her, rather that he'd taken a fancy to her. Why that should be, when she was supposed to be a married woman and Antoinette was a very pretty single girl, she could not imagine, and she wished it were not so. But having the approval of the German commandant could be useful, she supposed – just as long as it didn't mean he took too much interest in her movements.

When the meal was over, de Savigny cognac was produced and poured. As someone whose only experience of brandy was the sips from a quarter-bottle her mother had kept in the sideboard for medicinal purposes, Pascale was no connoisseur, but she found it far more pleasant than she remembered. And General Buhler was certainly appreciative. He swirled the balloon between his soft white hands, sniffing in the aroma, then emptied it with great gulps that made his Adam's apple bob beneath the tight collar of his uniform shirt. Pascale suspected Louis might be secretly horrified to see his precious cognac swallowed so carelessly, but if he was, he gave no sign of it, smiling benignly as he refilled Buhler's glass.

Just when she thought the German would never go, he checked his watch and rose to his feet. 'Forgive me, but I must leave.'

'Must you?' Alicia feigned regret.

'My driver will be waiting for me.' He laughed, a brittle sound that reminded Pascale of the snapping of a twig. 'It's his job, of course. He shouldn't complain. And if I find him asleep at the wheel . . .' He tailed off, leaving the company to imagine what fate would await the errant driver. 'I thank you for your hospitality, Louis. And if you could see your way to . . .'

'You'd like a bottle to take with you so that you can enjoy a nightcap, I expect. A pleasure, my dear friend. I'll have it brought out to your car.'

Buhler kissed Alicia's hand, but it was on Pascale that his eyes lingered.

'Good night, Herr General,' she said sweetly. Her eyes were beginning to droop, partly from having been up half the night before, and partly from the effects of the cognac.

'You look exhausted,' Paul said, when Buhler had left.

'I am! Did it show too much?'

'Not at all.' He squeezed her hand. *You did well*, that squeeze said, and Pascale experienced a sharp twist of pleasure, at both his praise and his touch. The brandy was singing in her ears; she felt slightly muzzy.

'Come on,' Paul said, 'let's get you to bed.'

She just grinned again inanely, enjoying the moment far more than she knew she should.

Afterwards, she had no recollection of saying good night to the de Savignys, only a hazy recollection of climbing the sweeping staircase.

'We'll talk tomorrow when you've had a good night's sleep,' Paul said.

Left alone in the bedroom, Pascale slipped out of her clothes and into bed. She pulled the quilt up to her chin and closed her eyes, listening to the soft sounds from the adjoining room as Paul prepared for bed himself. She hoped he would not be too uncomfortable on the chaise.

What a day it had been! I got myself all the way here on the train, Pascale thought. I had dinner with the German commandant and didn't do anything to let myself down. And I couldn't have a better sector leader if I'd chosen him myself.

The brandy-fuelled euphoria was making her muzzy again. Before she knew it, Pascale was asleep.

SIXTEEN

Paul's new circuit was growing, but beneath a veil of total secrecy. Always conscious of the risk that a member of a cell, however loyal, could be broken under interrogation and disclose the cover names and whereabouts of other members, he planned to set up a network of small, independent groups in an ever-widening circle that straddled the demarcation line.

These groups knew him only as 'Le Capitaine' or 'Avocet', the name he had given his circuit, and had no idea where he was living; they could contact him only by leaving messages for him in 'post boxes': with people who were sympathetic to the cause and in a position where visitors were unlikely to arouse suspicion – a hair-dresser's, a cycle repair shop, a café – or, more often than not, in a hiding place in a dry-stone wall or a hollow tree.

It was Pascale's job to collect these messages; she would cycle around the countryside under the guise of a botanist investigating the flora, give a pre-arranged password to the postmaster to retrieve the message or dig it out of its hiding place, and relay it back to Paul. She soon became a familiar sight in the lanes around Savigny, pedalling along on the old bicycle Paul had obtained for her, cotton skirt billowing around her bare – and now sunburned – legs, straw hat jammed low over her eyes.

The post boxes were used too to keep in contact with Claude, the 'pianist' who had been dropped in with Pascale. He was still holed up in the farmhouse, though he never transmitted from there – it was far too dangerous, even if the messages were kept brief and different wavelengths employed. Instead, he lugged the suitcase that contained his transceiver to various locations spread over as wide an area as possible. His only contact with Paul was through Pascale.

The system was as safe as Paul could devise, as tight as possible. But he still found himself worrying about Pascale as he never did about his other agents and was always glad to see her return safely. His concern for her perplexed him a little, but he preferred not to wonder why that might be. Personal involvement was a luxury he could not afford. The job in hand had to be his first and only priority.

The escape line was taking shape too, and Paul had put security arrangements in place to safeguard it. He decreed that no member of a cell was to visit a safe house without first telephoning ahead to ensure everything was as it should be; he didn't want anyone walking into a trap. So far, no Allied airmen had been passed down the line, but when a request was made, he had plans to ensure the escapee was genuine. Infiltrating escape lines was something the Germans had become rather good at, particularly the ones run from start to finish by French nationals, who could be fooled by an English-speaking 'plant' in an RAF uniform.

What Paul needed most now were supplies of arms and ammunition and a couple of good agents to whom he could delegate the running of the more far-flung cells of his ever-growing network. Pascale passed the request to Claude, and delivered the reply when it came. The drop was scheduled for the next clear night, at an isolated site Paul had identified as perfect for the purpose – a long, flat field close to the confluence of two rivers – the best possible navigational aid for the British pilot. Accommodation had been arranged for the two incoming agents, and they could do nothing more but wait for the message on the BBC French service that would confirm the drop was going ahead.

'Have you any idea who they're sending in?' Pascale asked.

She and Paul were hunched over the little crystal set in the sitting room of their suite, monitoring the stream of apparently meaningless messages. 'My little sister has a red dress.' 'Uncle Gaston will smoke a pipe with you tonight.' Not the one they were waiting for, though, and hearing all the others was both frustrating and oddly comforting. So many messages – so many groups of resistants huddled, as they were, around a wireless set, waiting for the one that would mean something to them. Somehow the knowledge eased the inevitable sense of isolation.

Paul shook his head, still listening intently to the wireless. Pascale knew she shouldn't be talking to him; if their message was broadcast and they missed it, it would be disastrous. But the compulsion was too great. She'd been alone all day, collecting and delivering messages to hidden post boxes, and hadn't spoken to a living soul. And a thought had occurred to her: what if one of the incoming agents was Simone?

On one level, Pascale would, of course, welcome her with open arms. She really missed the companionship of the other girls, and Simone in particular. She'd thought, on that first night at the château, that she had found a bosom mate in Antoinette, but after only a couple of days Antoinette had left to stay with friends in Tours, and Giselle, Charles's wife, was distant and unapproachable. No, it would be nice to see Simone.

But on another level entirely she didn't want Simone to be one of the agents. For in spite of herself, in spite of everything, Pascale had developed strong and disturbing feelings for Paul.

They had crept up on her, those feelings, over the weeks they had been working together, almost unnoticed. The glow that suffused her when he praised her – that was just pride in a job well done. The constant striving to do even better – that was driven by patriotic zeal. Or so she tried to tell herself. But there was no way she could explain away the constant longing to be in his company, nor the sharp darts of excitement that prickled in her at his slightest touch. No way to explain the crazy, soaring desire or the fact that she couldn't get him out of her head.

Pascale had tried very hard to resist all these unsettling thoughts and feelings. For one thing, he was spoken for, engaged not just to some faceless, unknown woman, but to Simone. Just by allowing herself to dream she was betraying her friend; it made her a shameless hussy of the very worst kind. And if that weren't enough, this stupid obsession could undermine their working relationship. They were here to do a job, for goodness' sake; she couldn't afford to let herself be sidetracked by her own emotions. And yet, she reasoned, the way she had come to feel about Paul made her all the more determined to do well. She *wanted* to please him, earn his approval. She *wanted* to succeed, not just for England, not just for France, but for Paul. She was desperate not to let him down. And her admiration for him was as potent as the physical attraction – an admiration she knew was shared by every member of his team, a fact that made her feel almost proprietorially proud.

Sometimes she fancied the attraction was mutual, though she had no evidence of that. Just wishful thinking, probably, propped up by the reasoning that feelings as strong as hers had become could not have been generated unless they were reciprocated. But that, she knew, was rubbish. Unrequited love was commonplace; to think otherwise was to deceive herself. All she was feeling was, if she was honest about it, no more than the product of circumstance. A man and a woman working closely together in a situation fraught with danger, having to trust one another and virtually no one else . . . It was exactly the sort of breeding ground for imagined romance to flourish. Nothing could come of it. Nothing would. Nothing must!

And yet . . .

And yet there was no way she could stop the treacherous thoughts.

'Perhaps one of the new agents will be a woman,' she said tentatively now.

Paul raised a warning finger; his head, cocked to one side, leaned closer to the crystal set.

'That's it. Our message. "The apple blossom is on the tree in the garden." It's on for tonight.'

The moon, clear and bright in the dark sky outside the window of their sitting room, fell across his bent head; for the first time Pascale noticed a few threads of silver amongst the dark hair. Her heartbeat quickened, her stomach contracted with desire and what she was beginning to think might be love.

'Good,' she said.

He switched off the wireless, straightened, stretching his back.

'What were you asking me?'

'If there's a possibility one of the new agents might be a woman.' He cocked an eyebrow at her.

'Are you missing female company, then?'

'No, of course not.' She didn't want him to think she was weakening psychologically. 'I just wondered, that's all.'

He stood up, rubbing the small of his back, stretched again.

'That's all right then. There's no chance at all, I should say. There are many more men who are agents than women, and besides, as far as I'm aware, the policy is always that a circuit leader should be a man.'

'It's *your* circuit. You're the leader.'

'Yes, but the new areas will be pretty well big enough to be circuits in their own right. I'll still have overall control, I hope. I don't want a newcomer doing anything to jeopardise the security I've built up. But I think I can say without fear of contradiction that the two agents coming in tonight will be men.' He grinned at her. 'You're just going to have to put up with being the lone woman in the madhouse.'

The relief was enormous; it shocked her. She hadn't realised until now just how much she didn't want Simone here.

It would be lovely to see her again, yes, of course it would. But to see her with Paul, knowing he belonged to her . . . Pascale acknowledged, not without shame, just how unbearable that would have been.

And, by the same token, just how much Paul had come to mean to her.

After Paul had left, riding Pascale's bicycle, she got undressed and into bed, but sleep eluded her. How could she rest when he was out on a mission? He'd been as certain as he could be of the security of the drop site, but there was no accounting for random patrols. What if he was stopped by one? The identity by which he was known in the district didn't really give him a reason to be out in the middle of the night. She hadn't asked him if he'd prepared a feasible excuse should he be stopped and questioned; knowing Paul and his meticulous planning, she assured herself he would have done, but she couldn't think what it might be, and the doubt niggled like a sore tooth. Generally an agent would assume the identity of a doctor or veterinary surgeon if he needed to be out at such an unearthly hour, but that wouldn't work for Paul in this locality, and he would never make the mistake of carrying more than one set of papers with him.

Then there was the danger that a low-flying plane would attract the attention of some vigilant policeman. It wouldn't take long for the area to be swarming with enemy forces.

Pascale paced the floor, nibbling on a hangnail until her finger bled. She wished desperately that Paul had taken her with him, but why would he? He had enough men to lay out the landing lights and hide the supplies until they could be recovered. As a mere woman she would have been no use at all, more of a hindrance than a help. But waiting was hard, very hard. Much less stressful to be in action, with no time to think and worry, with rushes of adrenalin buoying her up instead of this debilitating anxiety dragging her down.

Pascale got back into bed. She must try to sleep. If she didn't, she'd be worse than useless tomorrow, and there was nothing she could do, nothing at all.

A small sound had her wide awake once more, a creak, followed by the click of the outer door. Was he back, or had she dreamed it? She waited, reluctant to satisfy her curiosity; she thought he might be annoyed if he knew she'd been waiting for him to return. But in the end she couldn't bear not knowing for sure.

'Paul?' she called softly. 'Is that you?'

A dark shape shadowed the connecting doorway.

'Pascale? Are you still awake then?'

'Yes. I couldn't sleep for worrying about you. Is everything all right? Did they come?'

'Everything's fine. I'll tell you all about it in the morning. Go to sleep now.'

'Paul?'

'Yes?'

She wanted to say: 'Don't sleep on the chaise. Come into bed with me.' She wanted to feel the warmth of his body, to reassure herself that he was really here, safe and whole, to have his arms around her, holding her, comforting her, loving her.

But restraint kicked in.

'Nothing,' she said. 'I'm just glad you're back safely.'

'I am, I promise.'

For a long moment he remained in the doorway, no more than a dark shape against the muted silvery light, and Pascale ached for him with fierce longing.

'Good night, Pascale,' he said at last, and was gone.

'Good night,' she whispered.

She wrapped her arms around herself and closed her eyes. But it was still a long while before Pascale fell asleep.

'Right. Now, this is what I want you to do.'

Paul and Pascale were in the sitting room of their suite. He had been filling her in with the details of last night's drop as he had promised. When they were discussing business, they always did it in the privacy of their own rooms – though the baron was a staunch and reliable ally, the fewer people who knew the details of any operation, the better.

Not that Paul had relayed the night's activity in any great detail. There was really not much to tell. The two new agents – Henri and André – had arrived as planned and left to make their way to their temporary accommodation; some of the fresh supplies had been secreted away for collection later, some had been transported last night to their destination. Everything had gone smoothly and to plan.

But something else that had come in was desperately needed by one of the outlying cells, and that something was money. It had to be delivered to St Sancerre, in the occupied zone, and Pascale, as the circuit courier, was the one who would have to take it.

So far, Pascale had not been to St Sancerre. The post box used for contacting the cell leader was a hollow tree midway between there and Savigny, which she checked regularly for messages as well as leaving coded instructions from Paul to his lieutenant.

'That's not an option this time,' Paul said. 'It's too important to get the cash to Jean-Pierre as quickly as possible, and in any case I don't like the idea of leaving a wad of notes in a hollow tree. I'd like you to go into the town and deliver the money to one of the postmasters there.'

Pascale nodded. 'I can do that.'

She was looking tired this morning, her eyes heavy-lidded and with dark shadows beneath. Paul, on the other hand, looked remarkably fresh for a man who had spend most of the night directing operations at a remote drop site.

'What we have to decide is the best way for you to get there,' he said, draining his coffee cup and reaching for the pot to refill it. 'You've got two options. One is to go by bus, the other is for you to cycle. Either way, you're going to have to cross the border into occupied territory.'

'I'd rather cycle,' Pascale said promptly. She'd ridden a few times on the country buses, and was not impressed. They were always horribly overcrowded, they were hot, and they stank of unwashed bodies.

'It's a very long way,' Paul said dubiously.

'I don't mind that. And people are used to seeing me on my bicycle.'

'Not as far away as St Sancerre. Nobody in their right mind would cycle so far unless they were trying to be inconspicuous. It might well attract suspicion. I think you should bite the bullet and take the bus.'

'If you say so. You're the boss.'

''Fraid so. And by the way, I may not be here when you get back. In fact, I may be gone for a couple of days, so don't worry about me.'

'OK.' She didn't ask where he was going or what he was going to do; he wouldn't tell her, she knew. He never did. It was safer that way.

In any case, her mind was full of her own mission. Cycling into occupied territory in the open countryside was one thing, going to a town was quite another, and she was worried about her ability to carry it off.

Perhaps her anxiety was showing in her face.

'Just take care, as you always do, Pascale, and you'll be fine,' Paul said.

His hand hovered over hers for a moment, as if he was about to squeeze it as a gesture of reassurance. Then he thought better of it and withdrew his hand without touching hers.

'I'll take you to the bus stop as soon as you're ready,' he said.

The bus was every bit as crowded as Pascale had feared. She sat squashed on to the hard bench seat between a fat countrywoman nursing a basket of eggs and a small boy who kicked his none-too-clean legs restlessly against the seat in front of them. One of the men sitting on it, who had a protesting hen squashed between his knees, turned to remonstrate with him, which put a stop to his annoying antics for a few minutes only, and returned to an argument with his friend about the political situation.

'I don't know why people can't just accept it,' he said, loudly enough for Pascale to be able to hear every word. 'They should respect Pétain and do as he says. He got us out of a mess in the last war. He's a good man, and he has our best interests at heart.'

'But de Gaulle,' the other man protested. 'He thinks we should be putting up a fight.'

'What for? The war's won. We have to look to Germany for our future now.'

'De Gaulle doesn't think it's all over . . .'

'What does he know? He fled the country. He's been sentenced to death by the government. And he's in England, not here in France. England!' He spat the word with disgust, the disgust of a man who thought of the English as the oldest enemy of the French. 'Who but a traitor would trust the English? They've always hated us. No, it's up to us to take care of ourselves. Do the best we can so they'll leave us in peace. I tell you, once this war is over, it's the Germans who'll be our salvation. They'll make sure we're all right, just so long as we respect them and don't do anything foolish.'

'Oh, I expect you're right, Gaston.' The second man sighed and retreated into silence. He had the defeated air of most of the local people, who didn't really care for what was happening, but wanted only to be left in peace.

They were approaching the border, the demarcation line between Vichy and occupied territory.

The palms of Pascale's hands were damp; she wiped them on her cotton skirt, horribly conscious of the bundles of French franc notes she had stitched into the hem. She'd checked in the full-length dressing mirror that they didn't make the skirt fall unevenly, and had been satisfied, but now she couldn't imagine how anyone could fail to miss the bulges, especially a sharp-eyed border guard. As the bus came to a halt, she crossed one knee over the other and arranged the folds of her skirt beneath it so that the offending bundles were tucked well out of sight.

The border guard was on the bus now, moving down the aisle between the crowded seats, his revolver bumping menacingly against his hip. Pascale had her papers in her hand, the same papers she'd been issued with before she left London. They had appeared absolutely authentic then, and had served her in good stead. The trouble was, the German authorities could make changes at any time to what was required, papers could go out of date and you'd never know it, and she hadn't had to present them for inspection for a long while now.

She stared out of the window with affected nonchalance as the guard came closer, but her heart was thudding so hard she felt sure he must notice it. He was in front of her now, legs splayed against the juddering of the bus as its engine idled. She held out her papers, looking at the buttons on the guard's uniform, not his face.

To her utmost relief, he glanced at them almost uninterestedly and handed them back to her. The man in the seat in front of her, the collaborator, was saying something to the guard – passing the time of day in an attempt to show solidarity, she thought – but this time his words were no more than a jumble, drowned by the pounding of the blood in her ears.

The guard ambled back down the aisle, stopped to exchange a few words with the driver, and disembarked. With a grinding of gears the bus began to move away and Pascale breathed again.

Got away with it.

But she was in occupied territory now, and she knew she dared not relax her guard for a single second.

It was midday when the bus reached its final stop in the Place St Sancerre and Pascale was one of only a half-dozen remaining passengers. She got off and looked around, trying to get her bearings. Paul had described the route she had to take in as much detail as he could, but it wasn't as easy as he'd made it sound now that she was actually here, in this unfamiliar place. A clock began to strike the hour and she located the source of the bell: a tower above what looked like a municipal building – the *hôtel de ville* that Paul had used as a starting point, she was fairly sure.

A little more confident, but still anxious, she started along the pavement, checking street names and landmarks as she went – a bar, the Pomme d'Or, a bank, the Credit Lyonnais. None of the shoppers or the business people, identifiable by their dark suits and high, tightly buttoned collars, took the slightest notice of her, but she still felt horribly conspicuous, mostly by virtue of not really knowing where she was going, but unable to ask.

It took a good ten minutes before she came upon the place she was looking for – a baker's shop on a corner – and the street name on a plaque high on the wall above. She turned into the street, her heart echoing again as a nervous tic in her throat.

The street was a long one; as Pascale went further from the centre of town it became more run-down, shabbier, and there were fewer shops. She was just beginning to think she had somehow made a mistake when she spotted two or three bicycles piled one on top of the other against the wall beside a narrow doorway, and guessed this must be the place she was looking for. A peeling sign on the wall beside the door confirmed it.

Clement Barnarde. Réparation du cycle.

The door was ajar; she went in.

It was dim in the outer room of the shop; it was also empty. Pascale went to the counter and rang the brass bell. A figure appeared in the doorway to the inner room, a short, wiry man with a thin, leathered face. He was wearing a grubby collarless shirt and trousers tied up at the waist by a length of string. A cigarette, half smoked, was stuck to his lower lip. Pascale's heart sank. The man didn't look at all as she'd imagined, and not a bit trustworthy.

'Yes?' he said, without removing the cigarette from his mouth.

Pascale hesitated for a moment, then made up her mind. She couldn't come all this way and then go back to Savigny with the rolls of francs still in the hem of her skirt.

'I need a repair kit for a puncture in my bicycle tyre,' she said. 'I was told Jean-Pierre would be able to help me.'

'Who told you that?'

'Avocet.' She had almost said Paul!

For what seemed a lifetime the man stared at her, giving no sign that he recognised the name or understood the password. Then he crossed to the door and stood looking out, wiping his hands on a rag that he pulled from his pocket. But for all his apparent casualness there was a wariness in the set of his shoulders, and Pascale saw him turn his head, looking up and down the street and back again – making sure she hadn't been followed, she knew.

He tossed the butt of his cigarette out on to the pavement, then turned back into the shop.

'You have something for me?'

'Yes.'

'You'd better come through.' He pointed to the inner doorway and Pascale went through into what was clearly a workshop – a bicycle stood on its handlebars and saddle. It was missing its chain, which lay on the floor beside it.

The man crossed to a workbench in one corner that apparently served as his office space. He opened a drawer in an old chest beside it, removed a box file and took out a pile of invoices.

'Put what you've brought in there.'

Pascale was a little shocked; it seemed a very casual hiding place for so much money. But that wasn't really her concern.

'Do you have any scissors?' she asked.

He gazed at her, obviously puzzled.

'I need to cut the stitching on my skirt.'

The man padded off, returning with a penknife.

'Will this do?'

Pascale nodded. She sat down on a rickety stool, turned her skirt up and cut through the cotton that secured the false hem. When she pulled it out she was able to extract the bundles of notes, which she placed in the box file. Then she unpicked the rest of the hem, returning the skirt to its original length. A slight crease showed where the fold had been, but it was barely visible and she thought it would soon fall out.

The man motioned to her to remain where she was while he made sure the coast was clear, then he hurried her out into the deep shadow thrown by the buildings on the other side of the street. Hardly a dozen words had passed between them and she had no idea whether the money would reach its intended destination or whether he'd use it himself to buy some luxuries on the black market. But that was out of her control; she'd done what Paul had asked of her – she could do no more. Her skirt felt light and frothy around her bare legs now, and it matched her mood. All she had to do now was buy the books that were her excuse, if challenged, for going to St Sancerre, and get herself safely back to Savigny.

She'd passed a bookshop on her way to the cycle repair shop; she retraced her steps until she found it again and went inside.

It wasn't an impressive emporium – most of the stock was second-hand, dusty and faded, but she managed to find a couple of volumes that fitted the bill, one a dictionary of plant life, the other a book on the history of the production of cognac. She bought them and walked back to the town square clutching them to her chest, anxious now to be on her way.

She couldn't see a bus in the town square, nor even what might be a queue for one. Not wanting to make herself conspicuous, she walked once around the square and hesitated outside a café. She was thirsty, and a cup of coffee would help to pass the time. But she didn't want to risk missing the bus if it came. She'd see it, though, if she sat at one of the tables outside . . .

The voice, close behind her, made Pascale almost jump out of her skin.

'Madame Jestin!'

She swung round, her heart racing, forcing a smile to hide her dismay.

'General Buhler!'

'Well this is a pleasant surprise,' he said silkily. 'What brings you to St Sancerre?'

Pascale tried to summon a twinkle of cheeky flirtatiousness.

'I could ask you the same question, Herr General.'

'You could indeed. And I would have no hesitation in telling you that I have come to meet a fellow officer, who is in charge of this district. We had business to discuss with regard to certain unwelcome developments. But you haven't answered my question. You're a long way from Savigny.'

His eyes were sharp now behind his rimless spectacles.

Pascale dipped her chin towards the books she was carrying, thanking her lucky stars that she'd been able to buy them before running into the general.

'I need to do some more research into local conditions. This disease of the vines is proving something of a problem. So far I haven't been able to get to the bottom of it.'

'A great worry for you – and more especially for the vine growers.'

'It certainly is.'

'How did you get here?' Another sharp look. He's still suspicious, Pascale thought.

'On the bus. I thought there was one to take me back about now, but it seems I was wrong,' she said, striving to keep her tone light.

The general's thin lips curled into that grotesque smile.

'Then why don't you allow me to offer you transport? My car and driver will be here in just a moment, and it will be a good deal more comfortable than the bus.'

It was the last thing Pascale wanted, but what choice did she have?

'That's very kind of you. Thank you.'

As she spoke, the big staff car cruised around the square, the driver gesticulating authoritatively to a small rattletrap of a car to move out of the way and allow him to draw up at the kerb. Then

187

he got out and came around to open the rear door, saluting the general as he did so. Buhler stepped back for Pascale to get in first, then climbed in beside her.

'This is very kind,' she said again, and to her own ears the words sounded fatuous.

'If I can't help my friends . . .' Buhler gave her another of the smiles that made her flesh creep, yet Pascale felt he was still testing her, still suspicious. And she didn't like how close he was sitting to her, either, invading her space. But she knew that going along with his unwanted attention was the best way of deflecting his suspicion.

'I feel like some sort of celebrity!' she said, smiling at him coquettishly as the car moved away.

'As, my dear Sylvie, I am sure you are. An expert in your field . . . I'm afraid I was never fortunate enough to have such an education.'

'And yet you've become a very powerful man.'

The smile then was one of satisfaction.

'I suppose you could say that.' His hand covered her knee, squeezing gently. Pascale shuddered inwardly, not only at his touch, but at the thought that a few hours earlier that questing hand would have encountered a puzzling bulk in the hem of her skirt!

If the bus journey this morning had seemed long, the drive home was endless. Pascale struggled to hide her revulsion and even managed to go on flirting as the car purred through the countryside and the general moved ever closer to her. The heat from his body seemed to hem her in, a suffocating shroud, and the slight but repellent odour of his breath nauseated her so that it was all she could do not to turn her head away. The only saving grace was that she did not have to submit to a check of her papers at the border control point; the car was waved through and saluted.

At last they were turning into the drive that led to the château, drawing up in the courtyard where the fountain played.

'Are you coming in to see Louis?' Pascale asked; it seemed a natural question.

Buhler shook his head.

'Not today. Though I may well need to speak to him soon on rather serious matters.'

Pascale's heart leapt into her throat.

'What sort of matters?' she asked, striving to keep the alarm out of her voice.

The general covered her hand with his.

'Let's just say that it would seem there are those in this district who are behaving in a manner that is distinctly unwise. Nothing you need worry your pretty little head about.' His fingers stroked hers; her skin crawled. 'This has been very pleasant, my dear. I hope you'll honour me with your company again soon – perhaps in more intimate circumstances?'

Pascale honestly did not know what to say. She pressed her fingers to her lips, giving him what she hoped was a flirtatious look.

'You are very naughty, General.'

'Please call me Franz.'

'Whatever I call you, you are very naughty!'

The driver, pretending deafness, was opening the door for her, and to her intense relief Pascale saw Alicia come around the corner of the house. Buhler would be bound to speak to her; there would be no more opportunity for seduction today.

As Alicia approached the car, Pascale gathered her bag and the books she had bought and gratefully made her escape.

SEVENTEEN

Though Paul had warned her that he was going to be away, when two days had gone by with no word from him, Pascale couldn't help worrying. How would she know if something had gone wrong? If he'd been arrested within the area where he was known, of course, in all probability a squad of Germans would have turned up at the door of the château to take the rest of them away too, and that hadn't happened. But she couldn't forget what Buhler had said about 'serious matters' and people behaving unwisely. Was it possible that he had discovered Paul was an SOE agent, and was playing a cat-and-mouse game with the rest of them?

Then there was the worry that Paul might have been arrested elsewhere, in a sector where he wasn't known. Pascale was certain he would never betray them; he'd take the cyanide pill hidden in his cufflink rather than put them in danger. Her stomach clenched at the thought.

Besides worrying about him, she missed him dreadfully. She tried to keep busy, cycling out to check all her post boxes for messages – there were none – but without fresh instructions the days dragged. She missed him at mealtimes; not that he was a great conversationalist – it was Alicia and Giselle who did most of the talking around the table – but the empty place loomed large, more solid somehow than the flesh-and-blood de Savigny family. It was at night, though, that she missed him most of all, missed hearing his even breathing and sometimes his snores, knowing he was there on the other side of the connecting door.

She was anxious, too, to talk to him about her visit to St Sancerre, her niggling doubts that the money she had delivered would find its way to the intended recipient, and her encounter with Buhler. She was less eager to tell him about the general's attempts to seduce her, but she knew she must. As leader of the network it was imperative that Paul was in possession of any information that might affect its security.

On the third day she found a message in one of her post boxes, a dry-stone wall midway between the château and the farm where Claude, the pianist, was still holed up. Messages from Claude always needed to be treated as a top priority – he was, after all, their only contact with England – and Pascale decided to decode it there and then, sitting on the scratchy grass in the lee of the wall.

The message consisted of a map reference and a time, today's date, and the single word 'boom'. Pascale frowned; she knew what it meant – HQ wanted something blown up at the precise time given. Which probably meant it was either a troop train or a big consignment of arms and ammunition, the details of which they'd received from someone in intelligence, a railway employee perhaps. A static target wouldn't have called for such specific timing. She tore the message into tiny shreds and buried them in the rough soil. Then she recovered her bicycle and started back for Savigny, worrying whether Paul would be back in time to organise the operation. If he wasn't, it would be up to her to deal with it.

As the sun beat down on her face and her feet flew on the pedals, Pascale worked on a plan of campaign. She needed to consult a map so that she could work out who to contact to set things in motion, then speak to them herself – there wouldn't be time to rely on a message left in a post box. Adrenalin raced in her veins. This was the first chance she'd had to prove she could work on her own initiative.

The château was slumbering in the warmth of the midday sun. No one seemed to be about – none of the family, none of the servants, though she could hear Agnes, the cook, singing tunelessly as she clattered pans in the kitchen. And Paul was not back.

Pascale found a map, printed on a square of silk, checked the location she'd memorised and saw that she'd been right. A railway line ran right across the spot she'd pinpointed with her index finger. She felt certain that tonight a train carrying a vital cargo of some kind would be passing over it.

She folded the map and replaced it in the drawer, where it lay unobtrusively amongst her underwear.

The man in charge of the sector where the sabotage was to take place was, she knew, a retired schoolmaster named François, and the village where he lived was mercifully only about a half-hour's cycle ride away. At this time of day he would, in all likelihood, be found in one of the bars or cafés in the narrow cobbled streets that spread out like a spider's web from the central *place*. Pascale slung her bag containing her papers around her neck and went back downstairs.

Alicia was in the hall now, arranging freshly cut roses in the vase on the bureau.

'Going out again?'

'Yes. I shouldn't be more than a couple of hours.' She hesitated. 'If Paul should come back, will you tell him I need to speak to him urgently?'

Alicia nodded. 'Of course.'

She didn't ask where Pascale was going, or what she needed to speak to Paul about; she knew better.

'By the way, I should warn you, we're expecting General Buhler for dinner tonight. He's invited himself again. He's got through the cognac we gave him, I expect, and is hoping to replenish his supply.'

Pascale smiled. 'That's probably it.'

But she was thinking, with a sinking heart, that Buhler's interest was in more than simply his supply of cognac.

There was more cloud in the sky by the time Pascale reached her destination, white fluffy ridges scudding to join a darker-edged mass, and the light had a different quality, so clear that the distant hills looked close enough to touch. There was rain on the way, she thought, and didn't know whether that was a good thing or not.

The cobbled streets of the village didn't make for comfortable cycling; Pascale dismounted and pushed. François wasn't amongst the men playing boules in the *place*, nor sitting at the tables outside the first café she came to. Anxious not to miss him, she peeked into the dark interior, but he was not there either.

'*Bonjour, mam'selle.*' The café owner was behind the bar, polishing glasses. 'Why don't you sit at a table outside? If you tell me what you want, I'll bring it out to you.'

Cornered, Pascale decided to take a chance.

'Nothing at the moment, thank you. I'm looking for someone. François. Do you know where I might find him?'

The café owner eyed her curiously.

'François, eh? What do you want with that old misery?'

'Don't talk about him like that! He's helping my son with his school work. He's very kind.'

'Oh well, if you say so. He doesn't come in here any more. I don't like his politics. But I suppose that doesn't make him a bad teacher.' The café owner put down the glass, polished to sparkling perfection, and threw the drying-up cloth over his shoulder. 'You'll find him at the Café Rose if I'm not mistaken, enjoying a glass of red wine.'

Pascale thanked him, left the café, and walked further down the street. To her relief, even before she reached the Café Rose she recognised the man she was looking for, sitting at one of the pavement tables.

'*M'sieur,*' she greeted him. 'I'm so glad I've found you. Alain is struggling again with his arithmetic, and I hoped that I might be able to persuade you to give him some more tuition.'

François shook his head, grizzled grey.

'Ah, that boy! He'll be the death of me! Let's have a drink and we can talk about it.' He led Pascale to an unoccupied table, signalled to the waitress and asked for a bottle of burgundy. His eyes followed the girl as she disappeared into the café, watching the undulating swell of her buttocks beneath her tight black skirt. Then he turned to Pascale.

'So, what did you want to talk to me about?'

Surreptitiously checking that no one was within earshot, Pascale told him.

He rolled his eyes and shook his head.

'They don't want much, do they?'

The waitress was back with the wine. He waited until she had sashayed back into the café, watching her go with the same studied appreciation as before.

'A lovely girl. She makes me wish I was young again.'

'I'm sure,' Pascale said drily. 'Well? I know it's a lot to ask, but can you do it?'

'I'll see what I can arrange.' He poured some wine. 'Now, why don't we enjoy some of this excellent burgundy and discuss young Alain's mathematical problems?'

As she pedalled back to Savigny, Pascale had a presentiment that Paul was back. Her spirits lifted, her heart swelled with joy. And she was not in the least surprised to see Alicia's car on the gravel turnaround. She ran upstairs, to the suite they shared. He was there, sitting at the little escritoire, obviously deep in thought.

'You're back!' Her voice was light and excited as a child on Christmas Eve.

He looked up, hazel eyes meeting hers.

'You noticed.'

'Well of course I noticed! It's been horrid without you. I really missed you.'

'So I gather.' The smile left his eyes; he looked deadly serious now. 'Is everything all right? Alicia told me you wanted to see me.'

'Yes. I do need to talk to you – about several things. But : . . . oh, Paul, it is so good to see you!'

'And you, Pascale. But let's get down to business, shall we? This isn't a social engagement, you know.'

'I know that,' she said, chastened and deflated. She flopped down on to the chaise and tried not to let her awareness of the fact that this was where he slept distract her. 'Right. Where shall I begin?'

'You took a lot upon yourself, Pascale,' Paul said when she'd finished telling him about the message she'd recovered this morning and her visit to François.

'What else would you have had me do?' she flared, defensive in her disappointment at his response. 'You weren't here . . . it was obviously urgent. I've set things in motion. If I hadn't, it would probably have been too late. Whatever is on that train would have got to its destination in one piece. I don't think anyone on our side would have been very happy about that.'

'You're right. But we have to weigh the odds.'

'I did. And I came to the conclusion that it was up to me to act on the message.'

Paul nodded.

'You did well. Just so long as you didn't blow your cover.'

'I didn't.' But colour was rising in her cheeks. 'I did have a bit of a problem when I went to St Sancerre, though . . .'

She told him first her concerns about Clement Barnarde, or Jean-Pierre, as he was code-named, and whether or not he would pass on the money to its intended destination, and then about her meeting with Buhler. Paul listened, not saying anything until she had finished, but the tight line of his mouth and the narrowing of his eyes was not encouraging.

'OK.' He took out his cigarettes, offered her one, and lit them both. 'Well, I don't think you need worry about Jean-Pierre. He doesn't look like the sort to inspire confidence, I agree, but he's passionate about resisting. I wouldn't have used him as a go-between if I'd had any doubts as to his honesty. Buhler, though . . . that's a different matter entirely.'

'I think I got round him,' Pascale said defensively.

'At the time, I'm sure you did. He's got a very soft spot for you. But when he's had time to think about it, or if something else should happen to arouse his suspicions . . . we're on a knife edge here, Pascale. I'm not sure that the excuse of you investigating the vine disease will hold water much longer.'

'But as your wife, surely it's only natural for me to want to be with you?'

'Maybe. But cycling about the countryside, especially when winter sets in? Living in the château? That's another thing. By being under Louis' roof we're putting the de Savigny family at risk. It's not an ideal situation, especially with Buhler turning up whenever he fancies.'

'He's coming to dinner again tonight,' Pascale said.

'Exactly. I know the very fact that we're here, right under his nose, is a plus point, but with the interest he's taking in you . . .'

'I can handle him.'

'But can you? To a point, perhaps, but you can't afford to antagonise him. There may come an occasion when . . .' He paused. 'You do know what I'm saying, Pascale? All these implicit promises to keep him sweet? You may have no choice but to deliver. And I'm wondering if it might be best to get you out now, while your cover story holds good. As a research scientist, it's perfectly feasible that you'd want to go back to academia.'

Pascale stiffened. 'You're sending me home!' She said it very quietly, but her voice resonated with shock and horrified disbelief.

'I'm thinking about it.'

'But . . . I don't want to go, Paul! I want to stay here . . .' *With you*, she wanted to say.

'Even if it means sleeping with Buhler?' His tone was hard, uncompromising.

Pascale's stomach clenched at the very idea – and with shock that Paul could suggest such a thing so dispassionately. It was that, she realised, that stung the most. But the success of his circuit was the only thing that mattered to him, she reminded herself. And he wasn't necessarily asking her to sleep with Buhler, simply reminding her that it might be unavoidable if she stayed here.

And he was right, of course. To spurn Buhler's advances might well be a very dangerous thing to do, and Paul wanted her to be aware of that.

She thought of how revolted she had been by the general's proximity in the back of his staff car – the heat of his body, the sour smell of his breath, the creeping touch of his soft, clammy hands. If the necessity arose, was she committed enough to submit to far, far worse?

Paul's eyes were on her, narrowed, steely, and quite suddenly Pascale made up her mind.

Men and women were dying every day in the fight against Nazi Germany. If they could give their lives, surely it wasn't such a big deal to endure a few hours' intimacy with a puffed-up little creep with a few badges of rank on the shoulder of his uniform jacket? The cause was more important by far than her sensibilities, and if she couldn't, or wouldn't, be prosaic about it, Paul would send her home. She didn't want that. It would be a crushing blow when she so wanted to do her bit to defeat the enemy. But more than that . . .

It was the thought of being separated from Paul that she really couldn't bear. Her feelings for him, which she had tried so hard to deny, hit her with the force of a sledgehammer. She couldn't bear to be sent home because she couldn't bear to leave him. And she would do anything – anything – she had to if it meant she could stay.

'Well?' Paul asked in the same hard tone.

Pascale swallowed hard.

'I'm prepared to do whatever is necessary,' she said evenly.

For what seemed like an eternity, Paul smoked in silence. Then he ground out his cigarette.

'OK, we'll see how it goes. Then I'll make a decision.'

Paul stood at the sitting room window, wide awake though it was well past two in the morning. In the bright moonlight the poplars surrounding the château and the tall, graceful cypress trees that lined the drive shone silvery, ghosts of a peaceful past, and through the open window he could hear the constant movement of the water in the fountain in the courtyard below.

A good clear night for a drop. Not that one was expected in his territory, but very likely in other parts of France, groups of men with torches and blackened faces would be waiting, watching the sky, risking their lives for the sake of freedom.

And perhaps there were groups of hotheads closer at hand, taking risks in the same cause. He'd tried to stamp out that kind of brave but foolish activity, as he knew Louis had tried, but it was impossible to contain it completely. Tonight, at dinner, Buhler had made it clear that he thought there was insurgence in the district, and even clearer that he would not hesitate to do whatever was necessary to stamp it out. It could mean severe retribution, Paul knew, and an added risk for his own well-ordered operation.

It was not that that was keeping him awake, though. It never did. Paul had long since mastered the knack of doing what had to be done and then switching off. To worry unnecessarily and lose sleep over it was counterproductive; he needed to be fresh and alert, his head clear, his judgement unclouded.

Which was why he thought now that he really should send Pascale back to England. All the reasons he'd given her were valid ones. But there was another that he hadn't mentioned.

She'd got under his skin. Into his head. And quite apart from the fact that he was engaged to someone else, he was afraid his feelings for her were going to have an adverse effect on his ability to run his circuit.

For one thing, he worried about sending her into dangerous situations, though at the same time he knew he must not allow that to influence his decisions. She was here to do a job. The important thing to remember was that she'd known the risks before she came. And she'd be furious if she thought he was holding her back from doing what was no more than her duty.

But what had really thrown him was this business with Buhler. He couldn't believe the anger he'd felt when she'd told him how the general had tried to seduce her. The cold, hard knot in his gut when she'd said, calm as you like, that if necessary she'd be prepared to sleep with him. The antagonism that had pricked under his skin throughout this evening's dinner, when he'd had to listen to Buhler direct suggestive remarks at Pascale, watch him slide his hand on to her knee beneath the table and whisper in her ear, and see her flirting coyly with him by way of response. He'd found himself wondering how long it would be before the general engineered her into a situation where he could get his way with her, if he hadn't already made the suggestion in those whispered exchanges. That was what he couldn't allow – being in a situation where it was all he could do to restrain himself from punching the man hard in his leering mouth.

Peculiar, really. To be able to hide his hatred of a Nazi over the big picture; fighting to conceal his fury when it came to that same Nazi's designs on a woman he knew only as a fellow agent. He'd felt out of control, and he didn't like it.

Of course, to a point he supposed that any antagonism he might have displayed could be explained away by the fact that Pascale was supposed to be his wife. But he couldn't afford to upset Buhler – the man was dangerous, and his patronage was too important to the operation. And Pascale might well prove to be the trigger for him to say or do something he would live to regret. The anger was simmering in him now, the thought of that little turd's hands on Pascale a slow-burning fuse he could not ignore.

Paul swore softly and turned away from the window, knowing that his impatience was aimed as much at himself as at anyone else. He couldn't afford this distraction.

He went to the connecting door, opened it. Pascale appeared to be sleeping. Her hair was spread out over the pillow; one arm, curiously defenceless, lay on top of the covers. Then suddenly she stirred, eyes flying open, body jerking up into a sitting position.

'Who's there?'

'It's all right – it's only me.'

'Oh! Sorry . . . I thought . . .'

'I know. You're on red alert even when you're asleep. One of the reasons why I think you need the chance to recharge your batteries.'

She lay back against the pillows, head propped on one arm. 'I couldn't sleep. I'm so worried you're going to send me home. Please tell me you're not.'

He grimaced. 'I'm seriously thinking about it.'

'But I've tried so hard to be a good agent. What have I done wrong?'

Got into my head in a way that isn't good . . .

'Nothing. You've done well.'

It was no more than the truth. She *was* a good agent, totally reliable, cool-headed and resourceful. She'd proved that by the way she'd organised the sabotage of the train without any input on his part. Perhaps he was over-reacting to emotions he wasn't used to dealing with, he thought. Perhaps he was jeopardising the smooth running of his sector because of his own personal discomfort.

'Don't send me home, Paul, please!'

She pushed back the covers, got out of bed and crossed to where he stood. For a brief moment the moonlight streaming through the window illuminated her, a slight figure in her oversized pyjamas – she'd lost weight these last weeks – hair tousled, face anxious with an expression that contorted his heart. Then she was beside him in the deep shadow, clutching his arm.

'I do so want to succeed at this,' she said urgently. 'It's really important to me.'

He fought, and won, the sudden overwhelming urge to take her in his arms.

'More important than going home safely to those who care about you?' he asked, the inner turmoil making his voice rough.

'There isn't anybody,' she said bleakly.

'There must be.'

'No, there isn't. Not any more. They were killed. By a bomb.'

Paul realised suddenly just how little he knew about this girl with whom he was sharing a life-and-death existence every single day.

'Who are "they"?'

'Well – my mother. And of course, I miss her dreadfully. But more importantly, my daughter. She was just over a year old when it happened. If she hadn't been killed, I don't suppose I'd be here. But she was.' Her voice cracked, then she went on: 'So you see, there's no one.'

'What about her father?' Paul asked, rather shocked.

'She doesn't have a father. There was only her and me.' Then, before he could digest this information, she went on: 'Doing this has given me something to live for again, Paul. Don't take that away from me too!'

Her hand, pleading, was still on his arm; sleepy warmth emanated from her. Instinctively he drew her close so that her face lay against his bare shoulder and his chin grazed her hair, torn now by yet more conflicting emotions, all new, but equally powerful. He wanted to protect her, he wanted to take away her pain. But these two things were incompatible. To send her home, where she would be safe, would be to return her to a barren world. And, overwhelming everything else was his desire for her. The longing to hold her, closer, far closer than he was holding her now. To make love to her. To drown in her.

Her breath was warm and soft against his skin. It was more than flesh and blood could stand. He released her and moved abruptly away.

'Paul?' she said, her tone pleading.

Paul was no longer sure whether she was asking him to hold her again, or to reconsider his decision that she should go home. The latter, he presumed.

'You're sure about this?' he asked, and wondered – if he was wrong and she had been inviting him into her bed – what her response, and his, would be.

'I'm sure. I want to stay here.'

He could almost have laughed at his disappointment if he hadn't been on the horns of such a dilemma. He blew out breath on a long sigh.

'We'll give it a bit longer,' he said. 'See what happens.'

'Oh thank you!'

'Perhaps I'll try to find somewhere else for us to live. Get us away from the château, somewhere where we won't have Buhler breathing down our necks.'

She was unsettlingly close again. He moved away, putting some distance between him and temptation.

'Go back to bed now. We'll talk about it in the morning.'

She came to him again, reaching up, kissing him on the cheek. Once more he had to summon the strength to resist her.

'Good night, Pascale.'

'Good night.'

He closed the door, a solid barrier between them, went back to stand beside the unshuttered window.

He knew it would be a long time yet before he was ready for sleep.

EIGHTEEN

Next morning, neither mentioned what had passed between them the previous night. Paul left telling her he would most likely be gone all day; Pascale cycled off to check her post boxes, wondering if the sabotage she'd arranged for last night had gone off as planned. She hoped it had; she felt quite proprietorial about it, the first act of defiance she'd carried out off her own bat, not merely acting on Paul's instructions. But she was also aware that if it had been successful there might well be reprisals, and she felt a weight of responsibility for whatever might happen too. She thought of what Buhler had said about teaching the people a lesson; she thought of the small, sleepy town she'd visited yesterday, where everyone seemed to be going about their business with as much normality as was possible, and shuddered to imagine some of the locals being taken, lined up in the little *place* and shot.

But she told herself she must put such things out of her mind. This was war; the future of Europe was at stake. It wouldn't be won without sacrifice, but what was the alternative? *Better to fight for the good than to rail at the ill.* She didn't know where the quotation that popped into her mind had come from, and couldn't be sure who'd written it, though from some long-ago poetry lesson she thought it might be Tennyson. It didn't matter. It was so apt that she found herself repeating it and taking comfort from it.

It was evening, and she was eating dinner with the de Savigny family, when Paul returned. They never talked SOE business unless they were alone – though Louis and Alicia were well aware what was going on under their roof, it was safer for all of them if it was ignored, and the conversation around the table never strayed on to dangerous ground. Pascale was burning with impatience to know if the previous night's operation had been successful, but she had to wait until Paul finished his meal and the party broke up, Charles and Giselle going to their rooms, Louis to his study, and Alicia to the salon.

'Well?' Pascale didn't need to qualify her question; Paul knew exactly what she was asking.

'Let's go outside,' he said.

They went out into the softly gathering dusk to Alicia's rose garden. Perfume, trapped by the heat of the day, hung heavy in the air, crickets chirped in the grass border, a flight of swallows wheeled overhead feasting on the myriad clouds of insects.

Paul got out his cigarettes and offered her the pack. She took one, and as he lit it for her, his hands briefly cupped hers. But there was none of the intimacy of the previous night now.

'There's good news and bad.' He lit his own cigarette and drew deeply on it. 'They got the train. A shipment of ammunition, judging by the way it went up, apparently.'

Pascale let out her breath on a puff of smoke.

'Excellent. But if that's the good news . . . ?'

'The bad is that a lad, a villager, was arrested.'

'Oh my God.' A chill shivered over Pascale's skin. 'Will he talk?'

'François doesn't think he knows anything. He wasn't one of ours. God knows what he was doing out there at that time of night – looking for rabbits to shoot, François thinks, that's what his distraught mother is saying, anyway, and François is as sure as he can be that the sabotage party wasn't followed from the village. Anyway, he must have seen the explosion and gone for a closer look, the little idiot. He was still there, hiding in the bushes, when the German patrols arrived on the scene. And they would have been in no mood to socialise, believe you me. Especially if he had a gun.'

'What will happen to him?' Pascale asked, though it was a rhetorical question.

'I don't give much for his chances,' Paul said flatly. 'He'll be questioned and then shot, I imagine. We can only hope he didn't see and recognise any of the saboteurs. They're a good cell. I don't want to see it torn apart.'

Pascale was slightly shocked by the coldness of the sentiment, though she knew she shouldn't be. The task in hand was Paul's primary concern. He'd do what he could to protect his agents and colleagues in arms, and innocent villagers too, but at the end of the day it was the organisation that mattered.

'"Better to fight for the good than to rail at the ill,"' she said, recalling the quotation that had come to her earlier in the day.

Paul threw her a baffled look. 'What?'

'Nothing. I just don't like to think of some poor lad in enemy hands.'

'It's not a pleasant thought, I agree. But that's what we're up against. What France will always be up against if we can't set her free.'

His cigarette tip glowed in the grey dusk as he took one last pull, then ground it out with his heel.

'I have a job for you, Pascale.'

So he wasn't going to send her home – at least, not yet. A rush of relief made her forget the unfortunate lad whose curiosity had put him in such terrible danger.

'Yes?' she said eagerly. 'What?'

'A British airman came down just south of Bourges a couple of nights ago. He's holed up on a farm at the moment, but with all the increased activity in the area, the farmer is anxious to pass him down the line as soon as possible. I've arranged for some papers for him, and civilian clothes, and spoken to Maurice Delors, the first safe house in the line. Trouble is, our airman doesn't speak a word of French. If he's stopped by a patrol, they'll spot him as an escapee right away. That's why I want you to escort him. If there's any trouble, you'll have to do the talking and pretend he's deaf and dumb.'

Pascale smiled grimly.

'That's not very original. I should imagine the proportion of the population afflicted that way has increased dramatically since the Germans came.'

Paul shrugged. 'Well, if you can come up with anything better . . .'

'I shall certainly try!'

'OK. I'm going now to collect the papers I've asked for. Then I'm going out to the farm where our airman is hiding. I don't want him blundering about, wrecking weeks of my hard work. Tomorrow I'll escort him to Savigny and then I'd like you to take over from me. I'll meet you outside the church at eight. You know the line, don't you?'

Pascale nodded.

'Just refresh your memory before you set out, though if everything goes according to plan, you'll be able to leave him at a safe house and another *passeur* will take over from there.'

'Fine. What do I call him?'

'His papers are in the name of Jacques Valla. I suggest if anyone asks, he's an academic colleague of yours, passing through. You've sought his advice about the problem of the vine disease.' He cocked an eyebrow at her. 'I did a spot of sabotage of my own on my way back last night, by the way. I thought it might be a good idea to make it look as if the problem is spreading to other vineyards. I'm afraid another grower will find withered leaves and dying plants today. A crime, really, so close to harvest, but in the good of the cause . . .'

Pascale smiled. 'Oh dear.'

Paul checked his watch. 'Time I was going. Get an early night, Pascale. You've got a busy day ahead of you tomorrow.'

There was none of the shared intimacy of the previous night; Pascale wasn't sure whether to be relieved or disappointed.

Next morning, she was outside the centuries-old church in Savigny a good ten minutes before the appointed time. The cobbled streets were still quiet, a slow dawn breaking pink over the red-tiled roofs. She passed the time of day with the *boucher*, who was swilling down the step outside his shop with a bucket of soapy water, then pushed her bicycle along the road she imagined Paul and the airman would be coming in on, and waited.

It wasn't long before Alicia's Citroën rounded the bend; Paul and a thickset young man in his early twenties got out. He didn't look in the least like an RAF officer; he was unshaven, several days of stubble scarring a fresh-complexioned face, his hair was tousled and he was wearing a Breton sweater that had seen better days and a pair of trousers, skagged at the knees and barely reaching his ankles.

'Hello there,' he said.

Pascale glanced around cautiously, relieved the meeting had taken place on the deserted road.

'*Bonjour*,' she replied. '*Je m'appelle Pascale*.'

'Ah. *Oui* . . .' His accent was dreadful; just that one brief word would have confirmed to a listener that he was certainly not French.

Pascale rolled her eyes. 'For goodness' sake don't say anything when there's anyone within earshot.'

His face fell. 'Sorry,' he said, in English.

Paul was unloading an ancient bicycle from the boot of the Citroën.

'This is Jacques,' he said. 'I'll leave him with you.'

'Heaven help me!' Pascale was confident Jacques would not understand a word of what she'd said.

They set out, Jacques wobbling slightly on the old bicycle, which hardly looked roadworthy. Once they were through Savigny and out on the deserted country roads, Pascale decided it would do no harm to speak to him in English.

'It's going to take us a couple of hours to get to the first safe house. Do you think you can make it?'

'I certainly hope so. It's a long time since I've ridden a pushbike, but I'm pretty fit.'

'Actually, I was thinking more of the bike than of you. It's not up to much, is it?'

'Better than walking!' He pulled a rueful face, but there was a twinkle in his eye. It was, she thought, a very British response, stoicism tempered with humour.

'Look,' she said, 'I'm hoping we won't run into any trouble. The way we're going is pretty isolated, and we are in Vichy France. But there are some German patrols, and the Vichy police can be bastards.

They're the ones to really beware of, because they'd know the minute you open your mouth that you aren't French. So I can't emphasise it enough. You must play dumb and leave the talking to me.'

'Gladly. To tell you the truth, when my plane came down I thought I'd had it. I was damned sure I'd be headed straight for a POW camp. Would have been if the farmer's wife hadn't seen me in difficulties. By the time I'd destroyed what was left of my poor old kite by setting fire to it, she had her old man out looking for me. They hid me in a barn for a couple of days while they contacted Avocet. And very grateful I am to them. They risked their lives for me.'

'There are plenty of people here willing to do that,' Pascale said. 'But there are quite a few collaborators too. And communists.'

'Hmm.' He pedalled hard for a minute or two. 'Bloody communists, eh?'

'You're from the West Country, aren't you?' Pascale said.

'How d'you know that?'

'Well, I recognised your accent, of course. Where's home?'

'Devon. Seaton. Do you know it?'

'No.'

'What about you?'

'Bath.'

'Bath! That's a bit posh, isn't it?'

Pascale laughed. 'D'you think so? I wouldn't have—'

'Definitely posh. No wonder you learned French at school.'

Pascale said nothing.

'What I'd like to know is how you come to be out here, though. Working for the resistance.'

Again Pascale was silent for a moment. The temptation to talk – to pass the time, to take her mind off her anxieties about this mission – was great. But she knew she must give nothing away.

'I think,' she said, 'that we should stop talking and concentrate on riding.'

'That's a no, then, I take it. Oh well, you're the boss.'

She grinned. 'And don't you forget it.'

The sun was beginning to grow hot. Sweat was pouring down Jacques' face; occasionally, as the decrepit bicycle jolted into a pothole, moisture sprinkled Pascale's bare arm like a fitful shower of rain.

They pedalled on in silence now, intent only on reaching their destination.

Long before she saw it, Pascale heard the approaching German patrol and recognised the throaty roar of the engines. Her heart began to pound; she looked around in vain for cover in which they could hide. There was none – or none they would have time to reach. But the vegetation grew thickly along the sides of the narrow road.

'Quickly! Get off and study the plants!'

She grabbed her clipboard from the satchel slung around her neck and crouched down, seemingly engrossed in the profusion of late summer growth. Jacques followed her lead.

The German patrol rounded the bend and she glanced up, feigning lack of interest as they came to a stop beside the two crouching figures.

'What are you doing?' One of the Germans was out of the armoured car, eyeing them with suspicion.

'I am a botanist.' Pascale turned the clipboard towards him, though she doubted he understood. 'This is my colleague, Jacques Valla.'

As she had expected, the German looked puzzled. His companion, however, who had now got out and walked round to join them, nodded. He said something in German, which Pascale presumed was a translation of what she had said.

'Papers?' The first German was intent on regaining the initiative.

A second armoured vehicle had pulled up behind the first and more soldiers were getting out. Pascale didn't so much as look in their direction. She wanted to appear nonchalant, though she was seriously worried. Half dozen German officers would not have been good news under any circumstances; given that she was escorting a British pilot who spoke no French and whose papers might or might not be acceptable, the situation was dire.

Her mind was racing. Desperate measures were almost certainly called for.

She bit down hard on to her inner lip until she tasted blood, then she covered her mouth with her hand and began coughing into it, all the while sucking hard on the tear in her lip. When her mouth was full of blood, she gathered it into a gob, spat it out on to the road and continued to cough harshly.

She'd attracted the attention of the first German, she could see. He took a step backwards, looking alarmed, and she bit, sucked, coughed and spat again.

'I'm sorry,' she said. 'I am not well.'

The soldier who spoke French, who was also looking worried, said something in rapid German to his friend. She couldn't understand the exact words, but she knew, all the same, what he was saying, and it confirmed that her charade was having the desired effect.

'Go on. On your way!' The first soldier made an abrupt gesture of dismissal – he couldn't wait to be rid of them.

Pascale feigned puzzlement; she didn't want to appear to be too anxious to escape.

'On your way!' he repeated brusquely, and retreated to his vehicle.

Pascale slung her satchel around her neck and retrieved her bicycle, almost daring to breathe again. Then, as she turned to mount, she saw for the first time the face of one of the soldiers from the second vehicle.

Her heart lurched, and for a moment she froze in utter shock. It couldn't be – surely? But it was.

Kurt.

Though it was so long since she had seen him, though he had put on some weight and was now wearing the uniform of a German soldier, there could be no mistaking it was him. All the blood seemed to leave her body in a rush, her legs were so weak she didn't think they would support her, and she felt sickeningly faint.

He had recognised her too – well of course he had! She could see her own shock reflected in his face, along with confusion and disbelief. At any moment he was going to say something that would give her away, either because he couldn't help himself, or because it was his duty.

'*Danke.*' Her voice, though utterly calm, seemed to come from a

210

long way off. She motioned to Jacques, mounted her bicycle and began to pedal along the road, expecting to hear the order to stop at any moment, but forcing herself to continue slowly. If the Germans chose, they could catch them easily; undue haste was pointless.

But the order to stop never came.

'What's going on?' Jacques asked. 'What did you do?'

'Not now,' she replied, not looking at him.

High hedges lined the road now; looking over her shoulder to ensure they were not being followed, Pascale stopped at a gateway, got off and wheeled her bicycle through. Jacques, puzzled, followed.

'I just need to get my breath.' She dropped down to sit in the scratchy grass behind the hedge, motioning him to do the same.

'I still don't understand,' he said. 'Why were those Germans so anxious to get rid of us?'

'What?' Pascale's mind was on Kurt.

'When you coughed and spat blood.'

'Oh – that.' She laughed, a harsh sound born of nervous tension. 'They thought I have TB. It's a trick Paul told me about. Of course, it won't work if too many people do it too often, but luckily they didn't seem to have seen it before.'

'You're amazing! So cool . . .'

'No, I just want to live.' On a sudden impulse of urgency, she scrambled to her feet. It was still possible that when he got over his first shock Kurt might betray her. He was, after all, a soldier of the army of the Third Reich; his first loyalty would be to the Führer. He'd probably been brainwashed, like the rest of them, and would consider it his duty.

'Let's get going.'

They set off again, but her nerves were shot now, though she thought she was managing to hide it. The last thing she wanted was to make Jacques nervous, though to be honest, he seemed remarkably calm and unfazed by their brush with the enemy. He was, she thought, all that was best about the British, and British men in particular – rock solid, immovable, pragmatic. She doubted he had much imagination, and that left him free to live in the moment and take things as they came.

In sharp contrast, her own imagination was now working over-time. When they left the main road and started down a narrow track across fields where the hay was baled for harvest and pastures where herds of cows gathered in the shade of the trees, the risk of running into another German patrol, or even the same one returning, diminished, but still she couldn't relax.

Everything seemed precarious suddenly, fraught with danger. The escape line had been open yesterday – suppose it had been compromised since then? Paul's rules that a telephone call should be made to a safe house before approaching it couldn't apply today – she had no means of contact out here in the open countryside. There could be German soldiers or Vichy police waiting for them at the farm, and she'd never know.

Calm down! she warned herself, but it wasn't so easy. Her emotions had been laid bare, too, she supposed. Kurt had, after all, been her lover, the father of her beloved child. Seeing him so unexpectedly had awakened memories, stirred up echoes of love and loss. Though she hadn't yet had time to acknowledge them – the pressing need to escape had been all-consuming – the citadel she'd built around her personal life had taken a battering. It wasn't necessary to think about something for it to wreak its effects on the deepest layers of your subconscious.

The track forked, forked again and at last the farm was in sight, a low old farmhouse and scattered outbuildings. In the heat of the midday sun, nothing stirred. Pascale's antennae prickled. Did that mean it was safe? Or were there German vehicles hidden behind the barns, soldiers waiting in the farmhouse?

Only one way to find out.

'Wait here,' she said to Jacques. 'I'm going to make sure the coast is clear.'

His stubble-covered jaw set. 'I'm coming with you.'

'No, you're not. If there should be enemy in the house, I'd have a chance of getting away with it. If you're with me, we wouldn't have a hope in hell. If everything is OK, I'll come out and wave to you. If I don't . . . well, you'll just have to try to make your way to the next safe house on your own.'

Jacques appeared on the point of arguing; Pascale could see the battle between male chivalry and the sense of what she said playing itself out on his face.

'Just keep out of sight,' she said, and set off across the farmyard.

Two dogs came rushing out, barking furiously; Pascale jumped out of her skin. Her breath was coming fast and shallow, adrenalin pulsing through her veins. Disaster seemed to be sitting on her shoulder, casting a long, dark shadow over the sunlit farmyard, crowing with the frenzied barking of the dogs.

The figure of a man appeared in the doorway of the farmhouse. For a moment Pascale could not see him clearly; it was as if there was a film of sweat over her eyes. But as the man emerged from the shadows, she saw it was the farmer. Her heart thudded with relief, but the residue of caution remained. He could have been sent out to lure her in; there might yet be German soldiers hiding inside.

'Be quiet!' the farmer shouted at the dogs. He was brandishing a shotgun, looking around, cautious, alert. His demeanour was, she thought, not that of a man who has been set up as a spider to catch a fly, but one anxious that he was not being observed.

'Is everything all right?' she asked when she was close enough to speak without raising her voice.

'Why shouldn't it be? Quiet!' he shouted at the dogs again.

'There was a German patrol on the road.'

He shrugged, shaking his head.

'They haven't been here. Did you bring a parcel for delivery?'

'Yes. Are you quite sure . . . ?'

'I said so, didn't I? Oh, les Anglais . . . ! You are a pain in the backside. Do you want our help or not?'

'Of course we do.'

'Then deliver your parcel and get back on your own territory.'

For just a moment Pascale hesitated. But the farmer's rudeness was absolutely in keeping with what she'd come to expect, and her instincts, which she'd learned to trust, were telling her that for all her doubts it was safe.

She turned, gesticulating to the stand of trees where Jacques was hiding.

He emerged cautiously and she waved again. As Jacques approached, the farmer asked Pascale:

'Are you sure he's not Abwehr? He's not a plant?'

'He's definitely English. You have my word for it. Take care of him, won't you?'

The farmer grunted non-committally. But he lowered the shotgun, though he was still eyeing Jacques with suspicion.

'That's it then,' Pascale said to Jacques. 'This is your *passeur*. I'm going to leave you with him now.'

'Aren't you going to come in, have a drink?' the farmer asked.

Pascale shook her head. 'I'm anxious to get back. If you could just fill my flask . . .'

The farmer took it from her, scowling, and went into the house, leaving her and Jacques alone.

'Just remember everything I've told you,' she said to Jacques.

'I will, don't worry. And thank you. I'll never forget what you've done for me.'

'All in a day's work.' With confidence returning, she could afford to be a little more offhand.

The farmer was back with her flask.

'Goodbye, then,' she said.

To her surprise, Jacques took her arm, pulling her towards him, and kissed her on the cheek. 'Thanks again.'

Inexplicably, Pascale was deeply touched.

'Good luck,' she said, and smiled at him.

She replaced her flask in her satchel and pushed her bicycle back to the narrow track, eager now only to be home.

NINETEEN

'You know what this means, don't you?' Paul said.

Pascale nodded, her expression grim.

'That now you are going to have to send me home.'

'Pascale – I've no choice. You must see that. For you to go on working in this district is no longer an option.'

She nodded miserably. He was right, of course. She'd known from the moment Kurt had seen her that her cover was blown. That he hadn't betrayed her there and then didn't mean that he wouldn't. It was far too dangerous for her to remain – not only for her, but for any of her associates. It was just fortunate that when Kurt saw her she'd been with an English airman who would now, with any luck, be well away from the area. If she'd been in the company of another agent or *resistant* it could have been disastrous. And if she'd been with Paul . . . Her stomach clenched. The prospect of what might well have happened to him and the de Savignys didn't bear thinking about.

'I'll get a message to London to ask for a plane to pick you up,' Paul said. 'In the meantime, you'll have to stay here, out of sight.'

'What if Buhler comes calling?'

'I need to think about that one. Let's hope he doesn't, but even if your friend does talk, there's nothing to link you to the château, is there?'

'No.' An awful thought struck her. 'Oh God . . . there might be. I told the soldier who questioned me that I was a botanist.'

Paul swore. 'Well, we'll just have to hope he doesn't mention it to anyone who can make the connection. And that your friend keeps quiet about recognising you. How close were you?'

'Very.' She didn't elaborate.

'What a bloody mess.'

'I'm sorry,' she said miserably.

Paul sighed. He didn't tell her it was all right. It wasn't, she knew. He picked up his jacket and shrugged into it.

'I'm going to go and arrange for Claude to send a message to London. The sooner we can get you out of here, the better.'

'OK.'

Then he was gone, and she was left alone with nothing but wretchedness and a terrible sense of failure for companions.

Dinner that night was a tense affair. Paul had been gone for an hour or so; when he returned, he told Pascale that the message was being sent to order her immediate recall. He'd obviously spoken to Louis, too, and warned him what was happening. Though it was not mentioned over dinner, it was clear from Louis' brusque manner and the sympathetic but rather strained smiles that Alicia bestowed on Pascale that they knew.

When they'd finished eating, Pascale could bear it no longer. She excused herself and went up to their suite, leaving Paul with the de Savignys. The guilt she felt at putting them in such terrible danger was overwhelming. And she couldn't believe the stroke of atrocious luck that had put her and Kurt in the same place at the same time. Yet didn't that kind of coincidence happen all the time – and shouldn't she have foreseen it?

The sitting room was full of Paul – his sweater draped over the back of a chair, a handkerchief bunched up under a cushion on the chaise, the butts of his cigarettes in the ashtray. She picked up the sweater, burying her face in it, inhaling the smell of him. The feeling of terrible loss at the prospect of leaving him was as strong as the guilt she felt for her failure and the shame of being sent home, and a tide of blackness welled up in her.

Pull yourself together, girl.

She put the sweater back where she had found it and went into her own room. She might as well begin packing. She pulled her suitcase out from under the bed and began piling underwear into it. She looked with distaste at the shapeless skirt she'd arrived in, and which she'd hardly worn since.

She'd better take it with her, she supposed; she might need it again, and even if she didn't, the SOE would probably want it back to reissue to someone else. Perhaps if she left it behind they'd charge her for it. Missing kit.

The idea amused her in a droll way, and she began laughing, silly, mirthless laughter that she was somehow powerless to stop. And then, seamlessly, the laughter had become tears.

Pascale sank on to the bed, hugging the horrible skirt, and sobbed helplessly.

'Pascale?'

Paul was in the doorway. She straightened up, but kept her head bowed. She didn't want him to see her tears.

'Oh – hello.' Her voice was thick and forced.

'You're crying! He sounded shocked.

'Don't be silly. Of course I'm not.'

'Oh, Pascale . . . There's nothing to cry about.'

'No?' she snorted.

'It's not your fault.'

'So that's all right then, is it?'

'Oh, for goodness' sake . . .' He felt helpless, and the helplessness made him irritable.

'I so much wanted to make a success of this! And look how it's turned out. It's a disaster. I'm a disaster.'

'Don't talk such rubbish!'

'You haven't a clue, have you?' she snapped. 'You're so sure of yourself. You don't understand what it feels like, knowing I've put my friends in danger.'

She saw his face harden.

'Well *do* you?' she demanded, angry suddenly with him as well as with herself.

217

'More than you know,' he said harshly. 'I lost three members of my last circuit.'

She stared at him, shocked.

'It's why I was back in England when I met you.' He told her about it. 'These things happen, Pascale. So for goodness' sake stop thinking you're a failure. I came back, and so will you.'

'Not here, though,' she said quietly.

'Well – no.'

'And I want it to be here.' Her head was bowed again; she couldn't look at him. 'Oh, it can't be, I know. But that doesn't mean . . . I don't want to leave you, Paul.' The tears were sparkling again on her lashes.

'Oh Pascale, you silly girl . . .' He sat down on the bed beside her.

'Please,' she said softly, 'will you just hold me?'

For what seemed like an eternity, he did not move or speak. A tear rolled down her cheek.

'I'm sorry. I shouldn't have asked.'

'No more apologies. Come here!'

His arms were around her, her face pressed into his shoulder. And then he was kissing her, and the first searing flickers of awareness were licking through her, a fuse setting light to the tinders of desire she'd tried so hard to suppress. For just a brief moment Pascale thought: This is wrong – we mustn't do this . . . and then: What does it matter now? In a couple of days I'll be on my way back to England, and I'll never see him again . . .

And then, as their need became more urgent, all-consuming, there was no place for thinking at all.

They slept together that night and the next, white-hot explosions of passion followed by peaceful closeness. When she woke in the middle of the night, Pascale curled her body around his and pressed her mouth against the salty skin of his shoulder, tasting him, smelling him, drinking him in. This had to last her a lifetime; in a few days it would be over, for ever. It was this that she clung to when the guilt at betraying Simone niggled at her; this was unreal, another world. They were two people who needed one another, that was all. At no time did she try to fool herself that Paul loved her, nor that they might have a future together – if they had a future at all. She lived only for the moment, and in that moment it was enough.

The danger and the desire and the reckless abandon all fused into one; she was almost euphoric. And she told herself that when it was over, when the plane came to take her back to England, Paul would forget her.

But she knew in her heart, in her soul, in every tingling nerve ending in her body, that she would never forget him.

The plane that came for her was small, unlike the bomber that had brought her to France, a twin-engined Lysander that landed on the field Paul had picked out with plenty of room to spare.

Pascale felt numb and every bit as divorced from reality as she had on the night she had parachuted in. It sustained her, that barrier of distance, so that her goodbyes to the de Savignys felt as mechanical as if she were a puppet dancing on the end of a string, and she was able to kiss Paul coolly on the cheek and wish him good luck. There couldn't be any passionate embraces or tearful farewells in the presence of the other members of his team who had turned out to light the Lysander in and watch it out.

It was only as the plane climbed, with the trees edging the field making a carpet of silvery green in the moonlight and the lights on the ground turning to no more than pinpricks, that the reality hit her and a great wave of sadness overwhelmed her.

'Glad to be going home?' the pilot shouted to her.

Pascale only smiled in reply. If she told him the truth, he wouldn't believe her, and she wasn't going to lie.

But the sense of loss yawning within her was akin to grief, and she knew that, like grief, it would be a long time in fading.

Part Three

TWENTY

MARTHA

Miss Leverton stops talking. She's looking rather tired – not surprising, really. It's been quite a marathon, and she is an old lady.

'So that was how Pascale came to win the Croix de Guerre,' I say.

Though it's a bit odd talking about her in the third person when she's sitting opposite me, I'm getting used to it. I've been carried along by the story, I suppose, though I still don't understand why that's how she wants to tell it. It seems a bit like American psychobabble to me – the way shrinks get their patients to externalise, or so I've heard. I've only ever come across one person who did something similar – a battered wife I dealt with when I was a beat PC. She described the treatment her husband meted out to her that way: 'he punched her in the stomach', 'he burned her with the iron', and so on. I had a hell of a job turning it all into a statement we could put before the court, I remember.

She's looking at me thoughtfully now.

'There's actually a great deal more,' she says. 'Savigny was only the beginning. The war was far from being won.'

'Pascale went back to France?'

'Oh yes. But . . .'

'You want to leave the rest of the story for another day?'

'I think I'll have to, yes.' She sighs. 'Being old is very frustrating. When I think of all the things I used to be able to do without a second's thought . . .'

'My grandmother says the same. She was always very active until she had her stroke.' I break off. Miss Leverton doesn't want to hear about Granny. 'She says old age isn't for wimps,' I finish.

'How true. It is, however, preferable to the alternative.'

'Well yes.' I think of all the sudden deaths I've dealt with – road accidents, bodies in the river, natural causes, suicides, even a teenage girl who was murdered – all people gone before their time. Miss Leverton, however, is thinking about her SOE colleagues who never came home from France, or so I imagine. The two girls in the photograph that hangs in her hallway, perhaps.

'You will come back so I can tell you the rest, won't you?' she says.

The urgency is back in her voice; I feel those tentacles again, reaching out for me, the tentacles that scare the hell out of me. But there's no way I can give up on this now. She's got me hooked, just as she intended. It's a fascinating story, but I still don't know the answers to my questions.

Well, I can see how she came to win the Croix de Guerre, and I suppose the curl in the locket belonged to the little girl who was killed in the air raid. But I'm none the wiser as to how it all came to be in Bolborough Lake, and I can only guess at who gave her the ring. The father of her baby, perhaps? Or her fiancé, Hugh Woodhouse? That would seem to add up, since he lived at Bolborough House. Maybe they had some kind of a bust-up and one or the other of them threw the box of treasures in the lake in a temper. And then there's Paul Randall, her lover. Might he have been the one who gave her the ring? In fact, for all I know, he and Hugh Woodhouse could have been one and the same. All these aliases to protect the true identities of the agents is very confusing. The Woodhouses would have been privately educated and well travelled, which could mean he spoke fluent French. And what happened to him, I wonder?

There's still an awful lot I don't know – and I want to. Miss Leverton has done a good job of getting me interested.

'I would like to hear the rest of the story,' I admit.

'Good. So when . . . ?'

'I have a long weekend off next week. I'm off on Friday, Saturday and Sunday,' I suggest.

'That's over a week away,' she objects. 'Couldn't you make it before then?'

I've got another rest day tomorrow, but I intend to go and visit Granny and Lucy, and in any case, tomorrow feels too soon to come back, even if I am bursting with curiosity.

'What about this Friday?' I suggest. 'I should be able to make it early evening, provided nothing urgent comes up at work.'

She nods. Friday is agreed upon.

'Would you like another cup of tea before you go? she asks.

'No thank you. I'm fine.'

She sees me to the door, leaning heavily on an ebony-topped cane. She must have tired herself out with all that talking. Truth to tell, I'm feeling pretty knackered myself.

As I'm driving home, my mobile rings. Naturally I don't answer it. I don't have a hands-free, and it wouldn't look good for an off-duty police sergeant to be caught talking on a mobile while driving. Though every other bugger seems to do it. I got cut up on a round-about on the way over by a white-van man steering with one hand, his mobile clamped to his ear. If I'd been on duty I'd have gone after him. Out of uniform it would have been just too much hassle.

I'm curious as to who's calling, though. I sneak a look at the display, but all it says is '1 missed call'.

I'm heading across the parking area at the rear of my block of flats when the phone rings again. This time I catch it, juggling it into my shoulder as I fit my key in the lock.

'Hello?'

'So – how did you get on?'

I know that voice. Pete Holbrook.

'What do you mean – how did I get on?' I'm pretending I don't know what he's talking about, though I can hazard a guess.

'You've been to see Miss Leverton today, haven't you?'

'How do you know that?'

'Ah, you'd be surprised.'

'Nothing about you could surprise me.'

I've got the door open now; the communal hallway reeks of curry.

225

The people in the ground-floor flat again, obviously. Ever since they moved in, the place has stunk of curry. Now I like a rogan josh or a chicken tikka as well as the next person, but I'm getting totally browned off with this constant spice smell. It gets everwhere, through the floorboards even, and hangs in my flat. Pity there's no law against it that I know of. Could be a by-law, I suppose. Causing a stinking nuisance.

'So?' he prompts me. 'Anything you'd like to share with me?'

'You never give up, do you? No, there's nothing I'd like to share.'

'Pity. I was hoping we could help one another out here.'

'Really? Don't you mean couldn't I help you out with your exclusive?'

'You really know how to stick the knife in, don't you?'

'I've learned in a hard school, yes.'

'And if I told you I've been doing a spot of digging re our mysterious Miss Leverton you wouldn't be the tiniest bit interested?'

I've opened the door to my flat now. I was right, that damned smell has wormed its way inside.

'Look, I've just spent the best part of the afternoon with her,' I snap, irritated both by the reek of curry and Pete Holbrook's persistence. 'I can't imagine—'

'And how much have you found out about her?'

'She's been telling me all about the SOE.'

'No, about her, personally.'

'Not a lot . . .' I bite my tongue. 'I'm not at liberty to say. You know the deal.'

'Suppose I was to tell you . . . No. On second thoughts, I don't think so. Change of subject. Are you going to have that drink with me? How about tonight?'

'I'm washing my hair.'

'Tomorrow then?'

'Busy. I'm going out for a drink with the girls.'

'Foiled again.'

'It's a bugger, isn't it?'

Call over. I close down my mobile, put it on the kitchen worktop.

The answering machine on my landline phone is blinking – one message. I switch it to play. It's Lucy.

'Just ringing to check if you're still coming over tomorrow.' Then, in a lower voice: 'I'm a bit worried about Granny. She doesn't seem at all her usual self.' Louder again: 'Perhaps you'll give me a call when you pick up this message.'

Normally I'd leave ringing back until I'd changed into something comfortable and poured myself a drink. But Lucy has got me worried.

I ring her number, but annoyingly it's her answering machine.

'Hi, Lucy. Yes, I'll be with you mid-morning.' I hesitate, on the point of asking about Granny, and decide against it. It's possible she's there, even if Lucy is not, and within earshot of the phone. I don't want my concerns broadcast into the living room if she is.

I settle for: 'See you. And give my love to Granny.'

I switch on the radio, tuned to Radio 5 Live, switch it off again. They're talking about football, which is of no interest to me.

I look in the fridge to see what I can have for supper, but it's pretty bare. A yellow pepper, wrinkled, a tub of Greek yoghurt that was threatening to grow things the last time I looked at it, a roll of goat's cheese well past its sell-by date and a bag of salad leaves, ditto. Luckily, I'm not really hungry – Miss Leverton's cucumber sandwiches and fancy cakes certainly filled a hole. Perhaps I should have agreed to go back to see her tomorrow! But tomorrow is taken care of anyway. Lucy will feed me, I'm sure. What I really want more than anything is a bath. Hot, deep, bubbly. A real luxury. Generally I don't bath, I shower. For speed. For the environment. But tonight I feel like spoiling myself.

It's not great, my bathroom. Very seventies, avocado plastic and tiles that need regrouting. But when I've pulled down the blind and the only light comes from a big white church candle propped up beside the taps, it doesn't look so bad.

I run the water, as hot as it gets, which is not exactly scalding, and pour in some of the scented oil that Lucy gave me last Christmas – a stocking-filler, she called it. It's a bit sweet for my taste, but at least it's better than the curry smell. Then I strip off, climb in and lie back with my head propped against a pink bath pillow, another present from Lucy, God-knows-when (do you get the feeling she thinks I need some girlie pampering?), thinking about all that Miss Leverton told me.

It seems unreal, another world. I try to imagine myself in that situation, but I can't. Not really. Miss Leverton said we had a lot in common, but would I have been able to do what she did if I'd been her? I'd like to think I would, but I'm not at all sure. Well, for a start, I could never have passed myself off as French, but even supposing I'd had a better grasp of the language than you get at a bog-standard comprehensive, the whole thing is pretty daunting. To be in an enemy-occupied country, more or less on your own for most of the time, is a far cry from being part of a team where assistance, if needed, is usually no more than a radio call away, and violent criminals with guns are still fairly few and far between, in this part of the world, anyway. It must have been really lonely as well as dangerous; no wonder she fell for this Paul Randall.

The warm water is making me sleepy. I'm drifting, trying to picture Miss Leverton as a young woman. She was quite a stunner, I should think. I must have another look at the photograph in her hall when I go back – perhaps if I ask her, she'll show it to me, identify herself and the two other girls. It sounds as though Paul Randall was quite a hunk, too. Perhaps she has a photograph of him somewhere, tucked away.

It really is quite a story. I can see why Pete Holbrook is so interested in it.

Drifting. Drifting. Almost asleep.

Pascale . . . Paul . . .

Paul, who for some reason looks exactly like Pete Holbrook . . . How strange! Pete Holbrook in the uniform of a wartime RAF officer . . .

I wake with a jolt. The phone is ringing. Why didn't I bring it into the bathroom with me? Shall I leave it? No, I can't. It's just not in my nature. I climb out of the bath, dripping water on to the bathmat and beyond as I reach for a towel and wind it round myself. Bet the phone will stop just as I get to it . . .

It doesn't.

It's Lucy again.

'Oh, you're there now.'

'Well, obviously. Didn't you get my message?'

'Yes, but I thought I'd touch base anyway. You are coming tomorrow?'

'I said so, didn't I?'

'There's no need to be like that.'

'I'm not being like anything.' But I know I am. Irritable with everything and everyone. There are times when I don't much like myself.

'What's wrong with Granny?' I ask.

'I don't know really. She's just not herself. She seems to be in a world of her own, and she's sleeping a lot . . . she's asleep now, or at least I hope she is. I don't want her to hear me talking about her.'

'No, quite.'

'I don't like it, though. There's something not right. I hope she's not going to have another stroke.'

'That's not likely, is it? I thought they said that after that treatment they gave her she probably never would.'

Lucy sighs. She sounds stressed.

'Oh, I don't know, Martha.'

'Well, I'll see you tomorrow, anyway. I can't stay talking now, I haven't got any clothes on.'

'What!' She sounds scandalised.

'I was having a bath when you rang.'

'Oh. Right.'

'Night, Lucy. Give my love to Granny.'

I smile wryly as I hang up. Did Lucy think I had someone here – a lover? I think she imagines I lead the sort of wild life she doesn't approve of. Fat chance!

Although I suppose I could have had someone here if I'd wanted. Nick seems to be angling for some kind of hook-up (which Lucy probably would approve of) and I don't think Pete Holbrook would kick me out of bed.

For a crazy minute I imagine getting together with Pete Holbrook. It's actually not an unattractive prospect. He is rather gorgeous, if

I'm honest. And I do rather enjoy the banter between us. It crosses my mind to wonder if the reason I'm so snappy with him is because I actually fancy him, and don't want to admit it, even to myself. Maybe I ought to give him a chance. Maybe I would . . . if he wasn't a newspaper reporter. If he wasn't just using me to get at a good story. But there you go. That's life. And sometimes it's a bummer.

I go back to the bathroom, finish drying the bits that the towel hasn't reached, get into my pyjamas and head downstairs for a glass of wine before going to my solitary bed.

TWENTY-ONE

ANNE

I don't know if it's just wishful thinking, but Sonia seems a little better.

I went home at the weekend for a couple of days – though I hate leaving her, it's not fair on Rod, me being away all the time, and to be honest, I need the break to recharge my own batteries. Looking after her and the children is just so demanding, both physically and emotionally.

When I got back to Sonia's on Sunday evening she was definitely brighter. The weather has been quite good, and they'd gone out as a family for the day – to a Noah's Ark farm that's within easy driving distance. It makes a nice day out – Rod and I took the children there last summer, and they loved it. There's a picnic area with hens strutting around the benches, pony rides round a paddock, rabbits and guinea pigs and baby animals. If there are lambs to be bottle-fed, the children can help. One of the barns has been turned into an adventure play zone and there are rides around the farm on a trailer pulled by a tractor. There's also a gift shop and café, so Sonia was able to sit quietly while Kevin went around the various attractions and activities with Harry and Abigail.

It had tired her, of course, but she'd enjoyed it, and she's caught the sun a bit so she doesn't look quite so pale. They'd taken photographs and this morning she actually went on the computer and downloaded them from Kevin's camera so I could see them. Abigail on a fat pony, Harry with a calf. She and the children at one of the picnic tables eating ice creams. It was so good to see her face light up as she looked at those pictures, shadows of the old Sonia, echoes of happier times. Please God they'll come again, and next time they visit the farm Sonia will be up to walking down to the paddock with the children and going with them on the tractor-and-trailer ride.

Whilst I was at home, I went over to see Mum. Not the best part of the weekend – going to visit her has come to feel like a chore. She has become so self-obsessed that I fall into a stupor listening to her rabbiting on about things that really have no importance at all. Her doctor has gone on holiday to France for two weeks and she had to see a locum when she went for her regular bi-monthly check-up – 'a little bit of a thing who looked like she should still be at school. Wasn't the least bit interested in my stiff knee. Didn't know what to do about it, I suppose.' The village shop has stopped stocking her favourite brand of butter. Thelma isn't doing such a good job with the cleaning these days, she's vacuuming and dusting round things instead of moving them, and Mum had found a spider's web in the corner of a window.

'She's getting very slack,' Mum said, tight-lipped. 'If it goes on, I'm going to have words with her.'

My heart sank.

'Don't upset her, for goodness' sake!' I warned. I know all too well how sharp and tactless my mother can be.

Mum bristled.

'She's got to be told. I'm not paying her good money for half a job.'

'I agree. But just be careful how you put it. You'd be really stuck if she gave notice.'

'I'm thinking of giving her notice myself,' Mum said tartly. 'I'm tired of her imagining she can get away with it just because my eyes aren't as good as they used to be. And she's been at the sherry, too, I'm sure. I'm going to mark the bottle, and if I find she's been helping herself, she's definitely going.'

'Oh Mum, don't do anything rash, please. You know how difficult it is to find cleaners out here in the country. It's different in

Bristol, with agencies with plenty of staff on their books. If you lose Thelma and can't find anyone to replace her, you'll be in a real pickle. And it's no good thinking you can rely on me to come over and help you out, because I can't.'

Mum sniffed.

'No, I don't suppose I can. I've known for a long time I'm a burden to you.'

'That's just silly. You are not a burden.'

'Well you make me feel as though I am. You can find the time to go to Sonia's, doing things for her that she should be doing for herself, but you never seem to have time for your mother.'

'Sonia is ill.'

'So you keep saying,' Mum said tersely. 'That's the trouble with young people these days. No backbone. Don't want to stand on their own two feet. Think the world owes them a living.'

I could feel myself growing angry. Mum hasn't even asked what is wrong with Sonia; she's so obsessed with the aches and pains of old age that she simply assumes that Sonia should be able to overcome illness by virtue of being what Mum considers to be young.

I was tempted – very tempted – to tell her the truth, but in the end I held back again. I'm still afraid it might send her into one of her depressions – if she believes me, which of course she might not. But there's another reason too, a selfish one. I really do not want to talk about it. Can't face explaining the diagnosis, the prognosis. It's something I'm living with, coping with on a daily basis, but I don't want to talk about it. Not to Mum, anyway, or anyone who isn't already in the know. Rod, Kevin, Sonia herself, that's different. But not someone who would ask me questions when I don't even want to think about the answers.

So once again I left without telling Mum just how seriously ill Sonia is, and heaved a sigh of relief as I drove away. I was feeling very guilty on all sorts of levels, though, which is probably what Mum intends. But she's got a point. What sort of a daughter am I, that I actually look on going to see her as a duty, and can't wait to escape? She's done so much for me, devoted her life to me really, and now she needs me, I can't find it in myself to be gracious about it. But I only have so much to give, and right now my priority is Sonia and my grandchildren.

It's a funny thing, but Mum seems to have very little interest in them. Because she has no emotional hold over them, I suspect. She used to make a fuss of Sonia when she was little, but when she got to her teens and went through the stroppy rebel phase, Mum lost patience with her and somehow never really got over it. Sometimes I wonder if her antagonism springs from a form of jealousy, if she feels somehow subconsciously that Sonia has taken me away from her. Bizarre, I know, but possessive as she is of me, it could be just that. Certainly she's always been very off with Rod, though he's always done his best to be a good son-in-law. As for Harry and Abigail, it's almost as if they don't exist, which is sad, really, considering they are her great-grandchildren.

Anyway, I really can't keep on beating myself up about it. I've got too much else to worry about. And I can't afford to crack up. That wouldn't do anyone any good.

At least Sonia being a little better the last few days has given me the chance to catch up on some of my work for the model agency. I've been able to deal with mail and e-mails and phone calls and I even got into the office for a couple of hours. The arrangements for the fashion show at the college of art are well in hand – Elaine has been playing a blinder – and basically all I've had to do is tick boxes on the checklist and make a few calls regarding details Elaine didn't feel competent to deal with, or where my position could sway things in the right direction. I'm very much hoping I'll be able to be around for the whole of the week of the show, though. Kevin has arranged some holiday so that I'll be excused duty with regard to Sonia and the children, and in theory I should be able to give the show my full attention. But supposing Sonia should take a turn for the worse? How could I concentrate if she should be back in hospital, fighting for her life?

Don't even think about it. Take each hurdle as it comes.

The next one is tomorrow. Sonia is due for her appointment with the consultant. Kevin will take a day off work to go with her, of course, and I shall be on grandma duty, doing the school runs, getting the children their tea and having something ready for Sonia and Kevin when they get home. I'm half tempted to cook something special in the hope that they might have positive news. But I also feel horribly superstitious about doing anything of the kind. Better to wait – I'm sure Kevin will go out and buy a bottle of bubbly to celebrate if it's warranted. To jump the gun is to tempt fate.

But I am daring to feel just a little bit hopeful. When I'd fetched the children from school we sat out in the garden for a bit, having a cup of tea while they played on the trampoline. Sonia's still there, I can see her from the kitchen window as I get their tea – the ubiquitous pasta, tomato sauce and cocktail sausages that seem so popular with them. Harry has abandoned the trampoline now to play with his Nintendo, but Abigail is still bouncing happily. She really is a very athletic little girl – I don't know where she gets it from. Certainly not from me! When I was at school I was always the last to be picked as a tennis partner, or for the netball or rounders team.

I dish up the children's tea and call them in. By the time I've sorted them out with drinks and so on and I'm back in the kitchen, I notice Sonia is no longer sitting on the sunlounger, but don't think anything of it, assuming she's come in to use the bathroom, or maybe gone into the den to watch the early evening news on TV. When I've loaded the dishwasher with the dirty pans and there's still no sign of her, I go to look for her. She's not in the den, and I call up the stairs.

'Are you up there, Sonia? Are you all right?'

No answer. I call again. Still no reply. My antennae start to prickle. It doesn't take much these days. I'm in a state of permanent alert.

I go upstairs and find her in the little spare bedroom where the computer sits on an IKEA desk unit. She's pulled up the photographs they took at the weekend again – the one with her, Harry and Abigail at the picnic table is on the screen.

'Oh, you're up here,' I say unnecessarily. 'I was getting worried.'

I break off as she looks round at me. Her eyes are full of tears.

'Oh, Mum . . .' Her voice cracks.

'Don't, Sonia. Don't upset yourself. You had a lovely day, the four of you. And you've been so much better . . .'

'Have I?' Her voice trembles. 'I don't think so. Not really.'

'You have! Look at you, enjoying your ice cream. Cuddling Abigail . . .'

'It's just a blip, Mum. It's happened before. I've got bloody leukaemia and it's not going to go away just like that.'

'You don't know that. The treatment . . .'

She shakes her head.

'It's not working. I know damn well what they're going to tell me tomorrow.'

'You don't. You can't!'

'I do. I'm getting to know my own body rather well.' She sniffs, runs her fingers across her face, wiping away the moistness on her cheeks and under her nose, then nods at the screen.

'Do you honestly think that I'll be there for the children this time next year, buying them ice creams, watching them enjoy a day out? Because I have to tell you, I don't, and it makes me so angry! What have they done to deserve this?'

There's a hard little edge in her voice now. Perhaps that's good. Perhaps it means she's gathering the will to fight again.

Abigail is calling from downstairs. They've finished their pasta – what is there for pudding?

'Go on, Mum, go and sort them out. I'm fine,' Sonia says.

'Sure?'

'Yes. Go on.'

I sigh. There's really nothing else I can say, nothing I can do. Except look after her children, smooth the path for all of them as much as possible. And pray that Sonia is wrong, and the tests tomorrow will show she's in remission.

TWENTY-TWO

MARTHA

I'm at The Channings with the girls – Penny Brooks, Delia Thorn and Sam Smith – for one of our regular nights out. It's unusual for all of us to be able to make it, since Penny and Delia are both serving police officers – Sam handed in her warrant card a couple of years ago and now works as an estate agent. We've been going to The Channings for years – it's good and central for all of us, it's got a nice atmosphere and a garden. Tonight it's nice enough to make use of the garden; we're on our second drink, having a laugh and a good old gossip.

It's just what I needed after a bit of a stressful day. I went to Little Compton this morning as promised, and Lucy's right, Granny didn't seem at all herself. When I told her about the holiday I've booked, she smiled and said: 'That's nice,' but she seemed preoccupied, as if her mind was elsewhere. Very odd. Though she hasn't been able to converse easily since she had her stroke, she's remained very alert, listening to everything that's said, her good eye as bright as a button.

Not today. Mostly she seemed to be in a world of her own. The only time she perked up was when I mentioned my visit to Miss Leverton.

'I went to see the lady who claimed the box I found in Bolborough Lake,' I said.

'No!' Lucy was all ears suddenly, the salad spinner stopping mid-revolution as she dropped the cord and looked at me, open-mouthed. 'Why did you go to see her?'

'She asked me to. For some reason I can't quite fathom, she wants to tell me her story.'

'How exciting! You've been talking to a heroine!'

'I talk to heroes and heroines every day,' I said drily.

'But a real one!'

'You don't think it's heroic, then, facing down a gang of yobs with knives in their pockets, or being the ones inside the tape when there's a bomb scare? The ones who go towards an incident when everyone else is getting the hell away?'

'Oh Martha, you know what I mean. She won the Croix de Guerre! That must mean she did something really special. You can't compare it.'

'No, I don't suppose *you* can. I can't see you going into a house where there might be an intruder, all on your own in the middle of the night, or manning a roadblock when there's an armed and dangerous criminal on the loose.'

Out of the corner of my eye I could see Granny looking distressed, and kicked myself for letting Lucy rile me. I know Granny hates it when Lucy and I argue. I hate it when Lucy and I argue – I just can't seem to stop myself, and I expect Lucy feels the same.

'Anyway,' I said, trying to get the conversation back on an even keel, 'you're right, the Croix de Guerre is something special. That's why I agreed to go and see her. And what she did *was* pretty amazing. She was in the SOE – an undercover agent in occupied France. And one of the very few who came back alive.'

'Go on.'

'I'm not sure I'm supposed to. She's quite cagey about it all. She doesn't want it splashed all over the papers.'

'Oh, right. Granny and I are likely to do that, are we?' Lucy was steaming up a bit again, but this time I made an effort not to retaliate.

'No, of course not. It's a long story, though. I was there the best part of two hours and we're still only halfway – to the point where she came back to England after her first stint in France. I'm going back on Friday so that she can tell me the rest.'

'Did you find out how the medal and the other things came to be in the lake?' Lucy asked, tipping the salad leaves out of the spinner into a bowl.

'No, not yet, though she did say they weren't stolen. And I did wonder . . . Apparently she was engaged to one of the Woodhouse family. Did you know them, Granny? You must have done. They were still there when we were children, weren't they?'

'Yes, they were,' Lucy said. 'They had a great big grey car, didn't they? You couldn't miss it in the village. He was a sir, wasn't he? Sir . . . oh, what was his name?'

'Hugh,' Granny said.

'That's it. Sir Hugh. He used to wear a tweed suit and he had a huge stomach with a watch chain stretched across it.'

'I don't remember that.'

'I was older than you. It was probably just about my eye level.'

'Did you know him, Granny?' I asked.

'Well, I knew him, of course,' Granny said, 'but not very well.'

'And do you remember a fiancée? Not the one he married, obviously.'

'Lady Julia,' Lucy said with a burst of inspiration.

'Not her. Miss Leverton. Stella.'

'I don't think . . .' Granny was faltering a bit now. It happens sometimes, a burst of coherent language followed by a sudden barrier.

'Anyway, I don't think Sir Hugh is a likely candidate for Paul,' I said.

'Paul?' Lucy asked, cutting open a vacuum pack of smoked mackerel.

'Miss Leverton's circuit leader in France. Who she was in love with, by the sound of it. From what she said, I don't think he would be the type to have a watch chain straining over a big belly, even if he was twenty or thirty years older than when she knew him.'

Granny is smiling now, in spite of having lost the power of speech temporarily. Remembering a slightly farcical character, perhaps, who thought he owned half the district – and probably did, at one time.

We chatted a bit more about Miss Leverton, but I was still careful about what I said. Though, as Lucy pointed out, neither she nor Granny was likely to run to the press, I was still mindful that Miss

Leverton had talked to me in confidence. Lucy might be tempted to pass titbits on to her friends and neighbours. There was, after all, a local connection.

Then we got on to other subjects, and Miss Leverton and the mystery of the box in the lake was forgotten.

When I left, Lucy came out to the car with me.

'You see what I mean about Granny? She's in a dream, isn't she?'

'She is a bit,' I agreed. 'She perked up when we were talking about Bolborough, though. Maybe she's more interested in the past than the present. That happens with old people, doesn't it?'

'I suppose. But still . . . I am worried about her, Martha.'

'I hope she's going to be OK for this holiday. Do you think it's going to be too much for her?' I asked anxiously.

'I don't know. We're going to have to play it by ear.'

'I've got it booked now.'

'If she's not up to it, you'll just have to cancel.'

But Lucy looked stressed again. She was banking on it, I know. As much a holiday for her as for Granny.

I was beginning to feel a bit wound up myself, and things didn't improve.

The traffic on the way home was horrendous. No particular hold-ups that I could see, like an accident or roadworks, just sheer volume. It was stop-start all the way. I called into the supermarket to pick up a few essentials and got stuck in a queue where there was some problem on the till. Then when I drove into the parking lot at the rear of my flat, I found that somebody had pinched my space. And when I picked up my mail from the communal letter rack in the hall, my credit card statement was amongst it – a horribly big one, because I had to do the tax and insurance on my car last month, and I splashed out on a new throw and cushions for my rather ancient sofa.

All in all, not the most relaxed of days off. Which is why I was ready for a drink with the girls. We're an irreverent bunch, and we've known one another for long enough to be totally comfortable in each other's company. Which is why I'm beginning to unwind at last. Until . . .

'There's a bloke over there who keeps staring at you,' Sam says.
'Over where?'

'By the steps.' The steps are behind me. 'No – don't turn round. I'll tell you when he's not looking . . . OK – now!'

I swivel surreptitiously, groan, turn back quickly. 'Oh no!'

'D'you know him, then? Who is it?'

'A reporter called Pete Holbrook. What the hell is *he* doing here? I can't seem to get away from him.'

'Do you really want to?' That's Penny, who's facing the same way as Sam. 'He's a bit of all right, if you ask me.'

'Looks can be deceptive.'

'Well if you don't fancy him, you can push him in my direction any time you like,' Penny says.

She's having a cocktail; she puts the straw to her lips, sucking slowly and seductively, and I guess he's looking in our direction again and the pantomime is for his benefit.

'I think he's coming over,' Sam says. Then: 'Oh no, he's not. He's changed his mind. But he's definitely got his eye on you, MJ.'

'Not for the reason you're thinking. He's after a story,' I say grimly.

Penny sighs wistfully.

'I could tell him a story or two.'

'Yes, a bedtime story, I suppose,' Delia says. 'Leave him alone, Penny. He's MJ's. She saw him first.'

'He is not mine!' I snap.

'You're blushing, MJ.'

'I am not blushing!'

'Oh yes you are. There's something going on here . . .'

'Give it a rest, do!'

But for some unknown reason, I actually feel quite pleased. And I don't think it's only because it's nice to put one over on Penny, who has a reputation as a bit of a man-eater.

'More drinks, girls?' Penny swirls her empty glass.

'Yes, but you're not having another cocktail unless you put some more money in the kitty,' Delia says. 'They're twice as expensive as what we're having.'

'Don't worry, I'll buy my own.' Penny is pushing her chair back.

'Only so you can get to walk past MJ's man. Sit down. Let MJ go.'

'Look, he is not my man, and I don't want—'

'He's gone now anyway,' Sam reports. 'And it is your turn, MJ.'

'Oh, OK.' I scoop up the remains of the kitty. 'What are you all having? Same again?'

'Why don't we have a bottle of wine between us? It works out cheaper that way.' Delia.

'Don't you ever think about anything but money?' Penny.

'Don't *you* ever think about anything but sex?'

'Not if I can help it. Are you sure you don't want a hand, MJ?'

'Quite sure, thank you.'

I walk across the lawn. There is no sign of Pete Holbrook now. But as I enter the bar, there he is.

'Are you following me?' I ask rudely.

He grins. 'Would I do that?'

'Yes, you would, and it's getting on my nerves. You don't usually come to The Channings. Why are you here tonight?'

'Because I thought *you* would be. You turned me down because you said you were going for a drink with the girls. So I thought—'

'And how did you know we'd be here?'

Pete Holbrook taps the side of his nose, still grinning infuriatingly.

'I'm a newshound, remember. It's my business to know these things. And I thought you'd like to know what I've found out about our Miss Leverton.'

'I've been wondering how long it would be before her name came into the conversation. Look – can't you find someone else to pester? I have to order drinks for my friends.'

'So order them, and then let me buy you one.'

'No! And if you don't leave me alone, I'll arrest you.'

'Promises, promises . . .'

'I mean it.'

'OK, I give in. But I'm warning you, there are some very black clouds coming up. Or there were, before it got too dark to see. Let me buy you a drink, and I'll drive you home. Save you from a soaking.'

'It's not going to rain.'

'Want to bet?'

'And how do you know I haven't got my car, anyway?'

'You've had too much to drink. And you always walk to the Channings.'

I'm about to ask how he knows that that, but I don't. I'll only get the same answer as before – that it's his business to know these things.

In any case, Penny is in the doorway.

'What's taking you so long? Oh, hello . . .' She's giving Pete a long, smouldering look. 'Aren't you going to introduce me to your friend, MJ?'

'No,' I say, and suddenly I really, *really* want to take the wind out of Penny's very sexy sails.

I look at Pete.

'Perhaps I will take you up on your offer after all.'

I pass a flabbergasted Penny the float money.

'You get the drinks in, Pen. For the rest of the evening, I'm otherwise engaged.'

'She's a bit of a one, your friend,' Pete Holbrook says.

We've settled at a corner table, and he's bought me a large glass of wine and a lemonade and lime for himself – since he's offered to drive a police officer home, I guess he's decided he'd better go easy on the alcohol. I don't know what he's had already, of course, but I don't much care. I am off-duty, and he seems comfortingly sober.

'That's not very nice,' I say, reference his remark about Penny.

He smiles, takes a long pull of his lemonade and lime.

'So – did you decide to take me up on my offer to talk about Miss Leverton, or because you find me irresistible after all?'

'I should think the answer to that is pretty obvious,' I say, although I'm not at all sure he hasn't hit the nail on the head. 'Except that I'm not the one going to talk about Miss Leverton – you are. You said you'd found something out about her.'

'Just a few bits and pieces. The internet is a wonderful thing.'

I mentally kick myself. Why didn't I think of that? But I'm not one of those people who spend hours surfing. I don't have the time or, to be honest, the inclination.

'Go on then.'

'Well, for starters, I found her on a website about SOE agents. She was in France, it seems, from 1942 until 1944.'

Tell me something I don't know . . .

'Sounds about right.'

'She's told you about it?'

'Come on, you're the one doing the talking.'

'She was awarded the Croix de Guerre for her activities in the field. After the war she worked for the Foreign Office in London, and later for MI5. She's never married. And that's about it, really. There was a photograph, though. A mugshot that I should imagine was taken for her identity papers at the time.'

My eyes widen.

'I'd like to see that. What was the website? I'll look it up when I get home.'

'No need. I printed off a copy for you.'

He pulls out his wallet, extracts a sheet of white copier paper folded in quarters and hands it to me. I unfold it. The picture is a bit grainy, but it shows a young, fresh-faced girl. Though it must have been taken nearly sixty years ago, it's possible to recognise the same woman who served me tea and cucumber sandwiches, but it's rather sobering, all the same, to see the damage the years have wrought. It makes mortality horribly real, somehow.

'There's a photograph hanging in her hall,' I say. 'Three girls.'

'I know. I saw it.'

I should have known he would have. It's the sort of thing any journalist worth his salt would mention. But somehow there's something about the way he says it, something in his tone, in the way his eyes avoid mine, that arouses my suspicion – about what? I don't know, only that my policewoman's instinct is telling me there's something he's not saying.

'What?' I ask directly.

'What do you mean?'

'You're keeping something back. About the photograph.'

'Why would I do that?'

'You tell me.'

He grins suddenly. 'I'm glad I'm not a criminal. You've got a good nose, Sergeant. It's nothing, really, it's just that I had the feeling I'd seen that picture somewhere before.'

'But you don't know where.'

'I don't, no. And that is the truth.'

This time I believe him.

'If I'm right – and I might not be – it will probably come to me, though,' he says. 'When I'm not thinking about it.'

'And if it does, will you share it with me?'

'Depends. On how much you share with me.'

Those bedroom eyes are holding mine, and I'm glad it's quite dim in here, and that the girls aren't here to see, because I have a horrible feeling that this time I really am blushing.

How bloody ridiculous! I don't blush! Plenty of men have said far more suggestive things to me, some downright crude, it has to be said, and it's never fazed me at all. Certainly not made me blush. This has got far more to do with me than it has with Pete Holbrook. My own thoughts, not his.

I remember how it occurred to me that the reason I get so prickly with Pete Holbrook is that I actually fancy him a little too much and don't want to admit it. Right now it feels as if I might have hit upon the truth, and that is definitely disconcerting.

I drain my glass.

'I really ought to be going.'

'Why?'

I don't really know why. And I don't actually want to go anyway. 'Have another drink.'

'I've had too much already. I've got to go to work tomorrow.'

'One more won't make much difference. Or have one of these.' He taps his lemonade-and-lime glass.

I shake my head. A long drink like that, and I'll be up and down all night.

'Oh go on, I'll have another glass of wine. Just the one, though, and then I really am going.'

245

Whilst he's at the bar fetching the drinks, the girls come through.

'We're going for a pizza, MJ.' Sam.

'OK.'

'You're not coming with us?' Delia.

'Think I'll give it a miss.'

'I wonder why that is?' Penny. She looks highly miffed.

Delia takes her arm, propelling her away.

'Come on, you. Let MJ have her fun.'

'Night, MJ. Behave yourself.'

'Don't do anything I wouldn't do.'

They trundle off.

Pete is back with the drinks.

'Right,' he says. 'Now we've got Miss Leverton out of the way, perhaps we can concentrate on you.'

'Me?'

'Yes. I want to know the facts before we go any further. You *are* divorced, aren't you? I'm not going to have a burly motorcycle cop roughing me up, am I?'

I hold his gaze, teasing.

'I thought it was your business to know everything.'

'Just want to check.'

I grin. 'Yes. I am divorced. How about you?'

'The same. Where did we go wrong?'

'Perhaps,' I say, 'we married the wrong people.'

'Perhaps we did. Anyway, just to set the record straight, it's not a mistake I intend to repeat.'

'Me neither. Far too much hassle.'

'Agreed.' He puts his hand up to give me a high five; I reciprocate, but instead of merely smacking my palm, his fingers close around my hand, holding it fast. For a minute we sit there like two stalemated arm-wrestlers, just looking at one another in a challenging sort of way, then we both laugh and he lets me go.

'So go on, tell me about you and I'll tell you about me.'

'I honestly wouldn't know where to start.'

'Well – what sort of music do you like?'

That's fairly safe ground.

'All sorts, really. Except rap. I hate, loathe and despise rap.'

'Me too. What's your favourite film?'

I really don't know how I got here. Just a couple of hours ago I thought I hated Pete Holbrook's guts. Now here I am, sitting in a pub with him, talking about music, and films, and foreign holidays. What I do know is that I'm enjoying myself. I have a funny feeling it's not going to end there, either, and you know what? I really don't care.

I was right. It didn't end there. Where it ended was in bed. He drove me home, I asked him in for coffee and the rest just followed naturally.

It's Friday morning now. He's gone, and I'm getting ready for work feeling a bit thick-headed and hung-over, but pretty pleased with life. I haven't had a night like that for a long time, and I haven't a single regret.

Well, maybe just one.

I can't make a habit of this. Not with a newspaper reporter who probably only wants me for the titbits of juicy information he can wheedle out of me.

Pity. Never mind. Just this once, it really was worth it.

TWENTY-THREE

ANNE

The news from the hospital is not good.

I knew it the moment Sonia and Kevin got back, before they'd said a word. It was written all over them. Kevin looking grim and sort of blank, as if he'd wiped his face clean of any kind of emotion; Sonia pale – even paler than usual, because of the red weals under her eyes that I knew had come from crying. I really didn't need to ask the question, but of course, I did.

'How did it go?'

'Not too well,' Kevin said flatly, but with typical understatement.

'It's back, Mum.' Sonia's eyes were brimming again.

'Oh Sonia . . .' I felt like crying myself.

'Come on, love, come and sit down.' Kevin had his arm round Sonia, steering her towards an easy chair. And to me he said: 'All this has taken it out of her. She's exhausted.'

'Well of course.'

Kevin was rather stating the obvious, but I know how worried and upset he is. He adores Sonia, and all this is taking its toll on him too.

Sonia chose to sit on the sofa and Kevin sat down beside her, an arm round her frail shoulders.

'So,' I ventured, 'what happens now?'

'We're looking at a bone marrow transplant,' Kevin said. 'Or "stem cell," as the consultant calls it.'

'If we can find a match,' Sonia added. 'And there's not much chance of that, is there?'

'Don't even think such a thing!' I said fiercely. 'We'll find one, Sonia, if we have to move heaven and earth to do it.'

'If only I had a brother or sister . . . They say siblings are the best chance of a match.'

'I know.' I turned my head, unable to look at her ravaged face when I knew it was my fault that that possible lifeline had been denied her. How I wished I'd had another child! That I hadn't been so work-obsessed that the time was never right. But beating myself up about that now is a waste of time and energy. It's twenty years too late; I have to look forward, not back, and concentrate on doing everything possible to find a bone marrow match for Sonia.

'Your father and I will get tested, of course,' I said.

'Oh Mum, that is really sweet of you, but I think you might be too old. I don't think they consider bone marrow transplants if you're over sixty.'

'It wouldn't be me having the transplant, would it? If there's a risk . . . well, so be it. You're the one who matters here.'

But I had a horrible feeling she was right. I *am* too old, and so is Rod.

'There might be a match on the donor register,' Kevin said, steering the conversation away from the fact that I can be of no use to my daughter.

'Well, let's hope so.' I hesitated. 'I think I'll go and talk to your grandma, ask her about family. Your grandfather had a brother . . .'

'Did he?' Sonia asks, surprised. 'I never knew that.'

'They fell out, years ago. Something to do with money. The big bust-up happened before I was born; I don't remember ever meeting him, and his name was barely mentioned at home. Even I might never have known of his existence if he hadn't phoned one evening when I was, oh, about ten. We were having tea and when the phone rang Dad went to answer it – we had just the one in those days, a big black Bakelite thing on the table in the hall. Well, there was quite a commotion. We could hear Dad getting angry – I was quite frightened, I remember. When he came back, his face was like thunder – he had quite a temper when he was roused, your grandfather. Mum asked him what was going on, and he said it was his brother asking for money again. Well, that was more or less that. Mum and Dad didn't talk about it in front of me, though I did ask Mum about it later, and she told me what I've told you. That they'd fallen out over a family inheritance years before – the inheritance that allowed Dad to set up his business, I've always thought. "Just because your father has done well for himself, Clarence thinks he owes him a living," was what Mum said. And: "He's nothing to us. Your father doesn't want any more to do with him."'

'So I might have cousins I don't know about?' Sonia said.

'Well, they'd be my cousins, but if they've got children, grand-children . . . I know it's a long shot, but they are family. There's got to be a better chance of a match, surely, than with a complete stranger?'

'They mightn't be interested in helping if there was so much bad blood between the brothers,' Kevin said.

'No, that's true. They mightn't. But I've got to try, at least. I haven't a clue who they are or where they live, but I'll go and see your grandma and find out what she knows about them. I need to talk to her anyway.'

'About me.'

I nod.

'You haven't told her yet, then?'

'No, but I can't leave it any longer. Especially if I'm going to try to find some long-lost relatives who might just be able to help.'

I went off to my room then on the pretext of doing some work. In fact I thought Sonia and Kevin needed some time alone together to come to terms with the latest developments. As I went up the stairs I could hear their voices, intimate and low, and knew I'd done the right thing. Anxious as I am to be involved in every aspect of what is happening to Sonia, I have to remember that Kevin is her husband, and there are times when a mother needs to take a step back.

He and I did have a heart-to heart, though, after Sonia had gone to bed.

'This is doing my head in, Anne,' he said. 'I don't know what the hell to do for the best.'

'You're doing all you can do,' I said.

'It's not enough, though, is it?' He slammed his hand down hard on to the arm of the chair and left it there, curled into a fist. His face was a mask of agony. 'I don't know what I'd do if . . . She's my life, Anne.'

'I know.' My heart went out to him. I covered his hand with mine. 'We'll get there, Kevin. We will!'

The defeated slope of his shoulders – a defeat he never allowed to show in front of Sonia – told me that however optimistic we might try to appear, in fact both of us were fighting the same demons of doubt.

I had a pretty sleepless night, and this morning, as soon as I'd taken the children to school, I rang Mum and asked if she'd be there around eleven. She was quite sharp, as she so often is.

'Well of course I'll be here! Where else would I be?'

'You could have been going out. I just wanted to make sure before I came all the way over.'

She didn't ask me then why I wanted to see her – she was too surprised, I suppose – but when I arrive, it's her first question.

'What's this in aid of, then?'

'I wanted to talk to you.'

'What's so important that you make the time to come and see me twice in one week? I thought you were busy with Sonia.' She manages to make it sound like an accusation, which I suppose it is. I bite my tongue.

'It's about Sonia. Look, shall we have a cup of tea?'

'I didn't think you liked tea.'

'I don't much. But I don't suppose you've got coffee.'

'Of course I've got coffee! Not the stuff you have, but there's a jar of Nescafé in the cupboard.'

'I'll have a coffee, then.'

What I really feel like is a gin and tonic, but I know Mum won't have gin in the house, and in any case it's a bit early in the day to begin on the hard stuff.

She boils the kettle, makes a cup of tea for herself and a coffee for me. We take it into the sitting room.

'You see?' Mum says, pointing to a barely visible spot on the coffee table. 'Look at that! Thelma is supposed to have polished in here. I've got some special stuff to get out marks like that, but will she use it? She says it's dried up, and she can't get the top off. Excuses, excuses.'

'Sonia,' I say. 'I wanted to talk to you about Sonia.'

'Oh yes, Sonia. Well, go on then. What's she been up to?'

I settle my coffee cup on a coaster, sit forward in the rather low armchair.

'You know I've told you Sonia is ill.'

'So you keep saying. What's the matter with her? I never seem to get to hear the details.'

'That's what I'm here to tell you now, but it's not easy. She really is very ill.' I pause, waiting for that to sink in before I go on. 'Mum, I haven't told you before because I didn't want to worry you unnecessarily, but Sonia has leukaemia. She's had a month-long course of chemotherapy, and we were hoping that might work. But it hasn't.'

To give her her due, Mum looks very shocked. For a few moments she doesn't say anything, just sits digesting what I've told her. I can see a muscle working at the corner of her mouth, and she's scratching at a patch on her lower arm where she gets eczema when her nerves are bad.

'You should have told me,' she says eventually.

'Like I said, I didn't want to worry you.'

She snorts. 'Because I'm old, I suppose. Sonia's my granddaughter, Anne. I don't like being kept in the dark.'

'I'm sorry. I thought it was for the best.'

'Oh well, you've told me now. That's something, I suppose. How long have you known? How did all this start?'

I tell her the details and explain Sonia's treatment so far and her need now for a bone marrow transplant. Mum listens, her fingernails still worrying at the inflamed patch on her arm.

'There was a boy in your class at school had leukaemia,' she says when I've finished.

'It was the brother of a boy in my class,' I correct her.

'He was – what? – about seven? I remember his mother pushing him round in a pushchair.' The muscle works again at the corner of her mouth, making her lower lip tremble. 'He died.'

'I know.'

'But that was sixty years ago. They can do things now that they couldn't do then. This . . . bone marrow transplant. That will put her right?'

'We can't be sure. There are no guarantees. And we have to find a donor. They can't use just any stem cells. They have to be a match. The best chance of that is from a sibling, but of course Sonia doesn't have one. So we're going to have to look further afield, and I was wondering . . . Dad had family, didn't he? A brother?'

'Clarence, you mean?' Mum says in a disbelieving tone. 'He'll be dead and gone long ago.'

'But did he have children? Grandchildren?'

'How in the world would I know? He and your father never had anything to do with one another.'

'Where did he live?'

'Swindon way, I think. But why do you want to know? You're not going to . . . ?'

'I'm going to try and track his family down, yes.'

'You can't do that!' Mum looks horrified. 'Your father would turn in his grave!'

'Mum,' I say, trying to contain my impatience, 'Sonia's life is at stake here. I don't know if I'll be able to find them, or if they'll be willing to help, or if they'll be a match. But I've got to try. I can't just sit back and do nothing.'

Mum is shaking her head vigorously, that rapid, jerky movement that's become more accentuated over the years.

'It wouldn't do any good.'

'Nevertheless, I have to try. The Swindon area, you say?'

'Why don't you ever listen to me, Anne? I might as well talk to the wall.'

'Oh don't be so silly. Look, I really can't be doing with this. Sonia could be dying and I'm going to do everything I can to make sure she doesn't.'

Mum shakes her head again. 'Looking for Clarence's family is a waste of time, I tell you. It won't do any good.'

There's no point in arguing with her any more. She is becoming very distressed, and annoyed and frustrated though I am with her lack of co-operation, I don't want to leave her like this. It will be just another thing to worry me. Anyway, I think she has told me all she knows. I'll just have to hope that I can find the family from the electoral rolls in the Swindon area.

'Your tea's gone cold,' I say. 'Do you want me to make you another cup?'

I half expect her to snap that she's perfectly capable of making it herself. But she doesn't. Instead, she nods. As I go out to the kitchen, she remains sitting in her chair, staring into space and scratching convulsively at the sore patch on her arm.

I've been back at Sonia's for an hour or so when the phone rings. I answer it; it's Mum.

'You got back there then.'

It's something of an improvement that she's finally clocked I'm at Sonia's, I think, a bit irritably. I assume she's feeling guilty about her negative reaction to my suggestion of contacting Dad's brother's family; though we parted on reasonably good terms, things were still a bit tense.

'I need to speak to you, Anne,' she says.

'I'm listening,' I say, though I could do without a long conversation just now; I have so much else I should be doing and I really don't think she has anything constructive to tell me.

'No. Not over the phone. It needs to be face to face.'

My heart sinks. 'Mum, I really don't think—'

She interrupts me, sounding agitated.

'No, Anne, I'm not saying any more. But it is important. For Sonia. Come when you can.'

And she hangs up. Unheard of for my mother. She usually keeps a conversation going as long as humanly possible.

I sit picking at a hangnail that's been annoying me for days.

Important for Sonia.

Does Mum know more about Dad's family than she let on, and has she changed her mind about filling me in? Or perhaps there's some other estranged relative I don't know about. But what can it be that she doesn't want to tell me over the phone? Or is that just an excuse to get me to go and see her again? Somehow I don't think so. Not this time.

Well, there's only one way to find out. I'm going to have to do as she asked and drive over again. Kevin will just have to cover for me here, and he will, I'm sure. After all, he is just as anxious to find a way of helping Sonia as I am.

For the first time since we got the bad news from the hospital, I feel a small spurt of optimism. Maybe whatever it is Mum has to tell me will be the first step in finding a cure for Sonia.

TWENTY-FOUR

MARTHA

I pull into the car park outside Miss Leverton's residential development. I'm in a really cheerful mood, looking forward to seeing her and pretty pleased with life in general.

Though I'd made up my mind not to get involved with Pete Holbrook, my good intentions went by the board. We've seen quite a bit of one another over the past few days, and I have to say I've enjoyed it.

He called me the very next evening.

'So when am I going to see you again?'

'What makes you think you are?'

'Oh Martha, I thought we'd got past all that negative stuff. I thought we got on pretty well once you stopped insulting me.'

'Hmm.' I was going a bit weak inside at the memory of just how well we'd got on, but I wasn't about to say so.

'Anyway,' he went on, there are some really good films on at the moment. I thought you might like to see one of them. Or we could go for a nice meal. Or clubbing. The choice is yours.'

'Definitely not clubbing! I grew out of that years ago.'

'I favour a nice meal myself.'

I thought for all of ten seconds. Of the miserable array of mouldering food in my fridge. Of having to cook it and clear it away myself. Of Pete's hot lips and athletic body. Of how much I'd enjoyed it. Of how, in spite of myself, I wanted to see him again.

'OK. I'm on for a meal. As long as you let me pay my way.'

256

'We'll argue about that later. I'll pick you up, shall I? Say half an hour?'

I had a quick shower, actually put on some make-up – well, lippy and mascara and a dollop of bronzer on my cheeks and chin. We went to an Italian, where I had seafood linguine and Pete had pizza, and I lost the argument about paying my share of the bill. I must admit, with that horrendous credit card bill hanging over me, I wasn't overly insistent. And then he came home with me and we had another night of passion.

A good result, taken all round. Which we've repeated, twice more. And my opinion of Pete Holbrook has changed considerably. Far from avoiding him, I can't wait to be with him again. Can't stop thinking about him either. I'm thinking about him now, and feeling spirals of excitement twist inside me. What a difference a week makes!

I ring the bell on the entryphone; Miss Leverton buzzes me in. She's left the door of her flat ajar; when I tap on it, she calls for me to come in as if I were an old friend.

I don't have time to look at the photograph of the three girls in the hall, though. She's ushering me into her living room.

This evening, instead of the sandwiches and fancy cakes, there are dishes of nibbly bits, glasses and a bottle of wine in a cooler.

'I hope you like Chablis,' she says.

'My favourite.' Which is the truth. Not that I buy it very often. It's too expensive. I usually go for whatever is on special offer at the supermarket or off-licence – Pinot Grigio if I can get it, or Sauvignon Blanc.

We make a little small talk. She's very interested in my job, but fortunately doesn't ask what I've been doing in my spare time. I wouldn't want to be forced into admitting I've been seeing Pete Holbrook. She also asks after my grandmother, which surprises me, since I only mentioned her in passing. Solidarity of the older generation, I suppose.

'She's fine,' I say, which I'm pretty sure is the extent of what she'll want to know.

She's poured me a glass of Chablis, which I'm trying to drink slowly – Chablis is far too special to down as if it were tap water – and she pushes a dish of olives towards me.

'Do help yourself.' She's sipping a glass of Chablis too. 'Well – are you ready for the second instalment?'

'I can't wait,' I say, and it's no more than the truth.

'Very well.' She takes another sip of wine and settles herself more comfortably. 'Here we go then. France – 1944.'

Part Four

TWENTY-FIVE

PASCALE'S STORY

At long last it looked as if the tide was beginning to turn. On June 4th 1944, Rome was liberated; a few days later, the long-awaited and meticulously planned D-Day landings took Allied troops on to French soil, and slowly but surely the German army was being pushed back from the coast by a tidal wave of men and fighting machinery.

The Germans, though, were far from finished. Their flying bombs, the 'doodlebugs', were devastating London, and in France a terrible price was being paid for the continued resistance – whole villages razed to the ground, cattle slaughtered and crops burned, and the menfolk lined up and shot. But nothing could destroy the spirit of the people. With each new atrocity, more and more ordinary folk joined the ranks of the underground army, no longer willing to lie down quietly under the German jackboot, and ready and willing to help anyone who was helping them, even if it meant torture and execution.

In the remote mountain regions, the ranks of the Maquis swelled into thousands, men who lived in hidden camps, run on military lines, surviving on food that was delivered to them by the villagers, whilst they carried out acts of sabotage that brought the wrath of the enemy down on their heads – blowing up railway lines, creating landslides of boulders to block roads, ambushing convoys and looting everything from sugar and tea to ammunition. They were also in training for the battle that lay ahead.

261

Some of these secret armies were well ordered and run. Some were lawless and undisciplined, with no thought for the consequences of their impetuous actions. All needed supplies, communication and direction.

One man was responsible for co-ordinating resistance over hundreds of square miles of wild and almost inaccessible terrain.

That man was Paul.

In the spring of 1943, Paul had been called to London to confer with the chiefs of the SOE. The previous November the Germans and Italians had occupied what had been the Free Zone, and Paul imagined the interview had been arranged because the powers-that-be wanted him to report on how it had affected his operations.

To his surprise, however, it was far more than that.

'We need a good man we can trust to co-ordinate all the resistance in the southeast,' Major Dickens told him. 'It's a massive job, covering the whole area from your present territory to the Swiss and Italian borders, but it's a vital one. The Maquis need money and supplies, and we need to establish overall control if the operation is to be successful. At the moment it's far too fragmented and undisciplined. What's required is someone with experience in the field who not only understands the set-up but can command the respect of these groups. Your name came up.'

At the outset, Paul had not been enthusiastic, but the major was very persuasive.

'Your network is one of our most successful. Surely with everything in place you could hand over command to one of your lieutenants?'

'I suppose I could, yes,' Paul said reluctantly. He felt highly proprietorial about his network.

'And if they still reported to you, we'd have an unbroken chain from coast to coast.'

'There is that.'

'I can't force you into this, Paul.' The major tapped the stem of his pipe against his teeth. 'But I'm convinced you're the man for the job. You have all the right qualities. It's not going to be easy – in fact, it's going to be damned difficult. The Maquis can be awkward as well as unpredictable, and our own people in the area might well resent having to answer to you. But I think I'm right in believing you like a challenge.'

Paul smiled wryly. 'And I'd be right in believing you know all the right buttons to push.'

The major sat back in his chair, looking directly at Paul.

'You'll do it, then?'

'I'll need to go back to Charente, sort things out there. It shouldn't take me too long – a week or so at most. I'll need new papers and a new cover story.'

'It's all in hand.'

'You were fairly sure I'd agree, then.'

The major smiled. 'I had no doubts at all. Knowing you, and knowing how things have changed there in the last few months.'

'Yes,' Paul said grimly. 'I'm afraid they have rather.'

It was an understatement. Since the Germans had taken control of Vichy France, the old, easy-going relationship between the enemy forces and the collaborators – or, in the case of the de Savignys, those who pretended to collaborate – had gone for good. Buhler, with his taste for cognac and the company of the local aristocracy, had been replaced by a hard and ruthless officer who had thrown the de Savignys out of the château and commandeered it for his staff HQ.

The new regime had made it impossible for Paul to continue with the fiction that had provided his cover. He kept on the move now around his area, never staying more than a few nights in the same place. Already he was a nomad – he might as well be a nomad in Savoy, Provence and the Languedoc, he reasoned. And, truth to tell, he was beginning to be excited by the prospect of getting to grips with the massive task that was being entrusted to him.

Major Dickens fished the ever-present half-bottle of brandy out of his desk drawer and set it down amid the paperwork on his desk.

'Not de Savigny cognac, I'm afraid, old boy, but good enough. Let's drink a toast to your new undertaking.'

* * *

263

Back in France, Paul had set about organising his new venture with the same meticulous planning he had used so successfully on the Avocet circuit. It was, after all, he reasoned, the same thing but on a much larger scale, and the very size of the area he had to cover made the security of each individual cell all the more vital. He took his time in selecting the right people to forge the links of the chain, watching them sometimes for weeks on end before approaching them in order to be sure they were trustworthy, and insisting that no one else should be brought in until they had in turn been watched. He spread his net wide, from local gentry to craftsmen, small farmers and shepherds, from policemen to poachers and petty criminals. He studied the geography and geology of the area. He established relationships with SOE officers in neighbouring areas. Eventually he had hundreds of men and women working for him, including an ex-army officer who trained the troops in sabotage.

At Paul's request, HQ had sent him a fully trained wireless operator and a courier. He'd specifically asked for a woman. His head told him this was because he'd been so impressed by Pascale's capability, his heart that he wanted it to be her. She would be working well away from the area where she'd run into the German soldier she knew; the chances of them once again being in the same place at the same time were minimal. But it wasn't Pascale; it was a girl whose code name was Maxine, and he soon discovered that she didn't measure up to Pascale in any way. She was short, thickset and frankly ugly; there was no way he was going to end up in bed with her, he observed wryly. But she also lacked Pascale's qualities as an agent. She seemed to resent taking orders from him – something he wasn't used to – and she lacked Pascale's intuition. These faults put together made her dangerous, he thought. On one occasion she only just escaped arrest because she continued to visit a patisserie that Paul had warned her wasn't, in his opinion, as secure as it might have been – she had been in the kitchen with the baker's wife when the SS arrived at the front door, and had managed to slip out by the rear entrance whilst the baker himself was being arrested. Then she was targeted by a German officer Paul was certain was Abwehr – the German secret service. He managed to convince her he was devoutly anti-Nazi and wanted to help the British in exchange for a passage to England. Completely taken in, Maxine argued strongly that it would be a marvellous coup for the SOE, especially as the man had said there were others amongst his fellow officers who were anxious to defect. Paul was adamant that there would be no deal and no further contact, but Maxine's sour face and insubordinate mutterings worried him. He wouldn't put it past her to disobey his orders and try to reel in the German by herself.

He felt nothing but relief, therefore, when, in the early part of December, she fell on a rocky mountain path in the Drôme whilst carrying a message to one of the groups of Maquis and broke her leg. The inconvenience of getting her out and of being without a courier was as nothing compared to the risk he felt she posed both to herself and the whole of the organisation.

In January, Paul went to London for consultations about the progress of his operation and also to lay down some ground rules about Maxine's replacement. He didn't want another disaster foisted on him, and hoped that HQ staff were not becoming so desperate for bilingual agents that they were relaxing their previously high standards.

'What I'm looking for is another Pascale,' he said when he'd outlined the problems he'd experienced with Maxine.

Major Dickens's gaze levelled with his.

'*Another* Pascale?'

Paul cottoned on to the major's implicit suggestion.

'Is she available, then?'

'She could be.' The major deliberated. 'She's a good agent, isn't she?'

'The best.'

'And wasted on what she's doing at the moment. Would you be prepared to take a chance on her running into this German soldier again?'

'I think it's highly unlikely.' Paul considered, weighing all that was good about Pascale against the disadvantages, which, in the main, were about his feelings for her. He couldn't afford emotional involvement. But surely he should be able to keep that under control in the best interests of his operation? What was most needed now was a courier he could trust implicitly. Both to carry out his orders, and to work, where necessary, on her own initiative.

'There's nobody I'd rather have than Pascale,' he said.

The major smiled. 'Very well. I'll see what we can do.'

Since her return from France, Pascale had become increasingly frustrated.

In the beginning, she'd been seconded to the training camps, helping to teach new recruits the skills she had learned herself, and pass on the benefit of her experience in the field. Then she'd been given short assignments, accompanying an agent whose French accent was not as perfect as it might have been until she could leave him in safe hands, temporarily taking the place in one of the networks around Paris of a courier who was ill.

There she had met up with Simone, who was attached to a cell based south of Rouen.

It had been an emotional experience. Delighted as she was to see Simone again, Pascale's enormous guilt at what had occurred between her and Paul was a cloud hanging over the meeting. Simone, who had had no real contact with Paul since she had come to France, naturally wanted to talk about her fiancé. Pascale did not. Whilst Simone was anxious to hear anything Pascale could tell her about his work, his welfare, and whether he ever mentioned her, Pascale was desperate to change the subject to safer ground.

Part of her longed to confess; she couldn't bear the chasm her secret had opened up between her and Simone. But confessing, she told herself, would only make things worse. It wasn't, after all, as though she and Paul had had a proper affair. She hadn't the slightest reason to think that her feelings for him were reciprocated. He'd made love to her because it was what men did, given the chance; it would never have happened at all under different circumstances. She mustn't make trouble between Simone and Paul just because she wanted to unburden herself. And she mustn't upset Simone at a time when her life was constantly in danger – the Paris networks were notoriously hazardous. Supposing Simone lost focus and was captured? Pascale knew she would never forgive herself. Besides which . . . a confession would almost certainly mean an end to their friendship. Whilst castigating herself for such selfishness, she couldn't bear to contemplate Simone's scorn and disgust at her betrayal.

Strangely, their relationship seemed to mean even more to her now. The affection, awe and admiration she'd always felt for Simone was heightened and enhanced because she was the woman Paul loved. Whilst she remained close to Simone, it felt to Pascale as if she was still somehow in contact with a part of Paul. And though she was consumed with envy for her friend, there was no corrosive jealousy, no ill-will. How could there be when they had shared so much, including Pascale's private grief? Pascale thought of how kind Simone had been that day in the train when she had been so upset at seeing the little girl who had reminded her of Lynne, and hated herself for cheating on her with her fiancé.

But for all that it caused her enormous guilt, her passion for Paul had not lessened one iota in the months since she'd been forced to leave him in France; if anything, it had grown stronger. An uprush of tenderness and longing consumed her whenever she thought of him; she ached to be with him or simply to hear his voice. Her need for him was like a lingering sickness; she carried it with her whatever she did, wherever she went.

But it couldn't be. Paul belonged to Simone, and that was an end to it.

When Simone left to return to Rouen, Pascale wept, and her tears were for all of them.

In mid-March, Pascale was once more summoned to Major Dickens's office in London.

The stress of running an army of agents was telling on him, she thought. His hair was thinner and his moustache was now shot through with grey; there was a sharper edge to his voice than when she'd first met him and he seemed more restless, pacing the office as he spoke. But she soon forgot any personal observations when she heard what he had to say.

'You're anxious to return to the field, I believe, Pascale.'

'I'd like to, yes.'

'And we'd like you to. Have you ever been to the south-east of France? Grenoble? The Drôme? The Vercours?'

Pascale shook her head. 'No.'

'It's a very unforgiving region. Mountainous, remote, some of it virtually inaccessible. The sort of terrain that demands an agent at the peak of physical fitness as well as all the usual attributes. Do you think you could cope?'

Pascale's excitement at the prospect of being a vital part of a network again, doing a proper job, was palpable.

'I'd love to try!'

'Yes, I'm sure you would. And I think you may be pleased when I tell you who you'd be working with. You got on well, didn't you, with Paul Randall?'

'Paul?'

'He asked for you especially.'

A glow of warmth flooded through her, of absolute, unmitigated joy. It meant nothing, of course, and yet it meant everything.

'When do I go?' she asked.

'We have to wait for the right conditions, of course. We'll let you know. But perhaps you could read up on the area, and hold yourself in readiness. Paul would like you to join him as soon as possible.'

'I'll be ready whenever you want me,' Pascale said.

It was in fact more than a month before Pascale was parachuted into France. The Vercours, the area for which she was headed, was snowbound; suggestions that she should be dropped further west came to nothing for one reason or another. She allayed the frustration of waiting by studying everything she could find on the area, as the major had suggested, and by familiarising herself with some of the new gadgets – 'toys', as they called them – that the boffins had invented to assist SOE agents. There were tiny telescopes that could be hidden in a cigarette, maps printed on ricepaper and wrapped around the lead of a propelling pencil, a minute infrared torch that allowed an agent to read messages invisible to the naked eye, a compass small enough to be concealed in a cufflink.

She landed on a plateau in the Vercours, so high that for the first few days she struggled to breathe in the thin, pure air. The Maquis reception party took her to a camp deep in the forest of beech and pine, where some thirty men were living in shelters made of parachute silk and the Maquis chief occupied a cave divided in two to separate his living quarters from the 'office', where all official business was conducted. They escorted her past an unarmed sentry and a second, armed guard, whose tricolour brassard displayed the Cross of Lorraine, and showed her to the smallest tent, her temporary quarters.

Pascale shivered under the blanket the men had given her, too cold and too wound up by excitement to sleep, and hardly had she fallen into an exhausted doze than she was woken by a wailing sound that startled her into alarmed consciousness.

She staggered out of the tent, adrenalin pumping, and discovered to her relief – and disbelief – that the racket came from an accordion that was serving instead of a bugle to call reveille. It was six thirty a.m., and Pascale had had less than an hour's sleep. The cooks were already hard at work, preparing breakfast over a fire that burned clear and emitted almost no smoke – a basic precaution to keep their whereabouts hidden – and the smell of bacon made her realise just how hungry she was.

More snow had fallen in the night, and the path along which the reception party had brought her was hidden now beneath a thick carpet.

'Do you ski?' the Maquis leader asked her.

'A bit.' She'd tried it once or twice in her youth, when she'd been in France, but honesty compelled her to admit: 'Not very well.'

'Then you'll have to remain here and wait for a thaw.'

So began another period of waiting, and Pascale fumed with impatience. This time, however, she was able to pass the time instructing the maquisards in some of the demolition methods she'd learned, but never been called upon to practise.

They were a motley crew. Some had been set on resistance from the very beginning, some had joined when the Germans had begun press-ganging men and boys into going to Germany to work in the

269

munitions factories. Amongst their number were shepherds and farmhands who knew the remote district well and were proficient skiers and mountaineers. Others had come from the industrial towns, such as Grenoble. The oldest – the leader – had been a schoolmaster; the youngest, a gangly lad who claimed to be seventeen but looked much younger to Pascale, had worked on the railway. All of them wore thick clothing that made them – even the gangly lad – look bulky: a lumberjack's jacket over two or three heavy jumpers, shapeless cords and woollen balaclavas, stout boots and several pairs of thick socks.

But all of them, without exception, treated her with enormous respect, a respect, she suspected, that was accorded to her because of her connections with Paul, whom they clearly held in the highest regard.

Pascale grew used to the way of life – and even the accordion reveille! Something about the closeness to nature, perhaps, curbed her natural impatience. But she was glad, all the same, when the thaw came and the roads and tracks to the outside world became passable again. Glad that she would at last be able to start on the job she had come here to do. And glad because she would soon see Paul again.

Paul had been travelling extensively, as he seemed always to be doing these days, when the message reached him that Pascale was with the Maquis, but that their hideaway had been cut off by a heavy fall of snow. He cursed the ill-luck of it, wishing he'd arranged for her to be dropped into one of the lowland areas. But he'd been sure of the absolute loyalty of the group who'd received her, and the remote countryside had been a much safer option. There were Germans everywhere now, and parachutes floating down on a clear night were a sure-fire way to attract unwelcome attention.

Now he knew she was in France, he was impatient for her to join him. He desperately needed her help; keeping tabs on this whole enormous network alone was virtually impossible. And he acknowledged, unwillingly, that he wanted to see her simply for herself, an impulse he knew must be controlled. Though he had come to feel it had all been an enormous mistake, he was, after all, still engaged to Simone. When he pondered it, he wondered just how he had managed to end up proposing marriage to a girl he didn't love. But there it was, he had been a different person then.

More important than his personal feelings was the fact that there was a job to be done, a huge and vital undertaking that would require his undivided attention – and Pascale's. If they were both still alive when all this was over, and if they still felt the same way, then that would be the time to sort out the tangle and explore a relationship, he decided. For the moment, the only thing that mattered was mustering a force that could help consign Herr Hitler and his dreams of a Nazi-controlled Western world to the dustbin of history.

With the single-mindedness that made him a first-class agent, Paul concentrated on the job in hand and waited for the message that would tell him the roads were open once more.

When it came, he punched the air with his fist and uttered a single triumphant shout.

'Yes!'

Their reunion wasn't at all what Pascale had expected.

The maquisards escorted her down hidden tracks through thickly wooded areas and precipitous paths where ravines cut razor-sharp drops to the rushing streams and rivers far below. Fit as she was, she was exhausted by the time they reached the village where she had expected to be reunited with Paul but was, in fact, handed on like a parcel to another *passeur*, the second-in-command of the region. He took her to the outskirts of Grenoble to a safe house, the home of a doctor.

The following day, very early, Pascale was awakened by the sound of a car's engine. Instantly she was alert, aware that she was in an enemy-occupied country, and very afraid that she had been betrayed. She ran to the window, fumbling the shutters open, but could see only the roof of a black car on the street below. She dressed as quickly as she could, already thinking of escape – the doctor had shown her a door that led to his surgery, which had its own entrance, and another that opened on to the garden.

She crept down the stairs, listening for voices; heard the doctor's stentorian tones. He didn't sound agitated, but then maybe his bedside manner extended to dealing with SS!

And then she heard another voice, one she recognised instantly, and which made her heart leap not with fear, but with joy.

She ran down the stairs. He was there in the doctor's salon, thinner, older, somehow, than she remembered, as if the weight of responsibility had borne down on him. But the same smile, the smile she'd carried with her to England and back again.

'Paul,' she said, suddenly shy.

'Pascale.'

He made no move towards her, and though she was aching to throw herself into his arms, she understood. He had to appear totally professional in front of the doctor.

'So you've finally made it,' he said.

'Finally.'

'Good. I've got a lot of work for you to do.'

'Good.'

'Well, if you're ready, we'll get on our way.'

'Surely you're not in such a hurry that you can't allow the poor girl a cup of coffee, and have one yourself?' the doctor interposed.

'If there's some made.'

'It won't take a minute. It's not very good, I'm afraid . . .'

His wife, still in her dressing gown, joined them. As they drank cups of bitter coffee, Pascale wanted only to be alone with Paul.

But when they were finished, and Pascale and the tote bag she'd brought with her this time instead of the heavy and battered old suitcase were installed in the Citroën — which was cunningly marked with the logo of the Red Cross — Paul's mask of stiff professionalism was still firmly in place.

'Oh, it's so good to see you!' Pascale said, covering his hand with hers.

He removed it, shifting the gear stick into first and pulling away.

'We've got a hell of a job to do, Pascale. I think we need to concentrate on that,' was all he said.

'Yes,' she said. 'Yes, of course.'

So there was to be no joyous reunion. Well, she could live with that. Just as long as she was here with him.

She smothered her disappointment and tried to follow Paul's example by thinking only of the assignment ahead of her.

TWENTY-SIX

Through the weeks that followed, it was the same. Paul and Pascale spent a good deal of time together, travelling huge distances to set up the lines of communication that were so essential if all the far-flung cells of Maquis and *resistants* were ever to come together to form a cohesive fighting force, but Paul never wavered from that cool professionalism. A barrier had gone up between them; it was as if those stolen days when she had been waiting to be sent home from her last assignment had never been. In fact, he was more distant than he had ever been with her. She thought that perhaps he was regretting what had happened between them. But she had too much pride to raise the subject, and too much good sense.

It was better this way, she told herself. Better to be colleagues and good friends than to snatch a little physical pleasure at the expense of their commitment to the job they were doing – and at the expense of her conscience.

'I saw Simone in Paris,' she said, trying to make her tone conversational.

'Oh, did you? How is she?'

He said it in much the same way he would have if Simone had been a casual acquaintance, not at all as if she was his fiancée, and it crossed Pascale's mind to wonder if his work and experiences had caused him to completely shut down emotionally. It would tally with the way he was treating her, too, and the thought was of some comfort and encouragement to her. But Simone was still very much on her mind. It just wasn't possible to cheat on a friend and not feel dreadful guilt, and even a sense of responsibility. Though there was nothing now between her and Paul beyond the strictly professional, simply feeling as she did about him seemed like a betrayal.

'I think she's rather enjoying herself,' she said now in answer to his question. 'Living on the edge seems to suit her.'

A corner of Paul's mouth lifted. 'It would.'

'She was asking about you, of course.' She hesitated, then: 'She's very much in love with you,' she said, and immediately felt guilty again, unsure whether she was championing Simone or testing the water.

But Paul made no response whatever. He bent over the map he was studying as if he had either not heard her, or was choosing to ignore the remark.

'Now, this is the section I want to visit today,' he said, and it was back to business.

The Maquis army was growing. In the interests of security, Paul had endeavoured to keep each group self-contained, and to have no more than fifteen or twenty men on its strength. Each group had its own landing site, and Paul arranged for supplies of explosives and weapons to be dropped in, and experts to train the willing troops. One of his main objectives was to cut off all communication with Italy, and railwaymen worked to derail troop trains whilst teams of maquis-ards blew up roads and swooped down on convoys and enemy columns. Along the Route Napoleon, avalanches of rock were sent crashing down to block the road, and snipers with Sten guns on the heights above fired ruthlessly at the trapped German troops. It was heady stuff, and one of Paul's most difficult tasks was keeping control of the various groups, whose excitement was growing along with rumours that the Allied landings were imminent, or even that they had begun.

The danger that the Maquis and their supporters would become restless and overconfident worried him, and when, on June 5th, he received a signal from London that he was to put his troops at the disposal of the Free French, his disquiet grew. The rumours might be about to become reality, but victory – and the Allied armies – was a long way off. It could be months yet before his area was reached, or landings on the Riviera brought support from the south. But the Free French were as gung-ho as the Maquis. It took all Paul's powers of persuasion to keep them in line, and even then he was not always successful.

In one small town a Free French commander, backed up by a British officer who had been dropped in to one of the Gaullist reception grounds, allowed the tricolour to be flown from the town hall, which naturally incensed the Germans. Tanks and armoured cars thundered in, mowing down anyone who stood in their way, and for all Paul's efforts there simply weren't enough arms and equipment to repel them. The British officer was amongst the hundred and fifty who died that day, and Paul knew that unless he could restore calm and restraint, similar massacres would follow.

But he also knew that it was no longer entirely his responsibility. The command had passed now to the military in its various guises; his role from now on would be little more than that of a co-ordinator. Things had changed for ever. The only thing that remained the same was his determination to do his best for France.

Now, in the heat of summer, the Vercours was a very different place to the one Pascale had been dropped into. The snows had gone, sheep roamed the steep gorges, and the air was perfumed with the sweet, pungent scent of thyme. Pascale loved it, as she loved the Drôme, where the perfume was lavender and a myriad of wild flowers. Here, where ruined castles clung to rocky pinnacles, life could sometimes feel as if it were standing still. The villages were picturesque, each with a church and a marketplace where old men gathered in the cafés to drink wine and play cards and dominoes; on the farms, men still worked the land, and the only sounds that could be heard were the chirrup of the cicadas and the drone of the bees.

It was almost impossible to believe a war was raging, Pascale thought, as she and Paul drove to La Montagne, a remote village, to meet yet another Maquis leader, and yet she knew the Germans were keeping a close eye on the whole area, furious at the efficiency of the resistance and the nuisance caused by their continued sabotage.

And she knew too it was only a matter of time before they came in with their tanks and armoured vehicles and highly trained soldiers, though she tried not to think about it. The prospect was too horrible to contemplate.

The moment she was introduced to the Maquis leader – Yves – Pascale had the strangest feeling that she'd met him somewhere before, but couldn't for the life of her think where. As he and Paul talked over a glass of rough red wine in the dim interior of a village café, she kept looking at him, at the oddly familiar features, the sallow complexion and the coarse dark hair. She hadn't met him before, she was sure. How could she have? And yet . . .

It dawned on her suddenly in a flash of recognition.

Marie! He was a male version of Marie!

Though their paths hadn't crossed since they'd finished their training, Pascale was able to picture her clearly, and remembered that Marie had said her brother, at home in France, was involved with the resistance.

'Do you have a sister?' she asked.

Both Paul and Yves looked at her, surprised to be interrupted.

'Yes.' Yves' brow was furrowed. 'Why do you ask?'

'Marie.'

'Non. Her name is Véronique.'

But of course, Marie had been a training name only.

'Did she go to England to join the SOE?'

He nodded. 'Yes, she did. Two years ago. More. Why – do you know her?' His face was alive suddenly, his tone eager.

'I think so, yes,' Pascale said. 'We called her Marie – I never knew her real name. We shared a room when we were training. But it's uncanny – you look so much like her.'

Yves laughed. 'We are very alike, yes. Everyone always said we should have been twins. I can't believe it! You trained with Véronique!'

'I can't believe it either!'

'It's a miracle. I haven't seen her since she left. We hoped she might come back here to help us, but it is too dangerous, I think, for her to be in a place where she is so well known. Do you know where she is now?'

'No, I don't. I haven't seen her either.' Pascale turned to Paul. 'Do you remember Marie? We were very close, she, Simone and me. Do you know what happened to her?'

Paul shook his head. 'France is a very big place.'

'Well, yes, but . . . I'd have thought she might have been sent somewhere in this area, with her local knowledge and accent, even if it wasn't so close to her home as to be dangerous.'

'Could we please get this conversation back on track?' Paul said shortly. 'We've got a lot of important matters to discuss.'

Irritated by his rudeness, Pascale raised her eyes heavenward. Couldn't he, just for once, think about something other than resistance? Marie was Yves' sister, for goodness, sake. Surely the war wasn't going to be lost if they took a few minutes off to talk about her?

And Yves, apparently, shared her sentiments. When he and Paul had finished discussing a drop of arms that should be coming in any day now, and tactics should the German army launch a full-scale attack, he turned back to Pascale.

'My mother lives here in the village. Do you think you could spare the time to come and meet her? It would mean a great deal to her to talk to someone who knows Véronique, even if you don't have any news of her.'

Pascale, sure that Paul was about to refuse, jumped in quickly.

'We'd love to, wouldn't we, Paul?'

She kicked him fiercely under the table as she said it. He glared at her, but nodded.

'All right. But we can't stay long. We've got a full schedule.'

'It won't take long, I promise.'

They left the café and walked along the narrow street. The village was built on the hillside, a road that fell steeply from the square to the valley below, and tiers of cottages lining the streets that fishtailed from it on either side. The street Yves took them to was only just below the square, barely wide enough for the three of them to walk abreast. The houses were of higgledy-piggledy design, some tall and narrow, some a long, low ramble of three or four cottages, which, although they shared a roof, each had its own identity. Shutters and some doors were open on one side of the road, closed against the fierce sun on the other. A mangy dog lay in what shade there was, flicking and scratching; another, mauling a bare white knucklebone, growled menacingly as they passed.

Yves' mother's house was perhaps halfway along the street. Three narrow rough stone steps led up to a stable-type door. Yves opened it and called inside.

'*Maman*! Are you there? I have some visitors for you.'

'Yves!' A stout, swarthy woman dressed all in black materialised from the dimness of the kitchen into which the door opened. 'Goodness me, you know how to give an old woman a surprise! Come in, do. Don't stand on the doorstep of your own home!'

Yves ushered Pascale and Paul in.

'This is Le Capitaine . . .'

'Oh my goodness!' The old woman looked awestruck; Pascale thought she was about to genuflect. Paul's reputation obviously went before him.

'. . . and this is Pascale. She knows Véronique. They trained together in England.'

'*Mon dieu*! You know my Véronique? Oh, do you have news of her?' Tears had sprung to the woman's eyes, but her leathery face was wreathed in smiles.

'No, I'm afraid not. I haven't seen her since we were together in England.'

'Ah, she is a very naughty girl not to be in touch with her mother in all this time.' She wrung her hands, then sighed, regaining possession of herself. 'Won't you come through? I'll get you something to drink.'

'Madame . . . I don't mean to be rude, but this is only a flying visit,' Paul said.

'But we'd love something to drink.' Pascale threw him a fierce look.

Madame ushered them through the kitchen to the room beyond, where long French windows opened on to a tiny balcony. Two or three ancient chairs were crowded on it; Madame invited them to sit down, then disappeared together with Yves back into the house.

'What's the matter with you?' Pascale hissed at Paul. 'Surely we can spare half an hour to talk to Marie's mother?'

'You're too fond of talking,' he snapped back.

'Oh, really! I thought you found it useful, me making friends with the locals.'

'Yves is already on our side,' Paul growled.

The return of Madame prevented further argument. She was carrying a round tin tray on which were four thick, stubby glasses filled with golden liquid, and a dish piled high with ripe apricots.

'Muscat,' she said with satisfaction. 'I've still got a few bottles in the cellar, thank the Lord. And the fruit is from our own trees. We have to be quick to pick it, though, before the Germans come and steal what they want. They'd have the clothes off our backs given half a chance.'

Pascale sipped the wine, thick, sweet and lemony, so very different to the rough red she had become used to, and bit into an apricot. It was very peaceful out here on the little balcony. On a patch of rough ground immediately below her feet, a few scrawny hens scratched in the dust; further down the steep hillside was a thick bank of trees – the ones from which the apricots had come, she guessed. Above the fruit trees, away in the distance, the mountains rose majestically, a green and purple haze that was lost at the summit in a band of cloud. Pascale thought of the Maquis hiding there in their caves and grottos and tents of parachute silk, training and planning for all-out war whilst surviving on what they could steal, or what the sympathetic villagers took to them. Even with Yves, in his rough-and-ready clothes and military-style beret, sitting on the balcony beside her, it was difficult to believe the whole thing was not a figment of her imagination.

'I worry about Véronique all the time,' Madame was saying, staring thoughtfully into her glass of muscat. 'Stupid, I know. She's old enough and ugly enough to take care of herself, and it's a long time since she took notice of anything her old mother told her. But you can't help it. I worry about Yves, too. They're still my children, big as they are. And they always will be, to the day I go to meet my maker. You don't have children, I suppose. But if you did, you'd understand.'

The pain of loss ached suddenly in Pascale, the pain she had little time to think about these days, but which would never go away. *I do understand,* she wanted to say. *I do know how becoming a mother changes you for ever. I know they are always there in your heart.* But of course, she didn't.

'I wish I had news for you, madame,' she said, 'but I don't. I'm sure wherever she is, she's very busy doing whatever is required of her. But at least things are moving now. The Allies are on French soil in their thousands. I think the Germans are beginning to realise they can't hold on for ever. With any luck, it will all be over soon, and Marie will be back, sitting on this balcony and enjoying a glass of your muscat.'

'I'd better be sure to keep a bottle back for her then, hadn't I?'

Paul was becoming restless. He drained his glass, set it down on the tin tray, and got up abruptly.

'Thank you for your hospitality, madame, but we must get on.'

At the door, Madame hugged Pascale. Close to she smelled of garlic, and Pascale felt almost claustrophobic as meaty arms pressed her into the squashy mountain of flesh that was her breasts. But she suppressed her faint revulsion, patting Madame's back comfortingly.

'If I should come across Marie – Véronique – I'll tell her to try to get to see you,' she said.

'Thank you.' Madame's eyes were brimming once more. Pascale was a connection, however loose, with her daughter – and she didn't want her to go.

Yves walked back with them to where their car was parked, and whilst he and Paul had a last exchange Pascale waited in the passenger seat. But once they were on the move, she turned on Paul angrily.

'What's the matter with you? You were positively rude to that poor woman.'

'I don't have time for pleasantries.' Paul was negotiating the bends in the narrow road and the steep, tree-lined hill that led back to the main valley road.

'Then perhaps you should make time! She's just an old woman, worried about her daughter. And anyway, I was enjoying it. Marie is my friend, and I don't have many of those.'

'In our business that's the best way.'

'Well it may be for you, but I don't want to live like that. And one day neither will you. When you're old and lonely you'll wish you'd made the time for other people.'

'Oh for God's sake leave it, Pascale,' he snapped.

'It's true!'

'Just leave it!' His tone was so aggressive it shocked her. He'd never spoken to her in that way before; come to that, she'd never before seen this ill-tempered side of him. First the coldness, now this boorish behaviour. Perhaps, she thought, she really didn't know him at all. Perhaps, like the maquisards who hero-worshipped him, she had invented a romantic and mysterious persona that didn't really exist.

She turned her head, staring crossly out of the car window, but he drove in frosty silence. Either he didn't know she was upset with him, or he didn't care. For the first time since they'd been working together there was no communication whatsoever between them, only a vast and hostile no-man's-land.

She couldn't keep her anger with him on the boil for long, though. There was no place for animosity in their working relationship, and in any case, she was too ready to make excuses for him. Within a few days things were back to what had become the norm: planning, talking to maquisards and *resistants*, establishing radio contact with London to ask for supplies, trying to glean information on the Allies' progress. The personal and private was off limits; every ounce of their concentration was reserved for the job in hand. The hot July sun baked the earth hard and distilled the scent of lavender and thyme into the thin, clear air; Provence, the Drôme and Vercours waited.

The end was coming, they could sense it. But it was to be more bloody and more devastating than they knew.

TWENTY-SEVEN

Bastille Day 1944 was a bright, clear day when larks sang in the perfumed air and hopes were high. It was a month now since the Normandy landings and the Germans were on the run. And though the occupation and the Vichy government between them had changed life for ever, people were determined that the old traditions should be upheld.

The maquisards of the Vercours, however, had no time for celebration. At long last the supplies of arms and ammunition they so desperately needed were on their way – tons of them.

It was to be an early morning drop. Throughout the night the men worked, preparing the strip, checking and rechecking every detail of the operation. Then, after a few hours of snatched sleep, they were back at their posts and eagerly watching the sky.

The first planes arrived at around 9.30 a.m. British Halifaxes and American Flying Fortresses, flying in groups of twelve and escorted by the little buzzing fighters. The noise of the engines was deafening, but it only added to the excitement, and villagers cheered to see the sky filled with bulky crates floating to earth beneath the swirling umbrellas of the parachutes. The drop completed, the Allied planes headed for home, but the work of the Maquis was only just beginning.

And so was the horror that followed.

As the bulky containers were being loaded on to lorries by willing hands, two fighter planes dived towards the landing strip – two planes marked not with the roundel of the RAF but with the black swastika. The spray of bullets directed at the men who were working on the exposed plain was shocking enough, but worse was to come.

The bombers that followed the fighters were intent not only on the destruction of the landing strip, the precious cargo and the maquisards who had been there to receive it. They were determined to teach the whole region a lesson it wouldn't forget.

Though the final arrangements for the drop had been delegated and there were other, more senior military commanders in charge now of operations, Paul still felt a sense of responsibility. On the morning of July 14th, he and Pascale set out early for Le Montagne. They had arranged to meet other resistants who had become their friends – Hue Gironde, a doctor, and his wife Arlette, a nurse. Hue and Arlette were staunch in their support of the Maquis, and could be relied upon to treat the wounded and the sick.

As it always did when they were in the vicinity of Le Montagne, the atmosphere between Paul and Pascale had grown frosty. She liked to visit Madame, and could not understand why Paul was so averse to doing so. If she called on the old woman, Paul invariably found some urgent business to occupy him, and if she was too long gone he became irritable or even downright bad-tempered. Pascale hoped that being with Hue and Arlette would mean he would at least be civil today.

At 9.30, when the first of the Allied aircraft appeared in the sky, the quartet were drinking coffee in a café in the village square. They watched the containers float down, first in a sparse shower, then a cloud of billowing silk, and raised their cups in a salute.

'This calls for a celebration,' Hue declared. 'Never mind the coffee, let's have something stronger.'

The café owner, who had been watching the drop with them, sprang into action. He disappeared through the jangling net curtain into the café and re-emerged with a jug of red wine, glasses, and a dish of fresh olives.

'On the house! God knows, you've earned it!'

Again they toasted the arrival of the supplies, again the café owner topped up their glasses.

'They're coming back!' Arlette said, sounding puzzled.

Sure enough, the air was vibrating with a distant drone. But even as she said it, her face was registering uncertainty. The heavy engines didn't sound English or American. They sounded . . .

'Oh my God!' Pascale said. 'They're Jerries.'

And the first bombs began to fall. The Germans were bombing not only the landing site, but also the village.

'Come on!' Paul pulled Pascale roughly to her feet. 'Let's get you and Arlette out of here.'

Pascale tried to protest, but Paul propelled her at a run up the cobbled street to where the Citroën was parked, Hue and Arlette following. One of the first bombs had partially demolished the village church; already flames were beginning to leap from the dry old timbers that were now exposed to the scorching July sun. Smoke was rising too in a thick black cloud over the hillside below the square, in the vicinity of Madame's house, Pascale thought.

'Can we take Madame with us?' she gasped.

Paul jerked open the door of the car.

'Get in. Don't mess about, Pascale.'

'But she's on her own. She's an old woman . . .'

He ignored her, pushing her into the passenger seat and going round to the driver's door.

Hue was bundling Arlette into the rear of the car.

'I'll stay here.'

Paul nodded brusquely. 'I'll be back as soon as I've got the girls to safety.'

Pascale was surprised. She'd imagined that Paul, as a commander, would want to retreat to a place of safety, the better to conduct operations.

'You're going back?' she asked.

'They'll need all the help they can get.' Paul's tone was terse. 'It could be the Germans will send in troops when they think they've done enough damage with their bloody bombs.'

Pascale's heart sank, wondering how the Maquis could hope to repel a concerted attack when their supplies of arms were so low. The new consignment might have arrived, but there would have been no time to recover it before the bombers moved in. In fact, the billowing silk of the parachutes would make unmissable targets.

The half-hour drive was hazardous; even when they left the village behind them there were bursts of shellfire from the German fighters that had escorted the bombers and their deadly cargo. Though she remained outwardly calm, the palms of Pascale's hands were moist with sweat. She wiped them on her skirt.

'I should go back too,' Arlette was saying. 'There are going to be many injured. I'm a nurse. I shall be needed.'

'You'll stay with Pascale,' Paul said shortly. 'When it's over, I'll come back for you – perhaps take you up to the landing site, if we can make it. There will be a lot of wounded up there, I should think. But until then, I don't want to have to worry about you two. You'll be more use later on.'

Another wave of bombers was coming in; looking over her shoulder, Pascale saw that a pall of ominously black smoke had settled over the village they'd left behind.

In a thickly wooded area, Paul stopped the car.

'This is as good a place as any for you to shelter. Stay undercover, and don't do anything stupid. I'll be back as soon as I can.'

And then he was gone.

It was, Pascale thought, the longest day she had ever lived through. And it was the enforced inactivity that made it so.

They talked a little, she and Arlette, but conversation was next to impossible. They drank wine from the flask Pascale carried in her satchel, they took turns to go to the edge of the woods to report on what was happening – the little they could see of it. It was mid-afternoon before the bombers went away for the last time, yet still they expected them to return. It seemed impossible to imagine a world where the air did not reverberate with the sound of the heavy engines and the ground tremble as yet another load of deadly cargo was unleashed.

And then began a different sort of waiting, more intense, yet sharper-edged than before, so that Pascale had to fight the spasms of rising panic and the dark dread that grew with every passing minute.

The silence was threatening now; it rang in her ears as she listened for the sound of a motor car engine on the road from Le Montagne. Several times she thought she heard it, but no car came. Against Paul's instructions, she ran out on to the road, looking this way and that.

Arlette, by contrast, seemed almost unnaturally calm.

'He'll come,' she said. She was sitting on the thick trunk of a fallen tree, plaiting her hair into two braids as if she were in her own bedroom. 'He'll come – he said he would. And so will Hue.'

'How do you know that?' Pascale snapped. 'How do you know they're not both dead?'

'I'd know if anything had happened to Hue,' Arlette returned with infuriating certainty. 'Don't ask me how. I'd just know.'

'Well, you know more than I do.'

'That's because he's my husband, and has been for nearly twenty years. I don't expect you to understand. But that's how it is when you've been so close to someone for so long. Perhaps one day you'll be lucky enough to feel that about someone.'

Pascale tutted. She was in no mood for such airy-fairy talk.

'You and Paul . . . ?' Arlette looked at her quizzically, the tag end of one plait squeezed between finger and thumb to keep it from unfurling. 'Are you . . . ? Is there anything . . . ?'

'No, of course not!' Pascale snapped.

Arlette went on looking at her thoughtfully.

'Of course there's nothing between us!' Pascale repeated. 'I don't know what gave you that idea.'

Arlette shrugged. 'OK, so I'm wrong. But I could have sworn . . . There's something in the way you look at one another . . . something very *intimate* . . .'

'That's ridiculous,' Pascale said, but she was startled. Intimacy? In the cold, barren wasteland between them? Arlette was either a hopeless romantic or she had an extremely vivid imagination.

'I'm his courier, that's all,' she said shortly.

'Mm. And he is just your boss. That explains why he was so worried about you, I suppose, and why you are so worried about him.'

On the point of snapping yet again at Arlette, Pascale froze.

'Listen! There's a car coming!'

She was about to dash out to the road when Arlette caught her arm.

'No, Pascale! It could be anyone – Germans even.'

Pascale stood stock still, aware that she had almost committed the cardinal sin of carelessness. For a moment nothing had mattered except finding out if the car was Paul's, finding out if he was safe.

'And you still say there's nothing between you?' Arlette said softly, but in tones that suggested amusement.

Pascale was too busy watching the road to reply.

The car was coming closer; it didn't sound like a German patrol. She caught at Arlette's hand, squeezing it tightly. The car was slowing. Stopping, surely? The engine was idling now. And through the thick mesh of branches she caught a glimpse of the Red Cross markings. Her breath came out on a gasp of joy and overwhelming, dizzying relief.

'It's him!'

She let go of Arlette's hand, running through the thick under-growth. Paul was out of the car, heading across the grassy verge. He looked dishevelled, dirty, weary, older somehow. But he was safe.

'Paul!' she gasped.

She ran towards him, throwing her arms around him before she could stop herself. 'Oh Paul, thank God you're all right!'

For a brief moment she thought he was hugging her back, though in her overwhelming relief it was hard to be sure of anything.

'Where's Hue?' Arlette had reached them. For the first time she sounded anxious and afraid.

Paul stiffened and was holding Pascale away, once more the remote commander. But she noticed now how drawn was his face, how hard the line of his mouth, how bleak the expression in his eyes.

'He's fine, Arlette, don't worry. He's tending the wounded.' He turned back to the car. 'Come on, let's get going.'

'What's happened?' Pascale asked, climbing into the passenger seat. Another inane-sounding question, and one to which she scarcely needed a reply.

'You'll see,' Paul replied grimly.

*   *   *

Even before they reached the village, the scale of the devastation was apparent. Thick black smoke from fields of burning crops blew in clouds across the road; at the foot of the hill leading up to Le Montagne, a huge crater made it impassable.

'We'll have to walk from here,' Paul said. 'It's lucky I left the car where I did after I dropped you off or I'd never have been able to come to fetch you.'

The main pall of smoke had drifted now so that it no longer hung directly over the village, but thin funnels spiralled upwards to join the mass; clearly there were fires still burning. The afternoon sun blazed down on them as they climbed; perspiration ran down their faces, and Pascale's blouse clung damply to her back. In one place a tinder-dry thicket burned, bare and blackened branches close to the road, a red glow and more thick smoke further away. The cottages that had been the outposts of Le Montagne had gone, collapsed into heaps of smoking rubble. And the village itself . . .

Pascale's eyes went round with horror, but she said nothing. She was beyond words.

The church, the houses and little shops, the café where this morning they had toasted the arrival of the Flying Fortresses, all were smoking ruins.

'They missed the school,' Paul said. 'We've turned it into a hospital.'

They inched around another crater in the road, clambered over masonry thrown haphazard as a child's box of building bricks hurled away in a tantrum.

In the school the wounded lay on makeshift stretchers or wandered, dazed and bloody. Hue was there, in the thick of it, assessing, tending, issuing instructions.

'Good. Two more pairs of hands,' he said when he saw them.

'Two?' Pascale glanced questioningly at Paul.

'I'm going to try to get up to the drop site,' he said. 'They'll need help there too. We've got to rescue the supplies before Jerry decides to use the parachutes for more target practice. I'll come back for you when I can, Pascale.'

Pascale's heart sank. After the long, anxious day when she hadn't known if he was dead or alive, she couldn't bear to be separated from him again. And she was no nurse. The sight of torn, bleeding flesh and shattered bone, the stench of burned pork, was turning her stomach.

'Couldn't I come with you?' she ventured.

'It's man's work up there. You'll be more use here. Hue will tell you what to do.'

He strode away and Pascale experienced a moment's absolute desolation. Then Hue commandeered her and she was too busy to think of anything but the moment and the task in hand.

It was late evening before Paul returned. After hours of assisting Hue and Arlette with whatever humble task she was capable of, from handing instruments, holding swabs to gaping wounds and washing bloodstained floors, Pascale was dropping with exhaustion. On Hue's instruction she had taken a rest, and was sitting, head in hands, on a low stone wall outside the makeshift hospital. She didn't see him until he spoke.

'Pascale.'

She jumped, inexplicably guilty, and annoyed that he should have found her shirking.

'I've only been here a few minutes,' she said defensively. 'Hue told me to take a break.'

'How are things?' he asked.

'Quietening down now. It's been mayhem. What about you?'

'The same. Dozens of casualties. Half the roads impassable. And the bastards have peppered the landing site with grenades so we won't be able to use it again. We've recovered most of the containers, though – the ones that didn't get blown up. The parachutes made perfect targets.'

'What a day!' Pascale ran her fingers through her hair, damp with sweat and dishevelled. 'And it started so well.'

'That's war for you.'

'Have you seen Yves? Is he all right?'

'I don't know. He and some of his men were on a part of the plateau that took a hell of a battering. There's a party out now, trying to get access. We'll know more tomorrow.'

'And Madame? She isn't among the wounded in the hospital.'

'I don't think she'll have made it,' Paul said flatly. 'Her house took a direct hit.'

'Oh God!'

'Are you still needed here?' Paul asked.

'I don't know . . .'

'Let's find out then. If you can be spared, I'd like to get you back. We've got a lot to deal with tomorrow. You wait here. I'll talk to Hue.'

A few minutes later he was back.

'Come on, let's go.'

Pascale forced a weary smile.

'Am I excused, then?'

'Yep. And Hue says you've done a brilliant job here today.'

'I wouldn't say that. But I've done my best.'

'We're going to have to walk down to the main road again. There was still no way I could get the car up here. Will you be all right?'

'Of course I will! I'm the cross-country champ, remember?' But when she stood up, her legs felt shaky and unsteady.

Paul put his arm round her. 'Come on, Mrs Gamp.'

It was the first time they'd had any real physical contact since she'd returned to France, but she was too weary to feel any frisson of excitement. Yet there was enormous comfort in his touch and the nearness of him; in the midst of devastation she drew on his strength.

He kept his arm around her until they had passed the ruins of Madame's road, then released her, taking her hand instead. And that was how they walked down the hill, hand in hand. The smell of burning still hung heavy in the air; the horror of the day weighed heavily so that they walked in silence. Paul was wrapped in his own thoughts, Pascale in a mind-numbing stupor. Neither did they talk in the car. It was only when they reached the little single-storey cottage where Pascale had been living for the past few weeks that she spoke.

'Are you going to come in?'

He hesitated, on the point of refusing.

'Oh please, Paul! Neither of us has had anything to eat today. I've got some cheese in the larder, and olives, and a loaf of bread. Come and share it with me.'

'All right.'

Pascale was getting a second wind now. In the tiny kitchen she set out the food – remarkably good under the circumstances, but then the farmers and shopkeepers always looked after the English Rose, as they called her. She found a jug of wine and a half-drunk bottle of a spirit, local to the area, the name of which she could never remember. They ate, and then sat smoking cigarettes on the veranda.

'Poor Marie,' Pascale said. 'Her mother almost certainly dead, her brother missing, her home . . . well, the whole village in ruins.' Tears pricked her eyes; the loss was one with which she could identify only too well. 'This is going to destroy her. To come home to this, after all she's been through . . .'

Paul was silent, batting at a mosquito. His expression was grim, and suddenly Pascale was remembering all the times he'd avoided going to see Madame, and the ill-temper her concern for Marie's mother always seemed to provoke.

'What is it, Paul?' she asked. 'What is it about Marie that makes you behave so strangely?'

'I'm not behaving strangely.'

'You are. You always do. What . . . ?'

Paul sighed.

'OK, I'll tell you. Marie was captured over a year ago. She was almost certainly tortured, and I should think it's highly likely she's been executed by now. So I don't think she will have to deal with the loss of her home and family. If by some chance they've survived, it's more likely that they'll have to deal with hers.'

Coming on top of all the other traumas of the day, it was almost too much to take in. For a moment Pascale felt nothing, her senses numbed, her mind a total blank.

'Oh my God,' she said. 'You've known this all the time? Why didn't you tell me?'

Paul's face was a grim mask again.

'I couldn't see the point.'

'But she was my friend!'

'All the more reason not to upset you.'

'And Yves and Madame . . . haven't you told them either?'

'Yves knows she was arrested. He agreed with me it was better to say nothing until we knew the full facts.' Paul said it quite aggressively.

'But – you should have told me! And Madame. That's why you never wanted to go and see her, isn't it? You couldn't face her, knowing what you did.'

'It wasn't for me to tell her, Pascale. Really, it has nothing to do with me whatsoever. She wasn't my agent; all I know is what I've picked up on the grapevine.'

'All the same . . . How could you sit there and listen to Madame talking about wanting Marie to get in touch?' It was beginning to sink in now, and shock and grief were making her angry. 'Have you any feelings at all? Are we just numbers to you, pawns to be moved around a chessboard?'

'Of course not.'

'Well that's how it seems to me. You don't seem to care about anything except getting the job done.'

'Isn't that what we're here for?'

'But you can still be human, for God's sake!' Pascale covered her mouth with her hand, closing her eyes, seeing Marie's fierce little face, imagining her suffering.

No, she couldn't do this. Not now. The anger was better. It was anaesthetising the unbearable, giving her a focus.

'You don't care about anybody, do you?' she flared.

'Oh, don't be ridiculous!'

'You don't! Why would you care about Marie and Yves and Madame when you don't seem to care a fig for Simone, your own fiancée? You never mention her. I don't suppose you so much as think about her. Has she been captured too, and you haven't bothered to tell me? You just use people, Paul, and discard them when it suits you.'

'Have you quite finished?' His tone was cold, dangerously so.

'No, actually, I haven't. There's the way you've treated me. I've never mentioned it before because I know we have to work together, and like you, I know just how important what we're doing is. But I'm not going to keep quiet any longer. You used me, Paul, just like you use everyone else!'

'What are you talking about?'

'You see? You don't even know! When I was here before – when I was waiting to be sent home – you and I . . . Don't tell me you've forgotten!'

His eyes were narrowed, his jaw set.

'Hardly.'

'Ever since I came back you've frozen me out, acted as if it never happened. I suppose you're going to tell me that's because of the job, too.'

'It is. It's not good for agents to be too involved.'

'There you are! You see what I mean? If you'd said that when I came back, I'd have understood.'

'You *do* understand.'

'With my head, yes, maybe. But what about my feelings? I can't help those. And to be truthful, I am very, very hurt. As I say, you used me – when it suited you.'

'I did not use you.'

The shutters of a window on the opposite site of the street flew open; someone had obviously heard their raised voices and was looking out to see what was going on.

'For goodness, sake, keep your voice down!' Paul snarled.

'Ah – you don't want the villagers who think you're the next Messiah to hear the truth about you, do you?' In full flow now, Pascale was past caring.

Paul got up, went through the French door into the living room.

'I'm going.'

She followed him. 'That's right, just turn your back and walk away. What do I matter? What do any of us?'

He swung round. She had never seen him look so angry.

'Actually, Pascale, you matter to me a great deal.'

'Well you've a funny way of showing it!'

'Why do you think I wanted to get you out of Le Montagne this morning?'

'It wasn't just me. It was Arlette too.'

'Granted. So perhaps I do have some finer points, after all. Not wanting to expose a woman to something like that.'

'Exactly! A *woman*. That was all I was to you, wasn't it? A woman, when you wanted one. Any woman would have done.'

'Not just any woman. You don't get it, do you, Pascale? If that was all it was, I could live with it. But you're not just any woman to me. Your safety and welfare are on my mind when I should just be thinking about what has to be done. It's interfering with my judgement. I'd get you out of here again if I could, but I doubt if that's possible now, and in any case, I can't spare you. So we've just got to do the best we can, OK?'

'What did you say?'

'We've just got to get on with it.'

'No – before.'

'How the hell do I know? I'm going, Pascale. I shouldn't have come in at all.'

Pascale's anger had deflated like a burst balloon. She was on the brink of tears suddenly, though she did not know why; staring at Paul, not seeing him, but hearing a rerun of what he had said – that she wasn't just any woman, that he thought about her when he should be concentrating on the job, or words to that effect. And though she could not yet take it in, she was desperately anxious for him not to leave.

'Don't go! Not like this! Please, Paul . . .' Tears were welling now, the events of the day, the dreadful news about Marie, her anger, her anxiety, her love for him all coming together in a huge wash of emotion. She buckled beneath it, turning away so he should not see her tears, squeezing her eyes tight shut against them, pressing her hand against her mouth. Her shoulders were shaking, there was no way she could stop that, and the tears spilled from her tightly closed eyes and ran rivers down her cheeks.

'Oh, Pascale!' She didn't hear him speak her name; it was no more than an anguished groan. But she felt his arms go around her, the solid wall of his chest against her back. For a long moment neither of them moved, then he turned her around so that her face was into his shoulder. He smelled of smoke and sweat and something else that she thought might be gunpowder. It was the most beautiful perfume she had ever smelled. The tears started again.

'This isn't like you! Sweetheart, don't cry.' He held her away, wiping the tracks of her tears with his fingers, then kissed her gently. 'I'm sorry. I didn't mean to hurt you. That's the last thing I want to do.'

She looked up at him, into the face of the man she was powerless not to love.

'Really?'

'Really. What I really want to do is . . .'

He kissed her again, more deeply than before, holding her close so that their bodies fitted together like pieces of a jigsaw puzzle, his hard, hers soft and yielding. The desire twisted in her, a physical pain as if an electric shock was sending sharp probes into the deepest parts of her. His hands moved over her back, one finding the curve of her breast, the other on her behind, holding her firmly against him, and her desire ratcheted up another notch so that nothing mattered but being closer, as close as two people could be.

Then he held her back a little, his eyes looking deeply into hers.

'I want you, Pascale.'

'Not just because I'm a woman?' she asked, half teasing, for she still could not quite believe that she wasn't reading something into his words and actions that wasn't there, just because it was what she wanted so much.

'No,' he said. 'Because you're you.'

She wasn't tired any more – well, she was, but it had ceased to be important. All that mattered was that she was where she wanted to be, with the person she most wanted to be with, for a beautiful hiatus in time when she could almost dare to hope that he felt the same way.

TWENTY-EIGHT

He'd given up resisting her; given up trying to deny his feelings for her. It was, he rationalised, more of a distraction than giving in to them could ever be.

Paul had never thought about romantic love; it wasn't an emotion that had ever figured in his life. Rather, he accepted certain conditions – attraction, lust, warmth, comfort, familiarity – and in the beginning, when he had first met Simone, she had fulfilled them all. He'd known her since they had been youngsters together in France, both the children of diplomats, and expected to socialise together, and she had always fascinated him, though he had always thought her out of his league. Then, later, when he had met her in England and they had both done some growing up, the fascination was as strong as ever, but the balance of power between them had changed subtly and he had found it heady stuff. But love . . . ?

She had asked him once if he loved her, and he had found the question embarrassing.

'Of course I do,' he'd replied, more because it seemed to be expected of him than for any other reason, except, perhaps, to shut her up. But it hadn't.

'Really? Truly?' she'd pressed him.

'Oh, Simone . . .'

'Say it, Paul. Say you love me.'

He couldn't.

'For goodness' sake, we're together, aren't we?'

He had presumed though that he did love her; certainly, for a while at least, he had been obsessed with her – the way she looked, the way she spoke, the way she excited him, the fact that this

297

glamorous, assured creature was not only on his arm, but desperate for him.

But somewhere along the line the thrill had gone out of being with her. The last time he'd seen her, at the training camp on Exmoor, had left him feeling flat and let down, somehow. His fault, he'd thought at the time. He'd been through too much, seen too much.

Or perhaps the gilt would have come off the gingerbread anyway. Perhaps this thing called love always ended in indifference and disappointment. He remembered, as a child, being taken to a travelling circus. He'd looked forward to it so eagerly he hadn't been able to sleep for the excitement, and when he was taken into the marquee – the Big Top, they called it – smelling pungently of animals and trampled grass and hot stale air, he could scarcely sit still on the hard wooden bench. But after a little while, the sinking feeling that something was missing began to nag at him. He clapped the prancing horses and the monkeys riding on the backs of brocaded elephants, laughed at the clowns simply because everyone else was laughing, was a little bored by the acrobats. The trapeze looked to him like an extreme version of the rope he and his friends had fixed up in a tree to swing across the river. The one thing that did catch his interest was the lions and tigers, but even then he was vaguely disappointed that no one was eaten. And when it was over, he was left with the awful flatness and a feeling of guilt that somehow he was letting down his mother, who'd paid a lot of money for the tickets, by not enjoying it properly.

The circus hadn't give him the satisfaction he'd anticipated as a child, and neither had his relationship with Simone as a grown man. Perhaps he was fundamentally someone who never would be satisfied for long; there was something lacking in him. It was the flip side of what made him a good agent, maybe. He could think and plan and command authority, he could keep a cool head in a tight spot, but he couldn't feel.

No more. He hadn't told Pascale he loved her either, but he knew, without even thinking about it, that he did. The way he felt about her was something that was, quite simply, an intrinsic part of him, and he could no more stop loving her than he could stop breathing. So what was the point in fighting it?

They didn't talk about the future, they didn't mention Simone. Instead they took the here and now with both hands, content to enjoy what time, short or long, they might have together. Paul moved into the little house he'd found for Pascale, and into her bed. And found, in the midst of impermanence and danger, the elusive content-ment he had thought would always be missing from his life, and a joy of which he had never dreamed.

For a week the bombardment of the Vercours continued and it was a battle Paul knew would be lost without help from outside. Supplies of arms and ammunition were desperately low and manpower was clearly insufficient to repel the massive deploy-ment of enemy troops to the area by air and overland. Holed up in their HQ in the tiny mountain village, Paul sent message after message to London for assistance; none came. He couldn't under-stand it – or didn't want to.

'I can smell politics in this,' he said furiously to Pascale. 'There are too many irons in the fire now. It was a damned sight easier before there were so many bloody chiefs . . .'

'And not enough Indians.'

'Exactly. This is going to get bloodier before it's over, I promise you.'

Pascale experienced a sinking feeling in her gut. She was used to Paul being positive, if not totally optimistic. To hear him talking of defeat frightened her.

'What are we going to do?' she asked.

'Keep asking for reinforcements. It's all we can do now.'

'And if they don't come?'

'Then we're looking at a disaster.' He ran his fingers through his hair, massaging the back of his neck with his fingers. 'We're going to have to get out of here.'

'Run away, you mean?' Again she was shocked. It wasn't at all the sort of reaction she expected of Paul.

'There are times when you have to look at the big picture,' he said

299

soberly. 'This is only a part of my area of responsibility. While I'm trapped here, the rest of it is going to hell in a handcart for all I know. I'd be no use to anyone captured, or dead, and neither would you.'

'I suppose.'

'I'm a resistance organiser, Pascale, not a soldier. We've done all we can do here. Whether you like it or not, it's a fact.'

He was right, she knew, but it still stuck in her craw like an undigested meal.

'It's so unfair! All those troops they sent into Normandy, and they can't spare us one battalion!'

'It's war, Pascale. The powers-that-be have to decide where and how to deploy their strength. Look at the big picture, as I said before. Right now, for one reason or another, the Vercours in not top of the list of priorities.'

'Bastards!'

He grinned suddenly, reaching for her.

'I love it when you're angry.'

'Of course I'm angry! I love this place, Paul. I love the people. I can't bear what's happening to them. They'll lose everything. Their homes, their crops, their livestock. It's just appalling.'

'I know,' he said, serious again. 'I feel the same. But apart from badgering London, there's not a thing I can do about it.'

They sat in silence for a moment, then she took his hand, turning it over so it lay palm upwards in hers, staring at it intently.

'What are you doing?' he asked.

'Trying to read your palm. Somebody told me once how to do it.'

He tried to pull his hand away.

'You don't believe in that rubbish, surely?'

'How do you know it's rubbish? Come here, let me look.'

She didn't know why she was doing it. An excuse to hold his hand, maybe, though surely she didn't need one? A way of pushing his dire predictions to the back of her mind? More likely.

'Go on then.' He spread his palm again for her. 'What can you see?'

'Well, a blister . . .'

'Nothing very mystical about that. I burned it the day Le Montagne went up in flames.'

'I know. Is it very sore?'

'Yes. Come on, I'm waiting for some predictions.'

'It's not like that really. I'm not a psychic. I'm just reading the lines.' She traced her finger across his palm, carefully avoiding the angry blister that he'd refused to cover with a dressing. 'Your head line. Very strong.'

'I'm not soft in the head, you mean. Good.'

'Shut up. Heart line. Well . . . a bit shaky to start with, but getting stronger. Fate line . . . I'm not sure which that one is. Perhaps you haven't got one. Children . . .' She turned his hand on to a slant, counting the tiny lines at the base of his little finger. 'Hmm. One child. Or it could be two if that line there counts . . . but one definitely.'

'Huh! I don't know about that!'

'Life line.' She frowned. 'Curl your fingers up, I can't see properly . . .'

'You mean I'm dead already.'

'Don't be silly.' But her heart had come into her mouth. The crease that she was sure was Paul's life line came to an abrupt end midway across his palm.

'Show me,' he said.

'Well . . . there.' She felt flustered; she didn't want him to see what she'd seen. Didn't want to admit it out loud. It was nonsense, of course. Just a silly game. He didn't believe in it and neither did she. So why did she suddenly feel so full of foreboding?

'Good grief, it's not very long, is it?' he said.

She tutted. 'Long enough for you to have one, maybe two children.'

'Well that's a relief. I'm not ready to go just yet.'

'I should hope not!'

'Oh goodness me, no. There are things I want to do first.' He turned his hand over, grabbing hers and pulling her towards him. 'Starting with you.'

'Oh Paul, you are impossible!' she tried to say, but his mouth was on hers, his hand rucking up her skirt. Desire started in her, small, sharp darts that were linked somehow by a taut cord to her breasts and the yearning, secret place between her legs, and her flesh seemed to be rising to his. Pascale gave herself up to the all-consuming pleasure and forgot about foreshortened life lines, burning villages and a treacherous command on whose aid they were totally dependent. She was here and Paul was here. For the moment, nothing else in the world mattered.

Afterwards they lay for a while in each other's arms, enjoying the warm intimacy, sharing each other's breath. After a while, Pascale shifted slightly so that her head rested on his broad bare chest. Beneath her left ear the steady, muffled throb of his heart pulsed with reassuring regularity. It was hypnotic and it intensified the feeling of closeness.

'So,' she said, softly mischievous, 'you *do* have a heart. I can hear it.'

'What?' He sounded drowsy.

'I said . . . oh, never mind.'

She wriggled back into the crook of his arm, but an edge of anxiety was beginning to cast a long shadow over her contentment. All this could be snatched away from her at any time, without warning, and she couldn't bear it. The moment, however precious, was no longer enough. Pascale ached suddenly with the need to know that there would be tomorrows like this for them, when they could share love, laughter, life.

The shadow became a knife edge, scoring a sharp dread across her soul, cutting a chasm between her and the happiness she had been basking in just a few short moments ago. She pulled herself up into a sitting position, so that she could look at him lying there, eyes closed, face, for once, in repose. His hair was tousled, his lips slightly parted. She thought he might have fallen asleep.

'Oh Paul,' she whispered, 'what is going to become of us?'

He wasn't asleep. He opened his eyes, looking up at her, and for a brief second she thought she saw her own desire for a future together reflected in them. Then he sighed, shrugging slightly, and his tone was as prosaic as ever.

'I can't answer that, Pascale, any more than you can.'

'I know. But . . .' She bit her lip. 'When this is over . . . if we're both still alive . . . will we . . . ?'

She waited, willing him to answer, but he remained silent. Tears pricked her eyes, tears of desperate longing for a reassurance she knew he could not give.

'We will be together, won't we?' she said, hating herself for her weakness, and then, with a rush of guilt, for the fact that she had cut Simone out of the equation entirely, and a wash of bitter jealousy.

'I'm sorry,' she said, turning away abruptly. 'I forgot. You'll be with Simone, won't you?'

His hand reached out, encircling her wrist.

'No,' he said. 'No, I won't be.'

She jerked her head back so that she was looking at him again. He sat up too, putting his arms around her.

'I won't be with Simone,' he said again.

'But—'

'I've known for a long time that marrying Simone would be a mistake. No, don't look so worried – you're not to blame for that. It's all about me, and my only excuse is that I was a different person then. I thought I was in love, and Simone – well you know her, how she likes to organise. I let myself get carried along by her. That's no basis for marriage. Even if I hadn't met you, I wouldn't have gone through with it.'

'Oh.' Pascale experienced a rush of relief that she wasn't entirely responsible, but was still unable to ignore the heartbreak that lay ahead for her friend. 'She's going to be devastated, Paul.'

'Perhaps. Perhaps not. Maybe this war will have changed her too. But whatever, it's better to be honest about it now than settle for a life that would make us both miserable. I don't love her, and I'm not going to try and pretend I do. That wouldn't be fair to either of us.'

'No, I suppose not . . .'

'And now,' he said, 'I have you.'

Tears were pricking behind her eyes. She pressed her fist against her mouth.

'I don't know if we're going to get out of this alive,' he said, 'but if we do . . . well, I know now that I have met the woman I want to marry. No mistakes this time. How do you feel about growing old with me, Pascale?'

The tears pricked more fiercely. There was nothing she wanted more. She forced a grin, tried to swallow the wash of emotion.

'You, old, Paul? I can't imagine it.' And then realised she was joking about something that, given their circumstances, wasn't in the least funny. In her mind's eye she saw again his palm, that shortened life line, and her heart felt like lead.

She turned to look at him, welling up again.

'I'd like it very much,' she said. 'I only hope we get the chance.'

It was his turn to lighten the moment.

'Are you sure you know what you're letting yourself in for?' She nodded, unable to speak. 'Well, in that case . . .'

He released her and she saw that he was fiddling with the signet ring he always wore on his little finger, wriggling it off.

'I can't buy you an engagement ring, Pascale. But if this will fit . . .'

Her eyes went round above her clenched fist. He took her hand, slid the ring over the tip of her ring finger.

'Will you marry me, Pascale?'

'Oh Paul, you know I will.'

He pushed the ring down into place and kissed her, holding it there. The moment he released it, though, she knew it was much too big.

'I can't wear it, Paul. Not on that finger. It'll slip off. I'll lose it.'

'Try the middle finger then.'

'What if it gets stuck?'

'Does it matter?'

'No.'

He took the ring and pushed it over the knuckle of her middle finger. It was still loose, but not in so much danger of falling off.

'That will have to do for now. When this is all over I'll get you a proper engagement ring. Anything you want.'

'I don't want anything else. This is special.'

He laughed.

'A too-big man's signet ring that you can't even wear on your engagement finger?'

'I don't care about that. *We* know what it means, don't we. That's all that matters.'

He laughed again.

'I love you, Pascale.' The words that were so difficult to utter in moments of passion came easily now.

She levelled her eyes with his, still holding the ring in place.

'And I love you.'

It was a long time before either of them thought of anything but one another.

The aid Paul had repeatedly asked for was not forthcoming; the battle raged on.

Paul met the military commander of the plateau to inform him of his plans to leave the area, and learned that the officer had reached the conclusion that the only way to put an end to the wholesale death and destruction was to disperse the soldiers of the resistance. Whether Paul went or stayed, the battle for the Vercours was lost.

It was late in the evening when Paul returned; Pascale had waited anxiously all day. His face was grim when he came into the tiny salon and Pascale could see he was exhausted.

'Sit down,' she said. 'I'll get you something to eat.'

'Later. We need to get everything together first.'

Pascale bit her lip.

'We're going, then?'

'Yes. It's all but over here. We'll leave first thing in the morning.'

Dawn had scarcely broken when Paul and Pascale scrambled down the rocky slopes to the farm in whose outbuildings Paul's car was concealed, but already they could hear gunfire in the distance. Once Pascale stopped and looked back at the cluster of red-roofed houses, half hidden by stands of trees, and was overwhelmed by a wash of sadness. For her, this would always be a special place, the place where she and Paul had finally found one another, the place where, in spite of everything, she had been truly happy. Stones skittered beneath her feet, starting a small avalanche, and with an inaudible sigh she turned her back on the village, concentrating on keeping her footing on the steep slope.

Please God there would be other special places for them. And – who knew? – perhaps one day when this was over, they'd come back, bring their children.

Mercifully the farm where the car was hidden had, as yet, been spared. Mercifully the engine, after a few protesting coughs, spluttered into life. But there was no celebration in their mood as they headed south-west. Though there was nothing more they could have done, both felt that they had failed the Vercours.

When he saw the roadblock ahead, Paul swore. So far the journey had been uneventful, and he had been hoping it would remain so.

'It's OK, it's Mongols,' Pascale said as they came to a halt. Mongols were the Oriental Legion, and since few of them either spoke or read French, the checks carried out by them were generally speaking fairly swift and cursory.

They produced their documents with the usual casual aplomb and sure enough, after just a brief glance, the Mongols waved them through. But Paul had seen something he didn't care for in the rear-view mirror – a Gestapo staff car coming up fast behind them. He swore again.

'We're not out of the woods yet.'

The staff car caught and overtook them, signalling to them to stop again. Three SD – German security forces – men surrounded them.

'Papers.'

'We've just shown them.'

'Papers! And get out of the vehicle.'

Pascale's heart began to pound. Though SD men were always curt and overbearing, she knew instinctively that this was no routine check. She didn't like the way two of the officers were levelling guns at them either. Or the sneer on the face of the one holding out his hand for their identification. It wasn't just the look of a bullying Nazi, it smacked almost of triumph. He was taking his time examining the papers, seeming to relish the moment. Then he looked Paul directly in the eye.

'False!' he barked.

Paul began to argue; the SD officer cut across him.

'Do you think we don't know who you are? It's Le Capitaine, isn't it? We've been looking for you for a long time, my friend.'

A wash of ice flooded Pascale's veins; she felt her knees go weak with horror. How these SD men had got on to Paul she had no idea; she couldn't believe any of the patriotic villagers had talked. But someone had. They'd been followed, it was the only explanation. And now that the SD had one of their most wanted enemies, there was no way they were going to let him go.

'Into the car, both of you. Come on, hurry it up.'

Because she didn't know what else to do, Pascale started towards the German vehicle, but Paul stood his ground.

'Let the girl go. She knows nothing.'

'Hmm, we'll see about that.' The SD man's lip curled. 'She'll think of a thing or two to say by the time we've finished with her.'

'Let her go,' Paul repeated. He raised his hand in front of him; shocked, Pascale saw that he was holding a grenade.

The SD man took a step backwards, looking less sure of himself suddenly.

'Let her go, or I'll blow us all to kingdom come.' Paul's voice was low but dangerous. Pascale knew that tone, that steely determination. It was no idle threat. Paul meant what he said.

'Don't be a fool,' the German barked. 'You'll kill us all.'

'That's the idea, yes. Let her go, and I'll come quietly.'

'Paul – what are you doing?' Pascale squealed.

'Go on, Pascale – get out of here. Walk, and keep walking.' He wasn't looking at her, he was eyeballing the German, who had backed further away, his hands raised in protest.

'I'm not leaving you!'

'Go! Don't you know an order when you hear one?'

Panic was misting her eyes, turning the sunshine blood red. This was all wrong. Paul was the important one here; he shouldn't be sacrificing himself for her. Besides, she didn't want to walk away and leave him, though at least if she escaped she would be able to raise the alarm. Paul's allies would move heaven and earth to try to get him out of whatever prison he was taken to. It was really his only hope – the Germans would show him no mercy.

'Go, Pascale!' he barked at her again. He was still holding the grenade high, his finger on the pin. The three Germans were frozen like statues; their eyes, fixed on him, reflected their fear. That, at least, was some small satisfaction.

'We'll get you out, Paul.' She was backing away, the distance growing between them. 'I love you!' she called back, then she turned and began walking down the road where the plane trees threw long, sharp shadows across the glare of the sun.

She never saw one of the soldiers raise his gun, aiming at her retreating back in an act of bravado. She never saw Paul's instantaneous reaction. But she heard the explosion all right, so loud that it shattered her eardrums, and felt the rush of wind that knocked her off her feet. The rough surface of the road came up to meet her, grazing her face and hands, jolting every bone in her body.

For a moment she lay face down, too stunned to move. Then she scrabbled around on her hands and knees, looking back to where the Gestapo vehicle was engulfed in flame. A tumbled bundle that might have been the remains of one of the Germans lay broken as a child's toy on the grassy verge some feet from it, but it was the only sign that a moment ago four men had been standing there in the road.

'Oh my God!' Pascale whispered. 'Paul!'

She was shaking with shock, tears streaming down her cheeks. There was nothing she could do for him now. The harsh reality was inescapable; it shivered on her skin with the beads of cold sweat

and twisted inside her like the sharpest of knives. And a steely determination suddenly gave her new strength.

There was nothing she could for him now but make her escape
as he intended. If she survived, something of him would survive
too, because he would live for ever in her heart.

Pascale took one last look at the ball of flame that was Paul's
funeral pyre, turned her back and walked away down the road.

Part Five

TWENTY-NINE

MARTHA

Dusk is falling as I leave Miss Leverton's apartment. I drive out of the parking area behind the apartments in a bit of a dream. What a lady! What a story! And what a sad ending. To have the love of her life sacrifice himself for her like that. No wonder she's never married. I don't suppose she ever met anyone who could hold a candle to him, certainly not Hugh Woodhouse, with his fat belly and stupid watch stretched across it.

It occurs to me that she still hasn't explained how the box came to be in the lake, but perhaps she's kept that back on purpose, hoping to entice me here again when I realise there are still some loose ends that haven't been tied up. I haven't really asked her about the photograph in the hall either, though I assume it's the one she, Simone and Marie had taken at the end of their introductory course. Once again she was looking pretty knackered by the time she finished the story, and I didn't like to press her when I could see she'd had enough.

'I do hope you'll come and see me again,' she said as she saw me out. 'I've very much enjoyed talking to you. You are a remarkable young woman.'

'I'd hardly say that,' I said. 'Compared to what you did, my life's pretty ordinary.'

'Oh, I don't think so.' She smiled, that rather sweet smile that makes her look almost young again. 'In any case, we didn't think we were particularly special at the time. We were just doing a job that had to be done to the best of our ability. It's really only with hindsight that I wonder sometimes just how we managed it.'

'I'm really glad you've shared it with me,' I said. 'When I found the box in the lake, I had no idea what a story there was behind it.'

'Well there you are. Life plays some very odd tricks sometimes.'

I didn't quite understand what she meant by that, but she really was looking very tired and I didn't think I should prolong the visit any longer.

'I will come again, very soon,' I said.

'Please do. Perhaps you could bring your grandmother. I'm sure she must have her own stories of the war.'

The war is not something I ever recall Granny talking about, and I imagine her own experiences of it must be pretty tame compared with Miss Leverton's.

I'm still thinking about all she's told me as I drive along the marina, where the lights on the boats twinkle twice, once from their own source, and once in the reflection in the dark water. As always, it draws me. I pull in and sit for a while, just staring at it. It looks very calm tonight, very tranquil, but I know from experience the murk and the danger beneath the surface. The secrets it may be hiding, along with the dumped rubbish.

Eventually I start the car and head back towards Bristol. It's a road I know pretty well, it's reasonably quiet tonight, and I'm driving on autopilot. There's a junction up ahead, a minor road joining mine on my nearside, but that doesn't worry me unduly. It's my road, anyone on it will give way to me. There's a car coming towards me on the main road. I dip my headlights.

And then, when I'm just yards from the junction, I am suddenly aware of more lights, on my left, and the dark sky above the hedges is flashing blue lightning. Alarm bells go off in my head and I stamp on the brakes, but it's too late. A car shoots out of the junction right in front of me, and with a flash of sickening panic I know I'm going to hit it. Then everything becomes a confused blur. The screech of tyres, a bone-jarring jolt, and a bang and the horrible crunching of metal. The driver's airbag inflates, thwacking me in the chest, the car spins so I'm facing towards the side road, wondering for a shocked moment what the hell has happened. But the flashing blue light has condensed now into the strobe of a patrol car and I know immediately: some gung-ho traffic officers must have been chasing the car – stolen, perhaps – and the driver took his chance with the main road rather than stop and let them get him.

I'd caught the rear offside of the car – that was how fast he'd emerged from the junction. He'd carried on across the road and been hit again on his nearside by the other car that I'd seen approaching. That driver had had more warning than I had, and it doesn't look as if he hit him too hard. But it's still three cars splayed across a main road.

The driver's door of the offending car opens whilst I'm still gathering my wits, and a lad in a hoodie jumps out and starts to leg it. He's obviously OK, thank God, and I think I am too. Whilst I'm struggling to free myself from the airbag, one of the traffic officers jumps out of his car and sets off after him; his partner positions the police car in front of the wreckage of the two cars, strobe lights illuminating the scene in eerie blue and flashing a warning to approaching motorists. A second police car has arrived on the scene with twos and blues, which confirms my suspicion that this was a chase of some description. He would never have arrived so quickly unless he'd already been heading this way on a call. He positions himself on the other side of the crash scene.

At last I free myself from the airbag, manage to get the door open, and stagger out on to the road. One of the traffic officers approaches me. I recognise him as Andy Loxley.

'Are you all right, love?' He does a double-take. 'Christ! It's MJ!'

'He came straight out in front of me!' I say, my voice shaky.

'I know he did. Bloody maniac. We'll get him, though.'

'You'll be lucky, the way he took off.'

'He's a drug dealer – we'd already called the helicopter for assistance, and it should be on its way. And the dog handler. Are you sure you're all right, MJ? I've radioed for an ambulance.'

'I don't want an ambulance. I'm fine.' That is not exactly true. I'm hurting all over, as if someone has hit me with a sledgehammer, and very shaky. But I'm in one piece, no bones broken, nothing that won't mend, and I hate being fussed. 'What about the other driver? Do you want me to attend to him?'

'If you're sure you're OK.'

The other driver is also out of his car, looking as shocked and groggy as I feel, plus he has a nasty cut on his face, streaming blood. Well, at least that should keep the paramedics busy, keep them out of my hair. I go into policewoman mode, which helps me forget about my sore chest and concentrates the mind. Later, I'll probably think about how lucky I was not to be seriously injured or even killed and have a few nightmares about it. Right now I'm getting on with what I do best – reacting to an emergency.

But it's not long before I'm superfluous to needs. The ambulance is quickly on the scene, and I beat a hasty retreat before they can coerce me inside. But there are enough on-duty officers here now to deal with the accident, so I return to my poor car, which looks as though it will be a write-off, and sit in the driver's seat with the door wide open, watching proceedings.

The helicopter is hovering overhead now, its searchlights flooding the area, and the dog van has also arrived. I watch the handler set off in the direction the lad in the hoodie fled, his German shepherd straining at the leash.

'I suppose I'd better breathalyse you, MJ, just to keep everything by the book.' Andy Loxley is back. 'You haven't been drinking, have you?'

'I've had a glass of wine, that's all.' But blowing into the bag is not a pleasant experience; I'm shit scared that somehow I'll turn out to be over the limit, and I'm ridiculously relieved when Andy tells me everything is fine.

'You really ought to let the medics check you out, though,' he says. 'You're bound to be in shock if nothing else.'

'No way. I don't want to end up stuck in A and E for three or four hours. I just want to get home.'

'You shouldn't be on your own.'

'I'll be fine. I'm a tough cookie, Andy. There's no chance of a lift, I suppose?'

'Not while all this is going on.'

'No, I thought not. Look, I don't know if you've called out a garage yet to recover the vehicles, but I'd like my own. Dave Hoskins does running repairs for me, he's a good chap – well, you know that.' A lot of police officers use Dave, who has his own business and is a whole lot cheaper than the big franchises. 'If he'll come out for my car, I can ride back with him.'

'I'll get it sorted. Do you want to sit in our car while you wait? Then you can listen to what's going on.'

'OK,' I agree, a bit reluctantly, because it feels like a betrayal of my poor car to leave it bent to hell on the side of the road. But although it's quite a warm night I am shivering, and at least I'll be able to close the door of the police car, and listening on the radio to developments will help take my mind off things.

So I sit in the police car and listen. The airwaves are busy; it sounds as if they're closing in on the kid in the hoodie, who has apparently taken off across the fields. With the helicopter overhead and the dog on his trail he doesn't stand much chance of getting away, and he doesn't deserve to, the bastard.

It seems like an age before I see the flashing orange beacon of a tow truck approaching, although it can't be more than a quarter of an hour or twenty minutes. I hope it's Dave, but I'm disappointed. It's another recovery outfit, come to collect one of the other smashed cars. Dave's not long behind though, and it's good to see a friendly face.

'You've made a bit of a mess of this, MJ,' he says drily, taking a look at my poor car.

'Don't! It wasn't my fault, anyway. That wanker came out right in front of me.'

'You wait there. I'll get it shifted.'

When my car is loaded on to the pickup truck, I climb up into the cab. With difficulty. My chest is hurting like hell and my legs feel a bit wonky. But I'm not about to let on to Dave, or anyone else. Dave, cheerful as ever, chats all the way back to Bristol, and I'm happy to let him. I don't feel much like talking.

Dave drops me off outside my flat; I let myself in. What I want most is a stiff drink. I rummage in the cupboard and find a bottle of whisky that's been there since Christmas. I pour myself a generous measure. The bottle of tonic water, also at the back of the cupboard, looks as though it's gone flat – I should know better than to put to it back half used. I don't think I've got any ice in the freezer either, and I can't be bothered to go and look, so I sip the whisky neat, and boy, does it hit the spot!

I take the glass – and the bottle, in case I want a refill, which I'm sure I will – over to the sofa, put it down on the little side table, and wrap myself up in the new throw to try and get warm.

I've only been there a couple of minutes when the entry phone buzzes. I groan. Who the hell is that? I hope it's not some local plod wanting to breathalyse me again! Still draped in the throw, I stagger over to the phone.

'Who is it?'

'It's Nick.'

'Nick!'

'Yep. Can I come up?'

I blow breath over my top lip.

'I suppose so.' I press the button to unlock the outer door, then open mine and stand listening to his footsteps on the stairs. He hoves into view like a mermaid emerging from the deep. He's wearing a sweatshirt and jeans – not on duty, then.

'What are you doing here?' I ask accusingly.

'Andy Loxley called me. He said you'd been involved in an accident.'

'He had no right to do that!'

'He was worried about you. He said you refused to go to hospital . . .'

'Do you blame me?'

'. . . and were on your way home.'

'Yes. So what?'

'You shouldn't be on your own. It was pretty nasty, Andy said. He got me worried too. So I've come over to check up on you.'

'I'm OK! And I'm not your responsibility anyway. We're divorced, remember?'

'Oh, for goodness sake, MJ, we were married for five years. I still care about you. Are you going to let me in, or are we going to have this conversation on the landing?'

Reluctantly I retreat into the flat. Nick follows, shutting the door behind him.

'Are you sure you're not hurt, MJ?'

'I got a hefty thwack from the airbag. Apart from that, and the fact that I'm totally pissed off ... My car's a write-off, I should think.'

'Never mind the car. It's you I'm concerned about.'

'Well I was pretty lucky actually. It could have been a whole lot worse.'

'So Andy said.' Nick nods at my glass and the whisky bottle. 'You're taking the medicine, I see.'

'Too true. Do you want one?'

'I thought you'd never ask.'

So, actually, did I. The days when Nick and I shared a nightcap are well and truly over. But funnily enough, I am rather glad he's here.

'I'll get you a glass.'

'No, you sit down. Just tell me where they are.'

Again, I'm rather shocked that I don't argue.

'Top shelf, middle cupboard.' I sit down again on the sofa, wrapping myself up in the throw, but this time leave room for Nick. He comes back with a glass, pours himself a whisky, tops up mine, and sits down beside me.

'What the hell happened then, MJ?'

I tell him. And about the chase, and the helicopter and the dog. He tops up our glasses again.

'What were you doing on that road anyway?' he asks curiously.

Normally I'd balk at being quizzed, but the whisky has mellowed me. It was good of him to come rushing over, and like I say, I'm glad he's here.

'I'd been to Portishead. You remember that box I found in Bolborough Lake? The woman who claimed it is a Miss Leverton – Stella Leverton. She lives in Portishead, in a swishy retirement complex. I've been over to see her a couple of times.'

'Whatever for?'

'For some reason that escapes me, she wanted to meet me. I only went the first time because Amanda Coles insisted I did, and it's gone on from there. Miss Leverton invited me back to tell me her story, how she was an SOE agent in occupied France. How she came to win the Croix de Guerre, and all that. It's fascinating stuff, but it's a bit odd really. I don't know why she's so anxious to tell me all about it.'

'She wants some recognition, I suppose.'

'I don't think so. Much to Amanda's chagrin, she's totally opposed to any publicity. I think it must be that she's just very lonely. She doesn't seem to have any family or friends. Her baby daughter was killed in the bombing of Bath, and as if that wasn't bad enough, the man she was in love with – her sector leader – was killed in 1944. Blew up himself and a posse of Germans so that she could escape.'

Nick whistles through his teeth.

'Sounds like something out of a war film.'

'It is. It's totally amazing. And very sad, really, that someone who was so brave should end up all alone with just a stranger to talk to about what happened.'

'And how did the Croix de Guerre come to be in the lake?'

'I don't know that yet. I'm not even sure she knows. Either that or she's keeping titbits back so I'll visit her again. She's very interested in me, too. How I came to be a police diver, what the job entails, that sort of thing.'

'Not surprising, really. You are a bit of a one-off, MJ.'

'I'm not sure how to take that.'

'It's meant as a compliment.'

'OK, I'll believe you. Thousands wouldn't.'

I'm beginning to feel very tired, though I'm not sure how well I'll sleep. I have a horrid feeling that when I close my eyes I'll see that bloody car coming out of the junction without stopping over and over again.

'I think I'm going to have to go to bed, Nick,' I say.

'Good plan.' But he makes no move to leave.

'Night, then,' I say pointedly. 'And thanks for coming over.'

'No problem. I'm not leaving you on your own, though.'

'What?' I give him a hard stare.

'I'll sleep on the sofa.'

'You'll do no such thing!'

'MJ, you are not fit to be left alone. And I've had too much whisky to be driving. Think of my licence if you won't think of yourself.'

This much is true. I look at the whisky bottle, three quarters full when I found it in the cupboard, now considerably depleted. If I turn Nick out now and he has an accident himself, or gets breathalysed, it would be my fault.

'OK,' I say. 'As long as you stay on the sofa.'

He grins. 'I know not to push my luck.'

'Night, then.'

'Night.'

I head off for the bathroom, and then bed. I'd thought I liked living alone, having my own space, doing my own thing. I do like it! But tonight there is something very comforting about knowing Nick is there, just the other side of my door. Not just comforting, comfortable too.

My head hits the pillow, and contrary to my fears, almost at once I am in a whisky-induced sleep.

It doesn't last long. I'm dreaming, as I thought I would, of lights in the darkness, a car shooting out on to the road in front of me. But then I realise it's a German car, armoured, and the road is swarming with men in Nazi uniforms. I can feel the panic rising inside me along with an awful, creeping dread, because I know something terrible is going to happen.

I scream, and it wakes me. I'm bathed in sweat, and I lie for a moment, rigid with fear, still lost in the claustrophobic horror of the dream. I wonder if I cried out aloud, whether I've disturbed Nick, and he'll be appearing in the doorway asking if I'm all right. I hope not, though at the moment I'd like to feel arms holding me, a shoulder to bury my face in. But everything is quiet.

Tired as I am, I don't want to go back to sleep just yet. I'm too afraid the dream will begin again. And my mouth tastes horrid and is very dry. I get up, go to the bathroom and draw a glass of water in the tooth mug.

On the way back to my bedroom I look round the living room door. There's a mound on the sofa, covered with my new throw – Nick, still fast asleep. Which is probably a good thing. I feel a bit needy at the moment – very unlike me – and it would not be a good idea to lay it on Nick. I'm grateful to him for coming over, but I don't want to give him ideas.

I take a couple of aspirins, drink another glass and a half of water, and go back to bed.

This time when I fall asleep there are no disturbing dreams. I sleep heavily until morning.

THIRTY

ANNE

'So what's this all about, Mum? What is it you want to tell me that you couldn't say over the telephone?'

'Let's have a cup of tea. There's no rush, is there?' Mum seems very nervy, very tense. I can hear it in her voice and her fingers are working restlessly, scratching at the sore place on her arm, pulling her sleeve down to cover it, pushing it up and scratching again.

'Well actually there is,' I say. 'I really don't want to be too long. I'd like to be back at Sonia's before it gets dark. I don't like driving in the dark. The lights of oncoming vehicles play havoc with my eyes.'

Mum sniffs, as if she thinks I'm making excuses, but it's the truth. For the last year or so, the headlights of cars coming towards me seem to splinter into dazzling coronas; I try to watch the side of the road and not look at them, but it's not pleasant, and it makes me feel unsafe. It's my eyes ageing, my optician says, and there's nothing to be done about it unless I develop cataracts, in which case an operation for that might well put the other problem right as well.

'You should have come in daylight then,' Mum complains.

I bite my tongue. I really don't want to repeat myself yet again as to how my days are filled.

'I'm here now,' I say. 'If you want a cup of tea, make one. But please let's get on with it.'

'Why do you have to be so impatient, Anne?'

323

She makes the tea, but with annoying slowness that I'm sure is deliberate. I can see her hands trembling, and for once she doesn't regale me with a catalogue of her woes. I find this strangely disturbing, given that it usually drives me mad. It's further evidence that she's wound up about whatever it is she wants to tell me.

It must be something to do with Dad's family, I imagine, something she's decided to share with me after all but is ashamed of for some reason. I really can't see what could be so terrible that it's got her into this state, but then it's a long time since I've been able to fathom my mother.

'How is Sonia?' she asks when the tea is poured and we've taken it into the sitting room.

'The same.'

'And this . . . transplant. They haven't found a match for her?'

'Not yet. That's why it's so important that I find Dad's brother, or any other relatives. I'm guessing you know more about them than you told me, and it's something you're uncomfortable talking about. But honestly, nothing you can say is going to shock me. It really doesn't matter to me, or to anybody else. The only thing I'm interested in is finding a match so we can give Sonia a fighting chance. So please, stop worrying about things that are over and done with and tell me how I can get in touch with them.'

Mum shakes her head, a small, jerky movement.

'I told you before, Anne, it won't do any good.'

'What are you talking about, Mum? It's got to be worth a try. They are family, after all.'

Mum shakes her head again. Her mouth is working. Incredibly, she appears to be close to tears.

'No. No, they're not, Anne.'

'What?' I stare at her, puzzled.

'They're not family. Not yours. Not Sonia's.'

'But . . . ? What are you saying, Mum?'

'Your father . . .' She breaks off, her lips a tight but trembling line. 'Well . . . he's not your father. There, now I've told you. It's a waste of time finding his brother because he's no relation to you and Sonia. So you might as well put it out of your head.'

For a moment I am literally dumbstruck. I stare at Mum, open-mouthed. Whatever I'd expected, it certainly wasn't this. In fact, I'm having trouble taking it in.

'You're saying Dad wasn't my real father,' I manage at last.

'No.' She presses her fingers against her mouth as if it was not too late to stop the words that had knocked the bottom out of my world.

'I can't believe this,' I say. 'I can't believe you've kept this from me all my life. I just don't understand! How could you? Why did you never tell me?'

'There was no reason to.' There's a slightly aggressive note in her voice now, her form of defence, I suppose. 'We didn't think you needed to know.'

'So you lied to me.'

'No, we never lied.'

'But you didn't tell me the truth.'

'There was no need.'

'There was every need! I had a right to know who I am!'

'Oh, don't be like this, Anne. He was a good father to you. That was all that mattered. He loved you as if you were his own. He couldn't have done more for you if you had been. He didn't want you to know, and neither did I.'

'No, I don't suppose you did!'

I'm remembering all Mum's exhortations to me when I was a teenager, trying my wings with boys and dates, that I should be careful not to 'let myself down'. She'd been really quite strict with me, warned me against the ways of young men, embarrassed me sometimes with what had seemed to me to be her old-fashioned stuffiness.

Now I can see where it all came from. She'd been afraid I would make the same mistake she did. The hypocrisy of it makes me almost as angry as the fact that she and Dad had deceived me into believing he was my father.

With an enormous effort I get a grip on myself and my seething emotions. Perhaps some good can come out of this after all.

'So – who is he?' I ask harshly.

'Who?'

'My real father. Who is he?'

'Oh Anne, there's no point—'

'There's every point! I am trying to find blood relations in order to save my daughter's life. So please, just put your reticence behind you and tell me who my father is.'

Tears are gathering in Mum's eyes. She takes off her glasses and mops at them with a handkerchief that she's found up her sleeve.

'Don't be so cross, Anne, please. We thought it was for the best. I never thought for one minute . . . I never meant to do wrong . . .'

'Mum, I really don't give a damn that I'm illegitimate, though I am certainly cross that you never told me. But the only thing that really matters now is finding a bone marrow match for Sonia. So will you please tell me who my father was.'

Mum is silent for a long moment, and I resist the urge to shake her. Then she mutters something into her handkerchief.

'I couldn't hear that,' I snap.

Mum lowers the handkerchief. She can't look at me.

'He was a German,' she says, so softly that for a minute I think I must have misheard her again.

'What!'

'He was a German boy. I don't know his name. I never did.'

'A German boy?' I repeat, stunned. 'But how . . . ?'

'I was working in Bath with the Admiralty. So was he.'

'A German? Working for the Admiralty?'

'No, no. He was a waiter. In a hotel. The Royal Grove. He went home when the war started. They all had to, German nationals. He'd have been put in prison if he'd stayed here.'

'Oh my God.'

All my hopes of finding a donor for Sonia are turning to ashes. A German. Whose name my mother doesn't even know, or has forgotten. A German who may well have fought, and been killed, in the war, without fathering any more children – even given that I can find him, which suddenly seems a very long shot indeed. But it's my only hope.

I reach for my bag, find a diary and a pen.

'Tell me again – what was the hotel?'

'The Royal Grove.'

I write it down on the flyleaf of my diary.

'And you're absolutely sure you don't know his name?'

Mum shakes her head.

'I don't know, Anne. I'm so sorry . . .' She's crying again.

Somehow I find it in myself to put my arms round her. I'm angry, frustrated, impatient, but I don't like to leave her like this. Not at her age, when you never know what's around the next corner, especially when she's upsetting herself so. But I'm finding it very hard to feel compassion for her. The deception she has practised on me is too great to be forgotten and forgiven so easily.

'You see now why I couldn't tell you over the phone?' she says.

'Yes.'

'Don't be cross with me, please . . .'

'It's been a shock, Mum.'

'I'm so sorry.'

'Well, it's out in the open now.'

'And you don't blame me?'

I sigh inwardly. We're back to it all being about Mum.

'I'll get over it.'

'You're everything to me, Anne. You know that, don't you?'

'Yes, Mum, I know.'

Dusk is beginning to fall.

'I'm going to have to go. I'll phone you, all right?'

'Please, Anne.'

I kiss her cheek. It feels cold and papery. Then I walk out into that falling dusk, and for once I'm not worrying about how I'm going to manage, driving in the dark. There's too much else on my mind.

Mum is standing in the doorway watching me go, a diminutive figure who seems to have shrunk in the last hour. My mother. Whom I thought I knew so well, but whom I really didn't know at all.

And me? Well, I hardly know myself. I am not the person I always thought I was. The shock is enormous, but for the moment the revelations are important in one context only.

Somehow I have to try to find my real father. Not for me, but for Sonia.

The first thing I do when I get back to Sonia's is phone Rod. From my mobile, in the privacy of my room, not on her landline, of course. I don't want her or Kevin to overhear the conversation.

'Are you all right, love?' he asks anxiously when he hears my shaky voice.

'I'm fine. But I have to talk to you. I've had a bit of a shock.'

'Why? What's happened?' He still sounds worried. 'Is Sonia . . . ?'

'Nothing to do with Sonia. Well . . . actually everything to do with Sonia. If it hadn't been for her, I'd never have found out.'

'Found out what?'

'It's just unbelievable really . . .'

'What's unbelievable? You're not making any sense, Anne. Come on now, love, calm down and tell me what you're talking about.'

Just hearing his voice is soothing me.

'Well, I went to see Mum this evening to ask about Dad's family. So that I could contact them and try to find a bone marrow match for Sonia. And she told me that Dad wasn't my real father at all. That my real father was a German boy. Can you believe it, Rod? They've kept it from me all my life! I'm just . . . well, to be honest, I'm just speechless. How could they keep me in the dark about something like that? All my life!'

'Blimey! You're right. That is a bit of a shocker.'

'To put it mildly!'

'What else did she say?'

I fill him in on the scant details Mum was able to give me. Then:

'It's not much to go on, I know, but I've got to try and find out who he was. It opens up all sorts of possibilities – a whole new branch of the family . . .'

'Oh Anne – don't get your hopes up. It's like looking for a needle in a haystack. A German boy you don't even have a name for, who worked in a Bath hotel for a short time more than sixty years ago . . . that's a tall order. And even if you can find out who he was, there's no guarantee he'd want to help . . . To be honest, I think you'd be wasting your time.'

'I've got to try, though. If there's any chance at all . . .'

Rod sighs. 'I don't want you putting yourself under any more pressure, love. You've got enough on your plate as it is without this.'

'The pressure comes from Sonia being at death's door,' I say crossly. 'Don't you *want* to try and find a donor for her?'

'Of course I do. I just think—'

'I know what you think. That I'd be wasting my time.'

'I'm only saying . . .' He sighs again. 'Look, leave it with me. I'll go online and see what I can find out. I just don't want you taking on more than you have already.'

'You will do it, Rod?'

'I said I would, didn't I? Now, I think you ought to try and relax while you've got the chance. Have a stiff drink to help you unwind. You've had a hell of a shock. Promise me you won't do any more tonight. Right?'

'OK, OK.'

We say good night and end the call. But I have no intention of keeping my promise to Rod. There's absolutely no way I can put my feet up with all this buzzing around in my head, and in any case I'm not entirely convinced Rod will do as he promised either. It's clear he thinks trying to find my real father is a lost cause, and to be honest, I really don't hold out much hope myself. But a quitter I am not. I didn't make a career in modelling, or build up my own agency, without being possessed of a very stubborn streak. The tougher the odds, the more I dig my heels in; the more someone tells me that what I'm attempting is impossible, the more determined I am to prove them wrong.

Tired as I am, I boot up my laptop and go online to look for the Royal Grove Hotel.

To my surprise I find it almost straight away – I'd thought that even if it was still there, it might well have changed its name. It's in the centre of town, I discover, a stately-looking Georgian building with canopies over the windows and bay trees in pots on either side of the main entrance. All done in accordance with the strict planning laws in the historic city, I imagine.

I print up the contact details and, just for good measure, write them in my diary too. It's too late tonight to make any enquiries, but I make up my mind to do that first thing tomorrow.

And I say a prayer that by some miracle the secret that Mum has finally revealed to me, some sixty-odd years too late, will help me save my beloved daughter.

I have something of a sleepless night, and I'm awake again when my alarm goes off at six thirty. I do all the usual morning jobs, and when I've taken the children to school I rush back, raring to make a start on my investigation. But I've scarcely taken off my jacket and made myself a cup of coffee when the phone rings. It's Rod, worried about me following our conversation last night.

When I told him I'd located the Royal Grove Hotel he was cross with me.

'I thought I told you I'd do that.'

'And have you?'

'Not yet, no. I was going to do it later. And you were supposed to be relaxing last night.'

'How could I relax? I knew you wouldn't do it.'

'Anne, I *was* going to do it.'

'Well, now you don't have to.'

'And what are you going to do about it?'

'I don't know yet. I haven't made up my mind.' But that's not true. I know exactly what I'm going to do. I just don't want to tell Rod and have him put a damper on my plans.

The next hold-up comes when Elaine rings – there are hitches with the organisation of the fashion show, it seems. It takes me over an hour to sort things out, and I'm still not sure if the problems are resolved. I'm expecting some more awkward phone calls, and I'll have to call in a few favours before I can be certain things are back on track.

Then Sonia comes downstairs. She wants to talk about a day out that Abigail and her class are going on next week.

'You will make sure nothing gets in the way of her going, won't you?' she says, and I know what she means. She's concerned that if she should take a turn for the worse and have to be taken back into hospital, Abigail might have to miss the trip.

'I just want things to be as normal as possible for the children,' she says. 'I don't want them looking back and remembering nothing but gloom. Happy times in childhood are so important, aren't they? Nothing can take them away.'

That chimes with me, giving me pause for thought. I had a very happy childhood, and though at the moment it feels as though it was all a lie, once I've got used to the idea my memories will still be there, intact. Dad might not have been my real father, but he was the one who was there for me, teaching me to swim in the days before armbands by wading across the pool with his hand under my tummy to support me until I found the confidence to strike out on my own, playing soldiers with me under the dining room table with a bicycle pump for a gun (sounds strange, I know, but it was in the war, remember), carrying me up to bed on his shoulders, pretending to be a horse. And he was the one who could be relied upon to make things right when Mum was in one of her funny moods.

I've now discovered the reason for those moods. I don't yet know anything about this German boy, why he left her in the lurch when I was on the way – though if she didn't even know his name, it sounds a bit like a one-night stand or even a rape. A rape could well explain her depressions and reluctance to tell me the truth.

But learning the details is for later. There will be time then to talk to Mum and find the answers to all the questions and perhaps give her the chance to unburden herself after all the years of silence. For now, I have to concentrate on Sonia.

I can't make the phone call I'm itching to make with Sonia in earshot. I don't want to raise her hopes until I have something concrete to go on. So I make the excuse of needing to go out for something for tonight's tea. I drive to the supermarket and park in the quietest corner of the car park. Then I get out my mobile and my diary for the details of the Royal Grove Hotel.

I start to shake a bit as I punch in the number. That is very unlike me, but this means so much. Though I'm desperately trying to remain positive, I can't help anticipating the stony plummet of my heart when they tell me there is no way they can help me. Implying, of course, that I must be a sandwich short of a picnic to think for a moment that they could.

The telephone is answered by what I imagine to be exactly the sort of young woman who would be on the reception desk at a rather posh hotel in a very posh city. She's beautifully spoken and respectful when I ask if I could speak to someone about any records there might be of past staff.

'I think it's extremely unlikely we'd have records going back that far,' she says.

'It's a long shot, I know,' I say. 'Personal memory would probably be a better bet. You don't know of anyone – a long-serving member of staff, perhaps – who might have been working in the hotel just before the war, and remember a German boy who was a waiter? They'd have retired long ago, I know, but if you could put me in touch . . .'

There's a long pause. I'm just wondering if we've been cut off when she says: 'Could I ask who's calling?'

'Anne Mayle.'

'And you are . . . what? A writer? Someone in TV or film?'

'Goodness, no! This is a personal enquiry.'

But I'm very alert suddenly, the skin on the back of my neck prickling. What I said had meant something to her, I was sure. Either that or she was paranoid.

'Why would you think I'm from the media?' I ask sharply.

'I'm sorry. I assumed that someone asking about the Liebermanns must be making a documentary, perhaps, or writing a book.'

The breath is tight in my chest.

'The Liebermanns?'

'The family who own the hotel, yes. Mr Liebermann senior worked here before the war. He came back and bought it when it came up for sale in the early 1950s. It's been part of the Liebermann chain ever since.'

For a moment I'm speechless. Then I gather myself together.

'From what you say, I think it's the Liebermanns I'm trying to trace. Are any of them in England, or do they all live in Germany?'

'Miss Liebermann – Angela . . .' The girl stops abruptly. 'I'm sorry, I'm not sure I should be . . . Let me speak to someone. Can you hold?'

The line goes dead for a moment, then Handel's Water Music starts up in my ear. I move the phone away, just far enough to leave room for my racing thoughts, close enough to hear when the music stops and someone speaks. Inwardly I'm churning. This is beyond belief. But I mustn't get excited just yet. There could have been other German waiters working at the hotel, and even if I have been so lucky as to have found the right one, it could still go pear-shaped.

I must be careful what I say, too. I don't want to alienate or frighten off the people who might be my family . . . Sonia's salvation. I try desperately to use the long minutes to work out exactly what I'm going to say. But my head feels like a seething cauldron and I can't string anything together.

I put the phone back to my ear. Still music. Then there's a click and the girl is back.

'I'm putting you through to Mr Boris Liebermann. He's our chief executive, and he's Mr Liebermann senior's son. One moment, please.'

Oh my God . . .

Another burst of music, another click, and a man speaks.

'This is Boris Liebermann. How can I help you?' The voice is deep, with a faint guttural accent.

I take a deep breath.

'Mr Liebermann. It's very good of you to take the time to speak to me. My name is Anne Mayle. You won't know me, but I believe my mother knew your father when he was in Bath just before the war. And I was wondering if it would be possible for me to contact him.'

'Really! Well I'm afraid that it won't be possible, Ms Mayle. My father died in 1985.'

My heart sinks. 'But he was a waiter here in 1938?'

'He was, yes. Our family owned hotels in Germany and he was

here to learn the trade from the bottom up. He fell in love with Bath, and after the war, when he was charged with rebuilding the family business, he learned that the Royal Grove had been put on the market. He bought it, and it has been part of our chain ever since.'

'Do you live in Bath, Mr Liebermann?'

'Sometimes. Mostly I live out of a suitcase.'

'And the rest of the family?'

'Pardon me, but I don't see . . .'

'I'm sorry. You must think this all very odd. And I'm not sure I can explain over the telephone. I know it's an awful imposition, but would it be possible for me to come and see you? It won't take up too much of your time, I promise. But it really is very important. And it would mean so much to my mother,' I add, lying.

'I have to admit I'm intrigued. But I am flying back to Hamburg this evening.'

'Oh. And you couldn't spare me a few minutes . . . ?'

'I have meetings all day. I'm sorry.'

I grasp at the last shred of hope.

'You don't happen to know, I suppose, if there were other German nationals working at the Royal Grove at the same time as your father?'

'I wouldn't know. I don't ever remember him mentioning anything of the kind, but . . . What is this all about, Ms Mayle?'

I hesitate. And decide to go for broke.

'I have a daughter who is suffering from leukaemia. If she doesn't have a stem cell transplant, she is probably going to die, leaving two young children of eight and ten motherless. I've just learned that my father was a German waiter at the Royal Grove in the year before the war. And I'm trying to trace him in the hope that one of his family might be able to provide a match for the transplant that could save my daughter's life. When I phoned the hotel today I had no idea that it was owned by the Liebermanns – I was just looking for a lead to follow. And I don't know if your father is the man I'm looking for, of course. But if not, the names of other possible candidates would be so helpful to me. That's it really. I'm on a desperately urgent mission and anything – anything at all – that you can do to help me . . . well, I would be so grateful.'

Boris Liebermann is silent for a long moment. Clearly he is so shocked he needs time to absorb what I've said. I wait, holding my breath, praying.

'I think,' he says at last, 'that the person you should speak to is my aunt, Angela. There is really nothing I can tell you, but she and my father were very close. It may be that he said something to her when he came home to Germany just before the war began that may be of use.'

'Oh, that would be wonderful! Where . . . ?'

'She has a suite here, at the Royal Grove. I'll speak to her, ask if she is willing to meet you. If you give me your telephone number, I will have my secretary call you back.'

'Thank you so much!' I'm overwhelmed. 'It's a mobile number . . .' I give it to him. 'This is really so kind . . .'

'No problem,' he says, and there is the hint of a smile in his voice. 'I suppose it is the least I can do. After all, if you are right, and my father is the man you are looking for, I imagine you must be my sister.'

THIRTY-ONE

MARTHA

I am not a happy bunny. As I suspected, my car is a write-off – all I need, since it's next week that Granny and I go to Weston-super-Mare – and my bruised ribs mean I'm not up to diving. I refused to take sick leave, but I've been reduced to standing on the bank directing operations whilst the rest of the team do the interesting stuff. Or perhaps not so interesting. Searching a very murky section of the docks for a knife used in a mugging is something I'm not really crazy about, and a training day at a quarry can be a bit of a bore.

I really should be grateful for small mercies. At least I'm in one piece when I could be in intensive care, or even on a mortuary slab. At least my insurance covers me for a courtesy car while my claim is sorted out (a wonder, really – I usually pare all the extras down to the bone to try and keep my premium low). And they caught the yob who caused the accident, too, a small-time local drug dealer who'd been trying to make a dishonest living – a goodly stash of heroin was found in the wrecked car, and knock-on information has led to the raiding of a cannabis factory in a flat in the St Paul's area.

Plus, things are still going well with Pete. So what am I complaining about?

The day after the accident he turns up at the docks where we are searching for the knife and collars me when I go back to the lorry for a cup of coffee.

'Are you all right, Martha? I heard about the accident.'

Well, he would, wouldn't he? As a newspaper reporter, he'd be party to the story, particularly as drugs were involved.

'I'm a bit sore, but otherwise OK.'

'Should you be at work?'

'I don't call in sick unless I have to. Sitting around feeling sorry for myself isn't my style.'

'No, it's not, is it? You shouldn't have been on your own last night, though. You should have called me. Why didn't you?'

'I'm not a helpless female either. And in any case, I wasn't on my own. Nick came over.'

I see his face change, a narrowing of his eyes, a tightening of his mouth.

'Nick as in your ex,' he says.

'What other Nick is there in my life? Yes, one of the traffic lot rang him, apparently, told him what had happened and he turned up at my flat to check up on me. Actually . . .' I pause, thinking I might as well be upfront about this, in case he hears it from some other source, 'actually he stayed the night. But don't get the wrong idea. He slept on the sofa.'

Pete shrugs elaborately, as if it doesn't matter to him one way or the other, which actually makes me think the complete opposite is the case and, to my surprise, pleases me. I rather like the idea that he might be jealous.

I am also pleased when I go to pick up my coffee, wince at the sudden darting pain in my ribs, and he looks concerned.

'You're not all right, are you?'

'I'll live.'

'But you need a little TLC. How about I get a takeaway tonight and bring it over to your place? You aren't going to feel like going out, and we could have a quiet evening. As long as your ex-husband doesn't turn up again.'

Gratifying though it is that he's prickly about Nick, I don't think I should push this too far. 'Pete, Nick knows he's history as far as I'm concerned. He was just being friendly, which is the best way for ex-partners to be. No point in harbouring bad feeling. It causes too much angst. Look, I've got to get on. I'm working if you're not.'

'I am working!' He pulls a hurt face. 'I'm hoping to see some spectacular, newsworthy find.'

'A knife? Hardly spectacular.'

'You never know what you might find down there, though, do you?'

He's referring to the Croix de Guerre, of course.

'Gotta go, Pete.'

'You're on for the takeaway, though?'

'As long as it's not Indian. I am so fed up with the smell of curry I couldn't face it.'

'Pizza? Chinese?'

'You decide.'

We don't find the knife, or anything else of any interest, though we do have a bit of drama when Ding-Dong's line gets tangled up with some debris some idiot has dumped in the docks. Fortunately Shorty, diving as his buddy, spots it and all is well.

By the time I get home I'm pretty tired, and half wishing I hadn't arranged for Pete to come over. I could have done with an evening curled up in my throw on the sofa with nothing more demanding than *Coronation Street* or *Come Dine With Me* on the telly. But when he arrives with a carrier bag loaded with containers of Cantonese beef, sweet and sour pork balls and special fried rice I reckon I made the right decision after all, and when we've finished eating and got cosy on the sofa I'm sure I did. There won't be any red-hot passion tonight, my ribs are too sore for that, but it is rather nice to have a shoulder to lay my head against and a hand to hold.

'I take it you'd been to see Stella Leverton again when the accident happened,' Pete says.

'Go to the top of the class. You should have been a policeman.'

'A talent for deduction isn't the sole prerogative of Britain's finest,' Pete says drily. 'It's pretty obvious anyway.'

'Mm. I guess.'

'I thought you didn't want to get sucked into her net.'

'I didn't. I don't! But she is an amazing person. What she has told me about her time with the SOE is absolutely fascinating, though it's really odd, she insists on telling it all in the third person. She says "Pascale" – that was her name in the field – instead of "me" or "I", as if she's distancing herself somehow. But they were so brave! Honestly, I take my hat off to her.'

'What did she do, then?'

'What didn't she do! Just imagine being undercover in an enemy-occupied country, never knowing from one minute to the next if you were going to be caught, tortured and executed. Never being sure who was friend and who was foe. And she had such tragedy in her personal life, too. It's like she was fated to lose everyone she loved . . .' I hesitate. I shouldn't be talking to Pete about this. 'Promise me you won't print any of this.'

'You think I'd risk upsetting you, Martha?' He nibbles my ear. I melt inside. And funnily enough, I feel I can trust him. But then if you can't trust someone you're sleeping with, what the hell is the point?

'Well, I certainly hope not. I would be upset. Very.'

'Go on. Her private life.'

'She lost a child in the war, killed by a direct hit by a bomb. And her mother was killed too. She used to look after the little girl while Miss Leverton was at work, and she'd taken her shopping when they had this daylight raid. How awful is that?'

'So she was married, was she?'

'No. Now that tells you what sort of a woman she was. Having the guts to keep an illegitimate baby in those days . . . that was a hell of a thing to do.'

'I suppose it was.'

'Anyway, she was recruited for the SOE after her little girl was killed. Her mother was French, so she was bilingual, which was absolutely necessary if she was to blend into the background in France. They were desperate for people who were fluent in French, it seems, and Pascale – Miss Leverton – agreed to sign up. If the little girl hadn't been killed, I'm sure she'd never have done it, what-ever the pressure. But as it was, she felt she had nothing left to lose.'

'Understandable.'

'Well, yes. She must have been absolutely devastated. Anyway, the tragedy doesn't stop there. She fell for her section leader in a big way, and then he was killed too. It was so tragic . . .'

I tell him how Miss Leverton's Paul had sacrificed himself for her. Pete whistles softly. 'That is some story.'

'Which you are absolutely not going to use. Really, I shouldn't have repeated it. I don't know why I have – especially to you.'

'Because you find me irresistible.' His tongue flicks into my ear.

'Will you stop that?' I say, though I don't mean it. Already I'm forgetting about Miss Leverton. Maybe I'll forget about my sore ribs too, given a little encouragement.

'Are you sure she hasn't got some ulterior motive for telling you all this?' Pete asks, shifting back a bit and looking along at me.

'What do you mean?' I ask. 'You surely not insinuating that she *does* want it made public and she's just playing coy, guessing that I'll tell you? Because if so, I'm sure you're wrong. I think she's just lonely. That's the top and bottom of it.'

'Are you going back to see her again?'

'I expect so. There's a lot I still don't know. I haven't had the chance to have a good look at that photograph either, though I'm pretty sure the other two girls are Simone and Marie – the ones she trained with.' A thought strikes me. 'You haven't remembered where you've seen it before, I suppose?'

'Whatever you might think, I didn't come here to talk about Miss Leverton,' Pete says, pulling me towards him.

It's only later that I wonder – was he avoiding my question? But I really don't care much. Things are looking good between Pete and me. For the first time in ages I am with someone I want to be with. Enjoying the moment, not looking to the future, but feeling pretty optimistic about it all the same.

For all my recent problems, it is a pretty good place to be.

And then, a couple of days later, the bombshell strikes.

'Here she is, then, our Z-list celebrity,' Ding-Dong says as I go into the squad room.

'What are you talking about?'

'Picture in the papers again. We shall have to ask you for your autograph soon.'

He stabs with his finger at a copy of the *Western News* that's spread untidily across the counter.

Even from here, now that I'm looking, I can see a picture that is unmistakably that awful photograph of me in full diving gear.

'Oh shit!' I say, annoyed. 'It's about the accident, I suppose. That bloody drugs dealer! But why do they have to drag me into it? Just because I happened to be the car he hit . . .'

'This isn't about the accident, MJ. It's about the stuff you found in Bolborough Lake.'

'What!' I'm horrified. 'Let me see that!'

I snatch the paper from under his nose.

'Take it easy, MJ,' Ding-Dong protests. 'No need to lose your rag.'

But I'm not listening. There's a headline, 'TREASURES IN THE LAKE IDENTIFIED', that picture of me and another of Miss Leverton, which appears to have been taken with a long lens outside her apartment block. She's wearing a coat, clutching her handbag and looking startled – some bloody photographer was obviously lying in wait and snapped her when she went out to the shops or what-ever.

Beneath the pictures is a half-page spread, recapping the story of the box I found in the lake and the fact that it contained the Croix de Guerre and 'other personal items', and referring to Miss Leverton as a 'tragic heroine' living the life of a recluse after the love of her life died in occupied France saving her from capture. There's even mention of her baby daughter, killed in the bombing of Bath.

'Oh my God!' I say. I'm shaking – with shock, and with white-hot fury. There's no byline, but I'm in no doubt whatsoever who wrote this piece. 'He promised me! He promised me he wouldn't use what I told him!'

'Who?' Ding-Dong asks, bemused.

'Pete Bloody Holbrook! That's who! Oh, I don't believe this!'

'Pete Holbrook?' Ding-Dong still looks puzzled. 'What's he got to do with it?'

'Everything!'

'She's been seeing him, haven't you, MJ?' Doug Hawthorn says. 'Calm down, MJ. It's not the end of the world.'

'How could I have been so stupid as to trust him! Miss Leverton has been telling me her story, but she absolutely did not want it publicised – and now it's all over the paper. The dailies will have it soon – he'll be doing a feature for them next! His big scoop, and I've handed it to him on a plate.'

'You know what reporters are like,' Doug says, sympathetically enough, but I know what he's thinking. That I've been a complete idiot. Well, whatever he thinks of me, it couldn't be more damning that what I think of myself. How could I have been so naïve? Actually thought he was interested in me? All he wanted me for was to winkle out the details that Miss Leverton was confiding in me.

Still raging – and desperately hurt – I rummage in my bag for my mobile. Pete's number is in the directory, has been for a few days now. I scroll down to it and stab the call button, but infuriatingly it goes to voicemail.

'You little shit!' I yell at it. 'How could you?'

The phone in my office is ringing.

'Do you want me to get that?' Doug asks.

'No, I'll get it myself.' I snap off my mobile, hurl it in the direction of my bag. It misses, and hits the tiled floor with an ominous crack. I groan and swear.

'I'll get the call, MJ,' Doug says, disappearing into my office.

I pick up my mobile. There's a crack right across the display screen and no light showing. I try to get a dialling tone. Nothing.

'Now my phone's buggered! That's all I need!'

'You want me to see if it will receive calls?' Ding-Dong has his own mobile out, ringing my number. Again, nothing. I can feel my stress levels ratcheting up another notch. Apart from having a load of contact details on it that I haven't got stored anywhere else, this is an expensive phone – pay out heavily for the handset, get a cheaper tariff on the call rates – and the insurance may well not cover accidental damage. First my car and now my phone – what next? And as I'm working, I don't know when I'm going to have the chance to sort out all these disasters.

But the thing that hurts, really hurts, is Pete's betrayal. And the awful guilt that comes from knowing I've let Miss Leverton down.

I'll have to go and see her, tell her how sorry I am, and do what I can to protect her from the fallout. But stopping Pete from capitalising on his story and selling it elsewhere will be something of a problem. The fact is – I can't stop him. If he cared two hoots for me he'd never have done this, and he's about as likely to take notice of my pleas to him to leave it there as a snowman would be to survive a heatwave. Besides, the damage is done. The story is out there, and every hack from John O'Groats to Land's End will be on to it.

I curse myself again. Idiot! Lured into a trap because I couldn't resist those bedroom eyes . . .

Doug comes to the door of my office, beckons me.

'We've got a job, MJ. A car has gone into a canal. They're not sure if there's anybody still inside, or whether it's been dumped by joyriders. Do you want to speak?'

'Have you got the details?'

'Yep.'

'OK, then. Tell them we'll be there.'

With the greatest difficulty I get myself under control. 'Right, team. When you're ready . . .'

We set to work, gathering our equipment, gulping down cups of coffee as we do so. The morning paper lies on the counter, still open at the offending story.

I make very sure I don't so much as glance at it.

THIRTY-TWO

ANNE

The Royal Grove Hotel is an impressive Georgian building in the centre of Bath, facing on to a tree-lined square that could, more accurately, be described as a small park. I know it vaguely – Bristol is, after all, a mere ten or twelve miles away. The hotel has a long frontage and a rather grand entrance flanked by potted bay trees and tariff boards encased in sparkling glass. If pigeons or the seagulls that have invaded the town have left calling cards, every last trace has been washed away; the grey paving slabs and the window ledges are spotless.

I go into the cool and frankly luxurious foyer and approach the reception desk – all dark wood and highly polished brass – where a young woman who could well be on my books as a model appears from behind a computer screen.

I tell her my name, and that Miss Liebermann is expecting me. She makes a phone call, then points me in the direction of the lift. I need the top floor, she tells me. The lift is mirrored, reflecting my anxious face. I look away. I don't want to be reminded of how nervous I am. Bad enough feeling the tension tying my stomach in knots. This is so important to me, and I'm terrified I'm going to come away disappointed.

The lift purrs to a halt, the door slides open and I step out into a corridor carpeted in silver grey. The walls are pale grey too, and hung with pictures – original watercolours that would probably command a high price at auction. I find the door to the penthouse suite and ring the bell. It is opened by a young Filipino woman in maid's uniform. She shows me into a spacious drawing room, which I imagine overlooks the square, or park, beneath.

An old lady sits in a reclining chair, the modernity of which is slightly at odds with the other, very traditional furniture. As I go in she presses a button on the remote control she's holding and the chair slides into an upright position.

She's silver-haired, the slightly sparse locks pulled back, ballerina style, into a knot at the nape of her neck. Her face is broad, very Germanic, and she wears little rimless spectacles. She's dressed all in black, a ruffled silk blouse and wide black trousers.

'Forgive me,' she says in a heavily accented voice, 'if I don't get up.'

'Of course.'

I'm a little shocked at just how old she looks, and, in spite of her not inconsiderable bulk, rather frail. It brings home to me just how fit my own mother is for her age.

'They want to give me hip replacements,' she says. 'They say it would make me mobile again. But I don't believe in hospitals unless there is no alternative. And why would I want to be mobile? My dancing days are over.'

I don't think she's expecting a reply, so I don't make one. I just force a smile.

'It's very good of you to see me, Miss Liebermann.'

'Not at all. A visitor relieves the tedium.' She glances in the direction of the Filipino maid, who has brought coffee and a plate of petit fours from the kitchen and is now hovering in the doorway. 'You may go now, Nene. I'll ring when I need you.'

'Yes, Miss Liebermann.'

The maid departs.

'So,' Miss Liebermann says, 'you wanted to talk to me about my brother.'

'Yes. My mother knew him – or at least, she knew a German who was working here before the war.' I hesitate. I don't know how much her nephew has told her of our conversation, and it's delicate to say the least.

'Well, certainly Kurt was here then,' she says. 'Our father owned a hotel chain in Germany and he wanted Kurt to learn every aspect of the business so that he would be well prepared to take control when the time came. Which of course he did. But he had fallen in love with Bath. He loved its beauty and its history. When this hotel, the very one where he worked as a waiter, came up for sale, he persuaded the other members of the board that it would be an asset. And so it has been. Not least, it has provided a retirement home for me.'

'I'm surprised you chose to live in England rather than Germany,' I say, thinking it is probably a good idea to establish a rapport before getting down to the purpose of my visit.

She smiles. 'I suppose I fell in love with Bath too. And there was nothing to keep me in Germany. The home I grew up in was destroyed in the bombing. Besides, Kurt needed me. His wife, Marlene, died when the children – Boris and Maria – were still quite young. Kurt and I were always close, much closer than either of us were to our sister Ingrid, and I moved here to help provide some stability for the children. If I hadn't come over, they would have been without a mother to help them grow up.'

This is a bit too close to home for me.

'That's very sad,' I say, trying not to think of my grandchildren, who might well lose their mother.

Her lips tighten a shade.

'A matter of opinion.' She raises a hand, still plump and white, with rings she can probably no longer get off adorning every finger. 'No, I mustn't speak ill of the dead. And in any case, you don't want to talk about Marlene. I'll say no more, except that Kurt should never have married her. He wouldn't have, I think, if he had found the girl he came back here to find. It wasn't just Bath he was in love with, you see. I sometimes think that it was because of this girl that Bath was so beautiful to him. In fact, I would think it was entirely that if I hadn't been entranced by the city myself.' She laughs, low and throaty. 'This, of course, is the reason I was prepared to meet you. From what you said to Boris, it seems to me entirely possible that the girl who was the love of Kurt's life, the girl he lost and could never find, no matter how he tried, might be your mother.'

346

I shake my head, confused. Of course I'd like to believe it was so, but it doesn't actually make sense. If my mother was the love of Kurt's life, as Angela Liebermann put it, then surely she would have known his name? Much more likely that something had gone wrong between Kurt and this unknown girl and he had turned to Mum on the rebound. A one-night stand that had resulted in . . . me. I was on even more delicate ground than I had realised.

'Did you know this girl's name?' I ask.

Angela Liebermann purses her lips.

'Well, I did, once. But it's a very long time ago.'

'My mother's name is Margaret.'

I wait, holding my breath, as she considers. Then she shakes her head.

'No, that doesn't sound right. I thought . . .' She's silent, struggling to plumb the depths of memory. 'I thought it wasn't an English name. Somehow I have it in my mind that it was French.'

'French!' I repeat, surprised.

'Well, I thought so. But as I say, it is a long time ago.' She pauses, fixing me with a very straight gaze from behind her rimless spectacles. 'My nephew tells me you had a special reason for trying to find your mother's lover. You believe it is possible that he was your father.'

So she does know the reason behind my visit.

'Mum said my father was a German who worked here as a waiter, yes. But to be perfectly truthful, I don't think they were in a relationship. I think it was more casual than that.' This is awkward. I don't want to imply that Angela Liebermann's dead brother was running around town getting local girls into trouble. I settle for the oblique approach. 'Do you know if there were any other Germans working in Bath at that time?'

'If there were, then Kurt never mentioned them, and he would have done, I'm sure,' she says bluntly. 'I think it must be him your mother is talking about. It's entirely possible, I suppose, that he was involved with more than one girl whilst he was here. He was young, you must remember, and in a foreign country. He would have been lonely, and young men will always be young men if the

347

opportunity arises. But I wouldn't know about that. It's not the sort of thing he would have talked about to me, his little sister.'

'No. Quite. I'm not finding this easy, Miss Liebermann, but it is dreadfully important. My daughter—'

'Yes, so Boris explained,' she interrupts me.

'Look, I know I'm asking an awful lot. I realise we're absolutely nothing to you, and you must think I've got a dreadful nerve, turning up out of the blue like this. I can't imagine how I'd feel if our roles were reversed. But the fact is that I'm desperate. If we can't find a bone marrow match, my daughter is going to die. Which is why I felt I didn't have any choice but to pursue this. And why I'm begging you to at least ask the younger members of your family if they would be prepared to be tested.'

For a long moment Angela Liebermann says nothing and I hold my breath. To be honest, I can't imagine a single reason why she would agree to help someone who is, after all, a stranger to her. Then, to my amazement, she nods slowly.

'I will help you if I can. I try very hard to do what I believe to be right in this life. If you are indeed family, then it's no more than my Christian duty.'

The rush of relief brings tears to my eyes.

'Thank you so much.'

'Don't thank me yet. The first step, I imagine, is to ascertain whether we are in fact related. I presume a DNA test would establish that one way or the other. I don't know how one would go about such a thing, but . . .'

'At the moment, neither do I. But I shall find out. I really can't tell you how grateful I am.'

'Don't let's go too far too fast. The DNA test is all I can promise for the moment. Anything beyond that would be down to individual members of the family. Boris and Maria would be the closest blood relatives, of course, since Kurt was their father. And they have children of their own – Boris has two sons, and Maria a son and a daughter. But they are all in Germany, and I can't speak for what their reaction to all this will be.'

'No, I understand that, of course.'

'I'll wait to hear from you then.'

Angela Liebermann reaches out a be-ringed hand to a bell that is located on the wall within easy reach of her chair. She's summoning the Filipino maid to show me out, I realise. The interview is over.

But I'm elated now, full of hope. Though there is a long way to go yet and nothing is certain, at last there is a glimmer of light at the end of the tunnel.

And as I leave the Royal Grove, I'm praying with all my heart.

Please, God, let something come out of this!

As I'm walking around the leafy square on the way to the car park, I turn my mobile back on. I'd switched it off while I was with Miss Liebermann; I didn't want to risk any interruptions whilst we were talking.

When it boots up, it trills and vibrates, indicating that I have messages on voicemail. Still walking, I go to the in-box and put the phone to my ear.

It's Sonia. To begin with she says only one word: 'Mum.' But she sounds distressed and my heart comes into my throat with a sickening leap.

'Mum, can you call me.'

And Sonia again.

'Where are you, Mum? Please call me. It's urgent.'

My optimistic mood shatters. I'm filled with sick dread. I stop walking, back up to the wall on the edge of the pavement, locate Sonia's number, and ring it. She answers so quickly that I know she's been nursing the phone, waiting for my call.

'Mum! Oh, thank goodness!'

'What's wrong, Sonia? Are you . . . ?'

'Not me. Grandma. I've had a call from the police. She's . . . she's . . .'

I go cold.

'She's not . . . ?'

'No, she's in hospital. But it's awful.'

'What is? What's happened?'

'She's in intensive care . . .'

'Where is she? Which hospital?'

'The BRI. But Mum, before you go rushing there, I need to tell you . . .'

'What?'

'She took pills. And quite a lot of brandy.'

For a moment I can't take in what she's saying. And yet, given Mum's history, I really shouldn't be this surprised. Isn't it really what I've always been afraid of?

'Hang on, Sonia . . . you mean . . . ?'

'She tried to commit suicide. Thelma found her and dialled 999 and they rushed her to hospital.'

Oh my God.

'Are you all right, Sonia, if I go straight to the hospital?'

'Yes, I'm fine. I wanted to catch you before you drove all the way here. I've called Kevin and he'll see the children are met from school, so you don't need to worry about that either.'

'If you're sure you're all right . . .'

'Yes. I said. I'm fine. You go and see Grandma. She needs you.'

'I'll ring you as soon as I've any news.'

I turn off my phone, head for the car park as fast as my high heels will allow. My thoughts are racing, my nerves jangling, and there's a huge black cloud again, suffocating me, weighing me down.

I'd been right to worry about telling Mum the truth about Sonia's illness. It's tipped her over the edge as I was afraid it might. That and having to tell me that Dad wasn't my real father. But I can't waste time castigating myself now. I have to get to the hospital and find out how she is. The rest will have to wait for later.

Parking for the BRI is an absolute nightmare at the best of times. I drive round the nearby streets looking for a space, not daring to park illegally in case I get clamped and towed away, and desperately wishing Rod was with me. He could have dropped me outside the entrance and taken his time finding somewhere to park. I could have used his moral support too. But he's not here; I've just got to get on with it.

Suddenly my luck changes. I see someone pulling out of a metered space and grab it, attracting furious honking from another car that had been waiting for it. I mouth 'sorry', but have no intention of relinquishing what is now my space. I feed the meter with the change I always keep in the well of the car for just such emergencies, and set out at a run for the hospital. Inside I am pushed from pillar to post, but eventually find the side ward where my mother is being treated, and get some much-needed information from the ward sister.

Mum is stable now, but critical. She'd swallowed a whole load of prescription drugs and washed them down with half a bottle of brandy. Fortunately she had been found before the effects proved fatal, but as yet they have been unable to ascertain how long ago she'd taken the overdose, and whether there is any irreversible damage. I can talk to a doctor later to get a clearer picture and a possible prognosis.

I go in to see her; she's not conscious and she's hooked up to all kinds of life-saving equipment. She looks dreadful lying there, very small and frail, very helpless. I sit with her for a while, feeling I'm living a nightmare.

I've seen too much of the inside of hospitals just lately; the smells and the sounds have become all too familiar, and the claustrophobic atmosphere, compounded by drawn curtains around the beds, is pressing in on me, making me feel a bit faint.

I ask a nurse when I'll be able to talk to a doctor; she says it will probably be another half-hour or so. I decide to go and get myself a coffee, or even a drink of water, and perhaps something to eat. I don't really fancy eating, but I think I should try.

I go in search of the café, and the first person I see when I go in is Thelma, sitting at one of the tables. At precisely the same moment, she sees me and waves frantically.

'Thelma!' I say, surprised to find her here.

'Oh Anne, thank goodness! How is she? How's your mum?'

I reply with a slight shake of my head.

'It's just terrible! Gave me the shock of my life when I found her there, in the sitting room. Thank the Lord I did, though! It's not my day to clean really, but she's been going on and on about a mark on the table, and when I was in the pound shop I found some stuff

I thought might do the trick, and I thought: I'm going in straight away to have a go! And I went in, and there she was! With all these empty packets of tablets beside her, and a brandy bottle, knocked over . . . oh my life! I nearly passed out myself, I can tell you!'

My heart sinks. If today hadn't been one of Thelma's days for working, then Mum had clearly chosen it so as not to be found before it was too late. Not just a cry for help, then, but a determined suicide attempt.

'I am so glad you went in today,' I say.

'Fate, innit? Well, of course, I called the ambulance, and give them their due, they were there in no time flat. They let me ride with her – well, there was nobody else to do it, was there? And I've been here ever since, waiting for news.'

'That is so good of you, Thelma.'

'Truth to tell,' Thelma says, looking straight at me, 'I don't know how I'm going to get home.'

'Oh, don't worry about that. I'll take you, of course. Look, I'm just going to get myself a coffee. Would you like something?'

'I wouldn't say no to another cup of tea.'

I go to the self-service counter, get the drinks and a miniature packet of Hobnobs, and pay for them. When I take them back to the table, Thelma is fumbling in her rather large, very shiny plastic handbag. She pulls out an envelope.

'I'm glad I've seen you anyway, Anne. This was on the coffee table beside her. A note, I suppose, for you . . .'

She pushes the envelope in my direction.

'I don't know what it says.' She sounds a little defensive. 'I haven't looked at it. But I picked it up quick, before those ambulancemen or the police could find it. It's addressed to you, and I reckon you're the one that should open it.'

She's waiting expectantly now, looking at me with bright beady eyes. My fingers close over what feels like quite a thick wad of folded paper.

'Thanks. I'll read it later.'

She looks a little disappointed. Suddenly, grateful as I am to her for discovering Mum and getting help, for riding with her in the ambulance and waiting here at the hospital, I really don't want her here any more. Talking to her, having her talk at me, calls for an energy I simply don't have.

'Thelma, why don't I get you a taxi?' I suggest. 'Goodness knows how long it will be before I can leave, and I'm sure you're anxious to get home.'

'Oh, I don't mind . . .' Clearly she's enjoying the drama of it.

'No, I insist. You've already done more than I could ever have expected of you.'

I get out my phone, pull up the menu, where the taxi firm I use is listed.

'He'll be outside in ten minutes,' I say.

I get out my purse, glad I went to the cashpoint yesterday, and pull out three ten-pound notes. 'That should cover it. And you must let me know if I owe you anything else.'

'As if I'd charge extra hours for doing my duty!' Thelma says, sounding quite put out, then adds: 'Of course, I have lost a whole morning . . .'

'I'll make sure it's taken into account,' I promise.

We finish our drinks, and I put the Hobnobs into my bag for later. We leave the café, Thelma in search of her taxi, me heading back to the ward.

There is no apparent change in Mum's condition and no sign of the doctor I want to speak to either. I take Mum's hand and squeeze it.

'Oh Mum, why did you do it?' I say softly.

And open the note that I hope will give me an answer.

Part Six

THIRTY-THREE

MARGARET'S STORY

My dearest daughter,

This is the hardest letter I have ever had to write. Not only because of what I have to tell you, but also because it will be the last one you will ever get from me.

Do you remember how I used to send you a letter every week without fail when you were in London? I wonder if you still have any of them? I don't suppose so; I expect those letters meant more to me than they did to you. You were young, and so excited to be starting at a famous modelling school, I expect you read them quickly and forgot about them. But writing regularly meant the world to me. I missed you so much. The house was empty without you, and I was so anxious about you, alone in a big city.

I need not have worried, though. I should have known you'd be all right. You were never one to do anything silly, not even as a child, and much too sensible to get into bad company. And I'd like you to know how proud I am of you, and how much joy you have brought me. That's one of the reasons for this letter, because by the time you read it, I shall no longer be around to tell you myself.

You mean everything to me, Anne. You always have. I've loved you more than I can put into words. Everything I've done, I've done for you. And although this is what it has led me to, I can't regret it. You are my lovely girl. You always have been and you always will be. Without you I'd have done this long ago – put an end to it all. I've thought about it more than once, the only way out of the mire of my own making, but because of you, I never did more than think. The closest I ever came to making away with myself was when you were just a little girl, not much more than a baby. I was *that* close, but there you were, with your golden curls and your big blue eyes and your chubby cheeks. You saved me, Anne, though you never knew it.

It's different this time though. I've reached the end of the road. There's nowhere left to hide. There are things I need to tell you and I can't face up to it. I'm too ashamed. This is the only way I can do it, knowing I won't have to see how shocked you are at the secret your mother has kept all these years.

Your father never knew it. He was a good man, your father. I mean Leonard, of course, not the German. It might be the German's blood in your veins, but it was Leonard who was always there for you. He loved you as if you were his own, never let you want for anything. He worshipped the ground you walked on, though he wasn't a man to let his feelings show.

He'd have liked us to have other children – well, we both hoped we would. We tried for years, but nothing came of it, and the sad thing is he thought it was his fault.

'It must be me,' he said. 'You've had a baby. There can't be anything wrong with you.' And no matter how often I tried to tell him that I thought I was all messed up inside as a result of that pregnancy, I don't think he ever quite believed it.

He made up for it, though, by doting on you.

'Let's not make too much of it,' he used to say. 'We've got Anne. Another one would very likely be a disappointment.'

Another time he said: 'When I started courting you, my friends and family all told me I was doing a stupid thing, taking up with a widow with a young child, but it was the best thing I ever did.'

In the beginning, you see, I'd passed myself off as a widow. Having a child and no husband was a matter for shame in those days. Truth to tell, I think it's a pity it still isn't. I don't agree with people living together and having a family without being married. Where's the security? There isn't any. The man can just up and leave if he feels like it, which he does, half the time. And the poor children don't know whether they're coming or going. No, though I was an unmarried mother myself, I still don't think it's right. But that's neither here nor there. If I wasn't to be looked down on as a girl who was no better than she should be, I had to pretend to have been married. I bought a cheap ring and put it on my finger and made out first that my husband was away fighting in the war, and then that he'd been killed.

I did tell your father the truth about that before we were married. Well, I had to, really, or things would have got very complicated, with him wondering why I didn't get a war pension, all that kind of thing. I was frightened to death, though. I thought he'd change his mind about wanting to marry me when he knew the sort of woman I was. But he took it all in his stride.

'These things happen,' he said. 'You're still the same girl I fell in love with.'

I should have told him the whole truth then, of course, but I never did. That would have been a step too far. So I kept it to myself and tried to forget I was living a lie.

Only one other person knew the truth that I'd let myself down – my oldest friend, Trixie Bond. I don't suppose you'll remember Trixie; though we did used to meet up sometimes when you were little – Christmas visits, that sort of thing – life came between us and then, sadly, she died, years ago now.

Trixie and I were school friends. We were in the same class at juniors, and we were the only two from our year to pass the exam and go to grammar school, so we got really close.

We shared everything, me and Trixie, the good and the bad. We got together to do our homework, testing one another on lists of French and Latin vocabulary, we went to socials in the church hall, we wrote notes to one another under the desk in lessons when we were bored – that was mostly in chemistry, which neither of us liked. We told each other our crushes and made out lists rating the boys in our class on a scale of one to ten, which ones we'd like to go out with and which ones we wouldn't touch with a bargepole. Not that either of us went out with anybody until we were in the fourth form. Nobody had asked us, and we were afraid nobody ever would. (Though even if they had, I knew my mother wouldn't let me go. Trixie's mother was easier-going about that sort of thing.) Finally, it happened. A boy we met at a church social asked Trixie out and told her his friend wanted to go out with me, so we went on a double date, a walk, that's all. Trixie only saw her boy the once; she said he'd 'tried it on' and she went very red when she said it, but I went out with mine for three weeks before he finished with me, and my heart got broken for the first time.

Trixie and I stayed friends even when we left school and went our separate ways. I was at the technical college learning shorthand and typing, and Trixie went off to do a catering course. We wrote to one another regularly and met up when she came home in the holidays, but then her family moved house to Somerset. Trixie met the man she later married, a farmer's son, and gradually we drifted apart.

By 1942 it was down to Christmas and birthday cards. But she was the first person I thought of when I needed a good friend, and somewhere to go with you where nobody knew us.

Trixie knew that I'd got myself into trouble back in 1938 – we were still writing then. She knew I was no war widow, but she also knew how people talk, and so she went along with the pretence. But she never knew the truth about you, any more than Leonard did.

It was through Trixie that I met him. As I said, she was married to the farmer's son, and he was friendly with Leonard, who, of course, had the haulage business, which he'd started in a small way but had already built up to a fleet of lorries by the time I met him. Ron, Trixie's husband, and Leonard both sang in the male-voice choir, and one night I went with Trixie to a concert they were giving in the village hall. I liked the look of Leonard straight away – I remember thinking how handsome he looked, standing in the back row with the baritones in his navy blue blazer, white shirt and red tie. I started taking an interest in going to the concerts, and he started taking an interest in me, buying me a drink at the local afterwards, and then asking me out. He was a good bit older than me, of course, but that only added to the attraction. I'd gone right off boys my own age, and it was nice being courted by somebody with a bit of money to spend, who treated me like a lady.

It wasn't all that long before he asked me to marry him. I suppose, being older, he knew his own mind. And I said yes. The rest you know. He bought a plot of land and had this house put up, and when it was ready we set a date, tied the knot, and moved in. I never regretted marrying him for a moment. He was a good man and we had nearly forty happy years together. The business went from strength to strength, so I never had to worry about money, and he was a wonderful husband to me and father to you – not that I have to tell you that.

He never knew my secret, though, and that's something I regret. But there was no way I could tell him. No way I could tell anybody. And in time I almost forgot about it myself. Over the years I came to live the lie, though some-times it did come back to haunt me, and when it did, I'd go right down low, didn't want to talk to anybody or go anywhere, couldn't seem to do anything but cry.

That's how I've been since you told me about Sonia. I've been in a terrible way. I know that this time the truth has to come out. You've got to know what happened. But I can't bring myself to tell you, and that's why I've decided this is the best way. I don't suppose you'll want anything more to do with me once you know, in any case, so it's for the best that I'm no longer around.

The trouble is, I still don't know how to tell you. You are going to be so shocked. The look on your face when I told you Leonard wasn't your real father tore me in two, and the whole truth is so much worse. So before I begin, I want to tell you again how much I love you. How proud I am of you. What a joy you have been to me. There is no one in the world who means as much to me as you do. Please, my love, hold on to that.

So, here goes.

I got into trouble when I was just seventeen. He was a boy I met on the bus travelling each day to the technical college where I was doing my shorthand and typing course. I started going out with him, one thing led to another, and I ended up pregnant.

I thought Tony (that was his name) would marry me. That was what couples did in those days when things went too far – well, all the girls I knew who got themselves in that situation married their boyfriends, anyway. But Tony had other ideas. When I told him I was in trouble, I didn't see him for dust. I don't know where he went – London first, I think, and later I heard he'd emigrated to Australia. It might as well have been the moon. I was on my own, and in a terrible pickle.

My mother and father were in an awful way. I think it killed my mother – she only lived a year or so after it happened, and my father followed her into an early grave. They were adamant I couldn't keep the baby – they didn't even want anyone to know I was pregnant, though I'm sure people did. Even if they didn't say anything to us, I expect there was whispering behind our backs. Getting in the family way without a ring on your finger was such a cause

362

for shame, and for as long as I could, I hid my bump, strapping myself up tight in a corset. It's a wonder I didn't kill my poor baby, and I do wonder if it was that that damaged me in some way so I could never have another. When I was about six months gone and really beginning to show, my mother told everybody some story about me going away to work and I was packed off to what they called a mother-and-baby home.

Oh Anne, it was a terrible place! It was run by nuns, and they treated us like dirt. That's what they thought we were, I suppose. Dirty girls who had to be punished. We were worked like slaves; I remember scrubbing the stone steps leading up to the house the same day I went into labour. I told the sister I was having these pains, and she said: 'You've got a lot worse to come, believe me. Just get on with it.' As she turned away, she kicked my bucket over, I know she did it on purpose, and then she shouted at me for being clumsy and told me to sweep all the water away and fetch a fresh lot.

And when I was giving birth they were so cruel. Twenty-six hours it took, I'll never forget it, and they never gave me so much as an aspirin. Every time I cried and asked for help they just sneered and said, 'It's your own doing' and 'Let this be a lesson to you next time you're tempted by the devil to sin.' I could cry now, just thinking about it.

But worse was to come. My little baby – Anne, I called her – was born, and she was so beautiful! I forgot all the pain when I held her in my arms and looked down at her little face peeping out of all the swaddling they used to wrap new babies up in in those days. I loved her so much, and I wanted to keep her, but I knew they were going to take her away from me, and I didn't know how to bear it. I used to feed her with tears running down my face, and many was the time I lay awake at night, sobbing my heart out and trying to work out a way I could keep her.

Three months I had her. Just three months. I still had to

work, of course, all the same menial duties as before, but I spent every minute I could with her. And then they took her away. A couple came in a big car, with a Moses basket to put her in and nice clothes – they didn't want the matinee jackets I'd knitted for her, or the poke bonnet or the mittens. They did let her take her little pink bear, but that was all. And I had to watch from a window as they got into the car with her and drove away.

I don't want to think about it really, even now, but I have to, because I must make you see just what a state I was in. Why I did what I did. I wasn't myself at all. All I could think was that I wanted my baby. It was a pain that never stopped. It was terrible. Terrible.

I left the mother-and-baby home then, of course, but I didn't go back to Maidenhead. Well, I did at first, but my mother and father couldn't forgive me and I think my mother was already suffering the first stages of the cancer that would kill her. They wanted me out of the way – 'We can't bear to look at you,' my father said – and truth to tell, I couldn't forgive them either, for forcing me to give up my baby. I went to London and got a job with the Admiralty, as a clerk, because I'd never finished my secretarial course. And then the war came, and the Admiralty moved to Bath, and I moved with them And that was how it all came about.

I was still in a terrible way, pining for my Anne, knowing I'd never see her again, and all alone in a strange city. That was when I started thinking about taking my own life, because I just couldn't face a future without her. To make things worse, down the road from where I was lodging there was a girl about the same age as me with a baby just about the age my Anne would have been by now. She wasn't married either; she'd had a fling with a German boy who worked in a hotel in town, or so I'd heard, but nobody had made her give up her baby. She worked at the Admiralty too, in one of the typing pools, and her mother took care of the baby during the day.

Oh, how I envied that girl! When I saw her or her mother pushing the baby out in her pushchair, I'd get this pain in my chest, like a stitch, or a heart attack, I suppose, so sharp I could hardly breathe. But I couldn't stop myself gazing at her and talking to her when I had the chance, and imagining she was my Anne. I really think it sent me a little bit crazy. I 'went funny', as my mother would have said. There's no other way to explain what I did. And no excuse. I lost my mind, I really think that's what happened, and by the time I came to my senses it was too late.

That day, the day when it happened, I should have been at work, but the depression was laying me very low. It wasn't just the black cloud of despair I carried around with me; it made me feel really ill too. To make matters worse, I'd had a big to-do with Mrs Gardiner, my landlady, the night before. The digs were Admiralty-approved, and under the terms of the agreement Mrs Gardiner was supposed to provide me with breakfast and one hot meal a day in exchange for a guinea a week, but she really scrimped on it, and the food was horrible. She blamed rationing and shortages, but I suspected she was using my food coupons for the benefit of her own family, and what I got were tasteless leftovers. That evening when she served me up overcooked swede, gone-to-smack potatoes and a single rasher of gristly, fatty bacon, I had it out with her, told her I was going to ask my boss if they couldn't find me alternative lodgings.

The row upset my already frayed nerves, and next morning I just couldn't face going in to the office, couldn't face going over it all again with Mr Parry, my boss, couldn't face the fug of smoke from the cigarettes he chain-smoked, couldn't face the chatter of the other girls and the pressure of work. Funnily enough, because I had it in mind I wasn't going to go back to Mrs Gardiner's, I made sure I had everything that mattered in my handbag: my identity card, my diary and address book, and all the money I'd managed to save from my wages – little enough, but all I had in the world. I also had the copy of my Anne's birth certificate that I'd secretly kept when I registered her, though I'd had to hand the original over to the people who were adopting her. I couldn't take my ration coupons, of course, Mrs Gardiner had those, but that couldn't be helped. I didn't take any of my clothes, either, but then I don't suppose I really intended leaving just like that. It was simply an idea I'd cottoned on to to cheer myself up.

There was a little café within walking distance of my lodgings. I went there, and sat for a couple of hours over a couple of cups of tea, feeling sorry for myself. Then I wandered aimlessly.

It was a nice clear September morning, blue sky, quite warm. When I came to the arcade of lock-up shops I dawdled, window-shopping, though truth to tell there wasn't much to buy. And then, outside the hardware shop, I saw you. You were in your pushchair, staring intently at a pigeon that was strutting about the pavement between the paraphernalia that Mr Packer always kept outside his shop.

'Hello, Lynne,' I said. That was your name then.

You looked up at me, wide-eyed, and held out your arms to me, anxious to escape the confines of your pushchair.

'Where's your grandma?' I asked.

You didn't reply, of course. You weren't much more than a year old. But I guessed that if you could have spoken, you would have told me she was in the shop. I took a peek in the door, and saw a figure that looked like her at the counter, talking to Mr Packer.

'Ma,' you said, very distinctly. 'Ma-ma.'

I don't know what got into me then. Suddenly you weren't Lynne any more. You were Anne. I stared at you, mesmerised, hesitated, then crouched down, fumbling with the strap on the pushchair. I lifted you out. You felt wonderful in my arms, firm and soft. I buried my face in your head and your lovely fair hair was soft against my skin. You smelled of soap, clean and sweet and wholesome.

Tears were running down my cheeks, not of loss and sadness now, but relief and joy.

'Anne!' I whispered into your hair. 'Oh my darling! Anne!' And I started away down the street with you in my arms, slowly at first, as if in a dream, then faster, as a half-acknowledged fear that someone might snatch you away from me niggled at the edges of my mind, until I was running. I heard the drone of planes in the calm September air, but I didn't register danger from them. They belonged to another world. Even as they came overhead I took no notice. And then, when I'd reached the corner of the street, the bomb dropped.

I couldn't ignore that. It shocked me back to reality. I spun round, horrified. Mr Packer's shop and the one next door had gone. Gone! There was nothing left of them but a heap of smoking rubble. You started to cry, frightened by the noise and the rush of air that could be felt even from where we were.

'Sh, Anne, sh!'

I held you close, hiding your face in my shoulder, stroking your hair, and looking back at the flames that had begun to shoot up, scarlet and orange amid the clouds of smoke.

And it came to me suddenly that if I hadn't taken you from your pushchair and run away when I did, we would have been right there when the bomb had fallen. In the crater it had made, covered with chunks of fallen masonry and choking debris that was now being consumed by flames. We would have been dead, both of us, as your grandmother and Mr Packer undoubtedly were. But by some fluke of fate I had saved you. Because you were meant for me. Because you were mine. I turned my back on the terrible devastation, still crooning to you. And I walked away.

I got a bus into town; miraculously, the buses were still running – it wasn't a full-scale raid. I found a telephone box

367

and some change and I rang Trixie. They were on the phone at her farm, and I had her number in my diary.

I told her we'd just been bombed, me and my baby, and we'd lost everything. I asked if we could come to her, and she agreed straight away. 'Of course you can. And you can stay for as long as you need to,' she said. 'You'll be safe here, Peggy.' (Peggy – that's what I used to call myself in those days.)

So that's what I did, taking you with me, pretending you were Anne, and coming to believe it myself.

Well, my darling. Now you know. Your name wasn't Anne, it was Lynne. Your father wasn't Leonard, but a German boy whose name I don't know. And I can't remember what your mother's name was either, though I've tried very hard. I suppose over the years I blanked it out. But your grand-mother was French, I think. I believe her name was Marianne.

That's all I can tell you, but it shouldn't be impossible for you to find out the names of the people killed that day. A grandmother and a baby. Because of course when what remained of your pushchair was found under the debris, it would have been assumed that you had been killed.

I've kept all this to myself ever since, and no one has ever queried it. But it's only right you should know now if it can help to save Sonia.

I only hope, my dearest Anne, that you can find it in your heart to forgive me, for what I did then, and for what I'm doing now.

Good night, my love. God bless.

Your ever loving mother,

Margaret

THIRTY-FOUR

ANNE

This is horrendous. I feel as though I'm living in a nightmare, rushing from Sonia's to the hospital and back again, worried sick about both Sonia and Mum, and still in shock over the contents of Mum's letter to me. I coped with learning that Dad was not my real father; though it shook me, I concentrated all my attention on trying to find his family, and told myself I'd deal with how I felt about it later.

But this is something else, something so fundamentally earth-shattering that I feel as if my whole world has fallen to pieces. I am absolutely not who I thought I was; my past, my present, my whole being has lost its shape and form, become fluid and murky. It isn't even as if I'd been legally adopted – I'd been stolen.

The enormity of it is almost too much to take in. Hard enough to comprehend the moment of madness that made Mum snatch me from my pushchair, but impossible to understand how she could have kept her secret all these years. No wonder she suffered from black depressions and 'nerves', as they used to be called. No wonder, when she was faced at last with a choice between saying nothing, and owning up so that there was a chance to find a blood relative whose stem cells might save Sonia, she decided to confess, then take her own life. She must have been in torment. I could almost feel sorry for her if I had an ounce of emotion to spare, and if I wasn't painfully aware of the terrible anguish she must have caused my real mother.

How could she have done it? How could she have justified herself all these years? I suppose she felt there was no going back, but to let my real mother believe I was dead . . . it was cruel, callous, selfish, downright wicked. To pass me off as her own child – the child who had been adopted – is beyond belief. Who am I? I wonder. Who was my birth mother, and what happened to her? Is she still alive? Did she go on to have other children? For Sonia's sake I have to find out. But how? My head spins; I feel totally overwhelmed.

The first thing I did after reading Mum's letter was to ring Rod.

'Before you start worrying, it's not Sonia, but I really do need you, Rod. Is there any chance at all you could come over?' I asked – no, begged – him.

'Anne? What on earth is wrong?' He sounded worried anyway. He knew I wouldn't drag him out of work lightly.

'Mum's in hospital. She's tried to commit suicide.'

'What!'

'And there's more. I can't talk about it on the phone. But I really want—'

'Where are you, love?'

'Still in Bristol. At the BRI.'

'OK, stay right there. I'll be with you in just the time it takes to get through the traffic.'

I almost burst into tears then. 'Oh, thank you, Rod . . .'

'Don't be so silly,' he said. 'Of course I'll be there.'

Knowing I was no longer alone gave me a tremendous boost. Whilst I was waiting for him to arrive I rang Sonia. I gave her an update on her grandma's condition, but didn't mention the letter.

'I think I should stay here for a bit if you're all right,' I said.

'We're fine, Mum. Kevin is picking the children up from school himself and not going back to work.'

'Good.' So Kevin was turning up trumps, too. In the last resort, where those we love are concerned, work commitment comes a poor second in our family.

I have never been so pleased to see anyone in the whole of my life as I was to see Rod. We found a table in a quiet corner of the café and I told him everything. He heard me out, just shaking his head in disbelief and holding my hand on the Formica tabletop. He was pretty much as shocked as I was, but, being Rod, he went straight for the practical.

'Well, at least it opens up a whole lot of new possibilities for finding a match for Sonia,' he said.

'If I can find out who I really am.'

'There must be records of the people who were killed in the bombing. That would be a start.'

We talked about it for a bit, and about the fact that the Liebermanns too might be willing to help if their DNA did indeed show a blood link to Sonia. Rod said he would try to find out how we should proceed, and I could then get back in touch with Angela Liebermann and set things in motion, though we were both agreed that compared to the new developments the German connection was likely to be a long shot. Then we went up to see Mum. There was no change in her condition.

'I don't think there's a lot of point you staying here,' Rod said reasonably, and though I felt awful about leaving her, I could see he was right.

'Do you want me to come back to Sonia's with you?' he suggested.

'That would be good. And she'd love to see you. But I don't think we should mention any of this to her for the moment. She's had more than enough stress for one day.'

'You're probably right.' He hesitated, thinking. 'I could stay the night with you if you like. I don't like the thought of leaving you on your own with all this on your mind.'

I was sorely tempted. But I was feeling much stronger now and I knew Sonia would think it odd if her father suddenly moved in too. Besides which, neither of us would get much sleep squashed together into that very small double bed. Rod is quite a big man, and the days when we slept like spoons are well and truly over; we both need our space.

We decided that Rod would go home and begin investigations, and I would return alone to Sonia's and try to carry on as normally as possible. But that night when I found it impossible to sleep, I got up and went on the internet on my laptop, trying to search the records. The trouble was, I was so anxious, so distressed, I found myself simply going around in circles. At the kitchen table, with a cup of Ovaltine at my elbow and a dozen sites that meant absolutely nothing to me, or which I was unable to access, or both, staring at me from the computer screen, I buried my head in my hands and wept with frustration, confusion and despair.

The first thing I did this morning was phone the hospital for news of Mum, and was encouraged to be told she is still holding her own. Then I called Rod. Good as his word, he had also been hard at work, with considerably more success than I had had.

The main raids, when hundreds of people were killed, were in the spring of 1942, and they had taken place at night. But there had been occasional bombs before that, in 1940 and 1941, which probably hadn't been meant for Bath, but for the aircraft factories and docks in Bristol, and had been dropped either by mistake or because the bomber pilot wanted to dump his load. He'd found a list on a memorial site naming the people who had lost their lives, but he wasn't sure if it was comprehensive, and in any case it gave no details beyond the names – no ages for the victims, no date of death, no location. He'd go on looking, but he wasn't overly optimistic.

Again the realisation of what a mammoth task this was overcame me. It would have been difficult enough if time was on our side, and it wasn't. But we couldn't give up. Somehow we had to find my blood family. Rod and I put our heads together and tried to be methodical.

'I think the first step is to pinpoint exactly where these occasional bombs fell,' Rod said. 'If we look at each one in turn and concentrate on the ones where a block of shops was destroyed, we can take it from there.'

'How?' I was feeling too overwhelmed to be able to think straight. 'We still won't have a home address.'

'No, but it would almost certainly be within easy walking distance.'

'People walked much further in those days than they do now.'

'Maybe so, but we'll start with a radius of say a mile and work out. I don't know if the electoral rolls for that time are still available, but I'll find out. And we can knock on doors, try to find someone who lived in the area back then.'

'It's a long shot. Anyone old enough to remember is going to be . . . well, very old.'

Rod ignored me.

'The pity is that we can't ask your mother for an address. Or even which Admiralty site she worked at. That would at least have pointed us in the right direction, since the lodgings they found her were probably not too far away.'

'There was more than one site, then? I always thought they took over the Empire Hotel.'

'They did, but they were at other locations too. I wonder . . .' Rod paused, thinking. 'I wonder if they've still got records dating back to the war? It might be classified information, of course, but it's worth a try.'

'The local newspapers,' I said, my brain suddenly functioning again. 'They would have carried full reports, surely? And they'll be archived. Either at the newspaper offices, or at the library – maybe both.'

'Newspaper!' Rod said sharply.

'That's what I just said.'

'No. Well, yes. The archives are a good idea. It would have been headline news, I should imagine, a grandmother and baby killed by a bomb, especially if it happened before the main raids. They'd have been overwhelmed with similar stories then, I would imagine, given that list of names. But that wasn't actually what I meant.'

'What then?'

'Why don't we go to the papers, radio, TV even, get them to put out an appeal? I don't know why I didn't think of it before. That way we'll have a much better chance of finding someone who knows who the little girl was.'

'Me.'

I'm already shuddering inwardly at the thought of the publicity. For someone who used to model for a living, I'm really a very private person. But whatever it takes . . .

'Do you want me to phone them?' Rod asked.

I only hesitated for a moment.

'No, it would be better coming from me. I'll do it.'

First, of course, I'm going to have to tell Sonia the whole story. Though I shrink from that too, I know it's something I must do if I'm going public. There are too many ways she might find out about it from someone other than me, and in any case, even if I could keep it from her, it wouldn't be right. This isn't just about me, it's about her too. I owe it to her to tell her what my mother never told me.

Fortunately, she's having a good day. I sit her down and warn her that, although there is an upside to what I am going to tell her, she's going to be shocked. Then I plunge right in. Sonia listens, speechless. Eventually I show her the letter Mum left me. As she reads it she utters little gasps, but she keeps on going to the end. When at last she looks up, her eyes are brimming with tears.

'Oh poor Grandma! What she must have gone through!'

I'm surprised that this is her first reaction; I'd never thought she and my mother were particularly close.

'She brought it all on herself,' I say tersely. 'What about what she put my real mother through?'

'Well, yes, of course . . . but we don't know her, do we? We do know Grandma. She's the one who's always been there. It must have been awful for her, keeping a secret like that. And to have been forced to give up her own baby and never know what happened to her . . . no wonder it sent her slightly mad. It's terrible.'

I'm still finding it hard to forgive my mother.

'But no excuse for what she did.'

'Not an excuse maybe, but certainly a reason. It's just awful, Mum. And now, to feel that the only way out was to take her own life because she couldn't face up to telling you the truth but felt she had to for my sake . . .' The tears spill over and run down her cheeks. 'It's my fault she's in the state she is now. All my fault!'

'Oh, don't be so silly, Sonia, of course it's not your fault.' I get up to fetch a box of tissues, hand it to her.

'But it is my fault.' She blows her nose, wipes her eyes. 'If I wasn't ill . . . if I didn't need this stem cell transplant—'

'I'd never have known the truth.'

'Would that really have mattered? In the long run, what difference does it make? You're still you.'

She's right, I suppose, but I'm not yet able to see it in that light.

'It matters to me. But I don't want to talk about that now. The thing is, I've decided to go public to try and find my real family.'

Sonia's face registers more shock.

'Oh gosh, Mum, are you sure about that? It's going to cause an awful upset.'

'If it means we can find a match for you, it'll be worth it.'

'But think what the repercussions will be! Grandma—'

'Your grandma obviously intended me to try to find my real family,' I say. 'It's what she wanted. And going public is the only chance I've got of identifying them in time to help you.'

She looks uncertain.

'Don't you *want* to find a match, Sonia?' I say bluntly.

'Well of course I do. But there's no guarantee we'll get one even if we do find your blood relatives. The stone will be overturned and everything underneath it will come out, and it may all be for nothing.'

'That's a chance we have to take.' I'm silent for a moment and then, partly to lift some of the burden of responsibility from Sonia's frail shoulders, and partly because it's what I feel deep down, I go on: 'In any case, I'd like to meet my real mother before it's too late. If it isn't already. I'd like the chance to get to know her, and to let her know . . .'

I break off, a sudden doubt striking me. How would it help my real mother to learn, after all these years, that I had not been killed more than sixty years ago by a German bomb? However grief-stricken she was then, she'd had a lifetime to come to terms with it. If I found her, it would all be raked up again and the lost years would be a cause for fresh grief. If, like Mum's own baby, I'd been adopted, it would be a different matter. She'd always have wondered about me and finding me again would, hopefully, be cause for a joyous reunion. But a child she had believed dead all these years? The pain the truth would bring might well outweigh the joy.

I shake myself mentally. I'm straying from the core point, the only thing that really matters. Which is finding a bone marrow match for Sonia.

'I'm going to make a couple of phone calls now,' I say. 'Then, if you'll be all right for a couple of hours, I'll go and see your grandma. What I'm hoping is that while I'm in Bristol I'll be able to talk to someone at the paper and get things moving. It's published every day and it covers the whole area, whereas the Bath paper only comes out once a week now.'

Sonia sighs. She still looks doubtful, but I'm not going to let that put me off. This is far too important. I have to stay single-minded.

'I suppose you'll do what you want to do, Mum. You always do,' Sonia says, smiling slightly. 'I always wondered where you got your stubborn streak from. Perhaps I'm about to find out.'

'I sincerely hope so, Sonia,' I say.

As they'd told me on the phone, Mum is still holding her own, and the doctor is rather more optimistic, though still cautious.

'It's too early yet to be sure which way this is going to go,' he says, 'but we haven't detected any signs of vital organ failure and we are continuing to do everything we can. It's just fortunate your mother was discovered when she was. Any longer and she might well have been beyond help.'

I nod, making a mental note to update Thelma as to Mum's condition and thank her again for what she did. I spend a half-hour at Mum's bedside before leaving to go to the offices of the *Western News*.

I phoned them before leaving Sonia's, and was put through to the newsroom. A man I spoke to – the news editor, I think – said they'd have someone talk to me if I called around noon. So at 11.30 a.m. I'm looking for a space in the multi-storey car park that is within walking distance of the newspaper offices. My heart is racing and I feel unusually nervy. They must use my story, surely? Though it's hardly news, I would have thought. But presumably they know their business.

I make my way along the street, busy with city traffic, to the impressive office block that houses the *Western News*, push open the glass entrance door and go into the foyer, almost colliding with a girl in a very short skirt with what looks like a camera bag slung over her shoulder. The interior, though modern and well appointed, has the sort of buzz and feeling of feverish acticity that I imagine is common to newspaper offices, where deadlines are vital. People clutching scraps of paper – advertisements, presumably, or birth or death notices – are queuing at a desk where two more girls are holding court. Telephones are ringing.

I wait my turn, feeling anxious and stressed. At last I'm at the desk, explaining that the news editor is expecting me. The girl picks up her telephone and makes a call; over the general hubbub I can't hear what she's saying, but when she replaces the receiver she tells me to take a seat and someone will be with me shortly.

I don't sit down – I'm too wound up. Instead I hover, glancing at notices displayed on the walls and piles of newspapers on wire racks.

'Mrs Mayle?' A man's voice behind me. I turn expectantly.

'Yes.'

'I'm Pete Holbrook. You wanted to talk to someone about a bombing in Bath during the war.'

'Yes.' I look helplessly around the busy foyer. The young man – well, perhaps not so young; anyone under the age of fifty looks young to me these days – picks up on my unease.

'We can go somewhere quieter if you like.'

'I'd rather, yes.'

'I'll buy you a coffee – or a proper drink. The cafés and bars shouldn't be too busy yet.'

A proper drink is exactly what I could do with.

'Actually I could kill for a glass of wine.'

'Let's go, then.'

We leave the frantic atmosphere of the newspaper offices, walk along the street and cross the busy road by way of a footbridge.

'This is the place I use,' Pete Holbrook says.

It's a pub, quite old by the look of it, and dimly lit. But he was right, it is quite quiet at the moment, though I imagine it will fill up with office workers as lunchtime approaches. We take a table by the window; Pete Holbrook goes to the bar and returns with a glass of Pinot Grigio for me and a pint of beer for himself. He produces

377

a notebook and pen from the pocket of the leather jacket he's wearing, and lays them on the table beside his glass.

'OK, fire away.'

Stupidly, now that my opportunity has arisen, I don't know where to begin.

'It's a very long story.'

'But it begins in the war. A child and her grandmother who were killed by a stray bomb.'

'Yes. Well . . . that was the assumption at the time. The grand-mother was killed, certainly. But the child . . .'

'Go on.'

'I don't think the child was killed. I think she was stolen, before the bomb fell.'

'What makes you think that?' He's looking at me intently, expect-antly, as if he already knows what I'm going to say, though I didn't mention any of the sensitive details to his editor.

'Because,' I say, 'from what I now know, that child was me.'

We go through the story; Pete Holbrook is scribbling furiously on his pad, a mixture of shorthand and longhand. I tell him everything that was in Mum's letter to me – I don't want to show it to him, not yet, anyway, it's too private – and explain the reason why I am so anxious to trace my lost family.

'I'm sorry to hear that,' he says, with what appears to be genuine sympathy, when I tell him about Sonia's illness and the race to find a donor.

'I thought that if you were to print the story, someone might come forward who knows the people who were killed, and the whereabouts of their relatives now. To be honest, I'm not keen on the thought of all the publicity it will generate, and neither is my daughter. As for what it will do to my poor mother if she pulls through . . . it doesn't bear thinking about. But I'm desperate, and I have a feeling that going through the official channels would just take too long, though I'll try that too, of course.'

Pete Holbrook pushes his notebook to one side and takes a pull of his beer, until now virtually untouched.

'I think I might be able to help you.'

My breath comes out on a sigh.

'Oh, thank you! But if you could be . . . well, if you could treat it as sensitively as possible, I'd be really grateful, though I appreciate you have a job to do.'

He looks straight at me.

'I won't publish anything at the moment.'

'But . . . ?'

'Look, just leave this with me.' He pulls the notebook towards him again. 'Give me your contact details.'

I do, and he writes them down, closes his notebook with a snap and slots his pen into the wire spine. I'm still looking at him, bemused.

'I can't say any more at the moment, but I'll be in touch.' He smiles at me – it's rather a nice smile – and points at my glass. 'Can I get you another?'

'Oh no, I'd better not. I'm driving.'

'Well I'm having one. I've got a feeling I'll be needing it. Oh . . .' (seeing my frown), 'nothing for you to worry about. Just a couple of dragons I have to slay.'

'I'm afraid you've lost me totally.'

'Sorry about that. The thing is, my editor passed you on to me because what you said ties in with another story I've been working on. Again, I don't want to go into details. But I think it may well be that . . .'

Breath is tight in my chest.

'Yes?'

'I think I might know the identity of your real mother.'

THIRTY-FIVE

MARTHA

My sister Lucy has often said she hates, loathes and despises packing to go on holiday. For at least a week beforehand she's washing, ironing, making piles of clothes and other essentials on the bed in the spare room, sorting medications – aspirin, insect bite cream, stuff for tummy upsets of every description – terrified she's going to forget something vital, humming and hawing over what and what not to take and still ending up with a suitcase full of things, half of which never see the light of day. By the time they set off, she needs a holiday to get over the stress of preparation, and another when she gets back to recover from sorting out everything that's piled up whilst she has been away.

Me – I can't be doing with all that palaver. I throw the barest essentials into a holdall and if there's anything I've forgotten, well, tough. I can either buy it at my destination or do without. The latter, usually. As long as I've got my toothbrush, clean underwear, a swim-suit and a few spare T-shirts, I can manage very nicely.

I suppose, though, that since this time I'm going away with Granny, I should expand my wardrobe a bit. I don't want to embarrass her by going into dinner at the hotel in shorts and flip-flops – heck, they might not even allow it! So I sort out a couple of skirts, a pair of wide-legged linen trousers and some tops and shove them into my bag, following the dictum 'roll, don't fold – less space required, fewer creases'.

I pack my camera too. I'm not usually a person who takes holiday snaps – what's the point? A whole load of clutter you never actually look at and that nobody else wants to look at either, unless they're a glutton for being bored rigid. But I think I'd like to get a few photographs of Granny. She is after all getting older; this could be the last holiday I'll ever have with her.

I drive out to Lucy's fairly early on the morning we're due to leave – we might as well make the most of the time we have there – and find Granny all packed and ready to go. It surprises me that she's so keen – generally speaking she's very much a home bird.

Eventually we escape Lucy's fussing, I stow Granny's case in the boot of the car beside my squashy tote bag and install her in the front passenger seat.

'This is very smart,' she says, quite coherently. Her speech is improving all the time, thanks to the sessions with the therapist.

'Clean, you mean,' I say ruefully. I haven't yet had the courtesy car for long enough for it to become the tip that my own car usually is.

'How are you?' she asks.

'Fine,' I say breezily, though my ribs are actually still rather sore.

'Sure?'

'Yes, honestly. Fine. It was only a biff from the airbag, Granny. I was very lucky.'

She shudders, sighs. 'It doesn't bear thinking about.'

'So don't. I'm not. Especially when I'm on holiday.'

But I can't help noticing that I'm much jumpier than usual, watching what the other traffic is doing like a hawk, being more cautious about pulling out at junctions, not overtaking unless the road ahead is clear and straight, and still breathing a sigh of relief when I'm back on my own side. There's nothing like being involved in a road accident to make you aware of the dangers of driving. It's a wake-up call, reminding you that you're not invincible, infallible, or immortal.

We reach Weston-super-Mare without incident and drive along the seafront. The tide is out, but the promenade is bright with flowers and there are quite a few holidaymakers strolling on the tree-lined walkways or sitting on benches enjoying the warm sun and looking out to where the sea will be in a few hours' time. There's a string of donkeys on the beach, and a little train chuntering along between the road and the sea wall. Not many children, though, thank goodness. It's not that I don't like children, just that I'd rather not have them screaming and charging about when I'm trying to relax. Come the school holidays, the place will be swarming with them, and I, for one, will be giving it a miss.

I find the hotel, pull up outside the main door and leave Granny in the car while I go in to find out what's what. It looks like I made a good choice: the receptionist is pleasant and helpful, and a porter comes out to carry in our luggage while I help Granny into the foyer. I sit her down in a nicely upholstered green velvet chair while I go off to park the car where the receptionist told me I could.

When we've registered, the porter, who's been hovering, takes our bags again. There's a lift – I made sure of that before I booked; Granny wouldn't be able to manage stairs – and it purrs us up to the second floor. Our rooms are next door to one another, both with sea views, and more or less identical. I tip the porter and go into Granny's room to see if she needs any help.

'That porter,' she says.

'He was nice, wasn't he?'

'He was old!' she says scornfully. 'He looked as if somebody should be carrying his . . .' The word she's looking for eludes her.

'Case?' I suggest. She nods.

'Case. Carrying his case for him!'

'Granny, you are wicked.'

But I'm glad to see she's still got her old, sparky sense of humour, that her brain is as sharp as ever, even if she has difficulty sometimes in translating her thoughts into words. And in spite of all her recent infirmities, I suspect she still feels young inside, hence her disdain for the ageing porter, who is probably a good ten to fifteen years younger than she is.

She's looking a bit tired though, and I don't want her overdoing things.

'Do you want me to give you a hand unpacking?' I ask.

'Get your own done first.'

'That won't take me two minutes.' I heft her suitcase on to the bed and open it. 'Just tell me where you want things to go.'

She doesn't argue.

'It doesn't matter, as long as I know where to find them.'

She sits down in a wicker chair by the window and I hang her frocks in the wardrobe and pile underwear into drawers. There's a small en suite bathroom and I put her toiletries bag on the vanity unit beside the sink.

As I go back into the bedroom, I hear my mobile ringing in my bag, which I've dumped on a small writing desk. After a lot of hassle I've got a new one, and though I felt lost without it for the couple of days it took to sort things out, now I can't help thinking it was actually quite nice not being so readily available to all and sundry.

'That's probably Lucy checking up on us,' I say.

'Probably,' Granny agrees with a wry, slightly lopsided smile.

But it's not Lucy. The caller display shows Pete's number.

'Hmm!' I snort, and toss the phone down, a great deal more carefully than I did my old one that day in my office.

'Aren't you going to answer it?' Granny asks.

Really, her speech has improved beyond all recognition.

'Nope. There are some calls I can do without.'

'But . . .'

'It's not Lucy,' I assure her. 'Anyone else can leave me a message, and I'll ring them back if I feel like it.'

Which I won't. I never want to speak to Pete Holbrook again. He's called a couple of times since I got my new phone and I've ignored those too. I said all I want to say to him the morning I saw the report in the paper about Miss Leverton. Now he can go . . . no, I mustn't say that, not even think it, while I'm with Granny. I must make an effort to be a bit more ladylike, not resort to the sort of language that's everyday parlance when I'm with the diving team but would sound very vulgar to her.

She's looking a bit worried now. She's of a generation who feels the telephone should always be answered, I suspect, a master, not a servant.

'We'll ring Lucy if you like,' I say. 'Let her know we've arrived safely. We don't want her worrying.'

Granny nods, her sweet face softening.

'Yes, I think we should.'

I retrieve my phone, call Lucy's number, report in.

'You're sure Granny's OK?' Lucy asks anxiously.

'She's fine. We're going down to find some lunch in a minute.'

'You won't forget her tablets, will you? They're all in a little container, colour-coded. She has two of the pink ones twice a day—'

'Lucy, will you quit worrying! We're perfectly capable of sorting out Granny's medication.'

'Well, just double-check she's taking the right ones. It's complicated.'

'Not *that* complicated, surely!'

'And can you make sure she's got a spare blanket in case she needs it in the night? She gets cold sometimes. I always—'

'Lucy!' My tone is warning.

'There's no need to get uppity, Martha.'

'Just leave us to it, Lucy, OK? I promise you we're fine.'

'Can I speak to Granny?'

I pass the phone to her. 'Lucy wants to speak to you.'

'Oh!' Granny holds it to her ear, rather awkwardly. She's not used to being able to communicate through something so small. 'Hello?' she says, very loudly, as if she needed to shout across the miles.

They talk for a few minutes but I notice that Granny's hesitancy over words has come back. Because she's not comfortable with my mobile, perhaps.

'Right,' I say, when they've finished and she hands the phone back to me to switch off. 'Just let me throw my bits and bobs in a drawer, and we'll go down and see about some lunch.'

I go to my own room. Whilst I'm unpacking, my phone rings again. Again, I can see from the display that it's Pete. Again, I let it go to voicemail. I'll be damned before I let him spoil my few days with Granny!

I dump the phone amongst my T-shirts and bang the drawer shut.

Normally my phone goes everywhere with me and I come close to a panic attack if it's not within earshot. But I'm on holiday, for goodness' sake. Nobody is going to call me with instructions for an urgent job. I've phoned Lucy and let her know we've arrived safely. There is absolutely no need for me to speak to anyone else, and I can do without the irritation of hearing it ring and seeing Pete's number come up on the display. For a couple of days at least I'm going to try and forget about him, though that might be easier said than done. The man has got under my skin in a way I thought nobody could ever do again. I really thought we were going somewhere, and it was making me happy. He's hurt me more badly than I care to admit, left a sour taste in my mouth and an ache of disappointment in my heart. He's made a fool of me, and I'm angry that I was stupid enough to let him. But I'm going to try not to think about that for this week at any rate.

This is my time with Granny, and I'm going to do my damnedest to make sure we both enjoy it.

And we do. For once I made a good choice of hotel – I've had some disasters in my time through opting for the cheap and cheerful – and the weather is still good. We've done a few short outings, to Sand Bay, and along the toll road to Kew Stoke Woods, but mostly we've just chilled out, taking gentle strolls along the promenade, sitting on a bench on the seafront or in comfort in the hotel grounds. One day we made it on to the pier, not as far as the noisy amusement arcade at the far end, but far enough to feel we were at sea, and I remembered how, when I was a little girl, I used to love looking through the cracks between the boards and seeing the sea – or more often, the mud – beneath my feet. One morning I even challenged Granny to a round of clock golf, though I knew she wouldn't take me up on it.

'I never could see the fun in that, even when I could hit the ball straight,' she said. 'All those silly little houses and castles – it's enough to drive you to drink trying to get past them.'

I laugh. Granny never did have much patience with what she used to call 'fiddly things', and I'm the same. I expect I get it from her.

I've really enjoyed spending this time alone with Granny without Lucy being there to fuss and interfere. And I think she has enjoyed it too, though at times she has got really serious.

'When we get home, I want to talk to you and Lucy together,' she said on one occasion.

We were sitting in the hotel grounds enjoying a cream tea.

'What about?' I asked.

'No,' Granny said, 'I can't say any more until you're both together. It wouldn't be right.'

She had what we used to call her 'Mrs Pepperpot' face on – our code for 'we're in for a lecture'. Not that I thought we were for the high jump now – those days are long gone. Most likely Granny wanted to talk about something gruesome, such as the hymns she wants at her funeral, or how she's divided up what she has to leave us in her will. Not I suppose that there's much to leave, and what there is should all go to Lucy – she's the one who's been there for Granny. There are a couple of things I'd like, though, namely the green pottery rabbits that used to sit on her dressing table. When I was little I loved those rabbits. They may have been broken by now, of course, or gone to the charity shop, and if not, and Lucy wants them, then as I say, I'm happy for her to have first call.

But the truth is, I don't want to think about the disposal of Granny's belongings. I don't want to think about Granny dying at all.

Another thing I don't want to think about is Miss Leverton. I phoned her the day after the article appeared in the newspaper – on my home landline because that was when I was without a mobile. I apologised, told her how shocked and angry I was, and drew a veil over the fact that I'd talked to Pete Holbrook.

She was really quite nice about it.

'I'm sorry too,' she said. 'But I suppose it was inevitable it was going to come out sooner or later. It's not your fault.'

Which only made me feel worse. So when Granny asked me how I was getting on with Miss Leverton, I just said I'd been to see her a couple of times and was going back again, though truth to tell, I'm not at all sure she'll want to see me after that bloody article.

'She suggested I should take you to meet her,' I said, trying to steer the conversation away from her revelations to me. 'She said she's sure you must have some stories of your own to tell about the war.'

'Did she?' Granny looked thoughtful. 'Well, it would be quite nice really, I suppose.'

I was surprised; Granny has never been one for visiting, even her friends. Some people in the village always seemed to be in and out of one another's houses, coffee mornings and Tupperware and Pippa Dee parties, but Granny always said she couldn't be doing with all that. Perhaps she's lonely, as Miss Leverton is. Though she's got Lucy and Phil and the boys, perhaps she misses the company of her own generation.

That particular conversation never went any further, though. An elderly couple who are also staying in our hotel were passing on their way to the bar – they're in there every evening pre-dinner, she with her G and T, he with his Glenfiddich – and they stopped to pass the time of day, and then invited us to join them. Which we did, me thinking Granny would enjoy the company, she, as she told me later, rather fancying a G and T herself.

That's been typical of the holiday really. No plans to stick to, just doing what we fancy when the mood takes us. And I'm really feeling pretty chilled out and relaxed.

Until, four days in, I'm in my room getting ready to go down for dinner and I hear my phone ringing, muffled by the pile of T-shirts in the dressing table drawer.

Oh shit. Perhaps I ought to check it out.

It's stopped ringing by the time I retrieve it, but the display shows a number of missed calls. They can't all have been Pete – can they? But there's also a text message that is definitely him. I open it.

'Plse contact me. Urgent. Pete.'

I can't believe this, I really can't. And whilst I'm still fuming, the darned thing rings again. It's the last straw. I've had enough. I punch in Pete's number. He answers more or less immediately.

'For goodness' sake, Pete, will you just leave me alone!' I snap.

'Martha—'

'No. Enough. I don't want to speak to you or have any more to do with you. After what you did—'

'I didn't,' Pete interrupts me. 'The piece in the paper – it wasn't me.'

I snort. 'Who was it then? The tooth fairy?'

'It wasn't me, Martha. But that's not why I need to speak to you. How long are you going to be away?'

'Until the end of the week, if it's any of your business.'

He swears. 'I can't leave it that long. I'm going to have to speak to Miss Leverton myself.'

'What!' I'm startled and outraged.

'I was going to ask you to do it. But it won't wait.'

'What won't wait? A follow-up to your bloody story? I just don't believe this!'

'I told you. It wasn't my story. And what I have to tell her isn't for publication anyway – at least not at the moment.'

'What are you talking about?'

'I can't explain over the phone, Martha. It would take far too long. I'll tell you when you get back.'

'If you get in touch with that poor woman again, you're dead!'

'I have to.'

A tap on my door. Granny, I imagine, coming to see if I'm ready to go down to dinner. I haven't finished with Pete, but I can't leave her standing outside in the corridor, and I don't want her to hear this furious argument either.

'I've got to go,' I say shortly.

'Call me back, Martha.'

I simply snort contemptuously, disconnect, and open the door. It is Granny. She's looking very smart in a nice dress, and her hair, which had been wind-whipped and straggly earlier, is now combed into soft curls around her face.

'Wow, Granny! You look fantastic!'

A wry smile. 'I do my best.'

'I won't be long. Come in and sit down while I just finish off. I've got to keep up with you!'

She comes in, sits in the wicker chair, a twin of the one in her own room.

'Is everything all right?' she asks.

I pause, my mascara wand hovering dangerously close to my left eye. From the reflection in the dressing table mirror I can see she's looking at me anxiously.

'Why wouldn't it be?' I ask breezily.

'I thought . . . while I was waiting at the door . . . I heard . . . it sounded as if you were shouting at someone.'

'Oh, that.' I give a small, forced laugh. 'It was nothing. Just somebody I'm cross with. Forget it, Granny. I have.'

Granny doesn't press me and I go on putting on my mascara. But of course I haven't forgotten. I'm still fuming. I could strangle Pete Holbrook with my bare hands. Next time I see him I probably will. But for the moment there's not a damn thing I can do to stop him harassing that poor woman.

I slick on some lip gloss, toss the tube and the mascara back into my (very small and beginning to look tatty) make-up bag, push it to the back of the dressing table and get up from the padded stool.

'OK,' I say. 'Ready. Shall we go?'

I offer Granny my arm and we head for the lift, a drink, and dinner.

THIRTY-SIX

ANNE

The last few days, I've felt as if I'm in a state of suspended animation, waiting, just waiting. To hear from Angela Liebermann; to hear from Pete Holbrook, the journalist; to hear from the hospital with news of Mum's condition. I am absolutely in the hands of others, and I don't like that. I'm used to taking control of the problems in my life, to coping with them by being proactive. But for the moment there's no more I can do, and the feeling of helplessness, so alien to me, is debilitating. I veer between wild hope and black pessimism. I pick up the phone a dozen times a day to call either Angela or Pete and ask if there is any progress, impress on them the urgency of the situation, then put it down again. I mustn't make a nuisance of myself; annoy them by my impatience. I need them on side. But it is so hard to just sit on my hands and wait.

Not that I'm doing much sitting. I'm still rushing around trying to juggle all the things I have to do – the school runs, the shopping, my business – and now, of course, running in and out of Bristol to visit Mum in hospital too.

And then Pete Holbrook rings.

'I'm sorry I haven't been back in touch before.'

My heart had begun racing the minute I heard his voice.

'That's OK,' I say, trying not to give away the fact that I've been on pins 24/7 waiting for his call, but hearing the eagerness and the strain in my own voice all the same. 'Is there any news?'

'Not as such, no.'

My heart sinks. 'Oh, I was hoping . . .'

'The thing is,' Pete says, 'there was somebody I wanted to speak to before I took the next step, and they've been incommunicado. But I've decided I can't wait any longer. I'm going to press on anyway, and hopefully I should be able to get back to you by this evening. I just wanted to let you know that I haven't forgotten you. I am on the case.'

'Thank you so much.'

'Don't thank me yet. I may be barking up completely the wrong tree.'

'Oh, I do hope not!'

'For your sake, so do I. I'll be in touch as soon as I have anything to report.'

That, of course, sets me off again on the roller-coaster of hope and the black terror of failure with the shallow dips and inclines of caution in between.

Around midday I drive to the BRI, so distracted it's a wonder I don't get involved in an accident. But somehow I manage to make it safely and find a parking space. I go in and up to Mum's ward.

'Mrs Mayle!' The sister, who is at the nursing station, attracts my attention. 'Can I have a quick word?' My heart does a somersault. Then she goes on: 'Your mother is back with us. Still drowsy, but conscious. Even talking a bit, though I have to warn you she's not making a great deal of sense. But that's quite normal. She's been in a world of her own these last few days. It's probably best to humour her. We don't want to do anything to upset her or tire her.'

'No, of course not.'

She smiles. 'So go and welcome her back to the land of the living.'

Mum is lying back against the pillows with her eyes closed. She looks very small and frail, her face drained of any colour, her cheeks sunken hollows. One crêpey hand, equally pale, lies on top of the bedspread, fidgeting rhythmically as if she is trying to work a thread loose.

I pull up a chair, sit down and cover that restless hand with mine.

'Mum?' Her eyes flicker; she turns her head towards the sound of my voice. 'Mum – it's Anne.'

'Anne.' It's just a whisper, like the crackle of a dead leaf. Her lips look dry, too, cracked and flaking. I hadn't noticed that while she was unconscious; now the movement is drawing attention to it. I must bring her something for it – Elizabeth Arden's Eight Hour Cream would do the trick, it's always been a beauty basic for me, the magic cure-all.

'Oh Mum . . .' I stop, realising I'm lost for words. What does one say to someone who is clearly still so ill, someone who tried to take their own life, someone who knows you now know far more about them than they ever wanted you to?

'Fancy frightening us like that!' I say, sounding more like a mother chastising a young child than a sixty-plus woman talking to her eighty-plus mother.

A little dry sob escapes those dry lips, but there is still moisture in her – a tear squeezes out from beneath the hooded veil of her half-closed eyes and trickles down her cheek.

'Oh Mum, don't,' I say, anguished. 'You're all right now. It's going to be all right.'

Her eyes open fully, but it's as though she's looking through me rather than at me.

'I shouldn't be here. Why am I here?'

'Because you've been very ill.'

'I shouldn't still be here. Why am I?'

I sigh. 'Because, thank goodness, Thelma found you in time.'

Mum huffs breath over her lip, a pale parody of her usual disgust.

'Thelma! What was she doing there? It wasn't her day.'

'No, it wasn't. But she came to get a mark off your table, and it's a jolly good job she did. What were you thinking of, Mum? Oh, I know you explained it all in your letter, but to do what you did . . . You should have just told me.'

'I couldn't, Anne. I couldn't!' Another tear squeezes out. At last, for a moment, her eyes focus on me; they are full of torment as well as tears. 'Whatever do you think of me?'

'Well, it's been a shock, of course. I can't deny that. But—'

'You must hate me.'

'Of course I don't hate you. Whatever you did, you're still my mum, the only one I've ever known. And I don't want to lose you.'

'I couldn't face telling you, Anne. I thought you'd be so cross with me. And everybody knowing what I did . . . I'm so ashamed. But I had to tell you, didn't I? If it means that Sonia . . . Have you found them? Your real family? Can they help?'

'I haven't found them yet, but I'm hoping that I will.' I hesitate, wondering how much I can press her for more details, and decide that had better wait for another day. I don't want to upset or tire her – I scarcely needed the sister to warn me about that. My hopes are pinned on Pete Holbrook coming up with the goods anyway, and allaying the need to make Mum dredge up more painful memories.

'I have traced my father,' I say instead.

'The German?' She sounds almost disbelieving. I wonder if she's thinking that she need never have revealed the truth about my kidnap after all.

'Yes. Would you believe, he came back after the war and bought the hotel where he used to be a waiter. He's dead now, but I've spoken to his son and met his sister, and we're organising DNA tests. If they're positive, as I'm sure they will be, they are going to try to persuade the younger family members to be tested to see if any of them are a match for Sonia.'

'Oh, that's good.' Mum's eyelids are drooping again. 'Anne, I don't feel . . . I need to . . .'

'Rest. Of course you do. Look, I'm going to go now and leave you in peace.'

'Anne . . .' Her hand moves restlessly in mine; she forces her eyes open again.

'What?'

'Can you ever forgive me?'

'Oh Mum, don't be silly. It was a crazy thing to do, but—'

'No – the other thing. Can you?'

To be honest, I'm not sure. To be honest, I think I misunderstood her deliberately. I don't know if I can forgive her. But I can't be so cruel as to tell her that.

'Of course,' I say.

'I couldn't bear to lose you.'

'I know. And you won't.'

'That's all right then,' she says. Her lips soften into what is not so much a smile as a look of satisfaction. It doesn't sit well with me. It reminds me that really, to my mother, everything is, and always has been, about her.

I wonder just how much thought she has given over the years to the pain she's caused others; not a lot, I suspect. She would have seen herself as the victim, the girl who was forced to give up her own child, the woman forced to suffer under a burden of guilt for snatching someone else's baby. Empathy has never been her strong suit; everything is seen only from her own point of view.

And yet, in the end, when it mattered, she had made the decision to tell the truth for Sonia's sake. This time, at least, she actually put someone else's needs before her own, even if she was unable to find the courage to meet the consequences of her revelation head on.

I am glad, of course I am, that her attempt to commit suicide failed. But I can't help wondering whether perhaps it might have been for the best if Thelma hadn't found her when she did. Caring as much as she does about the good opinions of others, she's going to go through hell. For all I know, she might have to face a police investigation. She did, after all, commit a crime – probably more than one. I would think they'd show her a certain amount of leniency – what purpose would it serve to prosecute her, an old woman, after all these years? But she'll have to answer their questions, for sure, and that will be dreadful for her.

'Try and get some rest, Mum,' I say. 'I'll come back and see you this evening.'

I kiss her on the cheek and she smiles again. But I think she's almost asleep again already.

As I leave the hospital I think maybe that her being on the road to recovery is an omen that things are turning for the better, that at long last there may be light at the end of what has been a very long, very dark tunnel.

I hope and pray that I am right.

THIRTY-SEVEN

MARTHA

Not such a nice day today weather-wise – it's a bit overcast and apparently there's a chance of rain later.

We've had breakfast – I must say I'm enjoying those huge fry-ups; normally a couple of slices of toast is the closest I get to a cooked breakfast. More usually it's a bowl of cornflakes on the run as I dash around getting ready for work. Now I've come back up to my room, leaving Granny chatting to her new friends, the Pinkertons, over yet another pot of tea. They're the couple who like their pre-dinner drinks – as, I've discovered, does Granny! Apparently Mr Pinkerton – Frederick – used to be in the diplomatic service and they've lived in exotic places all over the world in their time. They go on about it a bit too much for my liking, but Granny laps it up. Since she's scarcely ever left England, she likes hearing about the adventurous lives other people have led, I suppose.

Perhaps she *would* enjoy coming along with me on a visit to Miss Leverton, and given how interested Lucy was in the box I found in the lake, perhaps she'd like to come along too, if Miss Leverton has no objection.

Lucy. I really ought to ring her. I haven't spoken to her for a couple of days, and knowing her, I expect she's fretting and wondering how we're getting on.

I switch on my mobile and click on her number, wandering over to the window and looking out at the grey sky and grey band of distant sea as I wait for it to connect.

There's no reply; her answering machine cuts in.

'Hi, Lucy. Just to let you know we're fine, and I think Granny is really enjoying herself . . .'

I break off, frowning. There's a car pulled up on the opposite side of the road, a silver RAV that looks exactly like Pete's. What is the matter with me? Paranoid or what?

'I'll ring again later. I expect Granny would like to speak to you,' I finish.

I've still got half an eye on the car that looks like Pete's. There's somebody in the driving seat, just a dark blurry silhouette from here. The door's opening; he's getting out . . .

Oh my God, it is Pete! I don't believe this! Why the hell would he drive all the way from Bristol to Weston-super-Mare to talk to me? He's got his story – he made it abundantly clear he was going to see Miss Leverton himself. Except that she probably gave him short shrift and he thinks he can sweet-talk me into getting whatever info he was after. And how did he find out where I was staying? I'm sure I never mentioned the name of the hotel. Oh, perhaps I did, and he remembered. He would! Journalists have memories like elephants as well as the same thick skins.

I switch off my mobile with an angry click and head for the door. Thank goodness Granny is occupied with the Pinkertons. I wouldn't have wanted to have a stand-up row with him in front of her. Perhaps that's what he's banking on. But I still can't understand what's so urgent that he had to come dashing down here at all. It's not as if it's hot news that won't wait.

For a treacherous moment, as I wait for the lift, another possibility sneaks into a corner of my mind. I wonder if perhaps the reason he's here is not because of his precious story, but because he wants to make things up with me. And I'm shocked at how hope leaps, making me feel almost excited.

Fool! He never was interested in you. He just wanted to use you.

The lift arrives. I push the button for the ground floor and zoom down. He's not in the foyer yet, thank goodness. I head smartly for the door and almost collide with him coming in.

'What the hell are you doing here?'

He raises both hands in a gesture of surrender.

'Don't kick off. I've got to talk to you.'

'I've got nothing to say to you, Pete. Zero. Zilch. What part of that don't you understand?'

'I know you're angry, Martha . . .'

'You bet I am!'

'. . . but you have to hear me out.'

'I don't *have* to do anything!'

'Will you just calm down and listen for once?'

'Calm down! After what you did?'

'I'm sorry you think that of me. I hoped you knew me better than to think that I'd take advantage of what you told me after I gave you my word I wouldn't. Obviously I got us all wrong.'

I snort contemptuously.

'If it wasn't you, who was it?'

'Actually the prime culprit, as I understand it, is your ex-husband. He drinks in the same pub as one of our keen young reporters. They got talking over a pint, and the rest is history. It was you who told your ex what you'd been up to, I take it?'

'Oh shit!' I can feel the hot blood rushing into my face. I *had* talked to Nick, the night of my accident. When he stayed over. When we were both a bit drunk. But it had never occurred to me he'd repeat it to anyone, least of all a newspaper reporter.

'I wasn't any more pleased about it than you were,' Pete goes on. 'Cheeky young bastard, pinching my story. He's been told in no uncertain terms to lay off now, though. And when this linked story came in, our editor made sure he put it my way.' His face is set hard. 'Ring him if you don't believe me.'

'There's no need.' I do believe him, and I'm feeling pretty much ashamed of myself. For talking to Nick, for being so ready to believe Pete guilty. But . . .

'What was I supposed to think when I saw it?' I defend myself, almost as crossly as when I went on the attack.

'You could have let me explain.'

'I'm sorry,' I mutter. Apologising doesn't come easy to me.

Pete shrugs. 'Oh well, it doesn't matter now. I'd have let you stew in your own juice if I hadn't needed to talk to you.'

I swear silently, willing the colour to go down in my cheeks, kicking myself for ruining what had been a very promising relationship.

'What do you want to talk to me about, then?'

A young couple are emerging from the hotel hand-in-hand; a family is just arriving, unloading suitcases out of the boot of their 4x4.

'Not here,' Pete says. 'We need to go somewhere a bit more private.'

'I can't leave the hotel. Granny . . . But there's a terrace at the back. I should think that would be fairly quiet this morning. The weather's not nice enough for people to want to have their coffee outside.'

'Coffee,' Pete says with a flash of his old insouciance. 'Now there's an inviting thought. I didn't stop for breakfast. I wanted to be sure of catching you before you went out for the day.'

'Come on then.'

We go into the hotel. Granny is in the lounge area outside the dining room, still sitting with the Pinkertons.

'Granny, if you want me, I'll be out on the terrace. With a friend who's come to see me.'

Granny looks surprised. She glances towards the doorway, where Pete is waiting for me. 'Oh – a young man!' She sounds surprised too.

'We won't be long.'

'There's no hurry. We've got plenty to talk about, haven't we, Gwendoline?' Granny says, including Mrs Pinkerton. 'And I can always go up to my room and read my book. Don't cut your visitor short for me.'

She smiles knowingly, and I can feel her watching as I rejoin Pete. *Don't get your hopes up, Granny!* She'd like me to meet someone, I know, or get back together with Nick. Preferably that, I should think. She comes from the generation who believe that marriage really is until death do you part, no matter how miserable you make one another. And who think that a woman can't be happy unless she's got a husband. Well, bollocks to that.

Pete and I go through to the rear of the hotel and out on to the terrace, stopping off on the way to order the coffee. As I expected, the terrace is pretty well deserted this morning. We take a table at the far end, overlooking the lawn, where pink roses climb over a trellis and a sleek tabby cat is asleep under a flowering shrub.

'OK,' I say. 'What's all this about?'

'It's a long story.'

'So you'd better get started.'

'Yes. I suppose so.' For the first time since I've met him, it strikes me that Pete looks uneasy. This is highly unusual for a journalist; they generally plough in feet first.

'Did you go to see Miss Leverton?' I ask, a little aggressively.

'I did, yes.'

'And she showed you the door?'

'No, actually. What I had to say to her was very awkward, though. That's why I was hoping to get you to do it. I thought it would come better from you.'

'What would come better from me?'

'That's what I'm going to tell you.' The coffee arrives. When the waiter has departed, Pete goes on. 'I mentioned just now that another strand to the story came up.'

'As a result of the piece in the paper?'

'No, actually. A lady called Anne Mayle got in touch with the paper to ask if we could help her trace her long-lost family. My editor, who is very much on the ball, spotted a connection to the Miss Leverton story. And because he knew I was pretty pissed off about having my territory trampled on, he pushed the new lead my way.'

'What are you talking about?' I ask, totally confused.

Pete doesn't answer for a moment. Instead, he stirs two heaped spoonfuls of brown sugar into his coffee. Then he sits back, still looking uncomfortable.

'Do you remember Miss Leverton talking about a little girl who was killed in an air raid in the war?'

'Of course I remember. If it hadn't happened, she would probably never have gone to France. And it was so terribly sad.'

Pete fiddles with his coffee spoon.

'Suppose I were to tell you that the woman who got in touch with my editor claimed to be that child.'

'What!'

'I know. It beggars belief, doesn't it?'

'It certainly does! The shop where the grandmother and child were killed suffered a direct hit.'

'But according to Anne Mayle, the little girl wasn't there. She'd been snatched from her pushchair moments before the bomb fell. By a deranged woman who had been forced to give up her own child for adoption. And who went on to bring Anne up as her own.'

'That's insane! It sounds like a made-up tale to me.'

'I don't think so. Why would anyone make up something like that?'

'God knows! There are some crazy people out there. We get them walking into police stations, confessing to anything that's made the news, the more ghoulish the better. Obviously your contact read the story in the paper and decided to get her fifteen minutes of fame.'

'No, there's a lot more to it than that. Anne insists that her "mother" has only recently told her the truth.'

'Exactly! After she read about it in your newspaper. Perhaps she's the one looking for a bit of celebrity.'

'Hardly. She actually tried to kill herself after writing it all down in a letter to Anne. And she had a solid reason for coming clean after all these years. Her granddaughter – Anne's daughter Sonia – is seriously ill with leukaemia. She needs a bone marrow transplant, and Anne is desperate to locate any family who might be compatible. Her mother felt she had to tell the truth so as to point her in the right direction. And then tried to commit suicide because she couldn't face the consequences.'

I whistle softly.

'Are you saying this woman, this Anne, is actually the baby Miss Leverton thought was killed?'

'It all fits the facts as we know them. Bath in the war. The Admiralty connection. The German father – actually that's another long story that I won't go into now, but I will tell you later. Plus apparently Margaret Maloney, Anne's "mother", has a history of depression. There's no doubt Anne believes her.'

'You're sure she's not clutching at straws?'

'I don't think so. She's very level-headed. Of course, it would take a DNA test to prove it one way or another, but I can't see any reason why Margaret would suddenly come out with a story like that and then try to take her own life if it wasn't true. Unless there were two grandmothers and babies killed in pretty well identical circumstances, which seems highly unlikely, I think we can safely assume that Anne Mayle is, in fact, Lynne.'

I blow breath out over my top lip, trying to take all this in.

'So you put her in touch with Miss Leverton?'

'No, of course not. I told her I might be able to help, but I couldn't give her any details until I'd checked something out. I wanted to speak to Miss Leverton first and break it to her gently. That's why I was trying to get in touch with you. You're the one she's been talking to. I thought you were the one who should tell her that the baby she believed dead is in fact alive.'

'But I wouldn't play ball, so you did it yourself.' I'm stunned by all this, but also ever-so-slightly peeved. I would have liked to be the one to break the amazing news to Miss Leverton.

'I had to. From what Anne said, finding a donor match for Sonia is pretty urgent.'

Hmm. A good excuse, I'd say. But there's no denying he did make every effort to contact me.

'What did Miss Leverton say?' I ask. 'She must have been . . . well, I can't actually imagine what her reaction must have been. To find out after all these years . . .' A thought strikes me. 'She won't be able to be of any help in finding a bone marrow match for the daughter, though, will she? She's never had any more children. That's very sad. To find her lost baby only to end up with another possible tragedy to cope with.'

For a long moment Pete says nothing. Then he looks at me directly.

'There's more, Martha. You don't know the whole story yet. There's something very important she hasn't told you. Which, when I'd explained why I was breaking the news to her, she had no choice but to tell me. And it's the reason why I'm here today. I didn't think it could wait until you came home.'

'What the hell are you talking about?' I ask shortly.

'I think,' Pete says, 'that you are probably going to need something a bit stronger than coffee. Shall I go and get you a whisky?'

'Pete, it's only about half past ten in the morning! I know I like a drink, but not this early!'

'Well, it's up to you.'

'Just tell me what you're going on about.'

'OK.' He sits back in his chair, looking at me levelly. 'You remember you thought it was odd that Miss Leverton was telling the whole story in the third person? "Pascale did this", "Pascale did that"?'

'Yes, but what . . . ?'

'There was a reason for that. It wasn't just a strange affectation as you thought. She really was talking about someone else. Stella Leverton wasn't Pascale. The Croix de Guerre you found in the lake wasn't hers.'

'What?' I'm outraged. 'You mean she's falsely claimed a medal she has no right to?'

'She did in fact win a Croix de Guerre herself. Just not that one. That one really did belong to Pascale, who had asked her, as an old friend, to claim it because she didn't feel able to do so herself.'

I shake my head, totally confused, and still angry.

'But why ask to meet me? Why tell me a pack of lies?'

'Martha, why don't you just shut up for a minute, and I'll explain. Miss Leverton was actually Simone. She told you the story at the request of her old friend, Pascale. Who, because she has had a stroke and lost a lot of her powers of speech, didn't feel capable of telling it herself.' He pauses, staring straight at me with a very strange look on his face. 'You weren't randomly picked because you found the box, Martha – although that was an extraordinary coincidence. You were picked because you are you. When Miss Leverton had finished the story, your grandmother intended to get you and Lucy together, ask you to repeat what Miss Leverton had told you, and then come clean with the truth. That Miss Leverton was actually Simone, and that Pascale . . .'

The hairs on the back of my neck are prickling.

'Pete.' I say it very softly, unable to believe what I'm beginning to think he's about to tell me. 'Pete, who is Pascale?'

'Now you know why I think you need a stiff drink,' Pete says. 'Pascale is your grandmother.'

Oh my God, he is right! I do need that whisky!

'You're winding me up.'

He shakes his head.

'No, no wind-up.'

'Granny! Granny – in the SOE? No! It can't be true! She couldn't have kept a secret like that all this time . . . I can't believe it!'

And yet, in a funny way, I do. Now that I come to think of it, I know nothing, really, of her past, before she married Grampy, that is. Somehow I never really questioned it much. They were an institution, she and Grampy. To a child, that had been enough. I think of how she was always reluctant to go on holiday, leave her home for any length of time. I'd thought it was strange she should be so unadventurous; she wasn't in any way a timid person. Now I think that if she really was Pascale, she'd probably had enough adventure in the war to last her a lifetime, and it had made her appreciative of simple home comforts.

I think, too, of what she said, just the other day, about wanting to talk to me and Lucy together. I thought she wanted to discuss funeral arrangements, but I know now I was wrong. With the end of her life approaching, Granny wanted us to know the truth. Perhaps my finding the box in the lake had been the trigger – she wanted us to have the Croix de Guerre and the ring and the locket, and she wanted us to know what they once meant to her. But with her speech so badly impaired by her stroke, she no longer felt confident about finding the words to tell us everything. So she had somehow got in touch with Stella Leverton and asked her to do it for her.

I cover my face with my hands, still reeling.

'This is just . . . mind-blowing.'

Pete pushes back his chair. 'I'm getting you that drink, Martha, half past ten in the morning or not.'

He disappears into the hotel and I sit staring into space with my thoughts churning in wild circles. Each time I come back to the realisation that Pascale was really Granny, it hits me with the same shock, absolutely undiluted, and winds me all over again.

'Martha?'

I jerk round; she's there in the doorway like some apparition. My granny, my very ordinary granny, who . . .

'Martha, I'm going up to my room now . . .' She breaks off, looking at me uncertainly, disconcerted, I suppose, by the way I'm staring at her. 'Are you all right?' she asks.

I shake my head.

'Granny – why didn't you ever say anything? I mean, I can understand why you might have had trouble explaining now, since your stroke, but before . . . All these years and you never said anything!'

Her face changes; she looks almost guilty. Then she sits down on the chair Pete vacated and says just two words.

'You know.'

'Well – I've just found out, yes. You . . . oh my God, Granny . . .' Like her, when she was at her worst after the stroke, I'm lost for words.

'You're a heroine,' I say, 'and we had no idea. We'd have been so proud of you! Why didn't you tell us?'

She fiddles with a handkerchief that's balled in her fist.

'There were things . . . I wanted to forget. And your Grampy . . . he wanted . . . I owed him . . . a fresh start.'

She's struggling a bit now, less coherent than she has been this last week, and suddenly I'm more worried about her than anything else. The last thing I want to do is stress her. Who knows, it might bring on another stroke.

'Never mind now, Granny. We've got the rest of the week to talk about it.'

'But . . . how did you . . . ?' She's looking puzzled.

This is something else I don't want to go into just now in any detail.

'It's a long story. I'll explain later. I am just so glad I know.'

Pete reappears with my whisky and a beer for himself. I make faces at him, unseen by Granny, warning him to be careful what he says.

I introduce them. Pete puts the drinks down on the table and offers Granny his hand.

'I'm very pleased to meet you.'

She smiles, takes his hand. 'You're looking after Martha, I see.'

'I'd certainly like to.'

A glance at me from those bedroom eyes and I feel my tummy tip.

Granny points at my whisky. 'Could I . . . ?'

'Granny!' I say in a pretend-shocked voice, but secretly I'm laughing. There is still some of the old Pascale there, though it's hidden from the outside world these days.

'Course you could.' He turns to go back into the hotel. 'Whisky and . . . ?'

'Cognac,' she says, and though rusty from years of disuse and a bit distorted by vocal muscles that don't work properly any more, the French accent is as authentic as ever.

For the first time since Pete's shocking revelation, I can almost accept the truth. There's still an awful lot I don't understand. But as I look at Granny, I can suddenly see the young girl she once was. Brave, determined, ultimately tragic. And hope that I have inherited a few genes that might make me half the woman she is.

When Pete leaves, I go out to the car with him. I thank him for not making a big deal of what he'd told me in front of Granny, and for not mentioning Anne, the woman who claims to be her lost baby. I need to break that news to her very gently; it's going to be one hell of a shock.

'But if you give me a contact number for Anne, I'll ring her,' I say. 'If this bone marrow match is so urgent, we ought to set things in motion.'

He gives me her phone number, but asks me to leave calling her until he's spoken to her and prepared the ground, which he'll do as soon as he's back in Bristol.

'You're not going to print any of this, are you?' I ask anxiously.

'It would be terrible if it became public before I've had a chance to talk to Lucy.'

'I won't be writing a word unless and until it's OK with you and everybody else concerned,' he says, and then adds slyly: 'I wouldn't mention it to your ex, though, if I were you.'

'You can bank on that!' I say grimly. 'The only words I'll be having with him would be unprintable.'

'No chance of a happy reunion there, then?'

'No chance! Not that there ever was. And Pete . . . I really think I owe you an apology for being so ready to blame you for the leak. I'd totally forgotten that I talked to Nick about it the night of the accident. I think I was a bit groggy, and drunk. But really that's no excuse. I should have trusted you.'

'You certainly should have.'

'Do you forgive me?'

'What do you think?'

He pulls me in, rests his forehead against mine. Such a tiny touch, yet somehow incredibly intimate. My stomach does a dive and somer-sault.

'Not here, Pete!'

'No, we'd be banned from Weston-super-Mare seafront for life. Just wait till you get home, though. I intend to make up for lost time.'

'Oh you . . .' I laugh, give him a playful push. 'Get out of here!'

'I'm going.'

He gets into the car, starts the engine. 'I'll call you later.'

I nod. And watch him drive away until he's out of sight.

Then I go back into the hotel in search of Granny.

THIRTY-EIGHT

ANNE

What a day! After all the waiting, everything has suddenly happened at once, and the telephone lines have been red hot.

First, a call from Pete Holbrook telling me he's identified my real mother. Apparently her name is Beatrice Lane, though she was once known as Pascale, which would tally with what Mum said about her mother being French. So it would seem I have quite an international heritage – a German father and a French grandmother. Beatrice doesn't yet know about me, but I'm to expect a call from her granddaughter, a policewoman called Martha Holley. This is doubly good news, since it has to mean that my mother married and had more children. Which will, of course, increase the chances of us finding a bone marrow match for Sonia.

Martha rang me early afternoon whilst her grandmother was having a nap, she said. As you can imagine, it was strange and a bit awkward talking to a complete stranger who could well be my niece. But she seemed very nice, very down to earth. She told me that her mother, who would have been my half-sister, is dead, killed in an air crash thirty-odd years ago, but she has a sister and three teenage nephews, and once she's had the chance to speak to them, she's sure they'll all be willing to be tested. At the moment, though, she is on holiday with Beatrice, and not due back till the end of the week.

She also promised to e-mail me some photographs of her grandmother – my mother! – if she can access a computer in the hotel, and then had another thought. If she took a snap on her phone, she could send me that, direct to my mobile. So right now I'm waiting – incredibly excited. I can't wait to see what she looks like.

I fill the time making phone calls of my own. To Rod. To Sonia's doctor. And, almost as an afterthought, to Elaine.

To be perfectly honest, I don't know whether I'm coming or going!

I'm getting tea for the children when my mobile beeps. I whack the fish fingers into the oven (no fancy meal tonight!) and set the timer before I pick up the call, thinking that if I get distracted, the food will burn. As I'd hoped, it's the promised photograph. I shade the phone with my hand so that I can see it better.

For such a tiny picture on such a tiny screen, it's remarkably clear. A head-and-shoulders shot of an elderly lady. Softly curling white hair, a still clearly defined heart-shaped jaw – my God! My jaw! The shape of our faces is almost identical. I'm like her – I must be! It's unreal. Uncanny.

For a moment I've forgotten all about the circumstances that have brought me to this – Sonia, the bone marrow. I am looking into the face of my mother, my real mother. And it is the most profoundly emotional experience.

The oven timer starts buzzing in short, stentorian bursts like an automated and very large bumblebee. The fish fingers are ready. I dish them up with baked beans and a salad and call the children. Then I leave them to it and go upstairs to change in readiness to go to the BRI to see Mum.

When I go back downstairs, Sonia is in the kitchen, sitting at the table with the children and nibbling some stray crispy crumbs from the fish fingers that have been spilled on the scrubbed board surface. She's been so much brighter since she's known there's a chance we may find a family donor for her; it's almost as if the healthy stem cells were already doing their work. I wonder if I should show her the picture, but I don't feel I'm quite ready to share it just yet.

'Will you be OK if I go to Bristol now?' I ask.

'Yes, fine. Kevin will be home soon anyway.'

'I'll get off then. The traffic should be easing by now.'

I leave them, a little family unit that will hopefully remain intact for a long, long time, and go out to my car.

I was wrong about the traffic. Rush hours seem to go on for much longer these days. Courtesy of flexitime, I suppose. But eventually I make it, find somewhere to park and go into the hospital.

As I make my way to Mum's ward, I'm wondering how we're going to manage when she's discharged. I can't imagine she'll be fit to be left alone in her own home, but I'm likely to be tied up at Sonia's for the foreseeable future, and there isn't anybody else. I'll have to talk to social services, I suppose, see if we can sort something out.

I go into the ward. The curtains round Mum's bed are drawn; perhaps she's on the bedpan, or a doctor is making a late round. Then I hear hurrying footsteps behind me and the sister calls my name.

'Mrs Mayle! Could I have a word?'

She looks a bit flushed and flustered, and I feel the first stab of alarm.

'Sister? What's wrong?'

'Could we . . . would you like to come with me?'

I look at the drawn curtains; look back at Sister's anxious face. And in that moment I know. My heart seems to drop into my boots; I've gone cold all over. I don't say a word. I just follow her. She opens a door to what I suppose is called the relatives' room.

'Mrs Mayle, I am so sorry. We've been trying to get hold of you . . .'

'It's Mum, isn't it?' I say. My voice seems to belong to someone else.

'I'm afraid so. We lost her . . .'

'But I thought she was getting better! What happened?'

'She had a massive heart attack. I'm afraid there was nothing we could do for her. It was very peaceful. Look, why don't you sit down? I'll get you a cup of tea.'

I sit down in one of the chairs where no doubt countless other bereaved people have sat before me. I feel utterly dazed.

'We rang your home number and your daughter said you were already on your way here. I'm so sorry that you should find out like this.'

'It's all right.' That same strange, faraway voice that doesn't seem to belong to me.

She goes – to get me hot sweet tea, I suppose – and I just sit there, staring into space. And all I can think is that while I was looking at a photograph of one of my mothers, the other was dying. As if I'd pushed her away, airbrushed her out of my life.

The tears start to prick behind my eyes. Later, I'll remind myself that it was what she intended, what she wanted. Later, I'll be thankful that she doesn't have to go through the trauma of police interviews, of living and reliving her shame. For the moment I can think only of the woman who raised me and cared for me, who had loved me more than she had any right to, and who had ultimately sacrificed herself to do the right thing. And who had died without me here to comfort and hold her.

Not my birth mother, but nevertheless the woman who will always, to me, be Mum.

MARTHA

'I expect you think it was a funny thing for me to ask Simone to tell you the story,' Granny says.

'Well, yes, but I can understand why you did it.'

We're sitting quietly on the terrace – the rain never did come to anything and the sky now is more blue than grey.

'I knew she'd tell it so much better than I could now.' Granny smiles ruefully.

'Actually, your speech is nearly back to normal.'

'Yes, but trying to tell you and Lucy all that . . .'

'I know.' I pat her hand. 'But how did you get in touch with Miss Leverton . . . Simone?'

'I wrote to her. Thank goodness the stroke affected my left side and not my right, so I can still hold a pen. We've always kept in touch by letter, though we haven't seen one another for years, so

Lucy didn't think anything of it when I asked her to post it for me. And I knew Simone would do it for me if I asked her. That's the way it's always been with us.'

'Even though you had an affair with her fiancé?'

Granny nods. 'There was a time when I thought she'd never forgive me, but after what we went through together . . . The bonds you forge are too strong to be broken. And she knew, I think, that it was over between her and Paul anyway.'

'I guess . . .' But I'm thinking that a friendship like that is a very special thing.

'Of course, I know now why she suggested I should take you to see her,' I go on. 'And I will when we get home, if you'd like me to. Lucy too.'

Granny frowns. 'I intended to tell you and Lucy the truth together. I hope she's not too upset that it didn't work out like that.'

'Me too.' It has been worrying me a bit. 'Never mind, we'll cross that bridge when we come to it. She'll understand, I'm sure.'

'I certainly hope so. She's been such a good girl to me.'

I hope so, too. I don't want anything else coming between me and Lucy.

'She is good,' I say. 'She always has been. I wish I could be more like her. Compared with her . . . well, I'm not a very nice person. I'm trying to be better, I really am, but it seems to be one step forward, two back. I always manage to end up getting annoyed and saying the wrong thing.'

Granny smiles and nods. 'You've always been fiery, Martha, and you always will be. But you've got qualities of your own. And however much you might try to hide it, your heart's in the right place.' She leans over and pats my hand. 'Just think a bit more before you speak and try not to judge others so harshly.'

'I'll try.' I grin bleakly. 'If I could be so wrong about you, Granny, what chance is there that I can be right about anyone else?'

'I think you're right about that young man,' she says sagely. 'From what I can see of it, you're ideally suited.'

'Mm. But I very nearly blew that. I really went off on one over the newspaper article.'

'You see? One of your good points. Honour.'

'Mm,' I say again, doubtfully. 'I'm not so sure I'm that honourable. Here I am, talking about not wanting to upset Lucy by finding all this out before her, and still itching to fill in the blanks, right here, right now. You see? I'm beyond redemption.'

'Oh Martha, you're so hard on yourself, aren't you? Every bit as hard as you are on everyone else. You know what? I'm going to tell you whatever you want to know. Just as long as you don't say a word to Lucy until I've had the chance to tell her too.'

'Granny! Are you sure?'

'I've had enough of secrets, Martha. Suppose something happened to me – another stroke, a heart attack? There are things Stella couldn't tell you and Lucy – and who knows, she mightn't be around to tell what she does know anyway. She's even older than me.'

'Don't say such things, Granny!'

'You've got to face it, Martha. When you get to my age, you just never know. Oh, don't look like that. Come on, ask away. I want to get all this off my chest.'

I take a deep breath.

'OK, for starters, how did the box come to be in the lake?'

'That was me,' Granny says. 'When I married your grampy. He was very good about everything, but I thought I ought to put the past behind me. Make a fresh start. I expect you think it was rather a drastic thing to do, but I suppose I was in a bit of a state at the time emotionally. Certainly afterwards I came to regret it. Not so much the medal or even the ring. They were things I felt I had to put behind me. But my baby's curl . . . I should never have . . .' She breaks off, tears misting her eyes, and I remember that I have to break the news to her that her child is not dead at all. But I don't think this is the right moment. All that emotional upset and excitement at the same time might be too much for her, and I don't want to make her ill again.

'Well you've got it back now,' I say soothingly. 'But it beggars belief that I should have been the one to find it. Coincidence or what?'

'Fate,' Granny says. Her eyes have gone very faraway and her voice is very soft. 'I do believe that some things are meant to be. That somebody is looking after us, and when the time is right . . .'

That's a bit deep for me. I don't go in for all that mumbo-jumbo.

'Anyway,' I say, trying to bring her back to reality, 'things worked out in the end, didn't they? You met Grampy and you were happy with him. You were happy, weren't you?'

'Oh yes. We were happy.'

There's a tone in her voice though that tells me that however happy she and Grampy were, she never forgot Paul.

'And you had Mum.'

'Yes.' She hesitates. 'There's something I have to tell you, though, Martha, now that you know about my time in France. It's the reason why I needed to prove to your grampy that I'd put the past behind me . . .' She hesitates again. I frown, waiting.

'The thing is,' she says, 'your mum . . . well, I already had her when I met Grampy. She was . . . your mum wasn't his baby. She was Paul's.'

'Oh!' I shouldn't be surprised, I suppose, but I am. This just gets more and more tangled.

'Why don't we have another cup of tea,' Granny says, 'and as long as you don't let on to Lucy that you already know it, I'll tell you the rest of the story.'

THIRTY-NINE

PASCALE'S STORY

Looking back, it always seemed to Pascale that her war ended with Paul's life. Though she remained in France, working tirelessly and bravely for the cause, her memories of those missions, the careful planning, the triumphs and the near-disasters, were painted in monochrome, a lifeless pastiche that faded rapidly into a meaningless blur, whilst her time with Paul remained clear and vibrant, each episode, every moment recorded in primary colours that would never be erased. With his death, night had fallen on her world, an inky darkness with no shadows of dusk to soften its coming, no gradual lessening of the light to ease her into its clutches.

With the vision of the leaping flames that had engulfed the German patrol still flaring before her eyes, and her ears ringing dully with the explosion of the grenade, Pascale had walked that day for a full eight hours, hiding, when necessary, from other German patrols, then pressing on again, driven only by an instinct of self-preservation and the determination that she must go on for Paul's sake. He had given his life for her; to give up now, or to allow herself to be captured, would be to fail him and his sacrifice.

At last she reached a village where they had a base, and it was only when she had staggered, exhausted both physically and emotionally, into the charcuterie owned by a friendly agent that her legs gave way beneath her.

It never once occurred to her to ask to leave France. If anything, she was more determined than ever to remain and do all she could to help defeat the enemy. She knew the country, she knew the people; the experience she had gained through working with Paul was invaluable to the movement. Though the pattern of command had changed and the soldiers of the Resistance had dispersed, many of them returning to the Maquis, it was still vital that the lines of communication were kept open and the growing army of ordinary people who wanted to see an end to German domination was supported and marshalled. Pascale soldiered on, working with new arrivals and old friends, as brave and resourceful as she had ever been, though her heart felt as if it had been frozen in ice and black grief swirled in an ominous tide around the periphery of her conscious mind. Until, in September, when the Allied tanks were rolling in and the German armies were on the run, she realised that not only was her work here done, but also that she had no choice but to return to England.

Paul might have died on that hot day in July, but a part of him was still very much alive.

Pascale was carrying his child.

Although she was a heroine of the SOE, Pascale had no expectation that she could turn to her superiors for help and support. She didn't even intend to mention her pregnancy at her debriefing, not because she was ashamed, but because she honestly didn't think it was relevant. Even if they were sympathetic – which she doubted they would be – she was no longer their responsibility. She'd got herself into this predicament; she'd have to find a way of coping with it herself.

But when Major Dickens suggested that she should work for the department on the home front in a clerical capacity, she felt obliged to tell him the truth.

'I won't be much use to you for very long,' she said bluntly.

The major, who seemed to have lost even more of his hair since she had seen him last, so that now just a few well-oiled strands threaded across the bony dome of his skull, eyed her speculatively and waited for her to go on.

'I'd be happy to work for you for the next five months or so, but after that . . . I'm expecting a baby in April,' she said, unconsciously twisting Paul's signet ring on the middle finger of her left hand.

'Ah.' The major reached for his pipe, tamping tobacco into it. 'I take it Paul is the father.'

Pascale started, surprised.

'You knew?'

'I would hardly be fit for purpose as an intelligence officer if I'd not realised there was something between you. And given that you were working closely together, it doesn't require great powers of deduction to make a guess as to the parentage of a baby you might be carrying. I'm just glad you decided to take me into your confidence.'

'I don't want to make a secret of it. In fact,' she added fiercely, 'I'm very proud to be having Paul's baby.'

'I'm sure you are, my dear.' The major applied a match to his pipe. 'Paul was a fine man and an excellent agent. The best. He'll be sadly missed. But it's not going to be easy for you.'

'I know that,' Pascale said tightly.

'Yes. Yes, of course you do.' He paused, puffing furiously for a moment or two. Pascale wondered what sort of a fallen woman he thought she was to have not one, but two illegitimate children.

'I'd still like to offer you a job here in the department,' he said at last as a stream of pungent smoke rose into the rather stale air. 'For as long as you want it, anyway.'

'Are you sure?' Pascale asked uncertainly. 'Won't I be an embarrassment to you?'

The major smiled.

'I think we can cope with that. And I think we owe it to Paul.'

'Thank you,' Pascale said.

The job would give her a focus – and an income – for the next few months, at least. And the time to make plans for when the baby was born.

Shortly after Pascale began working for the HQ staff of the SOE, who were now based at Baker Street, Simone returned to England and was also offered a desk job. When she heard the news, Pascale's stomach churned with mixed emotions. If it weren't for what had happened between her and Paul, she would have been delighted; as it was, she dreaded having to admit the truth to Simone. She wondered if Simone already knew, if somehow she'd heard on the grapevine, but doubted it. They had worked with different circuits, and the agents whose paths did cross would have had more on their minds than a romance between colleagues.

When she and Simone met, however, she knew at once from her slightly offhand greeting that Simone was indeed aware of the affair, at least. Pascale's heart sank. She wished that she had been able to break the news herself. It wouldn't have been easy, but it would have been far better than her finding out about it at second hand. At least Simone would have known she was going to be honest and upfront about it.

'I need to talk to you, Simone,' Pascale said.

'I don't really think I have anything to say to you.' Simone's tone was icy and final.

'I never meant for this to happen,' Pascale said. 'I tried to fight it – we both did – but—'

'It was too big for both of you, I suppose.'

'Simone – please . . . I can't bear to think of us being bad friends.'

'You should have thought of that,' Simone said coldly, 'before you started sleeping with my fiancé.'

'Do you think I didn't?'

Simone shrugged. 'Really, I haven't the slightest idea. And it hardly matters now, does it? Paul is dead. End of story.'

'Except that it's not the end of the story. Perhaps you don't know yet, but you soon will. And I'd rather you heard it from me. Couldn't we—'

'For goodness' sake, Pascale, whatever you have to say, just say it.'

'All right. If that's the way you want it. I'm pregnant. I'm going to have Paul's child.'

There was a moment's stony silence when Simone's face froze with shock and her eyes darkened with pain. Then she lowered them to Pascale's stomach, already beginning to grow round, and raised a scornful eyebrow.

'And there was me thinking you were getting fat,' she said in the same cold, hard tone.

'Oh Simone, I am so sorry,' Pascale said softly. 'I understand how angry you must be with me, and I'm sorry about that too. Your friendship means more to me than you could ever know. But I'm not sorry I'm going to have Paul's baby. I loved him too, though I had no right to. And this baby is all I have left of him.'

'Well lucky you,' Simone said bitterly. 'I have nothing at all. Not even my memories. You've seen to that.'

'Oh, please don't! I feel bad enough as it is.'

'And so you bloody well should. There's a name for women like you, you know.'

Suddenly Pascale was angry.

'Hang on! I'm not entirely to blame here. I didn't set out to seduce him, and even if I had, it wouldn't have worked if—'

'Don't kid yourself,' Simone interrupted. 'I know how lonely life in the field can be, remember. How dangerous. If you were there, throwing yourself at him, it's no wonder he took what was on offer.'

'It wasn't like that. I fell in love and so did he . . .'

'Spare me the details.'

They were shouting now, glaring at one another. Office doors were opening, heads poking round. A very senior officer appeared.

'My office – now!'

They had no choice but to obey, Simone stalking furiously ahead. Even when they were lined up in front of the big Civil Service desk, she kept shooting furious looks at Pascale.

'What is going on?' the senior officer demanded.

Both girls remained silent.

'I'll ask you again. What is all this about?'

'Nothing, sir.'

'Nothing, Colonel.'

'Hmm.' He snorted. 'In that case there will be no more of it, do you understand? I will remind you that we have a war to win. It's not over yet, and whatever our private differences, we have to work together until it is. Get back to your desks, both of you.'

'Yes, sir.'

'Yes, Colonel.'

'Go on then.'

They turned, marching single file. As Pascale opened the door, the colonel put out one passing shot.

'Can you imagine what Paul Randall would think if he knew the two of you were fighting like fishwives? So cut it out, in deference to his memory, if nothing else.'

As the door closed after them, Pascale glanced at Simone.

'He's right,' she said softly.

But Simone's face might have been carved in granite. She gave a small, disgusted shake of her head and turned away.

It would be some time before either of them spoke to the other again.

Time, as the old adage goes, is a great healer. Just what brought about Simone's change of heart, Pascale was never entirely sure. Perhaps the colonel's comment regarding what Paul would have thought had gone home; perhaps, when she had time to think about it, Simone recognised the truth in what Pascale had said; perhaps deep down she had known that Paul's feelings for her had already cooled before he and Pascale had begun their affair. Perhaps in the end the closeness of their friendship overcame Simone's perfectly understandable feelings of betrayal. Or perhaps, in a strange way, she felt as Pascale had once felt about her – that Pascale and the baby she was carrying were a link to the man she had loved and lost.

Whichever, or all, of these things it was, her hostility gradually lessened, her icy aggression thawed, though Pascale still felt she was walking on eggshells.

One evening, at the end of a long shift, they were alone together in the office. Pascale was feeling dreadfully weary and rather emotional, and when she realised she'd made several mistakes in the document she was working on, she ripped it out of the typewriter, tore it in two and burst into tears. For a few minutes Simone ignored the fact that she was bent double over her desk, head buried in her folded arms, and Pascale was too upset to care. She seemed to be drowning in a deep black place where no chink of light beckoned. Her grief for all those she had lost overwhelmed her, and not even the baby growing inside her could be of any comfort. What sort of a world was she bringing a child into? A world of pain and misery, a world at war, a world of loneliness and heartbreak. The thought that she was condemning her innocent baby to the sort of torments she herself had endured made her cry the harder.

'Pascale?' An arm round her shoulders. She froze momentarily, but the weight of tears was too heavy to hold back. 'Pascale, don't,' Simone said gently. 'You'll harm your baby.'

Pascale raised her head a fraction.

'Perhaps that would be for the best,' she muttered thickly.

'Don't say such a thing!'

'Why not? It's true!'

'It is not true! That baby is the most precious thing you have.'

'Yes? And how selfish is that – to put another little soul through living, just so that—'

'I won't listen to this. Oh, for goodness' sake . . . come here.'

And somehow, without knowing how it had happened, Pascale and Simone were in each other's arms, just as they had been that long-ago day on the train when Pascale had told Simone about Lynne. For long minutes she sobbed into Simone's shoulder; when she raised her head she saw that Simone, too, was crying, the tears running long, silent rivulets down her powdered cheeks.

'Oh Simone, I am so sorry.'

'I know you are. I'm sorry too.'

'What for?'

'Giving you a hard time over Paul. I know now . . . well, I think I always knew really . . . it wouldn't have worked out between us. But it's hard to let go . . .'

'And it made it worse because it was me.'

'Well . . . yes.' Simone brushed the tears from her cheeks impatiently. 'But now I'm glad. I'm glad it was you. And I can do one last thing for him, can't I? I can look after you, make sure you're all right. And that you don't harm that baby of his by getting yourself so upset.'

'Oh Simone . . . it means so much to me that we can be friends again. Do you honestly forgive me?'

Simone's expression was bleak, but she cupped Pascale's face in her hands, looking into her swollen and reddened eyes.

'Pascale, there's nothing to forgive.'

From that moment on it was Simone who was there for her. Though in the beginning there were moments of awkwardness, times when Pascale knew Simone was struggling with her own emotional journey, the closeness that had existed between the two girls almost from the day they had met began to grow again, little by little. And in the end it was Simone who came up with a solution to the knotty problem of what Pascale was going to do when the baby was born.

The daughter of a friend of Simone's mother, widowed in the war, was looking for live-in help to act as nanny to her three young children. She was forward-thinking, non-judgemental, and another baby in the house would make little difference. Simone arranged an interview and Pascale struck up an immediate rapport with the friend, who rejoiced in the name of Claudia Cuthbert-Smythe (pronounced, to Pascale's amusement, as plain, honest-to-goodness Smith), and for this she was glad, since the many miles that separated her new home from London meant that she would be able to see Simone only occasionally.

When her pregnancy became too obvious for her to continue working at Baker Street, she moved to her new quarters, a self-contained flat in an impressive old manor house. Three months later her baby was born, and a few weeks later Victory in Europe was declared.

The irony of it was not lost on Pascale. One of her daughters had come into the world just as the war was beginning; the other at its end. It seemed an omen for a new beginning, and Pascale had imagined that the new baby – whom she had named Wendy – would bring her nothing but joy. So she was shocked to discover that instead she was drowning in a pit of black depression. Her grief returned, magnified, it seemed, a thousand-fold, grief for both Paul and for

Lynne, for holding Wendy in her arms brought back memories of both of them, and with it came a terrible sense of guilt. That Paul had died to save her, that she had somehow been responsible for Lynne's death by not having been there on the day the bomb fell, that she was still alive when both of them were dead. There was the guilt, too, that came from the bursts of love she felt for Wendy – as if she was betraying Lynne, replacing her, in her life and in her heart.

She confided the way she felt to Claudia one evening as they sat drinking cocoa in the big, comfortable kitchen after the children were all in bed and Wendy was sleeping peacefully in a Moses basket by the big old Aga range.

'I feel as if I'm pushing Lynne aside, and I don't want to,' Pascale said. 'I don't want to forget her!'

'You won't,' Claudia said. 'How could you? But you mustn't take it out on Wendy. Loving her won't mean you love Lynne less. No matter how many children you have, there's room in your heart for all of them.'

Pascale knew Claudia must be right, but it didn't change the way she felt. She continued wearing the locket containing the snippet of Lynne's hair around her neck, and when it grazed the top of Wendy's head as she suckled, the ridiculous sense of guilt made her feel she was betraying both of them.

When she first met the young policeman, it never occurred to her that she would marry him. In fact, in the beginning it didn't even occur to her that he was arranging his beat so that their paths crossed, though he did seem to walk by rather often when she took the children to the bridge over the river to feed the ducks.

The friendship – though afterwards she learned that it was always his intention that it should be far more than that – developed slowly, with Pascale gradually finding herself looking forward to seeing him and being disappointed when she did not.

His name was Jim Lane, he had been in the navy during the war, and he was now one of the three constables who, with a sergeant, were stationed in the town. He was twenty-four years old and good-looking enough for several local girls to have set their cap at him. But from the first moment he laid eyes on Pascale, none of them stood a chance. He took things carefully, though; he knew instinctively that to rush in would be to frighten her off.

When eventually he asked her out, it was to the Divisional Police Ball, and he put it to her that she'd be doing him a favour – if she turned him down, he'd be the only one without a partner. Even so she refused at first, and it was Claudia who talked her into going. She'd look after Wendy, she'd even lend Pascale a dress to wear, she really should go, it would do her good. In the end Pascale was bullied into submission; it was easier than arguing with both of them. She went to the ball in an ice-blue satin gown and silver sandals belonging to Claudia, her hair fastened in an elegant knot on top of her head.

Much to her astonishment, she enjoyed herself immensely, perhaps because she'd never been to a ball before, or indeed even had much of a social life; perhaps because she felt comfortable in Jim's company. Other dates followed – to the pictures, to dances, for walks, for rides on the pillion of his motorbike. Pascale worried a little that he might be getting too serious about her but was still reluctant to put an end to things – their outings were a lifeline to her, a crack in the clouds that still hung over her world through which the sun could shine.

They'd been seeing one another for about six months when he asked her to marry him. He was being posted to Little Compton, a small market town some fifteen miles away, and he wanted her to go with him as his wife.

Pascale was in a quandary. She didn't want to lose him, but she didn't feel ready to marry him either. She was very fond of him, but he wasn't Paul.

'I'm really flattered,' she said, playing unconsciously with Paul's ring, which she still wore, 'but I can't. It wouldn't be fair on you.'

His jaw tightened. 'Because of the chap who was killed in the war. Wendy's father.'

She nodded. 'I still love him. And I think I always will.'

'I know that,' he said, 'and it doesn't make any difference. I love

424

you, Bea. You're the one I want. I wish you felt the same way about me, and I hope in time you will. But until then . . . well, I won't put any pressure on you. I don't want you to think I'm trying to take his place. I just want you to give us a chance. Because I think we could make a go of it.'

'Oh Jim . . .' Pascale buried her face in her hands, and suddenly she was thinking of what Claudia had said about there being more than enough love in her heart for both Lynne and Wendy. Perhaps the same went for romantic love. Though she would never stop loving Paul, perhaps in time she would come to love Jim too. Certainly the thought of him moving away, of losing contact with him, was a blow she didn't want to face up to.

Besides that, Wendy needed a father, and Jim was very good with her. Perhaps she should take this opportunity; if she didn't, she might well spend the rest of her life regretting it.

'I can't make any promises,' she said.

'I'm not asking you to. But give me a chance, Bea. Give us a chance.'

'Well as long as you know . . .'

He put a finger on her lips.

'Don't say it. Just say you'll marry me.'

Tears burned behind her eyes but she forced a tight smile.

'All right, Jim. I'll marry you.'

But it wasn't fair. She knew it wasn't. He was good to her, patient, kind, loving. She couldn't make him live all his life with the ghost of Paul, and she couldn't make Wendy live hers with the ghost of Lynne.

They'd been married six months when she made up her mind. The mementos of the past must go; it was time for a fresh start. She put the things that meant the most to her into the box with the medal that meant nothing at all and walked one gusty after-noon to Bolborough Lake. She hurled the box as far as possible towards the centre of the lake. It struck the dark water, sank, and was gone.

And with it the girl who had been Pascale.

Beatrice, as she thought of herself now, never expected to see the box again. Yet more than sixty years later it was her granddaughter, Wendy's daughter Martha, who was to find it by some strange quirk of fate.

A fate that Pascale could not help feeling was preordained.

FORTY

MARTHA

'And of course, I did grow to love him,' Granny says. 'We had fifty happy years together. I've been very lucky. Some people live their whole lives without finding that sort of happiness. I was blessed twice.'

She gives me a straight look. 'I hope you will be too, Martha.'

She's thinking, I suppose, about Nick, who I was so much in love with when I married him, and someone else I have yet to build a relationship with – Pete perhaps. But I don't want to talk about me.

'Did you ever regret it?' I ask. 'Getting rid of your treasures like that?'

'I had my moments,' Granny says drily. 'But I had to do it. It left me free to get on with my life. Now . . .' She smiles again. 'It can't do any harm for me to have them back again now, can it? Goodness knows what I'll do with the medal, give it to you or Lucy, I suppose.'

'Lucy,' I interpose quickly. 'She's the eldest.' What I actually mean is that, much as I would treasure it, I feel Lucy is the one who has earned the right to it.

'We'll see what she says. And the ring . . . that won't be much good to me now.' She looks down ruefully at her hands and the knuckles that have swelled with age. 'One of you can have the medal, and the other the ring. You can work that out between yourselves. But the locket . . . I think I'd like to keep that myself. It's very precious to me. Well, not so much the locket as what's in it. Lynne's curl.' Tears fill her eyes suddenly. 'It was a curl from the first time I had

427

her hair cut. She had such beautiful hair . . . well, she was a beautiful little girl. I never got over losing her. Not really. You can't get over something like that, can you? Such a terrible waste.'

My throat closes. I hadn't been going to say anything to her yet about Lynne – Anne. Now I see that she has provided me with the perfect opening.

'Granny,' I say gently, 'there's something I have to tell you about Lynne.'

And I tell her.

ANNE

And still the roller-coaster speeds on, totally out of control. I'm in an emotional whirlpool, and now, on top of everything else, I have to make arrangements for Mum's funeral.

Thankfully, Rod comes to my assistance. By the time I get back to Sonia's from the hospital, he's there, my rock. He has a stiff drink waiting for me and the kettle on the boil too in case I opt for a cup of tea, and he gives me a hug that I think will never end, just holding me with my head against his chest. Then we get down to discussing such necessary details as which funeral director to use, and Rod calls them. He knows I'm sinking in a quagmire, in danger of being overwhelmed, and I would be if I'd had time to absorb all the momentous revelations, stresses and traumas of the last few days, though right now I'm running on autopilot and a tank that's almost empty

But the day hasn't ended yet; the roller-coaster is still charging on.

The phone rings early evening. Rod answers it. I hover, thinking it's probably the funeral director with some query about our wishes. Then I hear Rod say: 'I'm sorry, I don't think she's up to it at the moment. Margaret died this morning,' and I know it can't be.

'Can I take a number and get her to call you when things have settled down a bit?' he goes on, turning to me, miming scribbling motions in the air and mouthing: 'Pen?'

I find one, and an envelope containing an offer from some motor insurance company that came for Kevin in the morning post and

I'd put aside for him. As Rod writes on it, I peer over his shoulder, but it's not a number I recognise.

'Who was that?' I ask as he finishes the call.

'Martha,' he says. 'Apparently she's told her grandmother about you. And she wanted to speak to you.'

'Oh my goodness.' Another great swell in the tsunami washes over me. I press my hand to my mouth. I'm shaking all over. 'Oh Rod, you should have put me on.'

'No,' he says firmly. 'Absolutely not. You're in no fit state. You've had quite enough for one day.'

He's right, of course, but still . . . I'm thinking of my real mother, the anguish she must have suffered, the years of thinking I was dead. And now, discovering that I am not, and wanting to speak to me.

I make a move for the phone.

'I must ring her back.'

Rod puts his hand unflinchingly in my way.

'No, Anne. She's waited all these years. She can wait another day or two. Come on, I'm getting you a drink. And then you're going to go to bed and at least try to get some rest.'

I'm too spent, too wrung out to argue. For once, I do as I'm told.

Another dawn, another day. I didn't sleep well – I knew I wouldn't. This morning I feel as if I'm on overload, my head bursting, my limbs heavy. Everything is the most dreadful effort and I'm probably not doing anything properly.

I can't go on like this. Somehow I've got to dig myself out of the pit I'm in. Too many people are depending on me for me to allow myself to buckle under. Sonia and her family. Elaine and the business. The funeral arrangements for Mum. My real mother waiting to hear from me . . .

The phone rings. What now? I pick it up, feeling at a great distance from it, from reality.

It's Sonia's doctor, with the most incredible news. Apparently once the DNA had been established the Liebermanns wasted no time in getting bone marrow tests, and one of them – a granddaughter of Kurt's – is a match. And is prepared to be a donor. What an incredible thing to do for someone who is really no more than a stranger. I can hardly believe it! They really are wonderful, this family of mine that I never knew I had.

Suddenly I am flying. The weariness, the grief, the feeling of sinking in a morass of never-ending problems and traumas, of being utterly helpless and incapable, have all sloughed away like a snake shedding its skin. Nothing matters but that we have a match for Sonia! I press my hand to my face; tears are running down my cheeks.

'Oh thank you, God! Thank you! Thank you!'

Sonia appears in the doorway.

'Mum – are you all right?'

'Oh Sonia, yes – yes! That was your doctor! The Liebermanns . . . they went ahead, just as they promised. And the fanatastic news is – we have a match!'

I enfold her in my arms and hold her tight, my dearest daughter, who has been given a chance to live.

MARTHA

Home at last. To a pile of junk mail and a vase of dead lupins on the kitchen counter and a bottle of gone-off milk in the fridge. To the coffee cup with dregs in it growing the sort of gunge that wouldn't disgrace a murky pond, and the bed I didn't stop to make because I was in a hurry to collect Granny the day we left.

And it's still the best place on earth because it's mine. Where I can kick my shoes off, wander about in nothing but a T-shirt and have no one to answer to but myself. Much as I've enjoyed spending the week with Granny, I have really missed having my own space, and having to constantly temper arrangements to fit them around another person is a bit of a straightjacket for me. I've got used to being single again and it suits me.

What a week it's been, though! Going back to work will almost seem like the holiday! But I am so glad I was there for Granny, so glad she had the opportunity to finish telling me her incredible story herself, and so glad that I was the one to tell her that Lynne was still alive after all. It was a terrifically emotional thing for her, as you can imagine. I was really worried how she would take it – couldn't imagine how I would react if it were me. But she is so unbelievably stoic – she always was, I suppose, and sometimes I think people actually become even more accepting with age. She cried a bit – unsurprising, really – and seemed a bit dazed, and then she wanted to speak to her. So I phoned, but Anne's husband answered. It seems the poor girl has had quite a time of it herself. But, the next day, she rang the number I left with her husband, and she and Granny spoke. And this time, though she was crying again, Granny's face was wreathed in smiles. 'My Lynne!' she kept saying, over and over again, as if she just couldn't take it in. 'My little Lynne!'

'Not so little now,' I said, trying to sound jolly.

'No, I suppose not,' Granny said.

I spoke to Lynne – Anne – too, and she told me there's no longer any urgency for us to have bone marrow tests, as a match has been found with one of the German family. Granny got a bit emotional about that, too – although she was so young at the time she was involved with him, he was her first love, and he didn't betray her when they ran into each other in France.

Anyway, I promised Anne that we'd fix a meeting between her and Granny when we got home, and Granny is also very eager to meet Sonia, who is, of course, her granddaughter, and, I suppose, my cousin. And I mustn't forget about Miss Leverton, either. I shall have to take Granny to see her. It is all so complicated I'm having trouble making sense of it, never mind Granny!

Today was particularly difficult, of course. When I took Granny home to Lucy's, we had to break the news to her of all that's been going on. Though I'd promised to play down my part in it, I was still very nervous that she would be upset at having been left out of the loop. But in fact she took it all rather well, probably due to the fact that Granny was amazing, tactful, and the most coherent she has been since her stroke.

When she broke off to visit the bathroom, I tried to do my bit too.

'You should have been the one to hear first, not me,' I said awkwardly. 'I'm really sorry it didn't work out that way.'

Lucy gave a small shake of her head. 'What does it matter? We both know now, don't we? The important thing is that Granny doesn't have to keep secrets any more. And to find her lost daughter like that, when she'd always believed her to be dead . . .' Her voice tails away into awe and disbelief.

'I know. It's pretty staggering, isn't it? I wonder what she's like? If she's nice? How we're going to get on with her?'

'We'll have to wait and see. But Martha . . .' she reaches for my hand, 'one thing is for sure – she won't be you.'

I grin. 'Hopefully.'

'No, I'm serious. I know we fall out sometimes, but when push comes to shove, you're still my sister. And we went through a lot together, didn't we? Nothing can ever take that away. There are times you drive me mad, I admit it. And I expect I do you. But that's life. Deep down I love you to bits.'

'And I love you. Mostly I just feel so damned guilty that you're the one who does everything, and I . . . well, I'm just rubbish at stuff like that.'

'Oh – come here.' Lucy puts her arms round me and we hug. I feel closer to her than I have in a long time. It's as if all this coming out, instead of driving us apart as I'd feared it might, has actually somehow thrown us back to being the two little girls who were orphaned, the two little girls who will always be there for one another, no matter what, even if things get a bit rocky between them from time to time. That's what family is, I guess, people who will always love you and be on your side in the last resort, never mind that they might not always agree with you or even like you much.

Granny came back then and we went on with Pascale's story, which of course was mostly down to me, since that was the way Granny had planned it, though she did take up some things herself and throw in the odd bit of embellishment.

Anyway, all in all it was quite an exhausting exercise, and now I'm looking forward to a quiet evening in with a bottle of wine and a takeaway pizza so I can begin to get my head round every-thing that's happened.

Someone, though, seems to have different ideas. My doorbell is buzzing. And when I answer the entryphone, it's Pete's voice that I hear.

'It's me. If I'm not much mistaken, we have a date.'

I grin. 'That's news to me. But seeing you're here . . .'

I press the buzzer and open the door. There's a tic of pleasure deep inside me. *You stupid girl!* I chastise myself. *Will you never learn?* And realise that I really don't want to. Being single is all very well, but it's not half as much fun as this.

'Right,' Pete says when we've got the preliminary greetings over. 'Shall I ring for the takeaway now or later?'

'Later,' I say. 'Definitely later.'

He kisses me again.

'That's what I hoped you'd say.'

Much later, we're talking about the incredible story that's emerged, the long-buried secrets that have finally seen the light of day like the items in the box that I found in Bolborough Lake.

'The picture in Miss Leverton's flat,' I say. 'Of the three SOE girls. You've never told me where you thought you'd seen it before.'

Pete grins. 'Oh, that. I just said that to get you going.'

'What!'

'I do love winding you up, Martha.'

'You,' I said, 'are a terrible man.'

'I know. And you just love it, don't you?'

'No, I don't! You're impossible.'

'Comes with the territory.'

I throw a cushion at him. And once again we forget about everything but each other.

EPILOGUE

2008

She stands at the edge of the lake, a diminutive figure in a warm winter coat and a scarlet pull-on hat, from beneath which soft white curls escape. Her hands are thrust deep into her pockets, the heels of her boots dig into the frosty ground. She is staring at the dark water that for so long concealed her treasures and remembering the girl who had seen no other way to leave the past behind and start afresh beyond disposing of them where she could no longer reach them.

It was so long ago now, yet it seems like only yesterday, and here, at the water's edge, the ghosts of the past seem very close. Yet they no longer haunt her as they once did; rather they seem like friendly angels watching over her.

She thinks of Paul, whom she loved so much, and who had loved her enough to give his life for her. She thinks of Marie, and all the others of the SOE who died for freedom. She thinks of Wendy, taken so tragically in the air crash just when she should have been watching her children grow up. And she thinks of Lynne, her firstborn, who is not dead at all, but a successful, caring, fulfilled wife and mother. Finding her again has been a blessing she never dreamed of. And not only Lynne – or Anne, as she must now call her – but a whole new family. A granddaughter who is now, thankfully, on the road to recovery from the terrible illness that threatened her, and great-grandchildren with all their lives before them.

She thinks of Kurt, her first love, whose descendants have provided the lifeline for Sonia, and who put his duty aside to protect her when they met in wartime France.

And of Simone, the best friend a woman could wish for, and of their reunion a few months ago when she was able to thank her in person for relating the story she had not felt able to tell herself and enjoy talking over old times and reliving events that only they could share.

I have been so lucky, she thinks, to lead such a full life, to have known the love of two – no, three! – wonderful men, and to have such a dear and special family.

Then she turns and looks towards the road, where Martha is waiting for her – Martha, who so reminds her of herself when she was young – and she prays that she will find the same rewarding happiness. There's been a glow about her these last months that seem to suggest it's on the cards.

Martha sees her looking, waves, and crunches through the frosty undergrowth towards her. She links arms, glancing at the dark water.

'I'm glad I don't have to go in there today.' She shivers, snuggling her chin down into the turned-up collar of her windcheater. 'Have you done here?'

A nod, a smile.

'Come on then, Granny,' Martha says. 'Let's go home.'